SOULS ON THE WIND

Roger L. Conlee

Pale Horse Books

Library of Congress Control Number: 2010938981

ISBN: 978-0-9710362-6-0

ALSO by Roger L. Conlee:
EVERY SHAPE, EVERY SHADOW
COUNTERCLOCKWISE
THE HINDENBURG LETTER

Cover Design: Mark A. Clements

www.PaleHorseBooks.com

www.RogerConlee.com

PROLOGUE

Nuremberg, Germany, October 1946

The men were as gray as the sky above them. They wore shabby coats of black and brown over rumpled civilian clothes and looked nothing like the powerful German leaders they'd been until a year ago. They were allowed one hour a day out here in the old garden for fresh air and exercise. A raw breeze whistled through the gloom, stirring up the musty smell of dead, damp leaves.

Wilhelm Keitel, tall, grandfatherly, stood alone. He gazed at the others. Career army man, never a Nazi insider, Keitel had little in common with the others. Everyone moved sluggishly except Albert Speer, who was running laps as best he could in the small yard.

Goering suddenly brushed against Keitel, which took him aback. Reichsmarshal Hermann Goering, the once-mighty air minister, the second most powerful man in all the Third Reich, had had little to do with Keitel—a mere hireling, a mere staff officer—during their Nuremberg captivity.

"Keitel," Goering whispered. Their eyes met. Goering had never looked Keitel in the eye before.

"Here." Goering slipped a small cloth sack, coarse, brown, and surprisingly heavy, into his hand. "Never tell them that I had this." The late afternoon light was bad—the guard hadn't seen. "Never!" Goering repeated, and walked away.

Keitel hid the sack in his tunic and walked back to his cell, twice looking over his shoulder. Once inside, he wasted no time loosening the drawstring to open it. "*Mein Gott*," he gasped. He pulled out a gemstone four, maybe five centimeters in diameter—as big as the Knight's Cross that had once adorned his tunic. It was fantastic. It must weigh *zweihundert gram*.

He'd known of this jewel and heard the rumors that Goering had it. And now *he* had it! He felt faint. Even in the dim light of the single forty-watt bulb, it was a deep pool of velvet green, pulling bewitchingly at his eyes. The Maria Theresa Emerald was even grander than he'd heard. Its six sides danced with light and seemed to throw off little sparks. It was almost the color of a tide pool he'd once seen at the *Wismarbucht* on the north shore.

Such rare, exquisite beauty. Was it any wonder that Goering, or any other person who laid eyes on it, would admire the Maria Theresa Emerald so?

Where could he hide this thing? Keitel wondered. He thought about it a moment, then put it back in the sack, closed the drawstring, and placed it in the bottom of his toilet kit, beneath the American-supplied tubes of Burma-Shave and Ipana toothpaste. He wondered where *im Himmel* the clever Goering had stashed it.

And why had Goering given it to *him?* Maybe because he'd thought that sycophantic Keitel, who always followed orders, would obey his "never tell" command. Honorable old Speer and some of the others were more likely to divulge Goering's culpability. But why *now?*

The answer came soon enough.

That night an American voice cried out, "Oh, shit. Get the doc! Quick." Footsteps hammered in the corridor. Agitated voices rang out. Doors slammed. "Damn it, it wasn't me on duty," someone protested.

The inmates weren't supposed to know what happened, but

they did. It was the only topic of conversation the next day in the yard. Goering was *dead!* He'd swallowed a cyanide capsule, just five cells down from Keitel, right under the guards' noses. Keitel thought bitterly that the Reichsmarshal hadn't been man enough to let the Allies execute him.

Back in his cell, Keitel's thoughts roamed. One of the world's great treasures had become worthless to Goering. Could he have used it to buy his way out of this prison under the eyes of the world, guarded by squads of Allied soldiers after the most conspicuous trial in history? Of course not. And Goering, who'd tried to portray himself as an innocent man, Goering with his martyr complex, couldn't leave such damning evidence of his thievery behind in his cell.

Keitel couldn't possibly buy his freedom with it either. So what could he do?

He wished for the thousandth time that he'd never become a staff officer. Surely it was the greatest mistake of his life.

He had become a field marshal and chief of the OKW, the High Command. These days Keitel often told himself he should have stayed with the artillery and gone to the Russian front. And died there doing his duty. He would be the honored dead now, instead of a sixty-four-year-old waste about to be crushed like the worm even his own people thought he was.

Everything had turned out wrong. Keitel, from Hannover in western Germany, had loathed the proud, arrogant Prussians. He'd been a loyal officer who never questioned orders. Maybe that was why Hitler had taken a liking to him and made him chief of staff before the invasion of Poland. He had admired Hitler then, that strong, mysterious man who'd risen from the common people to restore Germany to her rightful greatness.

He, Keitel, had been at Hitler's side through it all. The annexation of Austria. The Munich Conference. The invasion of Russia. He had officiated at the hugely satisfying surrender of the

French just six years before.

Now it all seemed eons ago. As the war had dragged on, Keitel hadn't been man enough to challenge any of Hitler's mad decisions. He'd just kept saying "*Jawohl, mein Führer*" while that fool dragged Germany down to utter destruction.

The only thing left for him was to die well. To climb straight onto the scaffold, every inch a German field marshal, and die without whimper or protest at the hands of the Allies and their so-called War Crimes Tribunal. Goering had begged for a firing squad. That was the honorable way for a condemned man to die. But cheating the hangman wasn't that important to Keitel. What difference did it really make how they ended his life?

His duty became clear. He had one last act to perform before that final day.

Keitel knew his history. The Maria Theresa Emerald had come from India. It had been presented to the young Austrian Empress Maria Theresa in 1736 by her father, Charles VI, Emperor of the Holy Roman Empire, on the occasion of her marriage to the Duke of Lorraine.

Many times it had beguiled prominent Viennese and visiting royalty when it dangled from the Empress's pale neck at the fabled balls in Schönbrunn Palace. Gemstone experts in the eighteenth-century courts of Europe claimed it was the most perfect emerald ever seen by Western eyes. It was said that the six-year-old Mozart stroked the jewel when the Empress allowed him to hop on her lap.

Legend had it that the emerald did strange things to people, made them slip back and forth in time. Keitel refused to believe it.

After Maria Theresa's death it became part of the Austrian Crown Jewels collection in the Hofburg, where it survived attacks by Turks, revolts by Magyars, and intrigue by cunning princes at court.

For a century and a half the emerald lay undisturbed in the Hofburg—until the German takeover in 1938. Then it became Nazi plunder, like so many other treasures in the lands swallowed up by Hitler.

Goering had confiscated the emerald and stashed it at Karinhalle, his hunting lodge north of Berlin. Keitel knew that Goering—who considered himself such an art expert—was nothing but a thief.

After the collapse of Germany, Keitel had heard, the Allies had begun cataloguing and returning the Nazi art plunder. But, to the sorrow of the Viennese, the Maria Theresa Emerald had not been found.

That night, as he tossed and turned in his sleep, Keitel seemed to find himself in an old Prussian uniform, manning an artillery piece outside Paris in the Franco-Prussian War. It frightened the *Hölle* out of him. His woolen tunic had a torn sleeve—and was smelly from weeks of sweat. Hunger rumbled in his stomach.

Bewildered but immensely relieved to wake up in the present, he heard footfalls in the passage beyond his cell door. In the long months of captivity, he had learned to identify some of the guards by the sound of their footsteps.

Keitel had grown fond of the cheerful young man whose approaching steps he now recognized. They belonged to the American military policeman Desmond Cavanaugh. Always smiling and joking, Americans like Cavanaugh seldom seemed to take life seriously. Perhaps if *their* homeland had been ravaged by war, their cities bombed to bits, they would act differently.

Cavanaugh, the only guard he trusted, peered through the judas window in the slab door.

"How are you, general, sir?" Cavanaugh always called him general, not field marshal, a little thing that no longer bothered Keitel.

In another time and place, he could have befriended this young soldier, so resolute and thorough, yet so good-hearted. He could have put him on his staff and made him a protégé. Cavanaugh would have made a fine officer.

Their conversations together were now the only bright spots in his last, lonely days. Keitel had even taught his visitor some German. He was bright and a fast learner. Cavanaugh had told him about his boyhood in a town near San Francisco—what a place that California must be—and Keitel had spoken of his own adolescence on the north German plain. How different their upbringings had been, how different the paths that had led them both to this bombed-out medieval city where the last miserable chapter of his life was being played out.

"Can I get you anything?" Cavanaugh asked. "Another magazine?"

"No, my young friend, no magazines tonight. But tomorrow or the next day I would be honored if we could have another little talk, a talk about something very important. If I can trust you completely, that is."

"You can," the American said with a firm, direct gaze.

Still shaken by the troubling Franco-Prussian War sensation he'd experienced in the night, Keitel decided there was one last decent thing he could do. The Maria Theresa Emerald would be the key to his redemption.

The stone couldn't go back to the Austrian people just now, of course, because he'd heard that communists and other foreign scum were tramping all over Vienna. No, a few years would have to pass, until the tangle of occupation was sorted out and a new Austrian government was in place.

At that point, Desmond Cavanaugh would carry out his last wish. Then Keitel's soul could rest.

CHAPTER ONE

1988.

Tom Cavanaugh had been seeing phantom sights for about a month now.

As he dozed off, they came again. Men and boy ghosts, stalking toward him out of a gray mist. Rifles up in firing position. Yellow flashes blinking from some of them. They vanished, every one, replaced by a cornfield. And that too, gone. Now a tiny white chapel. There. Gone.

Cass touched his arm. "Hey, you okay?"

Tom opened his eyes. He'd never had these visions until a month ago. But now . . .

The interior of the Swissair DC-10 came into focus. The engines thrummed away as they had for hours. Cass Nesbit slipped her headset from her ears, the sleeve of her jacket brushing his shoulder.

"Yeah, fine," he answered. "Where are we? How long was I out?" Steam rose from the coffee cup on the fold-down tray in front of him.

"Where are we?" Cass said, running a hand through her rust-colored hair. "Still about an hour out of Munich. You only closed your eyes for a few seconds. Were my tales of woe that boring?"

Tom remembered now. Cass had been telling him about the backlog of work in her office at the Capitol—he'd been getting drowsy.

"You had a weird look on your face," she said.

Something was going on in the hollows of Tom's mind,

hovering just beyond his grasp. "There was a flash of something," he said, "something real interesting, but I've lost it."

"Something interesting in your mind?" Cass squeezed his hand. "That's a breakthrough."

Teasing jabs like that were just one aspect of this complex woman who'd swept into his life with all the serenity of a tornado. He often joked about her needling a narc, Tom being a narcotics detective.

"Yeah, they were just fragments, flickers, like a slide show on uppers. When I try to focus, they slide right off like those little floaters in your eye you can never quite catch hold of. For the life of me, all I can remember later is some guys with rifles in a cornfield, and sometimes a chapel."

"I think your vivid imagination just makes for weird dreams." Her eyes turned playful. "But you're supposed to dream about me."

"Oh, I do." Tom smiled defensively. "These other things, though, I don't think they're dreams. I can remember dreams if I concentrate as soon as I wake up. These little devils are something else, something a little scary."

Cass mentioned the various theories: how all life is one vast continuum and each of us is connected to all human experience; or that we have parallel lives being lived out simultaneously in shadow universes; reincarnation; genetic memory.

Tom nodded. He hated to think what his fellow cops back in Sacramento would say if they knew he was developing an interest in these theories.

She leaned over and kissed his cheek. He felt blessed, lucky that she so willingly put up with him and his crazy ideas—and this trip. She hadn't wanted to come. As a top aide to the governor of California, Cass Nesbit had a damn big job and the workload was a monster. She's a trouper all right, he thought, glancing at the ring on her left hand that had cost him a nice chunk of his cop's pay.

When they finally reached the Munich airport, Tom was glad to get up and stretch his jeans-clad legs. Traces of cold seeped into the jetway, reminding him it was still February. In the terminal, he took Cass's hand and smiled into her hazel-green eyes.

Then he noticed the stern-looking Customs men in their dark uniforms, staring hard at each passenger before stamping their passports.

Ninety minutes later, Cass was yawning as their rental car headed south for the Alps and the resort of Garmisch-Partenkirchen.

She reached in front of her and turned the heat up a notch. She knew she should be happier. Skiing in the German Alps, then Vienna—a dream trip—but it wasn't coming at a good time. The governor had hesitated a few seconds too long before saying, "Go. You deserve it. The state will get along." Cass knew she should be mad at herself, not Tom, for feeling guilty. She could have just told him no.

As the car droned on, she saw frequent signs warning of *Schnee*. "That means snow, doesn't it?"

"Right babe, snow," Tom said. "And tomorrow we'll be out there on it." She caught his sideways glance at her. "Then you'll be glad you came. You're a great skier."

She kept her face neutral.

"What?" he said. "Still thinking about those meetings you're missing?"

"I guess so. Sorry. But we're in the middle of the budget."

Tom said, "They have telephones and fax machines in Austria, I believe." It sounded like he was going to say more but had stopped himself with an effort. A moment later, his right hand reached over and squeezed her thigh.

The road wound higher and higher. Patches of snow appeared in the larch- and birch-studded hills, hills that soon gave way to granite mountains.

Conversation gradually resumed. Cass brought up the extraordinary story that Tom's father, a retired police chief, had told him.

"I'd heard a lot of Dad's war stories," Tom said, "but never this one."

"And you never had those visions before—"

"Hearing that particular war story from Dad? The one that brought us here? Nope, not before then."

At dinner in an old lodge in Garmisch, they sipped Franconian white wine, studied the menu, and listened to light classics from the piano. All the while, Tom scanned the huge room, which was half filled, and their fellow diners. He said he admired the high, timber-beamed ceilings and the Bavarian and Tyrolean flags that hung every which way.

"What I like best is that roaring fire," Cass said, glancing at a huge fireplace of gray stone, drawing in her shoulders and rubbing her arms. "And those wooden skis mounted crisscross up there on the wall. They look ancient."

"Probably from the Twenties. That kind of leather binding hasn't been used for years."

Tom saw two men come in and look around. One was slight, dark-haired, wore glasses, probably late thirties. The other was older with a rounded, prosperous-looking face.

Tom studied the other people around them. A chubby couple with a bored-looking teenage girl. A dark-skinned pair eating in posture-perfect silence, a red dot in the center of the woman's forehead. A relaxed group of six sunburned beer drinkers, animated and noisy, looking as if they'd skied all day.

If these people knew what I'm here to do, Tom thought, they wouldn't believe it.

"You're casing the place again," Cass teased. "Can't stop being a cop, can you?"

He cased her lustrous eyes and smiled his crooked smile. "That huge bed with the down comforter looked pretty inviting, didn't it?"

"Now that you mention it." She touched his hand, mischief in her smile.

"Aha, you *are* glad you're here."

The two men who'd just come in seated themselves at the next table. Why did they take *that* one, Tom wondered, when so many were available?

The waiter broke that thought, appearing and refilling their wine glasses. "*Danke*," Tom said. He'd been advised that ordering German wine would please the locals and it seemed to. Besides, it was good stuff. "*Wie hier ist der Schnee?*" he asked, trying out his college German.

"*Sehr gut*," the blond youth replied, adding in English, "a five-meter base and good powder."

Tom glanced at the two men at the next table. The older one had a straight, milky scar—as if cut by a saber—on the left cheek.

"So, you're going native on me already," Cass said. "How much German do you really remember?"

"Not much, I'm afraid, but I'm going to try." He took a sip of wine. "This trip will do us both good. A little skiing tomorrow, then on to Vienna and the main event. One of the curators at the *Kunsthistoriches* Museum should be a good place to start."

"The *Kunst* what? Can't you just say the Fine Arts Museum?"

He returned her smile. "Anyway, if they can't tell us how to do it there, they can probably steer us in the right direction."

"What about Salzburg, the biggest carrot you held out?"

"That's on the way back, remember? First, the slopes of Hausberg. Tomorrow will be great," he said, opening and closing his fingers as if gripping ski poles. "I've wanted to do this ever since I saw a downhill race from here on TV. You'll have a great time." Stop that, he told himself. You're selling too hard.

"So, in Vienna," she said, "you're going to walk up to the curator and tell him in your schoolboy German that you'd like to return a—"

Tom stopped her with a quick "shh" shape on his lips. He fished a pen from his pocket, scribbled something on a cocktail napkin, and slipped it in front of Cass.

"Those guys at the next table are listening to us," it said.

CHAPTER TWO

Tom saw he wasn't the only one who was unnerved when the large gondola carrying two dozen skiers up the mountainside swung as it tugged upward above rocky outcrops and deep snowy gorges. It slowed and bumped at each tower. Tom had some trouble with heights, except in a plane. This oddity had always surprised him—he was a pilot himself—until one day when he realized the acrophobia struck only at times when he wasn't in control. Like now.

He was surprised to see a hang-glider floating into view under the bright morning sun. One of his fellow cops had taken up that sport, something Tom would never do—the very idea made him shiver. He'd sit inside a sealed-up plane, thank you.

Cass snuggled against his shoulder, and he turned his gaze to the church steeples and snow-cloaked rooftops of Garmisch and Partenkirchen on the valley floor. It was a Currier and Ives engraving come to life. He drank deeply of the sight, etching it into memory. He didn't ask Cass if she too was stirred by the panorama. Words now would spoil the moment.

A lacy cloud like spun glass was slipping across the top of the Hausberg summit when they reached the lodge.

Tom and Cass proceeded to ski most of the slopes, except for the black diamond runs. They were good skiers, but not daredevils. He studied Cass, her tall, slim body twisting and turning gracefully with the terrain. He appreciated her quick mind, magnetic personality, the intelligence and inner strength. The way she helped him on cases, bringing in fresh approaches.

At one point, he leaned the wrong way at the fall line and took a spill. Cass snapped to a halt a few yards below him, sending up a roostertail of powder. "The world's greatest skiing cop, huh?" Laughing, she added, "Need some help?"

Tom grinned and pulled himself up. "I was too busy admiring the view to watch where I was going."

"Yeah, I saw the view you were admiring. That goldilocks in the blue powder suit that looked like it was painted on."

Tom grinned, adjusted his grip on the poles, stuck his tongue out at her, and shoved off.

During their lunch break, they plopped themselves down at a long picnic table.

"Angie O'Graham," Tom said after the orders were placed. It was a game they played.

Cass wrinkled her nose. "Angie O'Graham . . . Cardiologist?"

"Right. Of course."

Cass closed her eyes for a moment, then said, "Porpoise Christy."

"Trainer at Sea World?"

"No, sorry, marine biologist. From south Texas, of course. But you get to keep the toaster oven as a parting prize, and thanks for playing along."

They were feasting on a rich, hot soup called *Jägersuppe*, thick slices of bread, and bottles of the local beer, when the blonde they'd seen in a skintight one-piecer came along with a young man to share their table. Introductions were made and she told them in accented English that she was Swedish. Her friend was an American soldier.

The day was clear and unseasonably warm, in the high forties, Fahrenheit. The waiter told them the *Föhn* was blowing, a warm wind from the south that made people do strange things. "They go a bit crazy, *ja*? It is on nights like this that stifled little husbands finger the edge of a kitchen knife and contemplate their wives' necks."

Cass gulped.

This guy's got his Raymond Chandler mixed up, Tom thought. It was the Santa Ana winds, and the wives were the ones thinking the deadly thoughts. Still, Tom had heard about the *Föhn*. It was said that its overabundance of positive ions made people go weird. When it blew, suicides, kidnappings and spouse-killings reportedly increased in this part of the world. Another legend was that the souls of the dead rode the *Föhn*.

This kind of wind was known in France as the *mistral*, in the Rocky Mountains as a chinook, and in California as a Santa Ana.

He and Cass skied the whole afternoon. I'm having a great time, Tom had to remind himself. Wish I could stop thinking about the strange task I'll try to pull off when we get to Vienna.

Later, in the parking lot, the *Föhn* riffled his hair. He felt its warm breath on his cheek. The souls of the dead? *Nah, that's just superstition.*

Driving through the streets of Garmisch at twilight, he gazed at the half-timbered houses with steeply pitched roofs, dormers, brick chimneys and hardwood balconies. The brightly painted flower boxes beneath the windows held no flowers, not in February.

He thought back to the day his father, now an invalid, had told him about the emerald. The retired police chief had been lying in bed, greatly weakened by cardiac failure. Tom could never get used to that image: his once robust father, a soldier, athlete and cop, now horizontal, on oxygen. His mother had died four years before and that had only made it worse for his dad.

Tom had always thought his father had more rapport with his older brother, Michael. He believed his dad would have gone to Michael with this problem, except that he was on active duty with the Navy. Michael had just finished a tour as executive officer of the carrier *Enterprise* and was somewhere—Norfolk?—on his climb up the career ladder.

After hearing the astonishing tale about the emerald, Tom had said, "What an honor that old Keitel would entrust you with this. You must have impressed him. But one thing, Dad, why didn't you take care of this years ago?"

For the first time, Tom saw vacillation in those pale blue eyes.

"I hope I can make you understand," Desmond Cavanaugh said at last. "Your mother was the kindest, gentlest woman I've ever known."

"I know, Dad."

"It hurt her deeply when she lost her twin brother in the war." Tom's Uncle Jack had served in the 12th Air Force in Italy.

"He was shot down and killed during a raid on an oil refinery near Vienna. For some reason, your mother—and this is the only shortcoming she ever had, God love her—blamed that whole country for his death.

"Twins have a psychic closeness the rest of us can't comprehend, son, and Jack's loss was a wound in her that never really healed. She always insisted the Austrians didn't deserve the emerald. It was her way, I suppose, of avenging Jack's death. So, call me an old wimp, but I just couldn't make myself return it while she was alive."

Tom was overwhelmed. *Must be damn hard for him to tell me this.*

"I never tried to exploit it or anything. It's been in the safe deposit box for years. The thing kind of scared me . . . my God, it's superb. Anyway, I still have to keep my promise to the old general to follow through. Except now, Thomas, you'll have to do it for me."

"Pop, thanks for telling me that. I never knew. Of course I'll do it, and when you meet up with Mom again on the other side, she'll understand."

Retelling the story to Cass, Tom missed his turn and had to drive around the block to reach the lodge.

"I wish I could've known your mother," Cass said.

Tom nodded. "She would've liked you."

He parked, and as they were about to enter the lodge—*there*— a quick glimpse of the blonde from the mountain, partially hidden by a car across the street. Odd. That was the third time she'd shown up—*if* that was really her. Maybe he was mistaken. He decided not to trouble Cass about it.

Back in their room, Cass sat on the bed and held up her long legs one at a time as Tom pulled off her pearl gray boots. Faces rosy, bodies tired but exhilarated from the day's exertions, their eyes linked. As she unzipped her jeans, he put a hand to her face, touching lightly with his fingertips. He considered her cheekbones works of art.

Arousal grew. When Cass was out of her jeans, he removed her sweater and bra.

Later, they lay entwined for nearly an hour. "Glad you came now?" he murmured.

"Mmm . . . Oh, on this trip, you mean?"

Tom laughed.

After a shower that included mutual back-scrubbing, Tom went to the dresser and opened a drawer. He froze. He always placed his shorts on the left, socks on the right. It was an old habit. Now the order was reversed.

Driving to Vienna the next day, Tom thought, wouldn't it be great if we could just keep the darn thing. It's so beautiful. *Knock that off*, he scolded himself. More seriously, he pondered the blonde who might have tailed him, and the men who'd been listening to them at dinner. Was there a connection?

About the time they crossed the border into Austria, he told Cass about the underwear.

"You're sure it was rearranged?"

"Positive. Someone was in our room."

"Well, sure, the maid."

"Why would the maid do that? Why would she open the drawer at all?"

"You're the cop. Looking for a camera or something to steal for some quick money. That's why they say never leave valuables in your room."

Her reasoned logic versus his gut feel. Tom knew cops got hunches others didn't understand.

Awhile later, Cass said, "Your father must have been very devoted to your mom. You've given me the impression he was a pretty cold customer, but that story sheds a whole new light."

"Dad always hid some self-doubt," Tom said, "under that tough-cop exterior. Men of his generation thought they had to look strong, be in control, and he was good at it, but some of it was an act. When I was a little kid in Novato, I came into his den one night and found him crying. He didn't know I was there, and I backed out very quietly. They'd killed a bank robber that day, a nineteen-year-old kid. Dad hadn't been the shooter, his partner did that, but it really affected him."

"Maybe he was thinking of you and Michael, equating his little boys to that poor dead kid." Cass fiddled with the heater knob. "Too bad you didn't feel closer to him."

"When I was in high school he was in his late forties and seemed like an old man to me."

"But the emerald, it just stayed locked up all those years and you never saw it?"

"Not till now. Imagine, that old fox keeping a secret like *that*."

The Danube lay just a few yards off to the left. A coal barge appeared, gliding east toward Vienna, making good time in the current.

"I'm glad you didn't bring it," Cass said.

"No way could I get an emerald through Customs. I just

want to find out where it properly belongs, and how it should be handled."

"Polly Hedron," Cass said as they passed an inn built in the Tyrolean style with an overhanging roof and flower boxes at the windows.

"Woman with multiple personalities?" Tom asked, looking in the rearview mirror. "Many sides to her?"

"Not bad, but I was thinking geometry teacher."

Tom chuckled. "Okay."

The first signs of Vienna materialized in the distance, a tall communications tower and the steeple of St. Stephen's Cathedral. Tom checked the rearview mirror again.

After taking their hotel room and having dinner, they bundled up and walked to a gilded concert hall called the Musikverein.

The Vienna Philharmonic played Schubert's *Symphony in C Major*—superbly. Tom appreciated it, but his mind kept wandering to their visit the next morning to the Fine Arts Museum. He found himself wishing this matter had been taken care of years ago.

Later, during the preliminaries to lovemaking, Cass said, "Pantyhose must have been invented by a madman who hated women."

"And I think bra clasps," Tom replied, "were invented by a madman who hated *men*."

Before falling asleep in the warm afterglow, he was gazing toward the ceiling when he thought he saw a dim image of a chapel up there in the murk. Blurry at first, it slowly grew clearer. A small white building with no steeple. It turned hazy again, and he squinted. The chapel had a hole in it, a jagged black hole near the peaked roof. The image disappeared. Nothing on the ceiling now but shadows. Had there been a brief glimpse of a cornfield too? He wasn't sure. Had there been anything at all?

Maybe his mind had just been playing tricks on him in the drab, grainy light. He used to see all sorts of faces on the ceiling of his room when he was a boy.

CHAPTER THREE

T his is it," Tom said as they completed the six-block walk from their hotel to the *Kunsthistorisches* Museum, arriving just after opening time. The museum hunkered next to the Ringstrasse, a wide thoroughfare that encircled the center of the city. "They built this boulevard where the old city walls once stood," Tom said.

Cass faced the art museum's domed, Italian Renaissance facade. "You nervous?" she asked.

Yes. His palms were clammy inside his gloves. "No. It'll be fine. Hey, maybe there'll even be a reward."

"I would be," Cass said. "Nervous. My heart's pounding, but you'll do fine." A cool breeze spun around the sculptures in the landscaped courtyard. She yelped and hopped aside when water from the wind-whipped fountain started spraying her.

"Come on, let's go in."

After buying tickets and museum maps, Tom was about to go up to a guard, when Cass exclaimed, "Oh, *look.*"

In the middle of the entrance hall stood a display of huge photo blowups beneath signs reading KÖNIGILICH JUWELEN VON OSTERREICH and AUSTRIA'S CROWN JEWELS.

The centerpiece was a color photograph nearly three feet high showing various gem-studded crowns, scepters, sabers, rings and necklaces behind glass, resting on deep fabric of ruby red. A sign explained in German, French, and English how to make reservations to see this actual display in the nearby Hofburg Palace.

Name cards identified each item, but Tom's eyes were pulled to the center of the photograph where the highest velvet-draped base, clearly the place of honor . . . stood empty.

Tom read the card: THE MARIA THERESA EMERALD. ROYAL GIFT TO THE EMPRESS OF AUSTRIA, 1736. STOLEN BY FOREIGN OCCUPYING FORCES, 1938. PERHAPS ONE GLORIOUS DAY . . .

Tom's heart trembled. He and Cass shared a terrible secret from the gawking visitors around them. All the sounds in the bustling room seemed to vanish as they stared at one another, alone in the powerful knowledge they shared. A weight pressed on Tom, a weight that was part guilt and part embarrassment for his father. The emerald, that beautiful, beguiling emerald his father had entrusted to him, belonged here. This was its home. He had to make this work.

At last he said, "I've got to get on with it. That looks like the business office over there."

"I wish I could be a fly on the wall," Cass said, "but I know you have to do this alone."

She gave him a peck on the cheek and clutched his arm. "Break a leg, Cavanaugh. I'll meet you in the room where they have the Dutch Masters."

A receptionist made a phone call, and soon arrangements were made for Tom to see the Curator of Middle European Art.

Minutes later, he was shown into a spacious, paneled office with high ceilings. Paintings of long-dead emperors glowered from two of the walls, seeming to examine him with icy disdain. Ancient oaken shelves holding hundreds of leather-bound books lined a third. In the fourth wall, a bank of arched windows overlooked the courtyard and the Natural History Museum opposite.

Tom was greeted with a firm handshake and a slight head bob. Doctor Gerhard, the curator, a thin, stiff little man, was younger than he'd expected. His gray, double-breasted pinstripe suit, the crease in his pants military sharp, made Tom feel underdressed in his navy blazer and conservative tie.

Gerhard waved him to a chair. "Foreign visitors seldom ask to see me," he said in precise English, smiling with his mouth but not his eyes. "They find the exhibits much more interesting than the simple bureaucrat."

A 1988 day-by-day calendar on the desk was turned to February 16th. Behind his wire-rim glasses, Gerhard had the grayest eyes Tom had ever seen. Like a wolf's. Disconcerting as hell.

"May I offer you some coffee?"

"No thanks, I've just had breakfast."

"Well then, how do you find our art museum?"

"I haven't seen much of it yet, but I'm looking forward to it. I understand it ranks right up there with the Louvre and the Prado."

"You are most kind. We do house one of Europe's finest collections. Have you been to the Uffizi in Florence?"

"No, I haven't had the pleasure."

"I hope that you can. It is magnificent." Gerhard leaned forward. "Now, Herr Cavanaugh, how may I serve you?"

"I have a friend who has something of value to the people of Austria and he'd like to see that it goes to the proper place."

"Something of an artistic nature?" Gerhard's eyebrows arched. He planted his elbows on the desk and made a steeple of his hands. "Please, can you be more specific?"

"I'd rather not at this point, until you can square me away on some procedure. Just who would have the authority to accept my friend's item for your country? He doesn't know about these things."

The man stared at him for a long moment. Travel fatigue gnawed at Tom's stamina.

"Forgive me, Herr Cavanaugh, you must realize that this entreaty is most unusual. I would need more information before I could proceed." Gerhard was stroking the inside tips of his first two fingers with his thumb. "What about the age of the object? It is from what period?"

Tom hadn't expected this to become a poker game. "I don't know. My friend didn't tell me." He felt a drop of sweat form on his brow. He knew he was a bad liar, that it probably showed.

"I am most curious about the item of which you speak. How your friend came to possess it, and its value, of course."

Man, he pronounced "value" with pure hunger. Tom silently said, "Up yours," but aloud, nothing. He felt he'd come ill-prepared, that he should have role-played in advance with Cass. This guy was a surprise. Cops didn't like surprises.

He also knew he didn't like the man. *He's a public employee, same as me, for God's sake.* Who did he think he was, with that superior air, that mendacious smile? And those eyes . . . could this small man have been in Garmisch the other night? He looked fortyish like the one who'd eavesdropped. No, too great a coincidence, he thought, though Tom never trusted coincidences. He didn't get that good a look at those two guys anyway.

"I repeat, I can't describe it in detail," Tom said. "Anyway that's not my purpose. I just want to know about the proper channels for returning it." Now he sounded like a fussy bureaucrat himself.

"This could be handled in any number of ways," Gerhard said. "Publicly . . . privately . . . perhaps even your friend a profit could make."

Tom was shocked, and afraid it showed.

"What is your price?"

"No, no, I . . . my friend . . . wants to *give* it to Austria. I thought I was clear on that. It belongs here."

"We are both men of the world, *ja*? You should consider it. A nice little profit for yourself, that is, your friend."

Tom made a face that didn't conceal his disgust.

Gerhard folded his arms across his chest, the wolf eyes staring directly.

Tom met his gaze. He crossed his legs. He remembered the

crown jewels photorama downstairs. *Damn, I hope he's not thinking of the Maria Theresa Emerald.*

When the staredown ended at last, Gerhard said, "Now, if it were the Badenberg Scepter to which you refer . . ."

Tom had never heard of the Badenberg Scepter, whatever that was.

"The scepter went missing more than a century ago." Gerhard tried to look sad. "Believed stolen by Hungarian separatists." He tilted his head. "Or, perhaps your friend refers to the Maria Theresa Emerald, a more recent and even greater loss for my country."

Tom felt panic, tried not to let it show.

"You are familiar with the Maria Theresa Emerald?" Gerhard said with a hard, inquisitive look.

Trying to look puzzled, Tom shook his head. *I don't ever want this guy's slimy hands on our beautiful emerald.* Shocking himself with his sudden possessiveness.

"The most extraordinary of all the Austrian crown jewels," Gerhard was saying, "like the Hope Diamond in its way. That extraordinary gem vanished after the *Anschluss*, a greater loss for Vienna than the bombing of the Opera. It was the Nazis, of course. Rumor has it that the emerald is now in America."

Tom's pulse was tap dancing. "America?"

"Yes. The story goes that Goering had it." Gerhard's gaze lasered at Tom and he did his best to meet it. "It wasn't found at Goering's estate by the Russians. Very thorough fellows, the Russians."

"Maybe the Russians just *said* they didn't find it."

"Serious students of the period say no, that Goering had the emerald with him when he fled. It is also widely believed that an American officer at Nuremberg slipped Goering the cyanide capsule he swallowed to, how do you say, cheat the hangman. Goering did not want the humiliation of hanging, so he persuaded the American, it is said, to fetch the capsule from Goering's luggage locked in a storage room."

Gerhard flicked both palms up as if to say, "So you see. . ."

After an uneasy silence Tom said, "I hadn't heard any of that. That's quite a tale."

"Oh, yes, but it is likely true. Goering was an engaging fellow, right to the end. It is widely accepted that he had charmed an American lieutenant."

Tom certainly had something new to ask his father about.

"But then this Goering business may all be a fairy tale." Gerhard smiled his non-smile—the eyes remote in their stoniness—and changed his tone. "Well, then, this is an international matter, and best dealt with by the foreign offices of the respective nations. I think I should advise your friend to go to the United States Embassy. Yes, that's just the ticket—isn't that the saying?"

Tom needn't have come all this way to see the State Department. He could have done that at home. He had wanted to set this up directly, behind the scenes with minimal fuss.

He got to his feet and said, "Since you can't help me, Doctor—"

"I wish that I could. Your embassy is best, I am sure. And where are you staying in Vienna?" Gerhard asked, trying to sound friendly and disarming, but not making it.

Tom wanted to say, "None of your damn business." What he did say was, "Just a plain hotel here in town."

"Do have dinner at Sacher's while you are here, and save room for dessert. Their famous tort is every bit as good as you've heard."

"Thanks," Tom said, getting up and heading for the door. Yeah, he definitely didn't like the fastidious Doctor Gerhard.

"But if you reconsider the possibility of a transaction, do come and see me again," Gerhard said to Tom's back.

Tom closed the door behind him. In the corridor, the air felt better already.

* * *

The museum was crowded now. On the second level, Cass admired a Rubens. Wonder if Tom would go for this statuesque babe? she thought. She knew Tom had a past but she didn't mind. He wasn't a lothario, but he'd had his share of at-bats between his divorce and meeting Cass. But the past was the past, period. She knew who turned him on *now*.

More than a year ago they'd met for lunch to discuss the death of a mutual friend. It took her twenty seconds to see that Tom Cavanaugh had a good soul, and twenty minutes to know she would marry him some day. There was much more than met the eye to that lanky narcotics cop who'd rather be teaching history, and she loved the discoveries she was making.

And suddenly there he was, his blue-eyed, sandy-haired head—Tom standing six-two—visible above most of the crowd.

"How'd it go?" she asked, striding up to greet him. "Uh oh, you don't look like a happy camper."

"Let's get out of here."

"Didn't go so well? It must be the curse."

"What curse?"

"Where there's a rare old jewel, there's always a curse. You should know that, Mister History Buff."

Tom shook his head and guided her down the broad stairs toward the exit.

Outside, people filled the plaza and band music was coming from somewhere. Tom winced when he saw a sign saying the courtyard was named Maria-Theresian Platz. That was one empress he was tired of hearing about. As they hurried down the steps toward the wide boulevard, he had the feeling that eyes were watching them from an upper window.

"You hungry, Cass?" He reached out for her hand. It wasn't there.

CHAPTER FOUR

Tom's forehead pinched with anxiety. He pushed through the crowd toward the source of the music, a touristy little band playing Strauss. Cass wasn't there.

He turned and hurried across the plaza toward the street. Tall enough to see over most of the people, he looked every which way. His hand felt the small of his back for his Ruger 9-millimeter semiautomatic, but of course it was back home, 6,000 miles away.

A headache began to pound. The crooked curator, and now Cass missing. Could Gerhard have had her snatched? Already? Where *was* she?

He saw a blue-clad Vienna cop and headed toward him with long strides. A voice cutting through the din stopped him.

"Tom! Tom, over here."

And there she was, standing near a statue, waving. He blew out a huge sigh.

"Tom, where've you been? I looked around and you were gone."

"Same with me." He hugged her like a million dollars. "You shouldn't wander off like that in this strange place."

"Oh, come on, this is a safe town and I'm a big girl." Pulling away and gesturing, she said, "These are great statues here."

"Yeah, great. Look, I just want to get the hell out of here. I didn't like that guy."

"Patience, my love, patience. Look at the old empress up there towering over the plaza. So lifelike. I wanta hear all about your meeting, but first let me get your picture here."

"Okay, a quick one." Tom took a casual pose.

Cass waited for a gaggle of Asian tourists to pass, then snapped the picture. "Perfect," she said.

Tom took her arm. He waited under a stone-gray sky, fidgeting, for a red tram to roll past, then they crossed the boulevard. Clinging together for warmth, they walked through the blustery Heldenplatz, a vast park fronting the royal palace. On through narrow, cobbled streets, where Cass picked out a coffee house.

Exposed brick walls, tall windows, beamed ceilings. Aromas of warm food, strong coffee and cigarette smoke. Pegs on the walls holding newspapers fitted into wooden spines like giant clothespins. Tom watched an old woman take one to her table and start reading.

Over cups of Mocha coffee fortified with brandy, Tom rehashed the meeting. Looking around warily, he lowered his voice and said, "He even mentioned the Maria Theresa Emerald." Cass's eyes widened. "I almost keeled over. Then he said there's a theory that an *American* has it."

Her eyes even larger. "That's when you *did* keel over, right?"

Tom related what Doctor Gerhard had said about an American getting close to Goering and added, "It's been half a century; I wonder if there's still any record of who the guards were. If a determined Austrian bought into that story, he would try to find out who the American guards were, and if he could do that, he could get dad's name."

"It's possible, I guess." Cass touched his hand reassuringly. "But if someone could find those names, your father's would be just one of hundreds. Anyway, those records are probably long gone."

"Let's hope so," Tom said. "Remember Mary Savage? The lieutenant in charge of Homicide? She had a classmate at the FBI Academy. German, I think. He's over here somewhere, Munich maybe. I'll see if she can ask him to run a check on Gerhard for me."

"Why?" They were leaning so close their foreheads almost touched.

"Because Gerhard *knows*. You should have heard him. I've been watching my back ever since I got out of there. He *knows*, Cass."

"Maybe not, Tom—"

"Yes, he knows."

"He could have been guessing. Think about it. Along comes a guy saying he's got something valuable—he doesn't say what— that belongs back here. The emerald is their famous lost treasure so, *voilá*, he thinks Maria Theresa."

Tom kept his voice low and looked around again. "You didn't see his eyes, hear the way his words toyed with me. Even if he doesn't know—and I still say he *does*—he definitely tried to buy me off."

Cass's face twisted in thought. "Maybe a little bribe's not frowned upon here. Like *mordida* in Mexico. We don't know all their customs."

"I always thought most German and Austrian officials were pretty straight. Anyway, you can see why I want to check him out."

That's when their salads and venison sausages arrived.

"What do we do next?" Cass said when the waiter had left.

"I'm going to call the American Embassy and make an appointment."

On the subway back to the hotel, Tom's thoughts swung right back to Doctor Gerhard. *A nice little profit for yourself, I mean, your friend.* Again Tom felt the desire to look on the emerald. At the strange, alluring, green light it gave off, as if from within.

He didn't know he'd made a fist and was smacking it into the palm of his other hand till Cass touched him and said, "Still reliving that meeting, aren't you?"

"What? Oh . . ." He gave an embarrassed little smile, opened his hands and flexed his fingers. ". . . yeah. Guess so."

In their room, he tossed his coat and scarf on a chair, went to the phone and punched a number. In a moment he said, "*Ja, ist Herr Cavanaugh im Zimmer dreiundzwanzig* . . . Okay right, Room Thirty-three."

He cupped a hand over the mouthpiece and said, "Everybody here speaks English."

"So I've noticed." Cass kicked off her shoes, lay back on the bed, yawned, and laced her hands behind her head.

Tom removed his hand and spoke into the phone. "Right. Could you get the American Embassy for me, please? . . . Yes, I'll wait here. Oh, by the way, what's the fax number here at the hotel?" He wrote it down, said thanks and hung up. He drummed his fingers on the maple nightstand and stared at the soft green walls.

When the phone rang moments later, he yanked up the handset. "Yes."

"This is Frank Lary of the U.S. Embassy, returning your call." The voice sounded young. "How can I help you?"

"My name is Tom Cavanaugh; I'm an American citizen and a police officer. I'd like to meet with an embassy official today or tomorrow. It's important."

"Well, officer, this is the Presidents' Day weekend, you know. We just have a skeleton crew on duty here. What is it you need?"

"It has to do with how to donate something of value to the Austrian government."

"I'm the weekend duty guy, sir, and about all I could do is help you send a message to the States or get an emergency advance of funds."

Tom ground his teeth. "There's no one else in authority?"

"Sorry, not really. I could set up an appointment for Tuesday."

"No, that won't do. Thanks anyway."

Cass searched Tom's face as he put down the phone.

"Holiday weekend," he said. "They can't do a damn thing till Tuesday and we're heading home on Monday." Tom made a fist. "Our tax dollars at work." He was having second thoughts about the State Department.

He looked at his watch. "Two-thirty. That's, ah, nearly midnight back home. I'm going to call the department and leave a message for Mary Savage."

A few minutes later he got the lieutenant's voice-mail. "Hi Mary. This is Tom Cavanaugh of Narcotics with your strange request of the day. I'm calling from Vienna. I seem to remember you have a contact over here, a classmate from the academy." Without mentioning the emerald, he told her about Doctor Gerhard, that he'd had a bad experience with him, and could she ask her friend to run a check. He gave the hotel's fax number. "I'll be here one more day," he concluded. "And thanks. I owe you one."

Cass sat up on the bed. "Time to change gears, Cavanaugh. Let's try to have some fun. We're in *Vienna*, for crying out loud."

Tom's face brightened. "Good idea, babe. There's this big park, the Prater, and we could check out their huge Ferris wheel."

Leaving the hotel, Tom left his key with the man at the desk and said, "I'm expecting an important call."

"Certainly sir. From Doctor Gerhard of the *Kunsthistorisches* Museum?"

"No!" Tom's face clouded. "Why'd you say that?"

"Because he just left a message for you, sir. Here it is: 'I apologize if I was rude or abrupt. Please contact me and let me make it up to you.'"

"Did he ask for me right off, or did he inquire first if I was staying here?" Next to Tom, Cass crossed her arms, her brow wrinkling.

"I do not know, sir. I did not take the call myself."

"In the future, please tell your operator not to divulge to anyone, except a Lieutenant Savage, that we're staying here."

"As you wish, sir. Lieutenant Savage. I will see to it at once."

Out on the sidewalk, Cass said, "You're going to ignore that message from Gerhard, right?"

"Damn right."

Later, on the Ferris wheel, Tom said, "I know I'm on edge about that character, but I'm going to compartmentalize it. Won't let it spoil our afternoon."

"You're very perspicacious."

"I am? Is that something dirty?" Tom said with a laugh—which felt good. The car stopped at the very top—which didn't feel good. That acrophobia again.

A panorama of the Vienna plain spread out below. They were all alone in their enclosed coach, as large as the gondola that had carried them to the ski slopes. "So this is the world's biggest Ferris wheel?" Cass said.

"One of them." The car jerked and Tom grasped the hand rail. Particles of animal fear fluttered in his gut, but still he surveyed the few people at the ticket booth far below. "Orson Welles and Joseph Cotten rode this thing in *The Third Man*," he said. "Maybe even this car. Remember that scene?"

"Yes, there was a lot of menace in it. Wasn't that where Orson told him to watch his step?"

"Yeah, slippery old Harry Lime."

Cass looked to the west. "There's the roof of St. Stephen's. Beautiful."

For a moment, Tom thought he heard something. A faint echo. It sounded like the *ketrack-a-tack-tack* of snare drums. How was that possible? They were enclosed in a coach a hundred meters above Vienna. He couldn't even hear the garish music from the carnival games down below. He shook his head, shocked by a prickly feeling of something sensed but not grasped.

"Did you hear something just now?"

"Sure," Cass said with a laugh. "Doctor Gerhard warning you

to watch your step."

"Funny . . . Say, I wonder how Orbison is getting along." Tom wasn't really thinking about his cat, but he didn't want to dwell on what he might or might not have just heard. "I hope Mrs. Potter remembers to feed him."

"Orbison's doing just fine," Cass said. "He knows you're coming back to him. You always do. Ha. Whoever would have thought I'd be living with a pair of rascally tomcats."

It was cold in the car, and she snuggled up, an arm around him, her head resting on his shoulder. Adrift in their own thoughts, they gazed at the hazy foothills of the Carpathian Mountains. Neither spoke for a long moment. Then the wheel began to turn and the car lurched downward. Tom was glad—he'd felt vulnerable up there at the top.

Again he checked the faces of those milling around below.

Tom didn't sleep well. In one of his dreams, nightmares really, he was falling off a cliff. In another, a bullet flashed toward him. No matter how he ducked or which way he turned, the silvery projectile tracked straight at him, closer and closer, larger and larger. He woke up in a sweat.

When morning came, still troubled by the half-remembered dreams, he called the front desk for messages. There was one—from Sacramento.

" 'Can't comply your request.' " the operator read. " 'Sorry, my friend unavailable for a week.' The name is Ms. Savage."

Tom thanked him and relayed the message to Cass, who was brushing her teeth.

"You don't look, uh, rested," she said, rinsing her brush and standing it in a glass.

"I look terrible, you mean. Had some bad dreams."

"Cornfield and chapel again?"

He told her about the bullet tracking him in his dream.

She stroked his arm, then touched his cheek with her other hand.

In the hotel restaurant, a bowl of fruit and a basket of croissants and muffins laid out before them, Cass said, "What now?" She fanned her fingers in front of his face. "Hello?"

"Sorry, what?"

"You're a million miles away, Tom. What is it? That bullet again?"

"No." His eyes regained focus. "Just thinking."

"The curator guy?"

"Um, I guess so. What were you saying?"

"I said what shall we do now?"

"Well, we've struck out in this town. We're supposed to be in Salzburg tomorrow and then fly home from Munich. Let's see if we can move the flight up a day."

"No way." Cass's face clouded. "You finally got me over here by promising Salzburg. We're not skipping Salzburg."

"You're absolutely right, sorry. We might as well finish up here today and meanwhile I'll"—he caught himself—"I mean *we'll* come up with a new plan."

Her clouds parted with a smile.

"When we get back," she asked, while Tom cut open a muffin, "will you contact the State Department?"

"I've been rethinking that. It's another rust-caked bureaucracy that might just screw it up with mounds of red tape. Maybe it was okay that most everybody was off this weekend. We still need to find a simple, clean way to do this that'll keep Dad's name out of it—ours, too."

"What'll we do today, then? I know, let's go to the Hofburg and see the real crown jewels."

"That's where they'd expect us to go," Tom said softly. "If we're being watched, we should avoid the obvious. Let's go out to

Schönbrunn Palace and see where Napoleon did all that waltzing after he beat these guys at Austerlitz."

So, in the suburbs, they were touring the summer palace, among a cluster of people trailing a guide like ducklings. The Hall of Mirrors, countless dining rooms, sumptuous bedchambers.

Tom checked the others in the party. Four couples: three of them older, and one young, touchy-feely pair probably honeymooning; a blond woman in a stylish hat and camel-hair coat; three teenage girls wearing backpacks; and a slight, dark-haired man in glasses carrying a slender black briefcase. He didn't seem to fit.

They were in a bedroom now, and Cass noted, "These beds are surprisingly small."

The guide, overhearing, said, "People were shorter in those days."

Tom whispered, "We'd have to lie real close together," and Cass shot him that smoky look she had.

As they filed into the next room—this place was endless—he checked on the man in the glasses. He'd hung way back and was talking softly into a mobile phone.

Later, as they tramped the vast park-like grounds, Cass said, "This would be a great place for jogging."

Tom looked for the man in the glasses but didn't see him. "No kidding," he said. "Let's come here every month and run."

"Right. On *your* credit card."

Tom glimpsed the woman in the camel-hair coat, partly obscured by a statue of a bearded man wielding a sword. Beneath the hat and dark glasses, she could be the blonde from Garmisch. He noticed glossy leather riding boots and gloves. *There!* She lowered a camera and looked away. Damn it, she'd sneaked a picture of them. He was sure.

The woman walked off at a fast pace.

Tom started after her, but jerked to a stop. He snapped his head both ways, looking at the retreating woman, then at Cass, whose face wore a question mark. He ran back to Cass.

"Let's head over and see if this zoo thing is any good," he said, taking her by the arm and steering her in the opposite direction, toward an ornate iron gate at the rear of the grounds.

CHAPTER FIVE

W hat was that all about?" Cass said. "Leaving me for another woman already?"

Tom's face told her he wasn't in a joking mood. "She took pictures of us. I wanted to grab her and find out what the hell was going on. I was really torn—go after her or stay with you. But I couldn't leave you alone out here, not with all the weird stuff that's happened."

Cass gave a meager smile. "I would've been fine."

They rehashed it the next morning on the way to Salzburg, Cass driving.

"You might have been embarrassed big time," she said, changing lanes to pass a truck. "Maybe she's a professional photographer and we'll end up in her portfolio. After all, we *are* an interesting couple. You've sneaked pictures of people yourself when they weren't looking. Don't deny it. People-watching is fun . . . Now Tom, about the emerald, why don't you just go to the Austrian Embassy in Washington, clean and simple."

"Call me overly suspicious, Cass, but remember, the emerald was stolen by the Nazis and it recently came out that Austria's president was a Nazi intelligence officer back in the day."

"Oh right, I remember now. Couple of years ago. Big national embarrassment."

"And Austria's foreign service is directly under the president," Tom said, "so nope, I don't trust 'em, don't wanta go to their embassy. I'd like the emerald to somehow go straight to the Hofburg palace."

Cass nodded.

They reached Salzburg after dark and checked into a hotel, where the concierge gave them a full dose of dining and sightseeing advice.

Tom told Cass he was tired, trying desperately to put the emerald business aside, and hoping to get a good night's sleep.

"No hanky panky, big guy?"

"Well, I didn't say *that*, babe."

The next day at lunch, Cass dipped a spoon into her dumpling soup and said, "We're putting away a lot of calories on this trip."

"Know why? Because a waist is a terrible thing to mind."

Cass groaned. "The Cavanaugh Curse strikes again. If you're part Irish, the other part must be Macadamian."

Once in San Francisco they had stopped in a coffee shop wedged between a Nordstrom Rack and a Hard Rock Café. "Know what?" Tom had said. "We're between a Rack and a Hard Place." That was when Cass coined the term "The Cavanaugh Curse."

Hohensalzburg Castle brooded above the town like an ancient tyrant. After visiting Mozart's boyhood home, they rode a funicular up the mountainside to this medieval fortress.

They spent three hours there, walking the grounds and inspecting the old buildings.

At one point Tom, looking over the precipice, leaned out to admire the sweeping view, and put his hands on a low rock wall. The incline below him was steep and sheer. A chill breeze ruffled his hair and music drifted up from somewhere down in the city. Far below, the River Salzach rushed lively and cold.

A large bird, maybe a hawk or falcon, began swooping around. Tom leaned out a bit more. Some of his vertigo appeared. His knees trembled. He lost his balance.

A bittersweet stench trembles across his senses. A blurry force encompasses him. He seems to be slipping through a dark tunnel.

It's not the River Salzach down there anymore. It's the Chickahominy. Tom glances down at his dirty blue dungarees and his high-topped shoes, scuffed and nicked from many months of marching, scrounging firewood, and digging rifle pits.

He and the Twelfth Massachusetts have just come through the terrible scrap with the Confederates now being called the Battle of Fair Oaks. They're a mighty long way from Boston now and just a dozen or so miles from Richmond. He's just helped to fix up a little farmhouse for General Mansfield to use as his headquarters. Kindly old General Mansfield, a damn good commander. Tom loves that fine old man.

It's a steep dropoff down to the Chickahominy, but a grand view. Down below, a large black bird is circling, playfully riding the air currents.

Tom steps up to the edge. He's never been bothered about heights. He's also not concerned about snipers on the far bank. Joe Johnston's Rebel rear guard was driven out of there yesterday by Company D in a splendid little action.

The Chickahominy is a lot wider and deeper than Antietam Creek. Antietam Creek? What the devil is that? He's never heard of anything called Antietam Creek. Where had that crazy thought come from?

Oh oh. Some rocks give way under Tom's feet. He loses his balance, arms windmilling uselessly. His weight, already shifted to his upper body, tilts him forward. He falls. Christ almighty!

Now his feet stand on nothing but air. Down and down he plummets. The rocky riverbank seems to be rushing up to meet him. He's always known he might get killed in battle, but not from falling off a stupid cliff. Arms flailing frantically. Almost to the rocks now. He knows he's about to die.

Again the rank but sweet smell, in his nostrils for a moment, then gone.

The riverbank vanishes. Someone has thrown arms around his chest.

It's Cass. Cass is tugging at him for all her hundred and thirty pounds are worth. She yanks him back from the edge.

Breathing hard, Tom regains his balance, looks over his shoulder, eyes wide, and utters, "What just . . . Hey, where did you come from?"

"Where did I come from? From South Pasadena by way of Sacramento, you silly goof."

"But I was . . . Well, hey, you just saved my life. Thank God for those great reflexes of yours."

Cass turned him around and hugged him from the front. "You started to teeter there, sure, but you're exaggerating a bit. Anyway, what's a medieval fortress without a thrill or two?" She grinned. "Hey, I finally got to use the Heimlich maneuver."

Tom shook his head, quivering from what he'd just experienced, or thought *maybe* he'd just experienced. The Chickahominy? General Mansfield? He wasn't going to tell her about this. She'd never understand. Hell, he didn't understand either.

In their room that night, Tom repeated that it had been a very close call and that she'd saved his life. "I'll probably have acute acrophobia forever." He still wasn't going to tell Cass about the weird sensation he thought he'd had that afternoon. He'd heard about genetic memory. Could he have been in the Civil War in a previous life? No, that was impossible. *Wasn't it?*

Cass was grinning. "It must have been the ancient curse of the emerald," she said.

"The only curse around here is the one you've applied to my exceptional sense of humor."

Later, as they lay nestled together in bed, anxious thoughts began to trouble Tom. The search of their room. That curator who knew too much. Crazy Civil War jumbles. Their pictures taken stealthily. Almost falling from that high castle.

Outside, a bare branch scratched against the window like a bony finger. Even here in Salzburg the *Föhn* was blowing.

CHAPTER SIX

s the plane took off, Tom gazed out at the green countryside, the River Inn, and the distant Alps. He'd just started to rehash all that had happened in the last five days, and especially the disturbing sounds and images he thought he'd been experiencing.

Sometimes he thought he should just keep the damned emerald. Or give it back to his father and say, "Sorry, I tried." He glanced over at Cass, who had her headset on but volume off, seat reclined, eyes closed. Let her sleep, he thought.

An hour later, somewhere over the North Atlantic, she stirred and gave him a sleepy "Hi." When she was fully awake, they talked again about Doctor Gerhard and his offer to buy "the item."

With a little grin, Tom said, "I wonder how much—"

"Don't even think about it."

"Five million? Ten?"

"Tom!" She punched his arm.

"You know I'm kidding." He grinned and touched her hand. "You pack quite a wallop there, babe."

"And you've got a lopsided smile."

"Crooked smile, honest soul," Tom said.

"So you keep telling me. What are you going to do now?"

"Regroup and rethink."

"If you're not going to the State Department, maybe the governor—"

"No, Cass, don't say anything to her. The more people who know, the more potential for trouble."

"But Governor Maggie's as honest as apple pie."

"Nevertheless—"

"All right, officer, I bow to your judgment."

They sat in silence awhile, then asked for red wine when the flight attendants pushed their cart up the aisle.

"Back to The Hole tomorrow," Tom said, biting his lip. The Hole is what he called his undercover narcotics location on the south side of town. He wasn't looking forward to it. Drug enforcement was more nightmare than occupation.

"And I go back," she said, sipping her wine, "to piles and piles of . . . insert the expletive of your choice."

Tom knew she thrived on the excitement of the governor's office, that her complaints weren't serious.

When they reached Sacramento—it seemed like a year later—they passed a bank of phone booths in the terminal. Tom thought about calling his father in Novato but decided against it. Too jet-lagged for a decent conversation. He'd see him soon enough.

Home at last, in their two-story Victorian near William Land Park, he punched the playback button on their answering machine while Cass unpacked her bags. Most of the seventeen messages could wait till morning and he fast-forwarded through them. On the last, the voice of a man who didn't identify himself said simply, "I hope you had a pleasant trip, the both of you." The voice, which Tom didn't recognize, had no discernible accent.

Across the room, Cass had been dropping wrinkled clothes into a hamper. She stopped and turned a puzzled face toward him.

In his palatial home, Kurt Neumann made himself laugh when his accountant said, "That looks a lot like the *Duquesa*, the lost Goya. Could it be that my best client is a cat burglar?"

"I'm glad you recognized it," Neumann said with forced ease. "It's a copy, you see, commissioned by a Barcelona merchant many years ago. The fellow hit hard times and I was able to buy it at a good price." Neumann lied well, but it surprised him that this young number-cruncher knew something about art. He'd have to be more careful, much more careful.

"A copy? That's disappointing," the accountant said, grinning as he closed his briefcase. "It would be cool to know a secret art thief."

"I suppose it would . . . I do appreciate your saving me a trip downtown," Neumann said, shaking the man's hand and ushering him out.

He closed the door and slid both deadbolts into place. "*Mein Gott!*" He pounded a fist into an open palm. Neumann hated surprises. That would not happen again.

He crossed the living room of his sprawling, cream-colored house on Camino Alegre in La Jolla, California, and returned to the den. He placed himself five feet from the Goya and locked onto the depthless brown eyes of the beautiful woman. They seemed almost alive. He loved that painting and was very pleased with himself for possessing it.

A tremor had shaken the art world in 1970 when a priceless oil by Francisco Goya, *La Duquesa de Catalonia*, vanished from the Prado Museum in Madrid. The Spanish government offered $20,000 for information leading to its return. None ever came.

Seven years later, Claude Monet's *Guyenne Pastoral* was stolen from the Yale University Art Gallery. When the security guards opened up one morning the painting was simply gone. Where it had hung, they found only an embarrassed rectangle of space, slightly lighter in color than the surrounding wall.

Both masterpieces, in ornate gilt frames, now hung in Kurt Neumann's very private den in La Jolla.

Neumann, still trim though nearing fifty, ran a hand through his close-cropped hair, now mostly gone from blond to gray. He glanced through a huge window at the Pacific Ocean stretching endlessly beyond Windansea Beach. He admired the artistic creations of both man and nature.

A flash of sunlight glinted off a fishing boat, a mile offshore. He gazed for a moment as the boat slid north toward the kelp beds. He loved to watch the sea crash against jagged rocks below his picture windows. *Such spectacular sunsets I see out where sea ends and sky begins.*

Neumann turned away from the window. Clad in a blue polo shirt, dove-gray trousers and Gucci loafers—no socks—he stood erect, clasped his hands behind him, and gazed lovingly at the two stolen masterpieces that had come into his possession four years before. They were greatly admired by the few select friends he allowed in that room, after determining beforehand that they knew next to nothing about art history.

Two years before his retirement, he'd met an international smuggler of stolen art while on a combination business and pleasure trip to his native Germany. Within a week of meeting the smuggler in Frankfurt, Neumann had purchased a rare vase from the Wan Li period. At $50,000, he considered it a bargain. The paintings came soon after, costing substantially more. He became a key player in the art world's black market and developed shady contacts in Europe, Asia and Latin America. When he became obsessed with an item—he always called things he wanted *items*—he would stop at nothing to get it.

Since the paintings, Neumann had acquired several other illicit items. Lately he'd become obsessed with the pursuit of gemstones.

He'd made his fortune through an electronics company he'd founded in Chicago in 1969. "I was shrewd enough," he often bragged to himself, "to switch from producing stereos to mobile phones just ahead of the big trend. No one is more astute than I."

When he retired to the Sierra foothills—La Jolla came later—he brought with him hundreds of millions of dollars and a feeble wife whose health was failing.

Then for once his judgment let him down. Even for a wealthy

man, the chance to turn two million dollars into a quick ten was too good to pass up. But the Colombian cocaine deal went bad and nearly ruined him. The botched affair cost him his wife, who soon died of heart failure. He told himself his stupidity had killed her.

Not a day went by without his thinking of the young narcotics cop who'd brought him down, a cop named Tom Cavanaugh.

CHAPTER SEVEN

Tom was back at work the next day, getting reacquainted with the drug wars and fielding questions about the trip. Was German beer better than the import stuff you get here? Were the *Fräuleins* real babes? When would he get his pictures back?

On his way home that afternoon he stopped at the bank just before closing time. He needed to transfer some funds, and wanted to see that his ailing father's insurance policies were up to date.

He filled out a safe deposit box form. A minute later a tiny Hispanic woman buzzed him through a security door and led him into the vault. Reaching his box, they each inserted and turned a key. The woman slid the box out and placed it on a table. "Take all the time you want," she said, and left.

Alone, raising the long metal lid, Tom began to get the same engulfed feeling he sometimes experienced in the quiet of a great library, or a cathedral. The stacks of locked boxes rising on each side of him could be ancient bookshelves, the soft fluorescent lighting, the sun filtered through stained glass.

He put aside a copy of his father's will and the deed to the house he and Cass had bought, and came to his insurance policies. He picked them up, glanced at their paper jackets, and put them down with the others. He picked up something else from the very bottom of the drawer. It was an old woolen pouch with a drawstring. The fibers were crinkly with age, the coarse brown cloth faded almost to gray.

He opened it and, shielding it from the surveillance camera with his left hand, removed the contents. An icy shiver trembled through his chest. He felt the weight of ancient eyes, catching him with a forbidden love. He stared for a long time into the Maria Theresa Emerald's warm deep pool of green.

As he turned the jewel in his right hand, it seemed to become a beautiful woman, aware of being admired. He'd always thought of the emerald that way, as a woman. It almost pulsed with vivid, inner light. Exquisite hues of verdant fire.

He actually felt the emerald's pull. A tiny green planet with a force field of its own.

Have you been waiting for me? Why are you so beautiful? You're an enchantress, aren't you? Did you taunt my father this way, did you? What games are you playing with me today? Several minutes passed in his reverie.

You would look so magnificent dangling from Cass's neck, nestled in that velvety valley between her breasts.

Stop this, Tom scolded himself. He thrust the emerald into the sack, jerked the drawstring tight, shoved it back in the tray, and covered it with the papers. He snapped the lid closed and slid the box back into its slot.

He punched the little bell indicating he was finished, and the bank clerk returned.

Driving away, he felt as if he'd skipped his grandfather's funeral to go to a matinee striptease.

"And who would be mastering whom?" Tom said. He was still talking to the emerald.

Two days later, Tom drove to Novato, a San Francisco suburb in hill country north of Mount Tamalpais.

He recognized the gray Jeep in front of his father's house. It belonged to Roy Oakley, one of his dad's closest friends. Both men were widowed and Tom was glad Oakley was a regular visitor. These two aging men, one gravely ill, still needed friends, maybe now more than ever.

Tom let himself in and made his way to the bedroom.

A cedar chest with a TV on top faced the bed, and a lamp, clock radio and remote control for the TV sat on a nightstand. Framed photos of Tom, his brother Michael, and his mother hung on the walls. One of those had been taken at Thanksgiving twenty years ago when his mother was still alive. Magazines and newspapers cluttered a chair and small table. Rich memories filled the room and flooded Tom's mind. He'd climbed all over that chair as a small boy, probably causing some of the cracks in its old brown leather.

"Thomas, welcome home," his father said. Two pillows propped up his head, and oxygen tubes snaked into his nostrils. His once-muscular arms were thin as rake handles, but the blue eyes twinkled and the voice hadn't weakened much.

"Thanks, Dad, good to be back. Hello, Mister Oakley."

"I keep telling you, Tom, call me Roy." The man was tan and fit at sixty-eight and his white goatee gave him a scholarly look. His handshake was robust.

"You should have seen the day nurse who left here a little while ago," Oakley said. "She was in black oxfords she could've got off a sailor. Never thought I'd see the day when guys wore earrings and girls wore men's shoes."

"Times change," Tom's dad said, "but this son of a buck has trouble dealing with it." He winked. "Old Twenty-Five-for-Twenty-Five was just telling me about his new shotgun." They both were longtime members of the North Coast Rifle & Pistol Club.

"You still break twenty-five straight clay pigeons?" Tom asked.

"Not as often as I used to, but pretty often."

"Your grandmother must have been named Annie."

"I wish I had a dollar for every time I've heard that one. Say, how's your young lady? Cass, isn't it?"

"Right, Cass. She's fine, thanks. You've got a new shotgun

then?"

"It's an antique," Tom's dad interjected. "French job, nineteenth century, double-barrel, four-bore . . . Get a beer for Roy and one for yourself, Thomas. You know where they are. Hell, bring me one too," he added with a grin. "What can it do, kill me?"

When Tom returned, he and Oakley leaned over the bed and clinked bottles with Desmond Cavanaugh, who said, "To family and good friends. Now, tell me how it went in Vienna, son."

It was the question Tom had dreaded. "Well, ah . . ." His eyes shot his dad a look.

"Now, you can talk in front of Roy. He knows all about it."

"It must have been very romantic for you and your lady," Oakley said diplomatically.

"Oh, it was, Mister, er, Roy." Tom talked about the sights and the Vienna cuisine for a few minutes before turning to the emerald. Again he sneaked a warning look at his dad.

"Go on, Thomas. Tell us how it went. State secrets are safe with Roy."

As Tom reluctantly told about the fiasco at the Vienna museum, Oakley listened with an intent but warm look.

Tom turned to his father. "Say, Dad, how many of you guards were there at Nuremberg?"

"How many? Hell, around two hundred I guess, counting the Brits, the Ivans and the Frogs."

"About fifty Americans then?"

"At least. Maybe more. Why?"

"Did any of them get close to Goering, like you did with Keitel?"

"Yes, I think Tex Wheelis did. He thought it was pretty special to sit and chew the fat with such a notorious personality."

"Could he have slipped Goering the cyanide capsule?"

"Conceivably. Some of the guys thought Tex might have. It really hit the fan when Goering poisoned himself. We were all told to keep our thoughts to ourselves—or else!"

Oakley put a paternal hand on Tom's shoulder and said, "You've had quite a trip, and you're handling this quite well. Dirty trick of the lazy old cop here, sticking you with this." This last line was uttered with a wink at his dad that jarred Tom. *I wish this guy would shut up about our emerald—it's family business.*

"If there's anything I can do to help," Oakley said, "anything at all, let me know. I have some contacts."

Tom didn't want to go any further down that road just now.

"Thanks. Nice of you," he said. "Can't think of anything, though. Just keep looking in on my pop here."

"Don't worry about that . . . Say, you're a sports fan, aren't you?"

"I follow the A's and the Kings a little, mostly on TV."

"Perfect. I'm getting a new home entertainment center and I'd like to give you my old TV. It's a giant-screen Sony."

"Take it, son," said his dad. "Thing's huge, like being in a movie theater."

"No, we couldn't."

"Sure you can. Des here doesn't have room for it, so I was gonna give it to the VFW. Take it. I insist."

"That's awfully generous," Tom said.

"Nonsense. I'm practically family, right, Des? It's settled. I'll have it sent out next week."

Tom hung around another half hour, hoping Oakley would leave. It was getting late, though, and he had to get back. When he left, the gray Jeep was still out in front.

Driving home, Tom gazed out across the north shore of San Pablo Bay, which was basically the northern arm of San Francisco Bay. The sky was overcast, the choppy waters somber and menacing beneath their shroud of gray. His mood matched.

They hadn't discussed next steps. He wouldn't do that in front of Oakley. *Dammit, Dad, we have to talk again soon—alone.*

Tom went over what he knew of Oakley. He'd quit police work early, leaving the San Francisco force in his thirties to start an industrial security firm. Now he lived off the interest from his investments and he also owned a lumber mill somewhere in the mountains.

Tom thought about Nuremberg. So there had been fifty or so American guards there. Someone like that Doctor Gerhard could maybe have got their names from old Army records, which probably wouldn't be classified. And one of the names would be Desmond Cavanaugh, who became a California police chief. From there it would have been easier than sin to trace his son Tom.

The thought shadowed him for miles.

When he pulled into the driveway, it cheered him to see the house he and Cass had bought six months ago, pooling their assets. Alone, neither one could have afforded this stately old home. Now they were slowly restoring it.

Over dinner, he recounted his afternoon, but didn't tell Cass of his concern over Oakley knowing about the emerald. He liked Oakley—a little.

"Do you think he means it about the big-screen TV?" she asked.

"I think so. He's a pretty straight shooter. Pun not intended."

"Nice try."

"Subconsciously intended?"

"That I might buy. The TV's nice, but I don't want it in the front room. How about the spare room you've earmarked for your study? I'll come in and watch *Nova* some time, or *Jeopardy*."

"You'll like Alex Trebek lifesize."

"Yes, I will."

After they cleaned up the kitchen, Tom channel-surfed on the old set. Cass, sitting next to him on the sofa, pored over a mound of files from the governor's office. Tom marveled at how she could shut out the TV and concentrate on office work the way she did. Orbison the cat snoozed at their feet. If the old silver-and-gray tabby was happy they were back home, he didn't make a big thing of it.

Tom came across a documentary on the Civil War and got hooked. It emphasized the European and Irish immigrants who'd fought on the Union side in battalions from New York, Pennsylvania and Massachusetts. He leaned back and cupped his hands behind his head while Cass flipped pages in a three-ring binder, speed-reading.

Minutes passed and he grew more engrossed. He also thought, with a quiver in his stomach, about that weird experience at Salzburg, where he thought he'd been falling off a cliff above the Chicahominy River in a Civil War uniform.

He suddenly threw his hands to his side and sat up straight. He was watching a segment on the Battle of Antietam, fought in 1862 near the little town of Sharpsburg, Maryland. He was entranced by old photographs of a whitewashed Dunkard Church where the Confederates had built a line of defense, and a cornfield through which Union troops had attacked them. The corn was high, tasseled, nearly ready for harvest. *Just as he knew it would be.*

The hair on his neck stood up and a shiver brushed his spine. Realization flooded over him; this was the church and cornfield he'd seen in sporadic flashes. He felt as if he'd been there. What did it mean? he wondered. *What's going on?*

The narrator mentioned the Twelfth Massachusetts and the weird feeling grew even stronger when a banner emblazoned with that name appeared on the screen. The Twelfth Massachusetts.

Tom heard a commanding voice cry out, "Dress ranks!" He shuddered. The voice came from inside his head, not the TV, he was sure of it. *What the hell is happening?*

His nostrils suddenly filled with the biting smell of black gunpowder smoke. His chest jolted. He threw a hand to his left biceps.

"What?" Cass blurted. She had dropped the office reading into her lap. How long had she been facing him? "You slapped your hand to your arm. You looked like you'd been shot."

"Just a small pain there for a second. Nothing to worry about."

"It's gone now?" Cass touched the spot.

"Yeah, I'm fine, but those flash pictures I've been having? I think they're subliminal glimpses of that battlefield there, Antietam."

"Really? What just happened? What did you feel?"

Tom did his best to explain.

"I don't necessarily believe in reincarnation," she said, "but I don't reject it either."

They discussed psychic phenomena and the like for several minutes, then Cass snuggled against his shoulder and glanced up at his face. "I think we'll have to go to Antietam," she said.

"What?"

"We should go to Antietam, wherever that is."

Tom thought so too. He took her in his arms and held her tight. Ever since Hohensalzburg Castle, he'd felt closer to her than ever.

Dress ranks?

CHAPTER EIGHT

L ieutenant Mary Savage, who headed the Homicide Department, was a cinch to make captain soon. Everyone was a little awed by her, including Mike Norfleet, a homicide detective and friend of Tom's. "She's so smart it's scary," Norfleet had said. "You and her are really on the escalator, the hottest cops we got."

"And you are a bullshitter," Tom had said.

Now he was about to have coffee with Savage in the employee lounge of the new downtown station. He missed the old station, a neoclassical stone and brick affair recently abandoned after almost a century of service. A Depression-era white globe with the word POLICE on it had stood out in front. At night, he used to envision Humphrey Bogart leaning against the pole, coat collar turned up, cigarette dangling from his mouth.

But time and Tom march on. In jeans and a San Diego State Aztecs sweatshirt, he slipped coins in the machine and filled two styrofoam cups with coffee.

Savage took hers black, the same as Tom. Her brown hair was bobbed and she wore a simple white blouse and navy skirt, cut slightly above the knee. Tom knew she was proud of her legs. Although she laughed and joked as they took seats at a vinyl-topped table, her brown eyes gave him a cool appraisal. Every time they met she asked about Cass.

"How's Cass?" she said.

"Fine. Feisty as ever."

"Feisty is good, especially in a woman." Savage wasn't an overly aggressive feminist, but she stood up for her gender.

"Yeah, most of the time it is," Tom said.

"You couldn't just agree without some small qualification?"

"Cass hasn't cornered all the feistiness in town," Tom said, meeting her glance.

Savage laughed. "So what's up, narc? Why you buying me a cup of coffee? You've already dashed my hopes that you and your statehouse sweetie were finished and you were here to ask me out."

"Flattery"—Tom smiled—"will get you anywhere. I don't figure on that happening, Cass and me breaking up, but if it ever does . . . Mary, about your cop friend in Europe."

"Great segué, Cavanaugh." She made a face in anticipation of her first sip of machine coffee. "He's a Luxembourger or whatever you call people from that little place. Charles Alzette. We were in the same class at the FBI Academy in Virginia. He's a pal as well as a professional contact. I helped him run down a fugitive from Antwerp a year or two ago. To save on hotels, I stayed with him a couple of nights the last time I went to Europe."

"The fugitive?"

"No, bozo. Charles."

"Sorry about that. It's this curse thing."

"What curse thing?"

"My amazing sense of humor is known in some circles as the Cavanaugh Curse."

"Maybe I'll leave you and your curse to Cass after all. But what's this about, your message from Vienna. What do you need?"

He told her about Rolf Gerhard and the Art History Museum, skipping a lot of detail and not mentioning the emerald.

"Charles is due back from Asia in a few days," she said. Then I'll ask him to see what he can find out about this Gerhard. I'll let you know as soon as he comes up with something."

"This is just informal, unofficial stuff. Don't let it get in the way of department business."

"No sweat. But what's this really all about? You get a bad feeling about a guy you meet in Vienna and suddenly you need a background check?"

"I'll tell you the whole story some day, Mary. Can't do it now."

"I'll hold you to that." Savage stood. "Next time I'm buying," she said with a sardonic glance at the coffee machine. Tom got a firm but warm handshake.

In his ocean-front home, Kurt Neumann, his fists clenched, was thinking about Tom Cavanaugh. *I hate that man. He robbed me of my peace, my dignity, and my wife.* His wife's death, however, didn't bother him as much as he let on—he'd been getting some on the side even before she died.

After his drug-deal fiasco, he'd changed his name from Richter to Neumann—literally a new man—and reinvented himself five hundred miles to the south. He still owned some property near the Sierras, but now he was ensconced in his sprawling seaside home in La Jolla.

As Neumann, he became part of San Diego's social set. He contributed to the symphony, the opera and the art museum, and he had a box at the Del Mar Racetrack.

His father, Willi Richter, had been a Nazi officer in World War II. In the last chaotic month of the war, he'd managed to spirit his wife and little Kurt to a cousin's home in Argentina, via Spain. The father said he would burn his uniform, change his identity and follow as soon as possible. Kurt was just six at the time. "I hardly knew my father," he later told his wife. "Maybe he was caught by the SS and shot as a traitor. Maybe he died in an Allied prison camp, or settled down in Switzerland—the bastard—with another woman."

Not knowing his father's fate hurt Neumann deeply. He had spent a great deal of time and money on trips abroad trying to find the answer, for both himself and for his mother. The lonely woman, now eighty-two, still lived with him. "Kurt, it is so extravagant," she would say each time he acquired a new art treasure. "You must be more thrifty."

I am a driven man, he admitted. *I will do anything to get what I want.*

He'd once had a man who stood in his way *managed*.

"My God," he said aloud, "some day I will have Tom Cavanaugh *managed*."

Late that afternoon, Tom slumped in the sofa with that day's *Sacramento Bee*. Troubles in the Middle East and the Balkans. A plane crash in Indonesia killed sixty people.

Orbison moseyed over and sniffed at Tom's feet before hopping on the sofa.

"How do you do that?" Tom said. "Take off straight up, then land soft as a feather?"

Orbison didn't answer, but simply curled up in a ball beside Tom's hip.

"And how do you do *that*, buckaroo? Put your head up against your hind feet like that? You got a rubber spine?"

Tom had saved Orbison years before from a black plastic sack that had been tossed out in the back of a parking lot. The little kitten's three siblings had already died. "But you were made of tougher stuff, weren't you, Orby? You were hanging on till your new buddy came by on his evening jog."

He stroked the cat's neck. Orbison, motor running, looked up and smiled, Tom could have sworn it.

He went back to the paper and turned to the sports section. The Kings might make the NBA playoffs.

He turned the page, mussing Orbison's fur. The cat looked up and cocked his head as if to say, "Watch it." Tom stroked him beneath the neck and Orbison purred. "That's better."

The phone rang and Tom went to his antique rolltop desk, switching on the green-glass Tiffany lamp as he picked up the phone.

"Mister Cavanaugh? This is Fred Hutchinson. I'm an attorney with Curry, Bickford & Marshall. I'd like to set up a meeting with you on behalf of one of my clients."

"A meeting? What about?"

"He has a proposal to make to you."

Tom's brow furrowed. "What kind of proposal? Do I know your client?"

"It would be best to discuss this in person."

"I'm pretty busy right now. You'll have to give me some idea—"

"Mister Cavanaugh, he wants to make you a generous offer"—storm warnings went off in Tom's head—"for something that's in your possession."

Heart racing, Tom said, "I don't know what you're talking about." All the light had gone out of the afternoon. Even the walls seemed darker.

"He's willing to place three hundred thousand dollars in your hands very discreetly."

This sounded like the voice Tom had heard on his answering machine. "I still don't know what . . . Who the hell are you fronting for?"

"Take some time and consider it, Mister Cavanaugh. Three hundred thousand dollars in cash, which the IRS will know nothing about. Talk it over with Cass."

Tom recoiled. *Cass? This guy knows her name?*

"When you change your mind, just call me." He rattled off the phone number.

Tom slapped the receiver down, surprise and anger flushed on his face. He leaned his chin into the palm of a hand, braced by an elbow on the desk. He looked at the number he'd taken down.

Area code 415. San Francisco.

"Three hundred thousand is a lot of money, buckaroo."

Orbison stared at him and frowned, Tom could have sworn it.

Two hours later, with Cass at his side, Tom climbed the grandstand ramp to the Cal Expo harness races. Each carried a racing program and a cup of beer. Tom also had a tabloid that listed past performances.

A Dixieland band they couldn't see barked out a spirited number. "Do you know who wrote that?" Tom asked.

"Wrote what?"

"That song. *The South Rampart Street Parade.*"

"Oh, is that what that is? I sort of recognize the tune . . . Pinetop Smith?"

"No, but that's a hell of a guess. It was Steve Allen. They should play Allen's other great song, *This Could Be the Start of Something Big,* since we'll rake in so much money tonight. Ha."

In the rare times they gambled, Cass invariably did better than Tom. He couldn't understand it. She operated on hunches while he studied everything out.

"Good idea, coming out here tonight," she said. "Chance to blow out a little stress."

They gazed out from beneath a huge overhanging roof at a mile-long oval track ringed by light poles. Beyond the state fairgrounds to the south, the American River coursed lazily around a wide bend. They found spots on the aisle, near the betting windows and concession stands. Tom folded Cass's seat down for her.

Three hundred thousand bucks, he thought, a lot of money. Invested well, that could set him up pretty nicely. He could take all the time he wanted getting a credential to teach history. He could travel. He could . . . *Stop it!* Damn, that was a disturbing phone call from that lawyer. That lawyer who knew Cass's name.

"Tom, are you okay?"

"Sure, why?"

"You act troubled. And except for naming that song, you haven't said ten words."

"I had a phone call today—"

"Tom, what do you say?" It was a young woman with curly black hair, denim shirt and blue jeans. A guy in cowboy boots, trimmed beard—a Vandyke—and a 49ers cap held her hand.

"April, hi." April was the lone woman in Tom's narcotics unit out in the boonies. Tom thought hers was a sweet little name that didn't fit a cop, so he'd labeled her April the Cop as if to remind himself that she was very tough and very good at her work.

"What are you guys doing here?" Tom said.

"Same thing as you. Running surveillance on some four-legged suspects."

Tom and April made the introductions. Her boyfriend's name was Rick and he was a bartender.

"Good to meet you," Rick said. "I got a tip for you, for what it's worth. *Purgatory* in the second race. A guy comes into my bar is a trainer."

After April and Rick left, Cass said, "You never told me April was so attractive," giving Tom a nudge with her elbow.

"I didn't know I was required to provide a full description of the people I work with."

"Just the females. I'll bet not many cops are named April."

"Her name is actually April May," Tom said.

"No kidding? Her folks must've had a perverse streak."

The first post was in ten minutes and they scanned their programs.

"I like *Jan Do* in the first race," Cass said. "Number Five, see? Jan's my sister and she always says five is her lucky number."

"Let me check that out. Ah, here we are. *Jan Do* ran third the time before last, the only time she's been in the money in nine races. They ought to call that nag *No Jan Do*."

"Tonight she *will* do, though," Cass said, eyes a-twinkle. Her hand stroked his back idly for a moment, then she got to her feet. "I'm going up to make a bet. Have you decided?"

"Not yet. Still checking these past performances."

"Well, I'm going on up. Can I get you something?"

"Not now, babe, thanks."

Tom had trouble concentrating. Who was trying to buy Austria's emerald from him? That attorney, Fred Hutchinson, had a hell of a nerve saying "*when* you change your mind."

How could I get my hands on Hutchinson's client list? he wondered. No way could he subpoena it. He was glad when Cass returned and diverted his mind.

She'd bet five dollars on *Jan Do* to show. After the trotter finished second at long odds, Cass collected twenty-three dollars in winnings.

In the second race, Tom put six dollars across the board on *Purgatory*, the tip from April's friend. It finished dead last. "I'm gonna give April some grief tomorrow about her friend and his inside information."

"Here's one for you," Cass said before the fourth race. "*Steverino*. No Steve Allen fan could resist that."

"You're right, I can't." Tom couldn't—and soon lost two dollars.

"Marty Rocks," he said, shrugging it off.

"Marty Rocks? Is that a horse or our little game?"

"The game."

"Miner?" Cass tried.

"Nope."

"Bartender then."

"Right, bartender."

"Heaven help me, I'm starting to understand how you think."

They left thirty minutes later. Going up the stairs, Tom made a fist and put it before his mouth like a microphone. "This just in:

Cavanaugh loses sixteen dollars at racetrack; Nesbit wins forty."

"Woman's intuition," Cass said.

"In Greek mythology, Cassandra had the power to foretell the future."

"You know it, buster. That's not a myth."

Tom didn't mention that Cassandra was abducted and murdered by the Mycenaeans. She'd know it, anyway. And he still hadn't told her about the call from Curry, Bickford & Marshall.

As they climbed the stairs to the exit ramp, a brunette woman about Tom's age with hard eyes and short hair peered out from behind a pillar, a camera strapped from her neck. She carried a SHOP SAN DIEGO tote bag, and she watched them closely.

CHAPTER NINE

T he next day, after sleeping poorly, Tom called the number he'd been given. The voice system said he'd reached the direct line for Fred Hutchinson, who wasn't available. To leave a message, press one, for further options, press zero. Tom chose zero and soon got an operator.

"Curry, Bickford & Marshall, Attorneys at Law," she answered.

"When do you expect Fred Hutchinson back?"

"I'm not sure. Would you care to leave a message?"

"No, I'll call back."

Curry, Bickford & Marshall. He hadn't thought about it before, but now something there rang a distant bell, though he couldn't put his finger on it.

So, apparently the caller was a real attorney and the law firm was genuine. Unless the man who called himself Fred Hutchinson was really someone else. He could have hired an answering service and a clever operator—a possibility.

Just to be sure, he called San Francisco information and asked for the number of Curry, Bickford & Marshall, attorneys at law. He was soon given a number and the operator added, "on Montgomery Street."

Tom thanked her and hung up. Okay, the trick now was to get the names of Fred Hutchinson's clients, but that was surely confidential information. He thought of Lan Nguyen, an eighteen-year-old California computer whiz whose hacking had been crucial to a big case last year. He was now a freshman at Princeton.

Tom called the university, putting it on his long-distance card. It took two calls and fifteen minutes to reach him. "It's pronounced

'When,' but it's spelled N-G-U-Y-E-N," he explained to a woman in a dormitory.

When Lan came on, he told Tom he was doing well at Princeton, after getting over some culture shock. He was hoping to major in engineering and applied science. When they got down to the real agenda, Lan said, "Another hacking job? Cool." He couldn't estimate his chances of cracking into Curry, Bickford & Marshall's system but he was optimistic. "Depends on how good their firewall is. I'll have to do this at a cyber café, so I won't be traceable. That will cost me some money."

"Don't worry," Tom said. "I'll cover that and more. This would be a big help to me."

"I wouldn't have mentioned it except I'm on a tight budget. I'll get back to you soon as I can, then, sir."

Two days later, Tom drove the department Chevy into the Land Park neighborhood and parked in front of his and Cass's two-story home. He hopped out and examined the house with pride. White siding, forest green shutters, one corner formed by a turret with rounded windows. The green accents had been Tom's idea and he glanced with quick approval before bounding up the concrete steps to a narrow, arched porch. The ornate door was inlaid with an oval window of etched glass.

Cass, whose job was to long hours what Arizona was to sand, wasn't home yet. Once inside, Tom felt eyes staring at him.

"Hello, Orbison, old boy," he said to the tabby perched on the stairsteps. He went to the refrigerator, reached for a bottle of chardonnay, changed his mind, and took mineral water instead.

He crossed the front room, his feet echoing on the hardwood floor he and Cass had refinished not long ago. He reached the mail slot and picked up the day's supply of credit-card offers and pizza coupons, plus a *Newsweek*. Orbison was at his feet now, rubbing against a leg in greeting. They had been together eight years and

Tom figured the cat was smarter than some people he knew. He stroked him between the ears. "Everything okay here on the home front, buckaroo?"

Orbison lifted his head, insisting that Tom caress the white patch on his neck, and purred when he did.

"Your motor's in fine form, Orby, you old Feline American. How's that for political correctness?"

Tom tossed the mail on the antique oak pedestal table, ran a hand through his hair, and climbed the stairs to the bedroom he shared with Cass. The old treads creaked beneath his feet.

As he hung his dun corduroy jacket on his side of the closet, he was ambushed by a thought about his ex-wife Sharon. Those sometimes sneaked up on him like bitter insect bites on the mind, but not as often as they once did. He had his happiness with Cass to thank for that.

Sharon always used to bicker with Tom over closet space. Cass wasn't like that, thank God. She had as many clothes and shoes as Sharon, maybe more, but stored a lot of her things in a spare bedroom, good-naturedly taking only half of the master closet. Okay, a little more than half.

Sharon! She'd lost interest in Tom a year or two after they were married, but they'd held on for another five bleak years before calling it off. Thank God she was gone, her clothes, her shoes, photo albums, Vivaldi tapes, hat boxes, collection of ceramic owls, all of it.

Tom brushed his ex from his mind and hopped back down the stairs, his hand sliding lightly over the varnished cedar banister. Back at the table, he picked up the mail. Among the junk was a small white envelope, addressed to him in hand-printed letters, with no return address. The postmark was Los Angeles. Looked like a wedding invitation. He tore it open and found a photograph, a grainy, black-and-white glossy.

A sudden tightness clenched his chest. He couldn't breathe. He pulled his fingers away and let the photo drop to the table. His eyes closed and he sank into a chair. Seconds passed slowly.

He finally willed himself to open his eyes, lean forward and examine the picture again.

It was Cass, mostly naked, taken in profile. She stood in front of a bench, bent at the waist, removing her exercise tights. Her short hair was wet, stringy, her bare shoulders and breasts glistened. This was Quorum Athletics, the health club where she worked out. It was a little dark—no flash had been used—and it was slightly off focus, but not much. This had been sneaked. A 35-millimeter telephoto shot, he was sure.

Was this a joke? Cass had a zesty sense of humor, but no, this wasn't her style at all.

Touching only the edges of the photo with his fingertips, he picked it up, looked again, then flipped it over. A message label on the back read: WE CAN SHOOT YOUR LADY AT ANY TIME, IN ANY WAY. ACCEPT THE OFFER AND SHE WON'T BE HARMED. A cold ice of anxiety grew in his stomach and the tightness continued to smother his chest. He smashed both his palms on the table and a vase jumped.

He closed his eyes again and forced himself to breathe slowly. Conquer the anger, he told himself, stay calm and conquer the anger.

A minute later, he re-read the note. The black capital letters were laser-printed on the label.

WE CAN SHOOT YOUR LADY AT ANY TIME, IN ANY WAY. *Who* can? Who the hell sent me this?

ACCEPT THE OFFER AND SHE WON'T BE HARMED. Has she been kidnapped? Tom sprang to the phone and called Cass at her office. His heart stopped until she answered.

"Hi," she said, sounding rushed.

"Cass, you're all right?"

"Just harried, that's all. I'll be about an hour late tonight.

Sorry."

"Be careful."

"Huh?"

"Drive carefully."

"I will, I will. Did you call just to tell me that?"

"Yeah, romantic, isn't it? Like unexpected flowers. See you later. I love you, Cass."

"Love you too, Cavanaugh," she said, sounding puzzled as she hung up. Tom felt foolish but relieved.

He was sorry he'd touched the photo, but at least he hadn't put more than two or three fingerprints on it. He picked it up by the sides and tilted it so that it reflected light from the overhead lamp. He saw no other fingerprints on the shiny surface, only his own near the edges. No surprise there.

He doubted if laser printers were identifiable by their printing, the way typewriters used to be. He'd have to check on that.

What to do now? Well, for starters he would call his friend Mike Norfleet in Homicide. Norfleet had great sleuthing instincts. But would he show him that photo? No, just a photocopy of the note. He would also go back to his father. Desmond Cavanaugh might be dying, but his mind was clear and he'd been a great cop.

Tom sank back into the chair, his insides still numb. Orbison sauntered over and stared at him. The cat seemed to look worried too.

CHAPTER TEN

ass was at the wheel of her "Burgundy Bullet," heading home. She'd bought the wine-colored classic Porsche 911 a year ago, second hand and below Blue Book, from an old friend of her father. She'd had a tough day. Governor Maggie had jumped all over her because a meeting with Oregon's chief justice had been canceled, although it wasn't Cass's fault—it was the chief justice who'd bailed. Thank God she'd soon be having a glass of wine with Tom.

The same blue car had been behind her on Riverside Drive for about four blocks. But when she turned off it didn't follow. She pulled into the driveway, hopped out, and strode across the lawn, thinking about the odd call Tom had made, asking if she was all right and reminding her to drive carefully. Her crazy, lovable cop was always surprising her, but it was the first time he'd ever called for no apparent reason.

Inside, Tom heard the car door close. He'd been agonizing over whether to show Cass the photo and note. She didn't need this, but she had to know for her own safety, so she would buy into the precautions he would insist on.

Why now all of a sudden? he asked himself. Dad had that blasted emerald for forty years and nothing ever happened. But as soon as he takes me into his confidence and we go to Austria, all hell erupts.

He thought about the men who listened in on their dinner conversation at Garmisch. About the oily Doctor Gerhard at the Vienna art museum. About the woman who snapped their picture on the grounds of the palace. That woman in Vienna—was she the blonde from the ski slopes?—had looked very much the well-dressed native. Could she be sneaking pictures here in California now? Someone sure as hell had—in a women's locker room.

These thoughts bounced around in his head like hot popcorn. This wasn't the kind of problem he experienced in Narcotics.

Cass scurried up the front steps and opened the door. After the day she'd had, it was good to see Tom, standing in the middle of the front room, waiting for her.

"Hi." She started to give him the obligatory tease about his call. "So, you love me so darn much you just had to—." She caught the look on his face. "Hey, what's wrong?"

"We have a little problem, babe."

She gave him a quick kiss, and said, "Okay, what's going on, Cavanaugh?"

His lower lip between his teeth, Tom handed her the picture.

"What's this?" she said. "Who's this half-naked—" She might as well have been hit by a bus. She went numb. Her throat emitted a whimper, a guttural sound she didn't know she'd made. She felt violated. Humiliated. Felt as if she'd been stripped naked in a stadium full of people.

A hand touched her shoulder tentatively, gently. Thank God for Tom, her rock. She felt weak all over. Empty. Debased. Knees barely able to hold her up. *Who would do something like this?*

Shock turned to anger. *Who the hell? They have no right.* Someone grabbed the bud vase from the table and hurled it against the wall. The vase exploded into a hundred glass splinters. She stormed to the front door, stopped, turned, stood still, looked back.

She'd done it. She'd smashed the vase. The anguish on Tom's fact told her that.

She stood there a long moment, then staggered back to him and drooped into his arms. It was better with his arms encircling her.

Safer. Her mind blanked out and she stood that way, wrapped in the silent embrace, for a period of time. Who knew how long?

I'll kill him, her mind said. *Kill the miserable son of a bitch.* And more time passed in silence.

She stiffened, strength welling up from somewhere. Get a grip, Nesbit, she told herself.

She leaned back in Tom's arms and looked into his face. She saw a mixture of anxiety, determination and devotion. The eyes were watery and streaked with veins of red. A tear bled from one of them. This touched her deeply. She said softly, "The poor demented fool. He must be very sick, whoever did this."

"Someone," Tom said in a thick voice, "someone has found my hot button—you. Someone who knows about the emerald."

A minute passed. Then, hoping she sounded more like her old self, Cass said, "Okay, Mister Cop, what do we do?"

"I'll get to the bottom of this. Meanwhile, you have to vary your routines, where you park, your route to the Capitol, your morning and evening departure times."

"But I've got an assigned space in the government garage."

"Doesn't matter. Switch around with somebody in the office. Park in a pay lot every few days. Take a cab sometimes. It'd be a good idea to rent a car for awhile. Study the surroundings before leaving a building or car, visually check dark corners, trees, side doors, alleys—trouble can come from anywhere. Look at people and settings the way cops do. If you catch anyone looking at you from a distance, form a mental description of their appearance, and stay away from them. Stay away from that gym too. Always carry your mobile phone. Your can of mace. And your pistol. Loaded."

"Should I talk to the governor's security people?"

"No, not now. Not till I, we, get a better handle on this thing."

The doorbell rang and Cass jumped, her eyes becoming large O's.

Tom gripped her arm reassuringly, then went to the door and opened it a crack without unfastening the chain. It was a uniformed delivery man; a truck stood behind him at the curb.

"Cavanaugh and Nesbit? I've got a huge TV here from a Mister Oakley. Also these."

As Tom unlatched the door, the man produced a bouquet of yellow roses.

Tom wondered why the hell Roy Oakley would send flowers. "Think we can find another vase around here?" he said.

Dinner consisted of rolled tacos with guacamole from Juanito's, a Mexican takeout, plus a salad Tom whipped together. Romaine lettuce, artichoke hearts from a jar, sliced mushrooms and tomatoes, sprinkled with lemon pepper and splashed with Italian dressing and Parmesan cheese.

"I've got this thing figured out," Cass told him, stabbing an artichoke heart with a fork. "I'll take all these precautions. After all, it's my skin they're threatening. But I won't live like a cornered rat. We'll still have a life. I insist. We'll go to the theater, skiing, and to the City"—that meant San Francisco—"for a nice dinner when we feel like it."

Cass sounded like herself again and it cheered Tom. He bit off a piece of taco and licked some guacamole off his lips.

"Tell me about the health club," he said. "Describe it, especially the area around your locker."

"Well, first of all, the room's enclosed on every side. No windows. There's the door to the lobby but no sightline into the locker room. Between the showers and the lockers there's a toweling-off area with sinks and mirrors where you can blow-dry your hair and put on makeup. It looks out on my locker. That's the only place that shot could have been taken from, but anybody taking a picture in there would be obvious as hell. A lot of people would have seen her doing it—including me."

"Her? Right, it had to be a woman."

"No way would a man be in there, Tom—though I know you'd like to be the first." Cass's grin vanished as quickly as it had come.

"The camera was probably hidden in a sport bag," Tom said, "with a tiny slit for the lens."

"CIA kind of thing?"

"Sneak photography's become a science. Just look at the junk magazines in the checkout line. That paparazzi stuff is commonplace now."

"So it was taken in the mirror room by a woman with a hidden camera."

"It wasn't Colonel Mustard in the library. Are any of the women you work out with camera buffs? Any of them talk about photography?"

"Not that I can think of."

"Remember that woman who sneaked a picture of us at the Schönbrunn in Vienna?"

"Barely. You steered me out of there so fast I didn't get a good look at her."

"Maybe I should have followed my first instinct—gone after her and grabbed her."

"I still say there's always a curse with a rare old gemstone," she said. Her face scrunched in thought a moment. "Hey, Tom, if we need to make ourselves scarce for awhile, maybe we should go to Antietam. I think you need to, anyway."

"Truth is, I'm a little scared to."

"That's one of the things I love about you. No macho bullshit. Not sure what you might learn about yourself when you get out there?"

Feeling caught out, like the time in junior high when he'd brought home a report card with a D on it, Tom nodded.

"Then I'll go with you. Antietam's somewhere near Washington, isn't it?"

"Yeah, pretty close."

"Okay then. I can spend a day or two in Washington, do some business for the governor, and expense account the whole thing."

"Well, maybe we can."

Two hours later, in bed, Cass propped herself on an elbow and drew a circle on Tom's chest with her finger. "Everything's going to be fine, isn't it?"

"Absolutely," he replied with a confidence she appreciated but knew was false.

CHAPTER ELEVEN

ow ya doin', kid?" said Mike Norfleet, a detective sergeant in Homicide and an old friend of Tom's. They were sitting at a small table in The Torch Club, a downtown watering hole. Willie Nelson coming from the speakers. Norfleet's curly black hair was thinning on top, his salt-and-pepper beard neatly trimmed, and his lively brown eyes shining with their usual private-joke glimmer.

After he and Tom clinked beer glasses, Norfleet said, "Punk wasted his old lady last night with a toilet plunger, up around El Camino and Northgate. Jammed the thing down on her face and held it there till she suffocated. One for the books. Not a pretty sight. Face all blue like that fake ice you put in your cooler. Eyes bugged-out, never seen eyes that scared, nostrils big as quarters. Tough way to check out."

"Tough way. His wife, huh?"

"No, his mother," Norfleet said. "Kid was fifteen. Said he was fed up with her naggin' him about school and hangin' out with dealers."

Tom pursed his lips, shook his head, and let a moment pass before saying, "Mike, you're the best investigator I've ever known, excepting maybe my dad."

"Geez, there's a setup line. No such thing as a free beer, huh?"

"Yeah, Mike, I might need a little help."

Ten minutes later Norfleet was up to speed on the Maria Theresa Emerald and the shocking photo of Cass.

"Ah, that sucks, Tommy." Norfleet drank off some beer. "The picture—dust it for prints?"

"Checked it myself, Mike. There weren't any of course, except my own."

"Predictable." Norfleet wiped some froth from his lips with the back of his hand.

"I've got a photocopy here for you," Tom said, reaching into his jacket.

"Predictable."

They laughed. It was a copy of the note, but not the photo. Norfleet could be pretty crude and Tom was relieved when he said nothing about absence of the nude picture.

Norfleet read the note slowly, and said, "Damned upsetting shit for you." He turned and checked out a slender blonde who stepped past in a short black skirt that fit her like a paint job. His eyes homed in like radar.

"Get a load of that equipment. Think she's a cop groupie?"

"Ask her," Tom said.

"Nah, with my luck, she'd go for you."

"Think so?" Tom said. "She's a babe all right."

"How do you know? You didn't even look at her. Must be that great perfidial vision you got."

Norfleet didn't always get things right in the vocabulary department but Tom knew those who thought his elevator didn't reach the top floor were sadly mistaken.

Norfleet slapped money down for another round over Tom's protests. "No, no, this one's on me, Tommy."

"Two more of the same, Sammy, and step on it."

"Keep ya shirt on, Mike," the bartender called back. "Who ya think y'are?"

"Get the hell over here with some beer, fuckhead, or I'll get Public Health out here, close this stinkin' place down."

Tom knew that was all a game. He then got all the expected questions from Norfleet. Why had his father delayed so long? What exactly was said to Tom in Vienna? Just how valuable *was* this emerald? Who else knew about it besides Cass and his father?

Did Cass have friends who worked out with her at her gym?

"What about the governor's security guy, the one who split to Mexico. Could that punk know about this?"

"Manny Díaz. Cass knew him but not real well. She'd never have talked to Díaz about this, never. Just to be safe, though, there's this FBI guy, Hector Esparza, who might know something about him. He's in the El Paso office."

"Call him. Now about this L.A. postmark. Who do you know in L.A.?"

"I've asked myself that. There's Cass's folks and her sister, of course, and my cousin Roger, the idiot sportswriter. Lan Nguyen, the computer geek—not him for sure. Besides, he's gone off to Princeton. That's about it. No L.A. possibilities I can think of."

"Well, this goofball wouldn't mail this thing right where he lives. I figure he's from any place *but* L.A.—Frisco, Phoenix, anywhere." Norfleet chugged some beer. "Maybe somebody who's in L.A. on business once in awhile. Cass took self-defense class, didn't she?"

"Yeah. She's a tough cookie, Mike."

"She's gotta take this serious. World's fulla nut cases, I don't hafta tell ya. If I thinka some other stuff, I'll let ya know."

When they stepped outside, a greasy, bearded man in a tattered flannel shirt staggered onto the sidewalk and blocked their path. Smelled like a month of dirty laundry. "Spare some change?" he said, filthy hands outstretched.

"Get outta my face, buttlick," Norfleet said.

"Damn, Tom," the greasy man said, "your Homicide buddy's a real sweetheart, isn't he?"

"He didn't want to blow your cover, Trammel," Tom murmured. "You shouldn't be talking to us."

"This shit's less fun all the time."

"Here, pal." Norfleet handed him a quarter. "Good luck to ya."

* * *

Tom's work station, The Hole, didn't deserve the name office. Six miles southeast of downtown, near Florin, it was behind a storefront in a strip mall that had seen better days. Or maybe not.

Weeds grew through cracks in the asphalt. Faded paint on the storefront glass said PEERLESS STAMPS AND COINS. The CLOSED side of a fly-specked sign perpetually faced outward in the door. The fly specks were fake. The place was air-conditioned and, although dusty, had very few flies. On one side was a dry cleaners owned by a Jordanian. On the other, a martial arts shop that went belly-up six months before.

Counters, merchandise displays and a cash register occupied the front half of Peerless Coins. The lights were never on in that half, which truly was a front, literally and figuratively. Tom's warren was in the rear behind a false wall painted black.

The four other narcs hung out in similar cubicles. Moses Porter and Muhammad Kamal were African-Americans, one from Sacramento, one from Oakland. Luke Monelli, whose grandparents came from Calabria, wore a ponytail and an earring. The fourth was April the Cop, who'd been at the racetrack. None of them ever came through the front door. They entered in the rear off a service alley.

They called Tom Mister Straight. He did more planning and organizing than undercover, although he did a lot of that too. A large map of the Sacramento area—roughly bordered by Lodi in the south, Vacaville in the west, Wheatland to the north, and Placerville, east—was tacked to one of Tom's walls. Cork board covered another wall. Numerous messages were pinned to the cork, along with a Kings' schedule and a snapshot of Tom and Cass at a Tahoe ski resort. A computer terminal, monitor, phone with four lines, and a radio set with a hand mike and headphones spread across a battered wooden tabletop.

Monelli suddenly began singing *April Love* in a bad, off-key mimic of Pat Boone. He did this a lot to needle April.

"Put a cork in it, Sinatra," she called from her cubicle. "Save that poor excuse for a voice for the shower, where it belongs."

"You wanta take a shower with me? Is that what you're saying?"

Muhammad Kamal—born Leroy Jackson—was staking out a crack operation near Grant High and Moses Porter was backing him up. Tom had to stay on top of it. But like a paperclip to a magnet his mind kept getting pulled back to the other matter. Who the hell could it be? Who knew about the emerald? Very, very few people. He and Cass, his father, his brother Michael, and his father's friend Roy Oakley. That was about it. Was there anyone else?

He tried to push it out of his mind and concentrate on work, but he kept seeing Cass's picture.

Cass couldn't concentrate either. She was supposed to be studying an insurance reform proposal and preparing a memo for the governor. She was good at that kind of thing. She loved it. Today, though, was another matter. She'd read the same paragraph over and over. The words wouldn't sink in. It wasn't just the verbose legalese; Cass could always decipher that garbage. It was that damn picture.

She gazed out her window at a patch of grass and shrubbery on the Capitol's south lawn. She stared at a squirrel fussing about without really seeing it. What she saw was herself, naked from the hips up, bending over a bench removing her exercise tights. She shivered involuntarily. What is going on? What the hell is going on?

Still sitting there, elbow on the desk, chin buttressed by her left hand, she suddenly realized the squirrel was gone. Her black mood wasn't.

*   *   *

The stakeout on the north side was over and Tom had a slow afternoon in The Hole. He called the FBI field office in El Paso and asked for Hector Esparza.

"*Bueno*," Esparza answered.

"*Hable inglés, por favor*," Tom said. "*Mi español es muy malo*."

"Oh, sorry. I was expecting a call from Guadalajara."

"Wrong direction. It's Sacramento. This is Tom Cavanaugh, remember me?"

"Of course, Mr. Cavanaugh. How are you?"

Esparza had been an electronics surveillance expert before going to the FBI. He and Tom had collaborated the year before in Mexico.

After they exchanged pleasantries, Tom said, "Hector, I'm calling about Manny Díaz. Do you have any idea where he is?" Manny Díaz had been a security man for Cass's boss, Governor Magdalena Artiaga Travis. He'd turned bad cop in a case Tom had been in the middle of, then vanished in Mexico. Tom thought he could be the guy sending those notes. "Is he in L.A. by any chance?"

"Manuel Díaz is hiding in the Federal District, Mexico City. We know he slips into the States once in awhile, but we haven't been able to catch him. He's very devoted to his wife Maria, who's still in Sacramento. He'd like to move her to Mexico, but she doesn't want to go. We think Díaz was involved in the death of Governor Travis' predecessor in California two years ago."

"Wouldn't be surprised, Hector. So Díaz sometimes smuggles himself across the line? And L.A., you know, is the easiest place in the world for a Latino fugitive to get to and hide in. You're shadowing him, then?"

"Asking questions in the right places. My first big assignment here is building up the Bureau's contacts in Mexico. You could help by watching his wife's place in Sacramento."

"Wish we could, but it can't be done, not officially. Sacramento PD has no reason to be involved. I could get some guys to check it once in awhile, but we couldn't stake it out. Besides, Díaz was a cop—he's too smart to show up at his old house. He'd have his wife meet him somewhere else. The trick would be to watch Maria. But we don't have the manpower, or a legal reason. No way."

"Yes, I know. I was just thinking out loud," Esparza said. "If you learn anything, though, please let me know."

"Sure will. I'll do a little checking up here myself."

"Good luck, Mr. Cavanaugh."

"Thanks again, Hector. Keep in touch."

It was still a slow day, and Tom found himself picturing the emerald. Well, Empress, he thought, you're causing us a hell of a lot of trouble, you and your lush, beguiling splendor. Why don't I just up the price to five mil, pocket the money, quit this lousy job, and become a gentleman history teacher in some small town?

That thought floated before his eyes and the corkboard in front of his face. He shook it away, telling himself, *stop that*.

Cass's body was telling her it was time for a good workout. Past time. It had been six days. Tom had told her to stay away from Quorum Athletics and go somewhere else, but Cass liked *this* gym. It was close to the Capitol; her friends went there; she was familiar with the machines. Besides, she wanted to do some sleuthing. Now that the original anger and fear were over, she wanted to take a good look at the club and the people there.

Toting her sport bag, she entered and picked up her key at the front counter. The college-age girl on the desk was new and had an innocent look about her. She didn't at all fit Cass's idea of a photo-sneaking suspect.

Cass made a circuit of the two rooms, one filled with weights and pulleys, rowing machines and stationary bikes, the other with stair-climbers, treadmills and stretching mats. It was six p.m., a busy time. She recognized only one person, a guy on an assemblyman's staff. They nodded how-you-doings at each other. As she found her assigned locker and slipped the key in, she examined her feelings. She was a little on edge, she admitted, a little scared but not terrified. She was in control.

She sank onto the bench in front of her locker and glanced around while pulling off her burgundy patent-leather flats. She placed the shoes in the locker and started to unbutton her charcoal gray vest.

There were two women beyond the arch in the toweling-off space outside the showers. One was plump, fully dressed, and was applying lipstick in front of a mirror. The other was in workout bra and panties, blow-drying her hair. Good body, nice legs, Cass noticed. Tom would like her. She smiled briefly at that thought.

Obviously the picture had been taken from that very spot. It couldn't have been an easy thing to do. A woman had taken it, no doubt about that.

Cass shivered for an instant. How unobservant she'd been. In a hyped-up hurry, not taking time to really notice her surroundings—until now.

She finished undressing and slipped into her workout gear: Lycra tights, workout bra, T-shirt, gym shoes. She went to a workout room and did her stretches, then forty abdominal crunches. Next, she worked out on several machines, spending most of her time on a bike and a stair-climber. She was breathing hard and deep, her lungs, muscles and sweat glands responding. She lifted eighty-pound weights twenty times, rested a few seconds, and pumped ten more. Then she changed into a bathing suit and topped off the workout with seven minutes in the lap pool.

It had been a great workout. In the shower, her body felt tired, good-tired. She was glad she'd come. She'd seen nothing out of the ordinary and no suspicious people. As she left, she felt relieved and yet a little disappointed. Oh, one guy had tried to hit on her, asking her name and what she did, but she'd deftly blown him off. That happened now and then. When it stops, as it will some day, she told herself, then I'll know I've become an old hag.

Passing the desk on her way out, she exchanged nods with a woman who'd just arrived. Cass thought she caught a flicker of recognition in the woman's eyes.

Stepping into the elevator, she had the feeling she'd seen that woman before. Maybe she's a cop, Cass thought, someone I met once with Tom. The elevator door slid closed.

At the desk, the woman signed in: Mary Savage.

Quorum Athletics was in an office building, one floor above the underground garage where Cass's Burgundy Bullet was parked.

Reaching the car, she suddenly realized that no one was around and there were plenty of pillars for someone to hide behind, a cliché scene right out of a Hollywood thriller. She jumped in fast, breathing hard, and jammed down both door locks.

When the car fired right up and carried her away, she felt silly.

CHAPTER TWELVE

Cass hadn't really wanted her parents to fly in from Los Angeles for the weekend. Too much on her mind. At dinner, she over-broiled the swordfish and tried to mask it with a little extra sauce.

"A lovely meal," her mother said, wielding her fork like a baton.

"I scorched the fish and you know it."

"A little blackened is quite acceptable these days, dear."

"But I *can* cook, even though I don't do it all that much. You taught me well, Mom."

"If I taught you *well*, you'd be doing it more."

Cass tried not to make a face. She'd wanted the meal to come out simple but gracious. Broiled swordfish in a wine and mushroom sauce, a huge Caesar salad, steamed broccoli and fresh, warm bread.

"Tom's a good cook too."

Cass's father gave Tom an appraising look. "Is that so?"

"Oh, not really. A few chicken and pasta things. I did make the salad."

Tom saw that Cass's nicely arched cheekbones and small mouth came from her mother, her height and long legs from her father. Ty Nesbit was now sixty and had been a banker most of his life. Two years ago, he'd been executive vice president at Los Angeles Mercantile Trust when it was swallowed up by a larger bank. He'd taken the golden parachute and now lived on a pension and the dividends from his investments.

"Never did much cooking myself," Ty Nesbit said, slicing his swordfish, "although I barbecue a mean steak. How long have you been a sergeant?"

"*Detective* sergeant," Cass corrected.

"Going on eight years now," Tom said.

"I'm more familiar with military ranks than police, but shouldn't you be making lieutenant or captain or something pretty soon?"

"It *is* different from the military, sir, you see—"

"Knock off the 'sir' business. Call me Ty."

"Yes, sorry . . . Ty. You see, to become a lieutenant I'd have to give up being a detective. I'd be a staff officer instead of a line officer. In other words, go into management."

"Nothing wrong with that. Anyone would want to advance himself, work his way up in the organization."

"Being a detective is important," Cass put in, "and Tom's a good one."

"Of course, dear," Edith Nesbit said, "but hasn't he done his bit? Just imagine, eight years."

"Do you hope to be a chief some day, like your father?" Ty asked.

Tom didn't. "I can't really say," he hedged. He knew the Nesbits were apprehensive about him in view of their other daughter's divorce. Jan's husband, a successful, aggressive trial lawyer, had dumped her for a younger woman.

Recognizing Tom's discomfort, Cass deflected the subject. "How's Jan doing, Mom?" she said while refilling her parents' wine glasses. "I haven't talked with her in a couple of weeks."

Edith Nesbit put on her sky-is-falling look and said, "I'm quite concerned, dear, but at least I think she's coming out of her lowlife phase. You know, for the longest time all she did was date plumbers and motorcyclists and things like that. Now she's had a date or two with an electrician."

"Not an electrician, Edith," Ty said. "An electrical engineer. There's a big difference."

"Well, anyway, he's a nice enough fellow, but you know—"

"Jan didn't do so well by white-collar types," Cass said.

"I'd always hoped that she and Dave would patch it up," Edith Nesbit said.

"No way, Mom. That bastard was screwing one of his paralegals—"

"Cass!" Edith Nesbit dropped her fork.

"Sorry, Mom, I could've said that better, but Dave *was*, and he told Jan he was going to keep right on. He told Jan he was bored with her. There wasn't any going back after that."

"I suppose not."

"Jan took a bad dive. Who wouldn't? She dedicated herself heart and soul to that bum and look what she got for her trouble. Anyway, she'll make it, Mom. It'll take some time, but she'll come out of this a stronger woman. Meanwhile, it's good for her to experience different kinds of guys. Who cares what they do for a living?"

This talk was making Tom, the mere cop, uncomfortable. "Cass and I are going to Washington in a couple of weeks," he said.

Taking that lead, Cass steered the conversation into politics.

The four of them dined out the next night at an Italian restaurant on Marconi Avenue. Afterward, Ty Nesbit insisted on picking up the tab.

Tom had tried hard with Ty, but always got the feeling he wasn't deemed good enough for his daughter. He and Cass were relieved when the weekend ended and they dropped her parents at the airport.

"Go for captain, Tom, go for captain," Ty said, shaking hands goodbye.

From her condo on a hillside in Fair Oaks, Mary Savage had a sweeping view of the American River and its green necklace of trees. She had slipped into jeans and plopped down on a canvas-backed chair on the balcony with a bottle of Coors and a pile of reports. She glanced at the view now and then as she flipped through the papers, making occasional notes in the margins.

Something on the river caught her eye, something round and yellow. Someone was rafting, one of the first she'd seen this year. Later in the season, when the water was warmer, there would be a lot of rafts and canoes out there. It made for a great outing on a hot day, which this wasn't. The April sun hung low and most of the water was in shade.

I'll give it a try, she suddenly thought, getting to her feet and stepping inside. She pulled a camera bag from a closet and returned to the balcony. She extracted her 35-millimeter camera and twisted off the lens, replacing it with a long black telephoto and snapping off the dust cover.

With her knees on the balcony floor, she supported the lens on the railing and played with the focus. Clarity came with a flick of her wrist. Two guys were floating downstream, past Sailor Bar Park toward the Sunrise Bridge. The lens brought them in close. One wore a sleeveless shirt, the other was bare-chested. He must be freezing, she thought. Good pecs. He must pump a lot of iron. Click. Click. *Gotcha.* Savage smiled.

She gulped some beer, put the camera down, and returned to her homework.

The next few days went by quickly for Cass. The trip to Maryland and Washington was a go, and she felt as good as she had since before the warning photo-note had come. She was confident, feisty, almost her old self, and she knew this had a positive effect on Tom too. Sometimes she imagined that the note hadn't come at all—but never for long.

Preparations for the trip occupied her mind. "I'm going to call on our senior senator," she told Tom at the breakfast table. "A couple of lobbyists," she added, her hands animated, "and maybe even the vice president. He's running interference for the president on a farm labor bill in the Senate. It's a big issue with Governor Maggie, you know."

"I called the Museum of the Confederacy in Richmond yesterday," Tom said, picking up his bagel. "I made an appointment at their research library." Cass knew he hoped to learn more about the Battle of Antietam from the Southern viewpoint. He felt he knew the Northern, history buff that he was.

That night, Cass shuddered when she saw the message light blinking on the answering machine. She reached for the playback button, but stopped. Drops of sweat formed on the back of her hand. At last, she forced herself to tap the button.

Later, in bed, she said, "You know, Tom, I had a strong feeling we'd have another weird message on the machine."

Tom put a hand gently on her cheek.

"I was scared to listen. God, was I relieved when the only call was from Jan."

"How's your sis doing? She dating a FedEx driver this time?"

Tom and Cass deplaned at Baltimore-Washington International. After collecting their rental car they got themselves to I-70 and drove west into rolling, wooded Maryland countryside.

Tom's spirits rose, each mile taking him farther from the dark world of ominous phone calls and threatening notes the damned emerald had plunged him into. Away from home and obligations, nothing felt insurmountable.

An overcast sky drew darker. A high ridge materialized in the distance, dimly backlit in the sulky gray afternoon, filling the western horizon.

"That must be South Mountain," Tom said. "That long ridge starts down in Virginia's Blue Ridge Mountains and runs all the way up into Pennsylvania. It's what shielded Lee's army when he invaded Maryland in 1862 and again when he marched to Gettysburg in '63. Pretty historic chunk of real estate."

"Is that what you call a massif?"

"A massif, yeah, I think so. I'm impressed."

"Does it look familiar to you? Any déja vu here?"

"Not really, not that I can tell." Tom felt her eyes searching his face.

"Maybe you'll have some tomorrow. It'll be interesting to see what feelings you get at Antietam. So this Winslow Homer thing going on up there," she said, tapping his temple with an index finger, "is a pretty new thing?"

"Winslow Homer? Oh, you mean the cornfield and chapel stuff. Right, just since Dad told me about the emerald."

Cass's brow knotted. "That's extremely interesting. Might be important."

Tom let that sink in for a long, mute moment.

Before long he turned off the interstate at Frederick onto twisting back-country roads—and proceeded to get lost.

"What happened to your infallible sense of direction?" Cass teased, while fumbling with the folds of the map.

"I think it turned left back there when I turned right. They don't have many good road signs in these hills, have you noticed? Maybe that's because Camp David is around here someplace, and they try to keep it sort of quiet."

Minutes later, Cass said, "Rosetta Stone."

"Archaeologist, right?"

"Of course."

"That was pretty bad."

"Bad?" Cass said. "They're supposed to be bad."

He found his way again, and it was raining lightly as they reached the hamlet of Boonsboro. When they took a motel room, the proprietor told them they were only eight miles from Sharpsburg and the Antietam Creek Battlefield.

They had dinner at a roadhouse on the edge of town, where the only menu selections were Southern-fried chicken, pan-fried steak and country ham. The walls were paneled in knotty pine and the hanging light fixtures were imitation ship's lanterns.

"Where y'all from?" asked a teenage waitress in a starched pink apron. Freckles danced on her cheeks when she spoke. "California? No kiddin'? Ah'd love to go to California after graduation."

"We love California," Cass said. "But it's good around here too. This is beautiful country."

"Yeah, but you can get purty tard of cows and chickens and antique stores. Decided what y'all want? . . . The frahd chicken? Good choice. We've got the most famous frahd chicken in Washington County. My uncle's the cook."

The waitress skipped off, a ginger-colored ponytail swishing behind her.

"The chickens are boring and yet famous when they're fried," Cass said. She smiled coyly and added, "I can't believe the Greatest Driver in the Western Hemisphere got lost like that today. I think we passed the same farm three times."

Tom shrugged and held his hands out, palms up. "I was counting on my trusty copilot and map reader."

"I've never claimed to be a great navigator." Cass fluffed the napkin into her lap and rearranged her silverware on a red-and-white checked tablecloth. "You know I can't tell south from east."

Nor fold up a road map, Tom thought, but kept it to himself. In his experience, women were congenitally incapable of properly re-folding a map.

The girl returned with two bowls of green salad and a pot of honey. "Be right back with your meals." When she reappeared, the plates were piled with biscuits, peas and gravy-smothered mashed potatoes, as well as heaps of fried chicken.

"Y'all goin' to Antietam?" she asked. "You'll have a fine day for it. Rain's s'posed to stop tonight. Lotta people come through here to see the battlefield. Usually older folks in Winnebagos. My great-great-granddaddy fought there."

"Your great-great-grandfather was with Robert E. Lee?" Tom asked.

"No, the North, actually. Most people here in western Maryland were Union. The secessionists were the plantation folks on the Chesapeake. Maryland never joined the Confederacy."

"I know," Tom said. "Say, you're really up on this stuff."

"Well, ah love history. Been accepted at George Washington, and that'll be my major."

"You've found a soul mate, Cavanaugh."

The waitress gave Cass a confused smile, but pressed on. "D.H. Hill's Confederate brigade was here at Boonsboro two days before the big battle, just down the road at Turner's Gap. When the Yankees showed up, Hill held the gap as long as he could, then retreated on down to the creek and joined up with Lee."

"Did your great-great-grandfather live through the battle?"

"No, sir, he died at Burnside's Bridge. Thirty years old. Left a wife and four boys, one of them being my great-granddaddy."

"Lucky for you, and the family line," Cass said, slicing a piece of the most famous fried chicken in Washington County.

"My mother's seen his ghost—my great-great-granddaddy's— two or three times. Blue uniform and all. Late at night. Makes her skin go all goosebumpy."

Tom knew the feeling. For a sliver of a second, he saw a field of tall corn behind the girl.

CHAPTER THIRTEEN

The waitress had been right; the rain was over. A tangerine sun peeked over the Catoctin Hills and ushered in a cheery dawn. Tom and Cass had a quick, light breakfast in town, then reached the Antietam National Battlefield shortly after nine.

As Tom made a right turn off the highway to head for the visitors center, Cass said, "What do you think about the ghost of that girl's great-great-grandfather?"

"Don't know what to think, but I like that kind of thing."

"Do you believe in ghosts?"

"I don't know, Cass. I'd like to."

"Reincarnation?"

"No. Well . . . hmm . . . nah."

Cass cocked her head at a funny angle and looked at him with an appraising smile.

Tom parked along the road. Getting out, his nostrils filled with the lush smell of wet grass. Droplets from the overnight showers sparkled like gems. A few creampuff clouds loitered in the soft sky. Orioles and whippoorwills chattered in the maples and dogwoods and among the brass field guns, no longer menacing, just archaic curiosities for the tourists. Spoked wheels dwarfed gun barrels long since turned green by oxidation.

They tramped all over the battlefield. The spot where the West Wood had once stood, the Sunken Lane, and the whitewashed Dunkard Church which had anchored the Confederate flank. The little church looked achingly familiar to Tom.

Cass tagged along without complaint, although Tom knew she wasn't much interested in this stuff. He appreciated that she was reciprocating for the times he'd gamely followed her through countless antique shops. He also knew the tables would be turned in the next few days as Cass ran around Washington, very much in her element, delivering messages to various politicos for her boss, Governor Travis.

Although cars and SUV's occasionally passed, their occupants peering at monuments or consulting their maps, Tom was struck by the quiet of the place. Only seventy miles from Washington but it might as well have been a million. It was truly peaceful. He knew, however, that there'd once been a day here that was anything but peaceful, a terrible day, a day of unparalleled fratricidal violence.

"Stonewall Jackson was dug in right over there on both sides of the church," he said, pointing, "with John Hood's Texas Brigade. Hooker's Union Corps was coming at him through the cornfield over there and the woods that used to stand about here." A squirrel stared at them, then scampered up a tree as if its feet were magnets.

When they reached the cornfield, they found it ringed by a weathered rail fence. Being late March, there was no crop, just plowed, muddy, reddish-brown earth, but Tom didn't need the small yellow sign reading STEWART HYBRID CORN to know what kind of field this was. When the armies collided, the corn had been tall and nearly ready for harvest. Somehow he'd always known that.

He stood beside the fence and gazed at the solemn ground, just a few yards away, where five thousand men and boys had perished on a hot morning almost a century and a half ago.

At the edge of this field, having these thoughts, Tom suddenly smelled gunpowder. A shiver trembled through him, a wisp of something reaching for his soul.

The feeling deepened. He glanced at Cass. Was she getting any of this? The air was suddenly sultry and hotter.

The grass began to stir in rippling waves, as though men were marching through it, although there wasn't even a puff of breeze. The cornfield tugged at him. He took a wavering step to the fence and rested his hands on one of the rails. Nerve endings tingled electrically and a sound echoed faintly in his ears. Snare drums. Rhythmic.

Ketrack-ketrack, ketrack-a-tack-a-tack. Attack, Tom. Attack, Tom. Attack attack attack, Tom.

Men and boys in blue come surging through tall corn that a moment ago hadn't been there. Blurry, out of focus, but real. "Dress up," a watery voice calls. "Company C, dress ranks." Clouds of black smoke blossom in front of them. A red and white battle flag appears. Artillery booms.

He glances to the left, to the little church. Men in gray and butternut are tamping balls into the muzzles of brass cannon. An officer in a plumed hat flourishes a sword toward their aiming point, the lines of blue tramping through the corn. Tom is wearing some kind of sweaty flannel uniform and is carrying a rifle.

Out of the roiling smoke he sees a bullet—rushing straight at him. He twists, jumps away from the fence. It doesn't help. The bullet keeps tracking him. He dives to the ground, a sharp stab of pain in his left arm.

The smoke begins to fade and slowly vanishes. The ghostly panorama dissolves into bright sunlight.

Cass had been puzzled by Tom's stone-still posture and the veiled, far-away look on his face. He'd seemed bewitched, not really there at all, a statue, where seconds before there'd been a lighthearted human being. She started to speak but nothing came out. Her hand went to her throat as if to touch the word that stalled there. Her brow wrinkled. She looked at Tom in wonder.

He suddenly hopped to the side, then fell to the ground. She rushed to him, knelt, felt his forehead, tugged at his hand.

Tom slowly looked up at her, blankly, as if he didn't know her. Cass shivered with worry. She had heard about *jaimais vu*, the phenomenon in which you suddenly feel you've never seen or heard things before, even though you have, like the sensation that you'd never met your spouse. *Please, God, don't let him be in something like that.*

His eyes took focus, he smiled thinly, and clutched her hand. She felt a surge of relief. Welcome back, her eyes said.

"You fell, Tom. Scared the life out of me. What happened? What the devil just happened?"

"The corn's gone," he muttered, getting to his feet.

"What?"

"Did you hear or see anything out there?"

"Out where? In the field just now? Only some songbirds. What was it?"

"They were calling me, Cass," he said, a queer look in his eyes. "Calling me. Those men."

"Men?" She looked at him searchingly. "What men?"

"I was in the middle of the battle. I saw them. I heard them . . . saw a bullet . . . I think. God, am I going crazy?"

She strengthened her grip on his hand. "No, of course not. Something awful happened here a long time ago and you felt it, had some kind of psychic connection. I don't know if the souls of the dead ride that *Föhn*, but some of them were calling out to you here."

"I don't know, but damn, I felt like I was floating right out of my shoes. Then for a moment I had this weird, lucky-to-be-alive feeling. I've only had that sensation once before, last year, when I really *was* lucky to be alive."

"When you got shot, sure," she said. "Well, you've just had a special encounter, a gift. I wish I could have felt some of it."

Tom remembered what he'd realized just yesterday: the fact that his visions of the cornfield and chapel started only after he'd learned about the emerald.

"Sharon would say I'm crazy." Tom rarely spoke of his ex-wife.

"Well, she's not here, soldier, and you're far from crazy."

"You always say the right thing," he said, wrapping his arms around her and hugging tightly.

Hand in hand, they resumed their stroll along the grassy berm of the narrow tar lane. Minute by minute, step by step, Tom felt himself again. They stopped occasionally to snap a picture at one of the monuments along the way.

At a small memorial to General Hooker's First Corps, Cass laughed and said, "Isn't this the guy who hookers were named for? Remember you telling me that story?"

"Yeah," Tom said with a grin. "It's true. Joe Hooker and his camp followers."

They reached the visitors center. Inside, Tom asked a thin, middle-aged attendant in a park uniform, "Do people ever mention something weird happening out on the battlefield, ghosts or anything like that?"

"Oh, there are many ghost stories here. Mr. Grady does a whole lecture on the ghosts of Antietam. The next one is Thursday, I think."

"Have you ever—"

The man looked around and lowered his voice. "One day about dusk, after closing time, I saw a dim light in the Dunkard Church, like a lantern would make. That building has no electricity and no one was supposed to be in there at the time. I was in the lane nearby so I went over to take a look. Just before I got there the windows went dark. I unlocked the door and shined my flashlight all around. Nobody was there, so I locked up again and left. When I was halfway back here to the center, I turned and looked. There was a dim light in there again. I took a step back in that direction and the light went out."

Tom's lips made a whistling shape.

"I don't tell that story very often, but it's absolutely true," the man said, holding up both hands and pursing his lips. Tom saw that Cass had been listening closely.

As they left, she hummed the first part of *The Twilight Zone* theme.

To reach their car, they had to walk down a long lane lined by monuments. Cass read from a placard, " 'the Twelfth Massachusetts lost 224 out of 334 men engaged.' Two thirds of their men? How horrible."

The Twelfth Massachusetts. Tom got the same ache he had when he'd heard about the Twelfth Massachusetts on that TV documentary two weeks ago—and felt a thrust of pain in his left arm.

Just beyond a tall obelisk that Cass called "a gray slab of ugliness," they spotted an elderly man striding in their direction. His black broadcloth frock coat came to the knees. He had a ruddy face, a thatch of white hair and ample chin whiskers of the same chalky color. He wasn't more than five-seven.

"He looks like General Mansfield," Tom said softly.

"Who?"

"Joseph Mansfield, one of the Union commanders in this battle. He was killed somewhere right about here. He was urging his troops forward when a Confederate bullet cut him down. Man, this is eerie."

"Oh, it's got to be a costume thing, Tom. He probably works for the park."

"Or maybe he's one of those battle re-enactors. Hundreds of guys are into that. Except I don't know of any re-enactment here any time soon."

"He must be a ghost, then," Cass said. She hummed *The Twilight Zone* again. "Look at the dignified way he carries himself. His posture. He's an elegant old ghost, I'll say that for him."

As the man reached them, Cass said, "Would you mind if we took your picture, sir? We've never had a picture of a real war hero's ghost."

The old man grinned at that and nodded, looking all the while at Cass with penetrating blue eyes. They were almost the color of the country sky.

"Great, sir. Now, Tom, stand beside Mister Ghost. A little closer. Back a step. There. Those distant trees make a good background."

Cass got the picture, then another to make sure. "Well, thanks a lot, sir," she said. "You do General—what is it, Mansfield?—real well." The man gave a dignified little nod, touched an index finger to his cap, and strolled off in his stately gait.

Cass shouldered her camera, faced Tom, stood on her tiptoes and kissed him. "Glad we came?"

"You bet. I've wanted to do this a long time."

"You've always been a little obsessed with the Civil War. Say, where's the old man?"

"I don't know. He must have walked in among the trees or something."

But the nearest grove of trees was a thousand yards away.

CHAPTER FOURTEEN

Reality slipped right out from under me, Cass," Tom said during the drive to Washington the next morning. "I had no solid footing. That's a scary feeling."

"I can see that, the always-in-control cop. I know we can't understand it, but try to just accept that somehow you were psychically attuned to the tragedy that took place there."

Tom shook his head slowly and puckered his lips in a silent whistle. They talked awhile about the funny old man in the black clothing.

"Feel like some music?" Cass asked.

"No, I feel like a thirty-eight-year-old man who's been driving a car for two days."

Cass "booed," turned on the radio and found a Baltimore oldies station. Roy Orbison was singing.

Tom joined in. "Pretty woman, kind I'd like to meet, pretty woman . . . "

"What he's really saying," Cass put in, "is, 'Pretty woman, *that* I'd like to meet.' "

"No, no, he says '*kind* I'd like to meet.' "

"I beg to differ. It's '*that* I'd like to meet.' And you're supposed to be such a big Orbison fan."

"Put your money where your mouth is, lady."

"Okay, you're on. Whoever's wrong buys dinner. Winner's choice of place."

"Fine. Song's about over now; he doesn't sing that line again, but here's what we'll do. I've got it on tape. When we get home, I'll re-record it on a slower speed and we'll find out for sure. I think I'll have you take me to Ernie's in San Francisco."

"You're thinking too small, Tom. When I win, I expect dinner at Robuchon in Paris."

Tom gulped. "France?"

"No less."

"Sure, Paris, France. Anyway, the night we met at that reception, that song started running through my head when I spotted you across the room."

"No kidding? I'm flattered. Know what was running through *my* head when I caught you scoping me out?"

"What?"

"*The Farmer in the Dell.*"

A look of mock pain crossed Tom's face. "You're vicious."

Cass smiled victoriously.

"What are you going to do the next two days while I make my rounds, besides go to Richmond?" she asked.

"Oh, I have some plans."

Cass's thoughts drifted to Nick Race, the man she'd been getting over when she'd met Tom. If she'd married well-heeled old Nick, she'd never have heard of the Maria Theresa Emerald and wouldn't have this anxiety in the back of her mind. She'd be buying her clothes in San Francisco's best shops, cost never questioned, dining in upscale restaurants, and *not* being photographed by devious, menacing criminals. Nor taking pictures of ghosts.

On the other hand, she wouldn't be having much fun. If she had challenged Nick Race about the lyrics in *Oh, Pretty Woman*, he'd have said, "Yes, you're probably right." That outlandish bet or the *Farmer in the Dell* crack would never have been made.

Thank God she wasn't married to Nick Race, spending her life with a man she half-respected and didn't really love. She'd take coach class and Tom Cavanaugh, thank you.

A sign told her the Beltway was one mile ahead.

* * *

Cass had a number of meetings lined up for the next day. The first, with California's senior senator, would start in an hour. After that was an appointment with an Arizona congressman who was an ally of Governor Travis on the Mexican immigration question.

She and Tom spent the interval in the visitors gallery above the Senate floor. Tom was surprised at how few senators were at their desks listening to the debate. And at others, who stood in little knots in the aisles and the back of the hall. "That's rude to the guy who's got the floor," he said.

"That's just the way it's done. Besides, a lot of them are out in committee meetings."

"Or back home collecting bribes."

Cass didn't answer that. "Oh, look, there's Ted Kennedy," she said. "God, he's huge. Isn't that Daniel Moynihan he's talking to?"

It was about time for Cass's meeting. They walked through a labyrinth of halls till they reached the right elevator. "Want me to get you Ted Kennedy's autograph?"

"Get me one from that pretty little page. The blonde."

"And her phone number too?"

"I'm off to Richmond, babe," Tom evaded. "See you at the hotel between five and six."

"Drive carefully, copper," she said, and gave him a quick kiss.

Tom took the rental down Interstate 95 through some of the greenest hills and woodlands he'd ever seen. He'd never been here before, but it somehow felt familiar, just as some of the Maryland countryside had the day before.

He reached Richmond by noon. It took Lincoln's army four years to get here from Washington, he thought, and I made it in just under two hours.

He found the Museum of the Confederacy, a neoclassical antebellum building fronted by a line of Roman columns. Inside, he was met by an aging librarian with a gray mustache, a blue bow tie and matching suspenders. He confirmed that Tom was the police officer who'd made an appointment. As he led the way to collections of books and manuscripts on the Army of Northern Virginia, he said, "You'll need to wear these cotton gloves, sir. Some of these old papers are quite fragile. And if you wish to take notes—pencils only."

Tom donned the gloves, pulled a notepad from his canvas carryall and began to scan the material. He didn't know exactly what he was looking for. It was 2:30 when he came on a bound packet of documents in protective sleeves labeled The Longstreet Papers.

He was well into them when the librarian approached and saw which manuscript Tom had. "James Longstreet. Not one of our more aggressive ginrals," he said. "Old Pete—Lee always referred to him as Old Pete—dawdled and fiddled away his attack at Gettysburg and thus caused the Confederate defeat."

Tom was getting the Southern viewpoint all right. "Okay," he said, "but my real interest is Antietam, or Sharpsburg as you call it."

"Sharpsburg, yes. Lee held off a Yankee army three times his size the whole day, then held onto the high ground and defied the Northerners to attack another full day before leaving the field."

"Longstreet was there too, wasn't he?"

"Yes indeed, commanded a brigade. Was promoted lieutenant ginral after that battle." He leaned over Tom's shoulder and turned several pages. "Here we are, young man, Longstreet's memoirs of Sharpsburg."

"Oh, much obliged. You've saved me a lot of time."

Much obliged? Tom never said much obliged.

The ink was somewhat faded; occasional words had been scratched out and others substituted, but the penmanship was bold and legible. He read eagerly.

A character of much charm and fascination was attached to my staff, Prince Rudolf of Belgium. He was with our army as an observer for Franz Joseph, the Emperor of Austria. Rudolf's sister, Princess Carlota, was married to Franz Joseph's brother, the Archduke Maximilian. The French were considering an invasion of Mexico, reasoning that the Yankee Army could do naught about it, being fully engaged with us in the War of Secession. He allowed as how France would put Maximilian on the throne as Emperor of Mexico. Carlota was much devoted to her husband. What matter a Mexican throne if it be merely a fatal trap for her Maximilian? And so she desired her brother's assessment of our Confederacy's chances of whipping the Yankees.

Prince Rudolf was much interested in infantry tactics. He possessed a probing mind and learned quickly. And, my, could he ride. Such a horseman. And quite the adventurer he was, too. On letters from the Swiss government, he was previous out in California visiting Colonel Sutter in New Helvetia, having sailed around the Horn.

Tom shivered and bit his lower lip. This guy had been in Sacramento? He knew that John Augustus Sutter, a clever Swiss, had acquired Mexican land grants and built a virtual kingdom in the Sacramento area in the nineteenth century.

Young Rudolf, a suspicious chap, told of mistrust between Austria and Belgium. He wasn't certain but what Franz Joseph was simply trying to get rid of him in the New World, so the wily fellow brought along an insurance policy, the damnedest insurance policy you ever laid eyes on, one of Austria's Crown Jewels.

Another shiver chilled Tom's neck.

Rudolf kept it tied around his waist beneath his fancy tunic, wrapped in an elegant little cloth pouch. The night before the battle, over brandy and cigars in my headquarters, a little Sharpsburg farm house (the brandy had loosened his tongue a fair bit), he showed me the jewel. 'With this in my possession, mein

Herr,' he conveyed, 'my safe return is assured.' It was the biggest and loveliest old emerald I had ever beheld.

Tom looked around, glad to see he was alone, then continued.

My eyes had never settled on anything so beautiful, saving of course for my darling wife's own sweet face. Rudolf vouchsafed it was called the Maria Theresa Emerald.

The emerald had been in America before. At the Battle of Antietam. And near Sacramento even before that! This was electrifying. He read the passage again. *Rudolf was the brother of Princess Carlota, the wife of Franz Joseph's brother, Maximilian . . . The biggest and loveliest old emerald I had ever beheld . . . It was called the Maria Theresa Emerald.* Tom copied it all down before continuing.

The paper went on to say the young prince made sure his father, the Belgian king, knew he had the emerald with him, so that any 'accident' befalling him could point to Franz Joseph.

The young man left our Army some six weeks later when we took up winter positions at Fredericksburg. I expect he and his insurance policy got themselves safely back to Vienna, Longstreet concluded.

Tom dropped his pencil and, cheeks puffing, whooshed out a big breath. "Jesus," he muttered.

As he copied down the last of it, the librarian padded in and said, "I'm sorry sir, but we're closing now."

Tom looked at his watch. Four o'clock! Rush hour on I-95 would be hell.

Kurt Neumann drove his twelve-year-old beige Mercedes sedan south on La Jolla Boulevard. He preferred German cars to American or Japanese, but wasn't impressed with newness or flash. He passed through Bird Rock, a section named for an offshore outcropping populated by seagulls and pelicans.

La Jolla ended and property values dropped a quarter of a

million. He veered onto Mission Boulevard into San Diego's Pacific Beach section. Nine blocks down, he turned onto a small street facing Crystal Pier and found a parking space between a Cherokee and a Harley.

Neumann checked his watch. He was a few minutes early. He liked that. He locked the car, stepped around to the sidewalk and almost got clipped by a near-naked woman on in-line skates. He turned his head and admired her physique and agility. Next to him, a biker in a sleeveless black leather vest scanned the same view. Neumann managed a small, conspiratorial smile, turned and walked off.

He passed a taco shop painted yellow and red—was there a law that all Mexican takeouts had to be yellow and red?—a T-shirt shop, a cabaret displaying a CONCERT TONIGHT sign, and a corner cafe advertising breakfast twenty-four hours a day.

He was stared at by a man of indeterminate age in a campaign hat with desert camouflage and stringy hair that hadn't been shampooed since the Mercedes was new. "Spare some change?" he asked. Neumann looked through him and didn't break stride, heading south on a wide sidewalk crowded with tourists, skaters and bicyclists. He came to an old motel that had rows of small patios with glass windbreakers facing the ocean. He pulled a card from his pocket and glanced at a number he'd written, then at the motel doors.

Looking about more furtively now, he passed five doors, stopped and knocked on the sixth. A brunette woman half his age opened it almost immediately. A hardness of the kind caused by too many divorces was overcoming traces of prettiness in her face. She looked up and down the concrete lane before inviting Neumann in with a movement of her head and a smile lacking in warmth.

Working with this woman was perfect, *perfect*, Neumann thought, after his botched drug deal up north.

* * *

In their room in Washington that night, Tom had just told Cass about General Longstreet's papers.

"Now I know why you felt so strange out at Antietam," she said. "Because your subconscious knew the emerald had been there."

He gave her a funny look.

"Neurobiologists say," she went on, "that we use only twelve or thirteen percent of our brains. Who knows what potentials exist in the rest of it? I think you were getting some kind of message, telepathic or whatever you want to call it, about the emerald."

"Mmm," Tom said. "I thought if I'd been metaphysically linked to anything at Antietam it had been a company of Union soldiers, not the emerald."

The next day was warm and breezy. Bloated clouds of charcoal gray were piling up on the Virginia side of the Potomac when Tom walked Cass from their nearby hotel to the Capitol.

"Looks like rain," he said as they reached the Capitol steps. "Got your umbrella?" They made arrangements to meet at noon for lunch.

"If you slip into another astral plane, call me," she said, grinning over her shoulder as she climbed the steps.

Tom smiled back, then set off on foot for the National Archives, where he spent a frustrating two hours going through the fragmentary surviving records on the Union Army. He found evidence of only ten Cavanaughs serving for the North, from Pennsylvania, Illinois and Ohio. Tom's people had been from Massachusetts.

Realizing he had just enough time to run one more errand, he stepped outside and hailed a cab. He told the driver, "State Department," and slipped into the back seat.

As the cab rolled west on Constitution Avenue, along the

Mall, Tom gazed at the National Art Gallery and the Washington Monument. His thoughts reached back to Antietam and his weird experience there. How different was the pastoral mood out there, two hours away, from the push and shove of this concrete and granite world hub. All they had in common were monuments. He flashed on the photo of Cass and the threatening note. That was never far from his consciousness.

The cabbie broke his reverie. "You said State Department, didn't ya, sport?"

"Right. Do they still call that place Foggy Bottom?"

"Oh, yeah. They say old William Howard Taft gave it that name."

"No kidding?"

"Whadja think of them Hoyas?"

"Georgetown? Yeah, they won the NCAA, didn't they?" Tom said. "I played a little basketball myself, quite awhile ago."

"Yeah, where?"

"Long way from here, place called San Diego State."

"I heard of it. Tony Gwynn, right?"

They were parallel to the Reflecting Pool when Tom blurted, "Wait a minute, I've got another idea! Do you know where Connolly and Butler is, the big PR firm?"

"Connolly and Butler? Yeah, up on New Hampshire Avenue, I think."

"I know a guy there. Let's go."

"Okay," the driver said, "it's your pony ride." And he pulled a U-turn that made horns honk and middle fingers go up.

CHAPTER FIFTEEN

T hat part about the prince visiting Sacramento before the Civil War," Cass said on the flight home from BWI that night, "is pretty amazing."

"Sure is. I'm going to ask a friend of mine, a history prof at Sac State, what he knows about that. He's either an authority on local history or he'll know somebody who is."

So, next day, Wednesday, Tom called the history instructor, who confessed he hadn't heard of Prince Rudolf. "But I have a graduate teaching assistant with a special interest in Sutter. I'll have her dig up whatever she can on the prince's visit to Sacramento and get it to you."

Then Lieutenant Mary Savage called and asked Tom to come and see her in the morning—she'd heard from Charles Alzette, her cop friend in Luxembourg.

Tom got up early and told Cass he was going to get in an hour of flying before meeting with Savage. Flying often cleared his head and improved his outlook.

Cass gave him a sleepy kiss without leaving the bed. "Okay, Neil Armstrong," she murmured. "I'll have the coffee on after splashdown."

"Just make enough for yourself, babe. I'll grab a muffin at the airport and then go straight in and see Mary Savage." Cass mumbled something that sounded like "okay" and buried her face in the covers.

Tom put on faded jeans, a Davis Aggies sweatshirt, his scuffed cowboy boots, and slipped out of the house. He'd been a licensed pilot for eight months after taking lessons off and on for years.

He reached Executive Airport at a quarter to seven and parked in the lot between the runway and Freeport Boulevard. Walking to the office of a flying service to rent a Cessna 172, he heard a familiar voice.

"Yo, Cavanaugh, you're up early." The voice came from the hangar of a helicopter school owned by his friend Dick McAuliffe.

"How about a cup of coffee?" McAuliffe called from beneath a rotor blade, a crescent wrench in his hand and a black smudge on his cheek. McAuliffe had been a cop but had gone into business for himself three years before. He'd taken a bullet in the shoulder after pulling over a speeder, and his wife had laid down the law—either police work went or she did. McAuliffe loved his wife.

Tom said, "Sure," and McAuliffe put down the wrench, wiped his hands on a rag, and went to the coffee pot. They swapped flying and police stories for several minutes.

"Say, are you any relation to Leon McAuliffe?" Tom said at one point.

"Who the hell is Leon McAuliffe?"

"Only the world's greatest steel guitar man. You ever listen to Western swing? Bob Wills and the Texas Playboys?"

"Not if I can help it, Tommy. Western swing?"

"Hey, it's good stuff."

"If you say so." McAuliffe shrugged. "Let me take you up in the chopper," he said. "I've got a slow morning."

"Thanks, but I need to do some flying of my own. I want to log an hour."

"What, in one of those boring fixed-wing crates? You should do some *real* flying in a helo."

"Those noise-makers? And with all those sticks and pedals? Too complicated for me, buddy."

When the banter and the coffee played out, Tom said, "I'll take a raincheck, though, on a ride in that egg-beater."

"Anytime, pal, give me a call."

Tom put the mug down, waved goodbye and went next door, where he signed out a plane and left a credit card at the desk. The blue and white Cessna was parked on the concrete apron with rows of other private planes. He checked the fuel mixture, freed the tie-down ropes and removed the wheel blocks. In the cockpit, he ran through all his preflight checks before cranking the starter.

In the air at last, he felt emancipated, soaring alone and free from earthbound anxieties. The sensation wouldn't last, he told himself, but enjoy it while you can.

He headed southwest over the Sacramento River Delta. The sun peeked over the Sierra in a pink sky, throwing long shadows behind buildings, hills and trees.

Seeing the Calaveras River and the many other fingers of water flowing into the Sacramento five-thousand feet below was a sight Tom always enjoyed. The meandering tributaries, lazing their way toward San Francisco Bay, were blue ribbons tossed helter-skelter on a soggy, wooded land.

He was about halfway to Oakland when he turned back, checked in with the tower and got clearance to land.

While he taxied to the tie-down area, the threat note and the shocking photo, as well as his meeting with Doctor Gerhard, swept back into his mind. The therapeutic minutes in the air had blocked that out. Now it was back—and he looked forward to talking with Mary Savage.

After signing in the plane, he walked past Dick McAuliffe's hangar again. "I'll take you up on that copter ride one of these days," he called.

"You got it, Tommy."

In the downtown station house, Mary Savage waved Tom into her small, tidy office. Mounds of files and papers were stacked on her desk and steel file cabinets along the side wall. Three framed photo blowups of outdoor scenes hung on the wall. A hat rack in the corner held a St. Louis Cardinals cap and a Garboesque wide-brimmed hat beplumed with a feather.

Savage went to her private coffee maker. "I told you I was buying this time," she said, pouring two mugs of coffee. "Believe me, my stuff is far better than you get from the machine downstairs. How's Cass?" she asked, handing Tom a steaming mug inscribed with "American River College."

"She's fine, just working damn long hours as usual."

"She still hasn't broken off your engagement?"

"Not yet, Mary, can you believe it?"

Savage snapped her fingers as if to say "darn."

Tom didn't mind the mild flirting, in fact he rather liked it. It *was* harmless, wasn't it? He wondered if it was her way of saying, "I'm a woman and I'm higher in the department than you, so here's a little sexual harassment, you mere male." She was a sharp professional and if she had some fun to boot, fine with Tom. Too many women executives took themselves too damned seriously. Besides, she was doing him a favor.

"Say, I think I saw her at the gym the other day," Savage said. "Doesn't Cass belong to Quorum Athletics?"

"Yes, she does."

"It was her then. I don't think she recognized me."

Tom gestured at the wall. "Nice photos. Ansel Adams?"

"No, Mary Savage, but I'm certainly flattered. I took those on the Snake River in Idaho three or four years ago on a hiking and rafting trip. Great country up there."

Savage glanced at her watch and picked up three sheets of fax paper.

"Well," she said, "I'm sorry it took him so long, but Alzette sent some stuff on your man. Rolf Gerhard has a degree in anthropology from Graz University and a doctorate in art history from the University of Vienna. He's forty-four and a native Viennese." She settled into her chair behind the desk.

Tom sat too, and pulled out a pen to take notes.

Savage waved that off. "I'll give you this fax," she said. "Everything's on it. Gerhard's father is a retired bureaucrat—he served in their equivalent of our Commerce Department. His one sister is a nurse in a Vienna hospital. She's older. Forty-eight. His grandfather, it appears, was a Nazi. He might have been involved in the 1934 assassination of their chancellor, Dollfuss. That's kind of murky. But when Hitler took over four years later, the grandfather became part of the Austrian Nazi government. Gerhard's wife works part-time for the UN in Vienna and they have a sixteen-year-old daughter in school."

"What about politics?"

"Gerhard claims to have no affiliations. His father, the retired bureaucrat, is a member of the Austrian People's Party, which is right wing and pro-German."

"Religion?"

"Let's see here, oh yes, Roman Catholic. I guess most Austrians are. It doesn't say if he's active, though."

"No record of course?"

"Sorry. Squeaky clean."

"Maybe so but believe me, he feels nasty," Tom said. "Does it say what Gerhard's grandfather did before this political assassination in the Thirties?"

"Right, ah, he'd been a clerk or a guard or something at the royal palace, a place called the Hofburg."

"Your friend Charles did a nice job here."

"He owed me. I gave him a ton of help at the academy. Oh, it also says that Gerhard's grandfather was one of the people responsible for the crown jewels," she said, pushing the fax toward Tom. "Now what the devil is this all about? You have any idea how fascinating this is?"

But Tom hadn't heard anything after "crown jewels."

* * *

"Hey, look at this," Tom said to Cass that night. "That's a great shot of you, babe. I'll have to blow that up and put it on my wall in The Hole."

They had just picked up their snapshots from the trip. A turkey and noodle concoction in the slow cooker filled the old kitchen with a savory aroma. It certainly had the attention of Orbison, who was rubbing against Tom's leg.

Cass flipped through the photos, made comments, and handed them to Tom one by one. There was a gigantic Lincoln reposing in his marble chair, the Ellipse, the majestic columns of the Supreme Court Building, an arty wide angle looking upward from the base of the Washington Monument, Tom leaning against the iron fence outside the White House.

Then came Antietam. The whitewashed Dunkard Church, Bloody Lane, Miller's Farm, two brass cannon guarding a rail fence, an asphalt road lined with monuments.

Cass stopped and her forehead wrinkled in amusement. "Look at these two shots of you here with the old man—General Mansfield, was it? I didn't think he'd show up in these."

"You mean ghosts can't be photographed?" Tom said with a laugh, leaning in for a closer look. "That's an old wives' tale."

Tom took a look at Manny Díaz' house in Carmichael the next day. Cass had known Díaz, who'd been the governor's senior security man before fleeing to Mexico.

Tom had never been on this street before. It was a typical neighborhood of low-slung ranch styles, Carmichael being indistinguishable from the rest of the suburban sprawl east of downtown. He was glad he and Cass lived in a Victorian in an older part of town.

He hadn't really known Díaz. He'd butted heads with him only once, last year, when Tom played a big part in bringing him down.

He pondered the cop gone bad. Díaz had helped to engineer the assassination of the previous governor, making it appear to be suicide. Could he be the one behind the threats? He has motive, Tom thought, must hate my guts. But opportunity? That I don't know.

He drove slowly past the Díaz house. What could have been a big lawn was dissected by a curving sidewalk leading to the door, a wide concrete driveway, and a mulberry tree, its base set off by a circular brick border. The lawn and flowerbeds hinted at Díaz' absence. They needed a good watering and trimming.

Tom rolled on to the end of the block, feeling uneasy being in this neighborhood. He knew he had zero chance of finding Díaz here, and he couldn't afford to be seen by Maria Díaz when she came home. The wife of a cop might make him.

He drove off. As he was about to turn onto Fair Oaks Boulevard, feeling he'd wasted his time, he saw a familiar figure on the sidewalk, staring at him. It looked like the old man from Antietam, the one who resembled General Mansfield. Tom slowed the car and looked closer. He looked *exactly* like the old man from Antietam.

Tom looked away because he was approaching a stop sign. No, he told himself, it couldn't be him.

CHAPTER SIXTEEN

S ounds as if you had a wonderful trip," Tom's father said
as he flipped through snapshots from Washington and
Antietam. Tom and Cass had brought Chinese food from
a takeout in Novato and given the home nurse the afternoon off.
They perched on the bed, on each side of Desmond Cavanaugh.
Still attached by tube to his oxygen machine, he looked weaker
and paler to Tom.

"Why so many shots of this cornfield?"

Tom answered cautiously. He hadn't told his father of his
strange feelings about Antietam—and definitely nothing about
the spectral old man there. Tom's father was a salt-of-the-earth
pragmatist who'd never been curious about what he couldn't see
and touch.

"It just seemed like a pretty spot, Dad, that cornfield. Lot more
greenery than we see around here."

"We had an ancestor at Antietam, I think," Desmond Cavanaugh
said.

"We did?" The same chill he'd felt on the battlefield snaked
down Tom's spine.

"I wish I'd had more interest in the family tree when I was
younger, Thomas, but supposedly it was my great-grandfather. He
was with an outfit from Massachusetts."

"Our people came from Ireland and landed in Boston sometime
before the Civil War, didn't they, Dad?"

"So the story goes. Now I wish to hell I'd paid more attention
when my granddad was telling me his tales. There's a letter around
here somewhere my father wrote to the family, passing down some
of this information. I read it years ago, when I was too young to be

interested. I'll have the day nurse look for it in my old trunk one of these days."

"No, Mister C," Cass said, glancing at Tom, "I don't think you'd want her going through your family things."

Tom felt the same. "Cass and I will do it." He still hadn't told his father about General Longstreet's papers, indicating that the emerald had been at Antietam.

The doorbell rang. Roy Oakley, his father's old friend, was at the front door. Tom greeted Oakley with, "That TV is great. Can't tell you how much we appreciate it." He led Oakley to the bedroom, gathering an extra chair from the dining room along the way.

The three of them assembled around the bed and visited for an hour, Cass slipping into the kitchen a couple of times to refill their glasses.

"I hope you marry that girl before I die," Desmond Cavanaugh said during one of her absences. The words caught Tom up short. He hoped so too. He and Cass had vaguely set the date for near the end of the year. Cass's folks were counting on a big holiday wedding. Maybe the Nesbits would pop for a TV crew and satellite time, so the ceremony could be downlinked to Dad. Ty Nesbit could afford it.

"Start up the van before you go, Thomas, and drive it around a little. The battery's probably running down."

"Dad, why don't I just sell that for you?"

"No, I want to keep a few of my things around me. Sell that old buggy after I'm gone and split the proceeds with your brother."

Cass returned and Oakley asked her about Washington. She described the vice president's office, and told about pitching Governor Travis's position on a Western farm-labor bill to a few senators.

Oakley was interested and asked some good questions. "Quite a daughter-in-law you've got here, Des," he said at one point, embarrassing Cass. "Future daughter-in-law, I mean." He then inspected the vacation pictures and made numerous remarks, especially over the battlefield shots.

"Roy is quite a history buff," Tom's father said. "Tell them, Roy."

"Yes, American history's always fascinated me. Your pictures remind me of my trips to Shiloh and Vicksburg. I haven't been to the sites farther east yet, but I know all about Antietam. Vicksburg is very impressive. Grant besieged it for months. I borrowed a Confederate arm patch from the museum there. The Fourth Mississippi."

"You *borrowed* it?" Tom said, confused. His father gave Tom a look that said, "Humor the child."

"Well," Oakley said, "they wouldn't give it to me or sell it, would they?"

He'd swiped it? Petty theft was a crime. If this wasn't way out of my jurisdiction, Tom thought, I'd run the guy in.

"Say," Oakley went on, "have you ever been to Canby's Cross here in California? Up at the Lava Beds? That wasn't the Civil War, of course—the Modoc War, one of the last great Indian fights. Forgotten piece of California history. You should go some time."

"I'm sorry, Cass," Tom's father said. "I shouldn't have gotten this old buzzard started. What did you 'borrow' *there?*" he chided Oakley. "An Indian headdress? He could go on for hours on this stuff."

"Look who's calling who an old buzzard." Oakley snapped a smile at Cass and said, "Anyway, I'll show you both my pictures of Canby's Cross sometime."

"Roy is a first-rate photographer," Desmond Cavanaugh said.

When Cass arrived home from work the next day, Tom wasn't there yet, so she sank into a chair, kicked off her shoes, and opened the mail. There were several items: bills, invitations and junk. A publishing clearinghouse said she might already be a millionaire. She had sliced open all the mail at once and hadn't noticed that a square white envelope was addressed to Tom. It didn't strike her as anything special until she pulled out a photograph.

Then it hit her like a truck. It was a picture of her. Her knees became Jell-O. If she hadn't been sitting already, she would have fallen. The same searing pain burned in her chest. In the black and white photo, she was unlocking the door of her Burgundy Bullet. There was the same bunched-up telephoto quality of the first shot, but this one was clearer and in sharp focus. It was taken from the front, her face visible.

This wasn't nearly as hard a shot to get as the one in the gym, she thought. Then she realized it was taken in another part of the Capitol garage, on an entirely different floor from her usual parking space. Her heart sank even lower. She'd begun randomly switching parking spots with a girlfriend on various days. And whoever took this picture *knew* that.

She looked closely at the suit and the scarf draped over her shoulder. She was pretty sure she'd worn that outfit the very first time she'd switched parking spaces. She thought about the night she'd gotten spooked in a different garage after working out at the gym. She looked at the envelope. Like the first warning, it bore a Los Angeles postmark. *Damn, damn! Some weirdo with a camera knows all about me. And it's a woman. Stalking me.*

Cass jumped to her feet, startling Orbison, who stared at her, cocking his silver and gray head at a curious angle. She hurried to the front windows and snapped all the blinds shut. Then she turned the lights off. She was just about to throw the deadbolt on the door when it opened.

She froze. The .38 in her purse was twenty-five feet away on the dining room table.

"Trick or treat," Tom said, stepping into the darkness. "You having a séance in here or what? No fair conjuring up General

Mansfield without me."

Cass threw herself into his arms. "Lock the door," she said.

"How can I? I'm your prisoner," Tom said as she clung to him with both arms. Quivering muscles communicated her fear.

"Cass, what's wrong?"

It took her a few moments to compose herself and tell him about the photo.

"There's another note on the back?"

"I don't know. Haven't looked. I started turning off lights and closing blinds as soon as I saw what it was."

Tom picked it up, touching only the edges, and looked closely. Then he flipped it over and looked at the back. As before, there was a message, in laser-printed capitals. WE REALLY CAN, YOU SEE. SHE DOESN'T HAVE TO BE HARMED, BUT IT'S UP TO YOU. INSTRUCTIONS COMING.

"What the hell am I supposed to do?" he said, before remembering what his father had told him long ago about being a cop. *Panic is the enemy. Keep calm. The other guy's got you if you panic.*

"You're supposed to give him the emerald," Cass said, "whoever he is. Or she. Or else they'll do something nasty to me. Well, the hell with that. I'm going to keep my eyes open like never before, and when I catch this creep, I'll blow him away."

"Cass!"

"I will. I've had it with this stuff. He's got no right. I'll blow his damn brains out, Tom. He's taken his last sneak picture of me."

"Remember, it's probably a woman, or one of them is, anyway."

"Right, I know. Madame X. Then I'll blow *her* damn brains out. Oh, this is so damn maddening."

"This is not just some wacko," Tom said, still holding her, but leaning back to study her face. "We're dealing with people, one or more—they always speak of themselves in the plural—who must know about the emerald. It's doubtful they're tailing you all the time. More likely just once in awhile to get their pictures and try to terrorize us."

"Try?"

Tom cradled her face in his hands and kissed her lips, then her closed eyelids. Cass always liked being kissed on the eyelids. He told her his father's adage about panic.

"He's right," she said. "I'd better cool my jets. I could probably never shoot anybody anyway. But damn, I wish they'd just cut to the chase and tell us what they want us to do."

"Right," Tom said."Then *we* could make a plan."

"But you're opening all the mail from now on."

"Okay, Cass, I have to ask you to tell me about your old boyfriends."

"Hmm, you've never done that before. I've always been glad you're not the jealous type."

"But maybe one of your old admirers is."

Cass hadn't wanted to talk about Nick Race, the object of her one romantic involvement before Tom. Race had been the special projects director for the previous governor. He was thirteen years older than Cass. Why did she always go for older men? Although she didn't think of Tom, who was thirty-eight to her thirty-one, that way. She and Tom seemed complete contemporaries.

Race was not at all her type. Six-two, like Tom, but stocky and a little overweight. He filled out his double-breasted suits like a wedge. Twice divorced and rather humorless, he nevertheless had style, and he knew everybody. He dined at the best restaurants, used valet parking, tipped big, and enjoyed lavish ski trips with Cass.

After sixteen months in the fast lane with Nick Race, Cass had called it off. It hadn't been easy, but she didn't really love him, never had, and couldn't imagine devoting her life to him. It was hard on him and hard on her—she'd been fond of the big oaf.

Cass had moped around for nearly a year until she met Tom. It didn't take her long to see that she'd met the right guy.

And now this right guy was dredging up Nick Race and a couple of others, all in the line of duty, part of trying to keep her out of harm's way. She looked at the slender, handsome, uncomplicated cop opposite her and was filled with the same feelings she'd had that first day. She was glad, right down to her marrow, that she was engaged to Tom Cavanaugh.

Fifteen minutes of talking about her old beaus didn't turn up anyone likely to be a camera-slinging stalker. Nor anyone likely to know anything about the emerald.

"We have some options," Tom said. "One is go to the department officially and get protection for you. Another: get out of here right away, move into a hotel, and keep changing every couple of days."

They could say they were going on vacation for awhile, Tom said, and ask Mrs. Potter, the neighbor, to take care of Orbison again. But would she buy it? After the trip to Europe in February and then Washington a couple of weeks ago?

"I don't like either of those," Cass said. "I've had enough packing and unpacking this year."

"Well, tomorrow looks like a light day for our unit. I'll tail you myself, most of the day anyway. If somebody's screwing around in your footsteps tomorrow, I'll stick his eyeballs up his fundamental orifice."

"Ah ah ah," Cass said. "Romans 12:19."

Though not very religious now, Cass had been a star pupil in Sunday school years ago and occasionally quizzed Tom on Bible verses.

"What's that? 'It's a sin to sodomize with eyeballs?' "

" 'Never avenge yourselves, but leave it to the wrath of God; for it is written, vengeance is Mine, sayeth the Lord,' " she recited.

"And I shall be Thine instrument, sayeth Tom."

CHAPTER SEVENTEEN

Tom tailed Cass twice over a period covering four hours. In the morning, he watched her walk two blocks west to the Capitol after parking in a state garage. The usual business-suited men and women bustled about, many of them carrying attaché cases or soft carry-alls with shoulder straps.

Tom wore jeans along with the brown uniform shirt and cap of an express-mail service, one of his many undercover getups. He even carried a small package.

He watched Cass go on foot to a mid-morning meeting in the Capitol Annex. After that, he changed into a blue button-down business shirt and navy blazer. No tie, still the jeans. He fancied that he looked like a young entrepreneur.

He saw all kinds of sights during his surveillance: homeless souls pushing their worldly possessions in grocery carts, a couple of teenage boys in baggy black shorts reaching halfway down their calves, a gun-racked pickup truck with a bumper sticker reading, *To Hell with Whales, Save the Cowboy.*

Stepping out from a convenience store with a styrofoam cup of coffee in hand, the thought hammered at him: *My great-great-grandfather was at Antietam?*

He saw Cass walk to lunch at Frank Fat's, where she met a well-tailored middle-aged man from the Beef Council, who Tom knew was courting the governor's help on some issue.

It all added up to nothing. He just didn't see anything or anyone, man or woman, out of the ordinary. He was convinced that Cass wasn't being watched all the time, that the sneak photos were hit-and-run affairs.

* * *

Ex-state security officer Manny Díaz peered down from his window seat and gazed at the hills separating Santa Cruz from the Peninsula and the marshy south end of San Francisco Bay. His Aeromexico flight from Mexico City had taken five hours.

The reading light reflected on the top of his head. He had a bald strip up the center, ringed by a crescent of black hair, and a ponytail tied in back. He hated going bald so young, and recently had grown the ponytail to compensate.

As the Stanford campus slid by, Díaz caught a glimpse of Hoover Tower and the oval stadium. Cars and trucks on U.S. 101 were ants crawling along at a uniform speed.

He would be on the ground in San Francisco in a few minutes. Moments after that he would have another bittersweet reunion with his wife Maria in a motel room in San Mateo, before going north on a big job, one that would bring him some good money.

A year ago, Díaz had been a state policeman, the senior security officer for California's Governor Magdalena Travis. But he'd turned, and gambled his future on a risky gambit that had gone bad. Now he was a fugitive hiding in Mexico. He moved about in shadows, sneaking in and out of California like a ghost. This was actually easy to do, but still humiliating, having to pretend, having to be on constant alert.

He loved Maria and missed her terribly. Their snatched moments together were both bliss and torture. They were too brief and the pleasure of lovemaking was always dampened by the inevitable discussions of their future.

Maria often said she would never desert him in her heart, would never divorce him, but she refused to live with him in Mexico or Nicaragua or wherever. A native of Fresno, she was a *Norteamericana*, an Hispanic American. The kids were established in Sacramento, two of them in school. They had bright futures in California.

A warm, painful mixture of longing and foreboding filled Díaz as he approached this reunion. He reflected that ten years ago he'd been a cop in Fresno, the son of a native Mexican cotton picker. Before becoming a state cop and ending up on the elite Dignitary Protection Unit, he had seen a young, intoxicated Mexican farm worker savagely beaten by white cops. They'd claimed the laborer had started a fight, then tried to resist arrest. Díaz always said that was the moment he'd learned about Anglo racism.

He recalled it bitterly as the plane descended over the choppy waters of San Francisco Bay, approaching the airport.

His fingers drummed against the arm rest so hard the older woman next to him must have felt the vibrations. She glanced over. "Landing isn't so bad, young man," she said. "I've done it hundreds of times. It's really quite safe, you know."

Stupid old *puta*, he thought.

Tom and Cass stood side by side at the kitchen sink, Cass rinsing the plates and glasses, Tom arranging them in the dishwasher. He had just filled her in on the non-results of tailing her that morning.

"We're playing the attorney general's office in slow-pitch tomorrow night at McKinley Park," Cass said, "and they really want me to play. What do you think?"

Tom knew she liked playing with the softball team from the governor's office. Cass hit like Ty Cobb and played a good first base. He'd played for them once himself, as a ringer, when they'd been a player short.

"They'd probably think something was funny if I didn't. I haven't been sick or anything and no one in the office knows about the threat notes. Besides, it'd give Madame X a chance to shoot me in my softball gear."

Tom smiled half-heartedly. Sometimes Cass carried this stiff upper lip/black humor routine too far. But in a way, she was right.

"Maybe you should. That's probably the worst that could happen out there, getting your picture taken. Nobody would be stupid enough to try anything in front of thirty or forty people at a softball diamond. I could hang out beyond the sidelines and check out the spectators, and anybody else who might be sneaking around in the trees with a long lens."

"Or across the street," Cass said.

"Or across the street."

"Okay, then, I'll play. Having you there will mean a lot. How about some dessert?"

"Dessert? We haven't had dessert in weeks."

"I picked up some great looking strawberries today, Tom, and there's still some whipped cream in the fridge."

"Sounds good. Haven't had strawberries since last summer." His eyes smiled deeply into hers. "Let's have 'em in bed. I can think of some other uses for that whipped cream too."

"Dirty old man," she said, and gave him a kiss full of collusion.

"What do you mean *old?*" Tom said.

The next day, Tom got a call from Lan Nguyen at Princeton, saying his hacking project had run into a snag.

"They had a virus at the cyber café that affected every computer—they were networked. It should all be cleaned up in a few days, then I can go to work on that law firm. I'm real sorry about this delay."

Tom told Lan Nguyen not to worry. There was nothing he could do but wait.

Cass stopped by the house after work to change into her softball gear. While putting her skirt on a hanger, she thought about her upbringing, how she and her sister Jan had been good students. How she'd become fascinated with politics after being elected president of her fifth grade class. By high school, Cass had decided that helping others get elected, guiding their campaigns, was more rewarding than being in office herself.

And now here she was two decades later, a key aide to the powerful governor of a large state. She had the ideal job and a good man. Her life should be perfect, not lived in fear, looking over her shoulder, jumping skittishly when the phone rang, afraid of looking at the mail or turning the key in her own front door. If only Tom hadn't had a father who'd once guarded an old German field marshal.

She slapped her open hand against the closet door. "Damn!"

That evening Tom wandered all around the softball diamond, the playground, and the rest of McKinley Park. He looked behind trees and the restroom building, checked the people walking along 33rd Street. Looked for people sitting in parked cars and SUV's. Nothing unusual, nothing at all. By the sixth and last inning, he perched on a bleacher plank close to Cass's bench, satisfied that he'd seen nothing suspicious.

Thirty or so spouses and friends were watching. A lot of beer was being consumed by fans and players alike, and the air was filled with good-natured bantering.

The governor's office trailed the attorney general's team, sixteen to fourteen, but had the last at-bats. Before the first pitch was lobbed in, the governor slid next to Tom. "It's nice to see you, Tom."

"Same here, Mrs. Travis." He was impressed that she'd showed up for the game. He knew how busy she was. He spotted her plainclothes bodyguard from the Dignitary Protection Unit standing nearby.

"You call me Maggie now. Everyone does . . . Come on, Randy, whale the tar out of that thing."

Tom had met the governor several times and liked the way she slipped easily between ceremony and informality as the occasion dictated. She always put him at ease. "Cass seems a little uptight these days," she said. "Anything wrong that I should know about?"

Tom glanced down at the bench. Waiting her turn at bat, Cass fidgeted, looking around nervously beyond the bleachers, beyond the outfield fence.

"Atta baby, Randy, atta baby," Governor Maggie shouted.

Tom hoped she'd forgotten her question. She hadn't. "How about it, Tom? Cass have a problem I should know about?"

"No, not really, Missus, er, Maggie. She's fine. Nothing to worry about. She's a little concerned about her sister and then of course there's our wedding plans. And the workload." Tom was sorry he'd said that last bit.

"I know it's a tough job, and we expect a lot from her, Tom. It's precisely because they're so good that the good people keep getting more work piled on them. The weak ones weed themselves out. I couldn't do without Cass. She'll have a job with me for as long as she wants, or as long as the voters want me in office."

Campaign speech for an audience of one, Tom thought. This was exactly how she'd sounded during the last election drive.

"She's worried about her sister then?"

Tom nodded agreement as Elena Ortega, Cass's favorite secretary, hit a line drive back to the pitcher, which he caught.

Now Cass strolled to the plate. Wearing shorts, the lean, strong muscles of her long legs were pleasingly visible as she stepped into the batter's box. She rapped her bat once at the plate—harder than usual—and took her stance. Her feet were spread three feet apart, her knees slightly bent, and she held the bat high. They had tied the game and the winning run was on second.

"Let's go, Cass, rip the cover off the ball," the governor called out.

"Come on, babe, give it a ride," Tom added.

"Tom, your fiancée is not only the prettiest person on my staff, and one of the smartest and hardest working, but she's also the best stick in the lineup."

I just heard that speech, Tom thought. "I know. I agree with most of that, except, well, you're the prettiest person on the staff."

"You heap it on thick, don't you, copper?"

Cass let the first pitch go. Tom knew it was too low for her liking.

"You're good for her." Governor Maggie put a friendly hand on Tom's shoulder just as Cass connected with an angry swing and lashed the ball toward left-center field. It dropped between fielders and the winning run crossed the plate before anyone touched it. Cass had loped around first base and was halfway to second when the game ended. She stopped and leaped in the air, her arms raised in triumph.

"Plus, she's a female Robin Yount," the governor shouting and hugging Tom, surprising him.

"Right . . . Excuse me," he said, jumping down and sprinting toward the field. A minute later, while co-workers slapped congratulations on her back and shoulders, Cass was the one giving Tom a hug.

"Nice going, babe," he said, and kissed her. "Game-winning RBI." When the others trotted off toward the beer cooler, he added in a whisper, "Apparently last night's dessert didn't wear you out. I've never seen you crush the ball so hard or run so fast."

"Know why? I was pissed off about all this stuff. At bat, I pretended the ball was that damn photographer." She looked around again, at the trees in deep shadow beyond the diamond. "Let's get out of here."

The next day was Saturday. They had planned to drive to Novato and go through his father's old Army trunk.

"Great," Cass said. "I need to get out of town, plus maybe we can find your grandfather's letter."

On the drive over, Tom said, "There wasn't much danger at the softball game, but you still need to be very careful every day."

"I know."

"Keep changing your routine. And wear that wig I got you once in awhile."

"Oh sure," she said with a frown.

"Seriously. Not in the office of course, but going to and from your car. And *always* check your surroundings."

"Yes, mother."

"Excuse me?"

"Honestly, Cavanaugh, give me some credit." Cass stared straight ahead. "Treat me like an adult, will you?"

A brittle silence filled the car for the next several minutes. Tom gripped the steering wheel tighter than usual.

At last, with a weak smile, Cass said, "Sorry," and put a hand on Tom's leg. The strain seemed to be gone by the time they reached Novato.

His head resting on a pillow, Desmond Cavanaugh told them, "That Army footlocker hasn't been opened in ten years. Have fun."

"Come on," Cass said, gripping Tom's elbow, "let's see what's in it."

In the attic, Tom glanced at a gooseneck lamp he hadn't seen in fifteen years, then moved cardboard boxes and orange crates away from the footlocker and brushed off some cobwebs. The locker was dun-colored with U.S. ARMY stenciled on the side. He undid the hasp, raised the creaking lid, and sat cross-legged in front of it.

Cass knelt beside him, her eyes alight with curiosity. "This looks just like an old-fashioned steamer trunk," she said, reaching in.

The locker proved to be a treasure trove. Tom's father's letters from overseas, written on flimsy World War II "victory paper," some words and sentences snipped out by the censors. An MP armband and a patch bearing sergeant's chevrons. Discharge papers from 1947. An elegant silver brooch. Commendations from the San Francisco Police Department. A letter from Novato's city manager dated 1968, offering him the police chief's job. One gold cufflink. A bank passbook, dated 1969, listing mortgage payments made faithfully on the fifth of the month for years.

"I'd like to have some of this stuff after Dad's gone," Tom said. "That'll be a sad day. Michael and I will have to go through all this and decide who wants what."

Cass smiled sympathetically and picked up something oval and flat, loosely wrapped in crumbling paper. She pulled away the paper and found she was holding a photograph, its wooden frame etched with ornate ridges and scrolls. Years of grime covered the glass, which was rough and imperfect, blotched by a couple of tiny air bubbles. She wiped at it with a Kleenex, held it up for a look—and gasped.

She composed herself and said, "Weren't having a good day, were you, Tom?"

"What?"

"Well, look here, what a face you're making about going to this costume party."

The aged photograph was more almond-color than gray. The young man in the picture stared straight ahead in a stern gaze. He had bushy muttonchop sideburns and wore a high, starched collar with a hand-tied ribbon tie. *And looked exactly like Tom.*

"It's you, the spitting image," Cass said, looking from him to the picture and back again. "Amazing."

Tom, his spine chilled, took the picture and turned it over. Some old-fashioned lettering appeared on the back. Cass leaned in close and they both silently read the words.

"Brennan's Gallery, No. 12 Oak Street, Grafton, Massachusetts."

And below that, hand-printed in pencil, "Padraic Cavanaugh, 1859."

Tom flipped the picture over again and they stared a long while at his great-great-grandfather, awed by the uncanny resemblance.

Cass started rummaging again and soon spotted an old spiral-bound writing tablet. She opened it and the edges of the pages were yellowed and brittle with age. "Tom, this is it," she exclaimed. "Look!"

It was dated January 29, 1919. "To my children," it began. The handwriting was flowery, with large, sweeping whorls, the T's and I's boldly crossed and dotted.

"People cared about penmanship in those days," Tom said.

They sat on the floor side by side, backs against the locker. Cass began to read aloud.

I am feeling foolishly sentimental on this Christmas, but you will forgive my rambling and perhaps one day find that these scribblings have meaning to you. This, of course, is not really Christmas Day, but this year our family observed it as such, because it found me safe at home again after the Great War. Because of my grandfather's fate, I had doubts that I would make it. On the actual Christmas I was aboard a troopship blustering its way through a stormy passage of St. George's Channel, somewhere off Cork on the land of our forefathers, happy for safe deliverance from that bloody continent, back to your beloved mother . . . .

A page or two later, Cass read,

You will want to know something of your forebears. My grandfather, Padraic Kavanagh, was born in the town of Kenmare in County Kerry, in 1840 or '41. I learned from my mother what little I know of him. The name was spelled KAVANAGH but that was changed by an immigration official in Boston, whence he came by ship with his parents in 1846, during the Potato Famine. We don't know much about them, although they had been tenant farmers at the time of the famine. Instead of receiving relief or succor from their English landlords, apparently they were evicted. They subsequently became domestic servants in Boston, and the Civil War broke out when Grandfather Padraic must have been about the age of 20. With a number of his young friends, he enlisted in the Union Army when the Twelfth Massachusetts Volunteer Regiment was formed.

Tom stared at Cass, changed positions, re-crossed his legs.

"You okay?" she said.

"Sure. Go on."

This regiment fought in all the important battles in the East, starting with First Bull Run. Legend has it, it was they who took the old Gospel song, eliminated the John Brown's Body *words in favor of Julia Ward Howe's and thus created* The Battle Hymn of the Republic. *I never knew my grandfather, because, I'm sorry to relate, he was killed at the Battle of Antietam in Maryland on September 17th, 1862.*

Cass stopped reading. A dazed look had come over Tom. She touched his hand and searched his face with her eyes. He looked as if his own death had just been described.

After a moment he said, "It's okay. I was expecting that. Go on."

. . . September 17th, 1862. His son, my father, was born one month later. I don't know much about my grandfather's death, except that it came in the morning, when the Twelfth Massachusetts and several other regiments were trying to drive off Stonewall Jackson, who had dug in around a Dunkard Church. It was a terrible battle, thousands dying on both sides. His body lies there yet as I understand, in a nameless grave, with so many . . .

"On second thought," Tom said, "that's enough for today. Let's go down and show Dad this old picture."

CHAPTER EIGHTEEN

Tom was back at work Monday morning in The Hole. The phone rang and he picked it up.

"Mr. Cavanaugh?" said a high-pitched and obviously disguised voice. "Listen closely."

Valleys formed on Tom's forehead. The receiver to his ear, he heard a sharp click, like a tape recorder being punched on. Three seconds passed, then a different voice, weird and higher toned, said: "Put the item in a paper sack, go to Land Park and place it beneath the blue trash can beside the picnic table directly opposite the entrance to Funderland. That's half a block east of the zoo . . ." This second voice sounded as if it had been recorded and speeded up. Sounded like Alvin and the Chipmunks.

Tom cupped his hand over the mouthpiece and called out, "Quick, April, trace on this. Line Three."

". . . at exactly 8:37 a.m. on Saturday. Land Park. Blue trash can, picnic table directly opposite Funderland, 8:37 Saturday. Don't even *think* about sticking a transmitter on it." Click. Dial tone.

Tom had scribbled the message on a pad. PAP SACK BLU TRSH CN, OPP F-LAND SAT 8:37.

"April, did you get that? April?"

"April's not here," said Luke Monelli. "What's up, Tom?"

"Damn." Tom slammed open palms on the desk. His coffee mug jumped. "Hell, the guy wasn't on long enough to trace anyway."

"What was it, Tom? What's going on?"

He didn't answer Monelli. They'd called him here at work, at this presumably secret location. Very few people were supposed to know this number. Tom was thinking in overdrive. These people sure as hell knew a lot about him and Cass. And now they'd told him exactly what to do. Funderland was a kiddie-ride place, little ponies and such. Opposite, across an asphalt lane, lay a big picnic area. It was only a few blocks from his and Cass's home.

Well, maybe they weren't so smart after all. It would be easy to stake out that picnic table. It was a wide-open place, very public. He could hide in the trees nearby and wait. They couldn't leave it there long after the drop. They'd have to come fast—that picnic area was popular.

Hours ahead of time, he would park his car a block away. Then he'd return on foot and be there at 8:37. After leaving a sack beneath the blue trash can—what would he put in it?—he'd hide in the trees and wait, armed with binoculars, his 9-millimeter Ruger and .25 caliber Astra.

Backup. He'd have backup too. Some of his friends, off-duty. April the Cop would do it. Debbie Hamilton too, the PO-2 doing high school undercover, and Mike Norfleet, of course. Luke Monelli was scheduled to work Saturday, but the other three would be enough. They'd be concealed among the trees well ahead of time.

Tom tried to persuade himself these people didn't know what they were up against. Their asses would be nailed. Or so he hoped.

Cass had been varying her routine, trading parking places with others in the office, and following most of the other precautions Tom had urged. She'd even worn a black wig a couple of times while walking from the office to her car. And hated it.

When Tom came in through the kitchen, she was sitting at the dining room table, her fists clenched, eyes staring toward the window.

It was several seconds before she realized Tom was in the room. She turned her head toward him. "Hey, you. I'm going stir crazy. We've got to do something."

"Let's go to the pistol range," he said. "I'd like you to get some more practice."

"Hmm. Yeah." Tom had pulled strings months ago and got her a carry permit for her Smith & Wesson .38. Cass being big in the governor's office, it hadn't been hard to do.

"The police range?" she asked.

"No, that private one near Executive Airport. It's closer."

Three other people were shooting when they arrived at the indoor range. Tom and Cass placed their guns and ammunition boxes on an enameled hardwood counter extending the length of the firing line, and put on sound-deadening ear covers. Cass placed safety glasses over her eyes and loaded her pistol carefully. She lifted it, felt the weight and balance, extended her arm and fired.

Even with earmuffs, the sudden echoing thunder of the first shot always startled her. While Tom watched and coached, she fired six shots, the pistol at arm's length, one-handed, as required in shooting matches. Brass shell casings clattered down after each shot.

"Okay, that's great," Tom shouted. To hear him, Cass raised the muff from one ear. "Everything on the paper and most of them in the black. Now reload and shoot two-handed, cop style."

She fired more than twenty shots that way.

When Tom mouthed, "Great, that's enough," she grinned, held the barrel upright near her mouth and pretended to blow smoke away, gunslinger style. Tom liked that—she was feeling better.

"It's fun plugging these bulls-eye things," she yelled above the din, "but don't they have any targets with silhouettes of men?"

"Not here. Only at the police range. You scored well, but I'm more interested in you getting off fast, accurate, two-handed shots than in piling up tens and X's on the paper. It's very different shooting at a man."

Tom picked up his Ruger 9-millimeter, saying, "My turn now." He called for a new target and fired off one clip's worth, all two-handed.

"Showoff," Cass said after every shot punched through the black circle near the center. "I'm still going to outshoot you one of these days."

"Probably so," he said. "Now let's police up the firing line."

"Police up?"

"That's target-shooter jargon for cleaning up after yourself." Thus enlightened, Cass helped him scoop up their expended brass.

At home, Cass dished up some ice cream.

"I'm glad we went down there," Tom said after gulping a spoonful of Dutch chocolate.

"I kept seeing that target as the creep with the camera," Cass said.

"I feel better, having you comfortable with that little cannon of yours."

"Shooting's growing on me," she said. "Remember how shocked I was last year when you said I should have a gun?"

"Yeah, and how thankful we were later that you did."

"Listen, Tom, whatever you're up to, I want to go with you. I want to do my part."

"No way, Cass. I like your attitude, but definitely not. Doing your part means lying low, not exposing yourself." Tom winced. Bad choice of words, considering that first picture.

Cass tried again later, but Tom wouldn't budge.

"The whole idea is to protect you. The president wouldn't stand on the running board with his Secret Service men."

Tom was at work the next day when Luke Monelli called out from his cubicle, "For you, Tom, line two. Somebody in the crime lab downtown." Tom had been waiting for this. He snatched up the phone.

"Cavanaugh? Virgil Trucks at the lab. Lieutenant Savage asked me to slow down a tape for you."

All incoming calls at The Hole were recorded on a master tape deck and Tom had asked Mary Savage if her crime lab could re-record the call instructing him to make the drop in the park, and slow it down to normal speed. Then he might be able to identify the voice.

"Got bad news for you. That message was produced digitally."

"What are you telling me?"

"That's a synthesized voice, computer-generated."

"So there's no human voice to identify—at any speed?"

"Right, sorry."

"Any way to identify the lab where it was made?"

"Not a chance."

"Who'd be able to produce that kind of thing?"

"High-tech audio labs, the kind that service businesses concerned about industrial espionage—or, hell, any ten-year-old kid with a computer. I'm sorry, man."

Tom thanked him and hung up. Any kid with a computer? He'd gained nothing and now at least two more people—Mary Savage and her crime lab guy—knew the contents of the call he'd received.

"Damn." He closed his eyes and kneaded his brow.

Mike Norfleet, April the Cop and Debbie Hamilton all agreed to help on Saturday morning, armed and in plain clothes. They met at April's apartment Thursday night and planned it out over beers, Tom bringing a twelve-pack. Tom had picked the meeting place. They were less likely to be seen gathering there than at a bar or his house. I'm not getting paranoid, he told himself, just taking smart precautions.

He felt better as the plan took form. There was confidence in the air. "This guy is fishing up the wrong tree," Norfleet said. "We'll take the bull by the neck."

"Let's hope," Tom answered.

In his motel room near the San Francisco airport, Manny Díaz was going through the usual argument with his wife Maria. The room was typical motel: off-white walls, cheap but serviceable furniture, the television set and wall paintings bolted down, table tent cards promoting pay TV channels and local restaurants.

Díaz knew Maria didn't like his new ponytail. He did, though. It was a symbol of his new lonesome belligerence.

"Okay, okay, you don't want to move to Mexico City. Not fair to you or the kids. Well, how about this? We could live in Tijuana; believe it or not, there are some nice neighborhoods there. The kids could cross over and go to school in the States. A lot of Mexican kids go to school in south San Diego and ours could too."

Maria shifted in her chair and crossed her legs. "Our children are not Mexican kids, Manny."

That hurt but Díaz didn't let it show. "You know what I mean. They'd still be in American schools and they could have lots of Anglo friends, if that's so important. I have some good contacts in San Diego now."

Díaz got to his feet and began pacing. "Look, Maria, I'm sorry this stuff went sour last year, but that's over now—I can't undo the past. I have friends in Mexico who'll help us and I'm making some big money on this next job. You could go to San Diego whenever you want, go shopping, go to the theater. We can get a doctor and a dentist there too, good Anglo doctors if you want. It's done all the time."

Maria didn't respond. She crossed her arms tightly in front of her.

"Look, honey, Tijuana is an okay town. You should see the money that's pouring in there from Japan and everyplace. One of my contacts in San Diego is a former businessman. He's onto something that could take care of us for the rest of our lives."

Later that night, Tom told Cass about the plan and his helpers.

"Debbie Hamilton, she's that looker who's got a crush on you."

"Oh, the hell."

"Tom Cavanaugh, I believe you're blushing." Cass's grin came and went quickly. "Anyway, now we're getting somewhere. I'm going to be there too, in the trees. Me and my trusty LadySmith."

"No way, Cass, I thought we settled that. Absolutely not. I love you too much to let you do anything that foolish."

"This has got my adrenaline pumping. I can help. You said yourself I've become a fine shot. You know damn well I scored as well as you last time we went to the range. Next time I'm going to beat you, just like I will next time on the tennis court."

"There's not going to be any shooting. Besides, you're not trained. No offense, babe, but would you let me write a speech for the governor? Or argue an issue before the Legislature?"

"It's my neck they're threatening, and I deserve to be in at the finish."

Tom took her shoulders firmly in his hands and held her at arm's length, shaking his head from side to side. "No," he said, and the discussion was over.

CHAPTER NINETEEN

The second Saturday in April found Tom up early. Slipping out of bed before Cass, he put on a battered pair of jeans, running shoes, and a green-and-white rugby shirt. In the kitchen, he made a pot of coffee.

While the coffee was dripping, a pair of arms encircled him from the rear and a warm mouth kissed the side of his neck.

"I wanta go with you," a sleepy voice said.

"Good morning to you too." Tom turned and pulled her face to his. He returned the kiss square on the lips.

They had gone over this subject for days and Tom had been unbending, so Cass pushed it no further as they had a snack of coffee and bagels.

"Go to the office like we planned," he said.

"I will, I will."

"I'll come there as soon as this is over. I'll follow you home."

Their parting hug was tight and warm. "Nail 'em," she whispered.

At 6:45, after making sure he wasn't tailed, Tom parked on one of the winding roads in William Land Park, a quarter of a mile from Funderland. He walked on out of the park, heading east, and went into a coffee shop on Freeport Boulevard near City College.

Mike Norfleet, Debbie Hamilton, and April the Cop met him there at seven. They took a booth in the back and went over the plan again.

Wearing a baseball cap, jeans and hooded sweatshirt, Norfleet looked like a weekender about to mow his lawn. April was in jeans, a Hard Rock Cafe T-shirt and sneakers, and Debbie looked svelte in a lavender jogging suit. Each woman wore a fanny pack large enough to hold a pistol.

"Nobody's ever picnicking before nine," Tom said. "The table's sure to be empty."

Twenty minutes later they drove to the zoo in April's Cherokee and fanned out to the east. April and Norfleet were on the south side of Land Park Drive, April on point. Tom and Debbie were on the opposite side, in the picnic grounds. All had good lines of sight to the picnic table.

Tom surveyed the entire area. The kiddie rides wouldn't start up before nine and there were no customers yet, just a few morning walkers and joggers from the neighborhood, some folks strolling with their dogs, others powering along to burn calories.

He saw Norfleet sit on a bench, open a newspaper, and pretend to read. April strolled in front of Funderland, looking like any other young mother whose kids might be running around nearby.

Across the road, Debbie was jogging, going several hundred yards in one direction before circling back. Tom leaned against a tree and tried not to think. Calliope music started up in a kiddie park nearby to the west.

Casey would waltz with the strawberry blonde, and the band played on . . . That innocent little tune couldn't be in greater contrast to the tension he felt. He kept glancing at his watch. Time barely moved. Debbie jogged by and gave him a shy "good morning" as if they were strangers.

Whenever Tom caught sight of Norfleet or April they ignored him. Good cops.

A young couple pushing a baby carriage approached Funderland, checked the hours on the sign, and strolled on. Then came a young white woman with a small black boy by the hand. A bird screeched from the zoo. Peacock, Tom thought. A horn honked somewhere. Three teenagers clattered by on skateboards. One of them cried, "Watch out, dude."

At 8:25 two Sacramento fire engines rumbled up from the west, pulled over to the side of the asphalt lane, and stopped about a hundred yards from the picnic table. Firemen and women wearing light blue T-shirts and navy blue sweatpants piled out and began stretching exercises. Tom remembered that they often came to the park for morning workouts. Maybe it was on Saturdays, he wasn't sure. After several minutes of stretching, they went into a calisthenics routine.

He checked his watch again.

8:30. Almost time now. He'd give it five more minutes, then he'd stroll over to the picnic table, hang around for a minute retying his shoelaces, slip the sack beneath the blue trash can and leave at exactly 8:37.

The woman with the black child crossed the lane from Funderland and—*Oh no!*—sat down at the picnic table. Why that one? There were plenty of others. *Jesus!* What are the odds that someone would use that table before nine o'clock? Helplessly, Tom watched her plop her purse down on the table, pull out a mobile phone and make a call. The little boy wandered close by, kicking at twigs.

8:33. She was waving an arm, agitated, arguing on the phone. The kid started to cry. Damn.

8:34. Tom shifted his weight from foot to foot. The last thing he wanted to do was show his badge and chase the woman off, but he couldn't stick the sack under the trash can while she was there. She was still talking. The kid was kicking at the legs of the picnic table. "Wanna go, wanna go."

"Shut your face," the woman yelled.

8:35. Tom felt his pocket to be sure his ID wallet was there.

Okay, damn, this was it, no more time. He started toward the picnic table. He glanced around looking for strangers, trying not to be obvious about it. As he approached the table, the woman snapped the phone in her purse, jumped up and seized the boy's hand. She stormed off, red-faced, jerking the boy across the street.

Tom glanced at his watch, then sat at the table, his back to the blue trash can. He stared at the pointless graffiti carved on the table.

8:36. He wondered where the guy was, what he looked like. He had to be close by. He could almost feel him. He swung his left wrist into view. When the sweep hand reached forty-five seconds past 8:36, he crouched beside the trash can, tilted it, and slipped the sack underneath. The earth felt damp and moldy.

He got up and walked briskly through the park for sixty paces. He reached an old oak tree he'd picked out earlier, a spot he knew couldn't be seen from the picnic table. He slipped behind the tree, turned, and waited a few seconds.

Damn! The firefighters were jogging through the park now, parallel to the street, toward the picnic table. A phalanx of blue. Across the way, Norfleet caught Tom's eye. His face flashed a what-the-hell look.

8:39. Twenty or twenty-five of them trotted along in ragged formation, roughly three abreast and spread out along sixty feet of space. Some jogged on the grass, some on the street. They ran along both sides of the table and the trash can. It took several seconds for them to pass.

8:40. Tom didn't see anyone suspicious hanging around, man or woman. A potpourri of sound rang in his ears. Children laughing, the calliope, the agitated whinny of a pony, a motorcycle starting up.

Tom hadn't counted on this. None of them had. They knew the lowlife would have to act fast, before someone else used the table, but they'd agreed to give it five full minutes. *Christ!*

He shifted his weight from foot to foot. May not have five minutes, he told himself.

The hell with it. He headed for the trash can. Was he was doing the right thing going now? This time he openly looked around for other people, questionable people. Butterflies scrimmaged in his stomach as he reached the picnic table.

He tilted the trash can and reached beneath it. There were rocks, twigs, dead leaves, gum wrappers, some startled mealy bugs. But nothing else. The sack was gone.

Debbie, April and Norfleet converged around him.

"It's gone, smooth as silk," Tom said. "Any of you see anything? Anybody at all? No? Let's get going then. He can't be far. Let's see who's dressed like a firefighter but not working out with that crew." Pointing one way, then another. "Mike, go north on foot, Debbie, south. April, get the Cherokee, take me to my car. Meet back here in ten minutes. Everybody haul ass." He knew all this was a longshot.

As his car careened through the park lanes, then up Freeport Boulevard and Sutterville Road, Tom remembered having heard a motorcycle moments after the firefighters had come by.

This was useless.

When they regrouped, no one had seen a thing. Yep, it had been smooth as silk.

"Guy must've been shielded by the firemen," Tom said. "Knew they'd be here, probably even dressed the same way."

The music was still playing. . . . *He'd marry the girl with the strawberry curl, and the band played on.* He wanted to smash that damned calliope. And get to Cass as fast as he could.

"Yes?" Kurt Neumann always answered his private line that way.

"The asshole didn't do it."

"No?"

"He left us a little rock, a fucking pebble."

Neumann looked over his shoulder. He wanted to be sure his eighty-two-year-old mother wasn't in the room. "Did he try to trap you?"

"Yes, like you predicted, but my little safeguard did the trick. The firemen are in the park every Saturday at that time, like I told you. It worked perfectly."

"Except for one thing."

"Yeah, except for one thing. You called that one too."

"I didn't think this man would give in that easily," Neumann said. "I would have been disappointed in him if he had. You know what to do now. Playtime is over."

That night, after rehashing the events in the park for the fifth or sixth time, Tom told Cass he was invited to a party the vice squad was throwing on Monday night. "Going to a cop party is the last thing I'm going to do right now," he said. "No way."

"No, you should go," Cass said. "You don't stand guard over me nine hours a day at work, and I survive. So what's a couple more hours at night? A night out with your buddies will do you good."

"April the Cop has been saying the same thing."

"Smart lady. Go on, have some fun. I insist."

"Come with me."

"Can't. Working on the Delta water legislation. I'll be there till seven or eight. But you go."

"Well, maybe I'll put in an appearance since you're working late—won't stay long. I'll try to get home about the same time as you. Meanwhile, be extremely careful. Carry your gun. Don't trust anyone you don't know."

"Come on, I'll be fine."

"Cass, damn it."

"Don't boss me," she said. "I know what to do. I'll be fine."

Tom started to say something, stopped, and hugged her. She accepted the embrace indifferently. Look what fear was doing to them, he thought.

CHAPTER TWENTY

Monday morning, after a quick breakfast of cantaloupe and cottage cheese, Tom bounded up the stairs to brush his teeth. In the bathroom, wet pantyhose hung from the shower bar and towel racks to dry. This was one of the very few things Cass did that bothered him.

"What's with the darn nylons again?" he said, hurling his toothbrush into the sink. It bounced up against his chest, where he trapped it with his hand.

When he stepped back into the bedroom a moment later, Cass was sitting at her makeup table, mascara brush in hand, her features a stern mask. How long had she been there? Had she heard his dumb remark?

"I'll see you tonight, babe," he said from behind her, trying to sound innocent. He put both hands on her shoulders and bent down to kiss the side of her face, but she jerked away and leaned forward.

"Go on, go to work. Catch some criminals. Maybe somebody's squeezing the toothpaste from the middle."

"Come on, I'm sorry, Cass. We're both on edge these days."

"Someone certainly is. Good-BYE."

Tom gave up, slouched down the stairs and out to his car, wishing he'd been able to find just the right thing to say, something disarming to save the moment.

Driving to work in the morning twilight, he was as bleak as a tossed-out Christmas tree in January.

I understand women like I do Etruscan sculpture.

* * *

That afternoon, her eyebrows rising warily, April the Cop told Tom he had a call.

"That wasn't a very bright thing to do, Mr. Cavanaugh," Alvin and the Chipmunks squeaked. Tom had dreaded this moment since Saturday morning in the park. "A plain old pebble? *Please*. And planting your worthless cop friends all over the park. For shame. Now you'll have to pay the fucking consequences." Some other time and place, the digitized chipmunks using that expletive would have been funny. Fucking funny. Not now. He slammed the receiver down.

"That was the guy, wasn't it?" April said. "The guy who slickered us at the park."

Tom had only half heard, but he nodded.

When April left his cubicle, he dialed Cass's office. She wasn't in. He got her voice-mail. "Hi, it's me. Sorry about this morning. I apologize. Profusely. Listen, have someone walk you to your car tonight, one of the security guys if possible. This is important, very important. I got another call."

Early in the evening, Tom stood by their bed, pulling on a V-neck sweater to go, with great reluctance, to the vice squad party. He stared at the makeup table where Cass had been sitting that morning when he'd committed his faux pas about the nylons. *Wish to hell I could have that moment back.*

Before leaving, he poured some dry cat food in Orbison's bowl and said, "You're lucky not being able to talk, you know that?"

The anguish of the last few weeks weighed heavily on his mind as he drove east to the home of the vice squad's lieutenant in Orangevale. Ribbons of cloud over the foothills of Loomis and Auburn were burnished yellow and sulfur orange by the late-day sun.

More than forty cops were expected to be there with their spouses and dates. "Hopefully not both at the same time," Luke

Monelli had cracked.

At the open front door, his hand raised to knock on the jamb, Tom decided, *No. I'm out of here. I've gotta get back to Cass.* He started to turn. Too late. The host materialized in the doorway.

"Cavanaugh, Narcotics, right?" He stepped out, draped an arm around Tom's shoulder and walked him to the back, pointing out the redwood deck and fish pond he'd just completed. Balloons, Japanese lanterns in the trees, lighted torches along the slat fences. People buzzing around tubs of cold drinks and tables piled with hot and cold hors d'oeuvres.

Mary Savage approached in a short, flowery dress. "Mary, take over, would you? I've got to look in on the kitchen." Mary complied, taking Tom by the arm.

"Where's your lady?"

"Had to work late."

"Too bad. Say, these stuffed mushrooms are great," she said, and popped one into his mouth. "I've got a joke for you."

Tom listened, and laughed at the right time.

"Oh, there's Lieutenant Hackett," Mary said. "I've got to talk to him. Excuse me, will you?"

"Catch you later," Tom said, and wandered off across the expanse of clipped Bermuda grass. The party was tame by vice squad standards, which was fine with him. In a corner of the yard, he listened in on a debate about department politics. Would sergeant so-and-so make lieutenant? Of course, he was Chief Pulaski's fair-haired boy. No way, he was a bozo.

A few minutes later, holding a cup of decaf coffee—he didn't want booze—Tom sat on a garden bench with Debbie Hamilton. Debbie had warm blue eyes, honey blond hair and a dimple in only her right cheek when she smiled. Although he hadn't told her exactly what the drop at Land Park had been all about, she had to know something weird and troubling was swirling in his life.

"You flying solo tonight too?" Tom asked. "Where's Larry?"

"Oh, he's history. He's going out with some bimbo who slings beer at a sports bar."

"Sorry to hear that, Debbie."

"Don't be. He wasn't the one. Mister Right hasn't come along yet."

"He will."

"Yeah, but sometimes I'm like, are the good ones all taken?" Tom's right hand was resting on his knee and he suddenly felt Debbie's hand on top of it. "Let me know if I can do anything else for you," she said.

Whether or not that was a come-on, it made him feel better, just as the attention from Mary Savage had.

"I mean it. Some off-duty legwork for you, anything you might need."

"Thanks, Debbie, I might take you up on that."

"I wish you could clone yourself."

Tom must have looked shocked. Debbie added, "No, I'm not sorry I said that. I mean it. I wish I'd met you first."

Not knowing what to say, Tom squeezed her hand, then released it. At that instant, he caught Mary Savage looking at him from across the yard, a wine glass in her hand. She shot him a funny smile and wagged a forefinger as if to say, "Don't even think about it."

Minutes later, Debbie was talking about a traumatized cop who'd been seeing a psychiatrist when Mike Norfleet, the Homicide detective, walked up with his wife Melanie.

"How ya doin', kid?" Norfleet said. "You too, Hamilton," he added, taking in an eyeful of Debbie's legs. Tom saw that Melanie didn't like that. It hadn't bothered Debbie.

"You know my wife Mel, don't you?"

Melanie wore the weary look of an unhappy wife, a look Tom decided was chronic. He felt sorry for both of them.

"You guys talking about whatzisname seeing a shrink?"

Norfleet sneered. "Anybody who goes to a psychiatrist oughta have his head examined."

Tom groaned, then looked at his watch. Before he could say his goodbyes and duck out, Mary Savage came over to join the group. Norfleet was telling a joke.

Cass had worked till almost seven, nothing new in that. There hadn't been anyone left in the office to walk her to her car, but daylight savings time had kicked in, so she'd be all right in the evening brightness. Still, she scanned her surroundings as she walked east, past Capitol Park and the Vietnam Memorial. The Convention Center tossed a heavy shadow across L Street. She saw no strangers, nothing suspicious.

She thought about Tom's little fit over her pantyhose. Had she ever exploded over his leaving the toilet seat up, which he did damn near all the time? She wished she hadn't reacted so badly. *He's a little boy in some ways, and I love him anyway*. A wicked little smile crossed her face. *I know how to square things with him.*

Nearing the state garage, she saw a blue van moving slowly. Inside, a woman with an open map in front of her, pointed in one direction, the male driver another. Looking for Sutter's Fort or something, Cass thought. The confused tourists were reminiscent of her and Tom on some of their travels.

Moments later, the van reappeared. These lost souls must have driven around the block. Or *were* they lost souls? Cass wondered with a trace of suspicion.

They stopped and the woman's head leaned out the passenger window. "Excuse me, can you help us?" she said. "How do we get on 80 West?"

Yep, lost souls, Cass thought. "That's easy," she said, stepping closer. "Go up here to Sixteenth, take a right. . ." Her peripheral vision caught movement beside her. *Oh oh.* Before she could back off, something clamped over her nose and mouth. Heavy cloth, reeking an antiseptic smell. Strong arms wrenched her off her feet.

Even though it was a warm night, Tom felt a sudden chill. His body shuddered for a moment.

"What is it?" said April the Cop.

Tom felt the hairs bristle on the back of his head—slapped a hand to his neck.

"What is it?" April repeated. "You get a bad eggroll or something?"

"No, it's nothing. Excuse me, okay?" Tom left without another word and sprinted around the house toward his car.

Cass feels herself falling—no, being pulled—backward.

Grab his arm, she tells herself, try a judo flip. Can't. Okay, get to his eyes. Same problem, he's behind me. I'm reaching backward, blindly. Countered too late. Caught by surprise. Stupid!

Panic tightens her throat. The hands, large and strong. Too strong. Suffocating. No strength. Desperate for breath. Almost sucking that cloth into her mouth.

She's jerked into the air, then pushed. The cloth is off. A quick, frantic breath. The sky turns over, then vanishes. Her back bangs onto something hard. A door slams.

Dark now. Back hurting. Cloth jammed over nose and mouth again. Can't breathe. Nostrils filling with, with . . .

CHAPTER TWENTY-ONE

Cass is floating now, remembering things. The time she'd had her tonsils out, years ago. The last thing she'd recalled before blacking out on her hospital bed had been the broad white disk above her head like a full moon. And this very same pungent smell.

"Return, O my soul, to your rest." Something from her Sunday school days.

Driving like Mario Andretti, Tom stole a glance at his watch. Seven-thirty. On his mobile phone, he hit the speed-dial button for his home. The answering machine came on and he heard his own recorded voice. Cass had told him she'd be home around seven or eight. A month ago he wouldn't have worried—but this wasn't a month ago. He'd been phobic since the botched operation in the park and the subsequent angry phone call.

He thought about the sudden jolt he'd felt minutes ago at the party. It was as if a message, some kind of a desperate message, had been nailed to his chest. He'd warned Cass to be extra careful and prayed that she had. Slowing for a red light at Fair Oaks and Sunrise, he saw no opposing traffic, a rarity. He punched the accelerator and ran it.

Wakefulness creeps into Cass's mind like a gray morning. She feels nauseous. Her nose and lips sting, temples throb. She comes to realize that she's bound, hand and foot, that she's lying on a carpeted, firm and yet springy surface—surely the floor of the van. Worst of all, some kind of a hood covers her face. This isn't the anesthetic-soaked cloth that had knocked her out. This is something different, softer, maybe flannel. She can't see.

Her lower back is stiff. Her hands are tied behind her—the bindings secure. Not tape, rope, or plastic cord, maybe pillow cases or scarves.

The painful lump in her back each time the van bounces turn out to be her hands, so she rolls onto her side. The relief is immediate.

Hell of a lot of good that self-defense class did you, Nesbit. *Next time. Next time.* Nobody will ever take you by surprise like that again. Okay, let's figure this out. Self-pity or panic won't do any good.

She hears the steady drone of the engine and the hum of tires. Feels occasional jolts to her spine and pelvis, irritating pressure on her lower back. Okay, Nesbit, you're in the van and it's making good time, so it's probably on an Interstate.

Now, which direction are they going? The road seems fairly straight—she doesn't feel turns to right or left. No engine strain of pulling uphill, or the braking of downhill, which would make her slide forward. Or maybe backward. *Which way am I facing?* They're going north or south, she believes. If they'd gone east on a freeway they'd be in the mountains by now, if west, they'd have reached San Francisco or Oakland.

But wait, how long has she been out? Come on, Nesbit, think. Maybe we've crossed the Sierra and this is the Nevada desert. No, she hasn't been unconscious that long, because she doesn't have to pee. Hell of a way to tell time, but she's pretty regular that way.

My God, this is really happening.

Except for the cat, the house was empty. Tom leaned down, gave Orbison a quick stroke on the head, then searched to see if Cass had left a note. Nothing. Not even on the refrigerator.

He called Cass's office for the second time in ten minutes, having called earlier from the car. Again, even on her direct line, he was shunted into Voice Mail Hell. "To return to the main menu . . . For other options, press . . ." Obviously, she wasn't there. He tried her mobile phone. No human response there, either.

As the van rolled on, Cass heard a train whistle in the distance, piercing the night, burying her heart. About the mournfulness of a train whistle in the dark, the cowboy songwriters got it right.

With the van's hypnotic rhythm unchanging, she thought about her parents—her prudent, Bible-reading mother and her pragmatic banker father. How he'd railed at the foolishness of getting mixed up in politics, but then made a complete about-face when she'd gone to work for the governor. She thought about the sobbing, incoherent call from her sister Jan, after her husband had dumped her for a younger woman. About meeting and getting to know Tom, the man she was going to marry. Hoping desperately that now, somehow, he would be able to rescue her. Or that she could escape.

She heard the rhythmic bells of a railroad crossing. The sound whirred past and was gone. Freeways don't have railroad crossings. In the San Joaquin Valley the railroad line flanked old U.S. 99, not the Interstate, so maybe they were around Stockton or Modesto, towns along 99.

But maybe they were north. She thought she caught occasional whiffs of hay and corn, stuff that grew in the Sacramento Valley, between the capital and Mount Shasta. A horn blasted from an eighteen-wheeler.

She thought about her kidnappers. She hadn't got a good look at the man. He'd been in the driver's seat when she first saw the van, but he wasn't there when the woman called her over. He'd obviously slipped out and gone behind the van to get the anesthetic, whatever it was. It wasn't chloroform; that would have burned her eyes and mouth. This is what Tom was talking about when he said be extra careful. Why hadn't she been more alert, more skeptical?

Tourists aren't sightseeing at six-thirty. They've taken their motel rooms by then.

She'd seen the woman. Short brunette hair, probably about forty, kind of hard looking. Something about her was vaguely familiar. Had she ever seen her before? She didn't know, couldn't place it.

The van accelerated and switched lanes to pass. Cass heard the rumble of the slower vehicle beside her, before it was left behind. She wondered how much time had passed. She wasn't hungry, though God knows she hadn't eaten in a long time. Thirsty, though—she'd love to wash away the sour, empty taste the anesthetic had left in her mouth.

Cass apparently wasn't in her office and Tom couldn't get into the governor's offices at this time of night anyway, so he went to the capital garage. He knew she'd been swapping parking places with friends, so he had no idea where the Porsche was parked, or even if it was there at all. Wild thoughts surged. What if it wasn't there?

He reached the garage and walked the first level methodically, then the second. He was on the third floor when he found the Burgundy Bullet. It was locked and the hood was cold. Hadn't been driven for hours. He looked inside and saw a red light blinking on the car phone, indicating messages. That meant nothing. Cass got lots of calls each day, and he knew one of the calls was his own from an hour earlier, asking where she was.

Dread weighed on him like a flak jacket. Drops of sweat formed on his brow. *Where is she?*

The van slowed. Cass felt deceleration pull her forward. It stopped, then accelerated slowly in what she thought was a left turn, made another turn, and bumped a bit as it climbed onto—what, a driveway? The van stopped and she heard one of the front doors open and close, felt the vibrations too. She heard roadside business sounds, a car horn, the thunder of a motorcycle, the hissing of a big truck's air brakes.

Several minutes passed, then the rear door clanged open. She felt hands on her and flinched, tried to jerk away. "Easy, your highness, I'm untying your hands so you can eat." Female voice, raspy, a smoker's voice.

Her hands were free! They throbbed. Pins and needles pricked them.

"Don't try anything. If you yell out, I'll remake that pretty face with a crescent wrench. That smart-ass man of yours really screwed you over this time, didn't he?" Whoever this woman was, she was trying too hard to talk like a guy. The hate in her voice was real, though. *Why hate us? Do you know us? Who the devil are you?*

The woman shoved a cold cylinder into Cass's right hand, which was just starting to get some feeling. The thing was wet with condensation, must be a water bottle. Hands raised the bottom of the hood just enough to free her mouth.

Cass strained the pupils of her eyes downward as far as they would go. She saw a white paper sack, and one of the woman's ankles, attached to a well-worn sneaker. She smelled french fries.

"Have some water and a little food, your highness. We don't want our high-class guest starving, do we?" Again Cass thought the language was bogus, that playing gun-moll was an act.

"How long have you been interested in photography?" Cass asked.

"Hmmph. You going to eat or what?"

The voice definitely wasn't familiar. Cass tried to take a drink but found the bottle was still capped. Before she could unscrew it, the woman's hand was on hers, brushing hers away, unscrewing the cap for her. The hand wasn't rough or calloused, it was office-soft.

Cass again forced her pupils to focus downward as far as possible. She saw more of the hand. On the index finger was a gold ring with a small watch inlaid upon it. Elegant and expensive. Hey, the time. It's . . . no, she couldn't make it out. And the hand was quickly gone.

Cass took a drink of water, a long, cool, delicious drink.

She'd learned a few things. The woman didn't do manual labor, she had a taste for nice things, and her voice wasn't familiar. That wasn't much. The air coming through the open door smelled like a spring night in farm country. She heard a metallic voice from somewhere nearby. "Welcome to Jack-in-the-Box. May I take your order please?"

"You didn't answer my question," Cass said. "How long have you been a photographer?"

"I don't know what you're talking about. Shut up and eat."

"Don't take pictures of people in locker rooms?"

"I said *shut up*."

"You sound like somebody's father," Cass said.

"Just shut the hell up."

Eating a few soggy fries, Cass realized she'd been hungrier than she knew. When she'd eaten several, she said, "Look, I've gotta pee."

"I was wondering when you'd say that," the woman said. "You must have a hell of a bladder." A large coffee can was shoved into Cass's grasp. "I'll turn my back, your highness."

Cass hated the sarcasm. And the humiliation of having to use a coffee can. When she was through—it hadn't been easy, her face covered, feet bound—the woman said, "Okay, let's tie your hands again."

"Like hell." On her knees, Cass threw a punch, hit something hard, maybe the slut's hip.

"You bitch!" the woman cried.

Cass swung her left fist, hit something softer, maybe a thigh.

Then something crashed on her head, the water bottle probably. She swung her right hand again, hit nothing but air. Then she was kicked in the back, fell over on her face. Squirming, she felt a knee come down hard and heavy on her back. It stayed there, the weight behind it pinning her down. The man. Had to be.

Someone grabbed her wrists, jerked them together. She tried to pull them apart, but they were forced together again—and bound. Quickly, roughly.

Cass was in a rage. But glad she'd resisted, even though she'd had no chance in a fight against two people, blind and with her feet bound.

A thin shaft of pain spiked the back of her right thigh. What the hell was that? A hypodermic?

"Told the bitch not to try anything." The woman's voice.

"Fiery little cunt." The man.

Feet shuffled. Fog drowsed across Cass's mind. She heard them step down from the van. The door clanged shut.

Orbison welcomed him with knowing eyes when Tom got home. He stroked the top of the cat's head, then checked his 9-millimeter Ruger, made sure it had a full clip. With a notepad and a pen in hand, he called the night desk at police headquarters.

Tom knew some of the desk sergeants but not this one. "Detective Sergeant Cavanaugh," he said, "Narcotics, Badge 401. You have any reports of an assault or anything like that near the Capitol tonight?"

"Let me check." Tom heard papers shuffling. "Ah, a purse-snatching at 15th and G, 5:55, old woman and a kid involved . . . a stabbing outside the Trailways Depot, 6:16, two black males . . . man striking a woman and shoving her into a van, Fourteenth and L, 6:54, probably a domestic—"

"Hold it. That one." Tom's heart dropped. "What's the status on that one?"

"Beat Sixteen. Patrol checked out the scene on L, didn't find anything. Nothing else to do till somebody files a complaint or we get a missing persons report. What's your interest in this, detective? Narcotics getting into this?"

"Who called in the report? Can you give me the eyewitness's name and number?"

"I think you better come down here and see my supervisor. I'm sure you're who you say you are, but I got rules to follow. Nothin' personal."

"Yeah." Tom hung up, a jumble of thoughts fighting for attention. Fourteenth and L. Between the Capitol and the garage. Exactly where Cass would've been. 6:54. About the time she'd have been there. Man striking a woman and shoving her into a van. *Shit!*

He picked up notepad and pen, slid the Ruger beneath his belt, and drove to the downtown station on Eighth Street.

CHAPTER TWENTY-TWO

ass had a weird dream, something about floating in a dark pool of water, suffocating, unable to break the surface and breathe. She awoke, her head cobwebby, stomach queasy. The van's rhythms had changed. They were on a winding road, with up and down grades, mostly up. The engine whined at a higher tenor pitch, the transmission reaching down for power on the uphill stretches. There was more of a chill in the air.

The hood covering her face had become maddening. She could no longer feel her wrists and ankles, but she did sense a sharp soreness in her thigh, like a bee sting. Then she remembered the jab there just before fading out. *The bastard!* She wondered about her purse, recalling grimly that her pistol had been in it.

The van turned onto a rougher surface, maybe gravel, and rumbled over something that felt like railroad tracks. It rolled to a stop. The back door clanged open and a rough pair of hands— obviously not the woman's—pulled her into a sitting position. As soon as the hood was jerked from her face, she caught a whiff of ponderosa pines, a smell she knew well from outings to Lake Tahoe. Smelled sawdust too.

Most everything was black, but a rectangle of gray filled the doorway, partly blocked out by a large, moving shape, the silhouette of a man. The shape grabbed her arm. She recoiled, but the grip was strong. A sharp cut of pain flamed in her thigh. "No, not again, not again, you *son of a bitch!*"

With her hands and feet bound firmly, she was defenseless. Her leg hurt. Her mind swirled, consciousness fading. One of the hands touched her cheek and caressed, the fingertips slowly working down to the lips and chin. Though drowsy, cold fear walked Cass's spine. She started to shake her head in terrified protest, but that's when her mind slid into a deep blackness.

Kurt Neumann repeatedly tapped his fingers on his antique rosewood desk, awaiting the word.

He thought bitterly about the drug deal that was to have made him an easy ten million when he'd first retired to northern California. The proposition had been brought to him by a South American contact he'd met through his art dealings. *Just be the middle man for a day or two, they told me. Take the shipment off the hands of the Colombians, then re-sell at huge profit to the Oakland Triad.*

But when the goods arrived at a cropduster's airstrip outside Sacramento, the police and the DEA were waiting. Tom Cavanaugh, a young Sacramento narcotics cop, had infiltrated the transportation end of the deal at the landing strip.

Kurt Richter—the name Neumann was born with—was ruined. His crafty lawyer, Ben Marshall, working a technicality on evidence handling by the DEA, got him off with a suspended sentence and a huge fine. But the publicity had finished him and was more than his wife's fragile heart could take. *The nights I spent in that holding tank were horrible.*

The festering memories of those traumatic nights had darkened the six years of his reinvented existence as Kurt Neumann of San Diego social prominence. *But now, all these years later, the fates have handed me my golden chance for revenge.*

When the old man who supplied much of his art information had told him that one Tom Cavanaugh possessed the fabulous Maria Theresa Emerald, he'd practically jumped with glee.

Now that delicious revenge was about to play out. He'd abducted Cavanaugh's woman, hadn't he? That was his thought when the phone rang. He picked it up before the first ring died. He didn't want to disturb his elderly mother, even though up in her room she had no access to this private line.

"Yes?"

"The bouquet has been delivered."

"Any hitches?"

"None at all."

"Good. Is it a lovely bouquet?"

"Indeed."

"As I expected. Water it well, then. It will wilt of course, but don't rearrange it. Above all, it must *not* be *managed*," he said. A euphemism he often used. "It's the next delivery that we want most."

"I understand."

"Good." Neumann put the receiver back in its cradle.

I'll have to inspect that bouquet myself, he thought, looking up at his prized painting, *La Duquesa de Catalonia*. Examine it closely.

Tom pulled into the police parking lot across the street from the station. Plenty of vacant spaces. He dashed up the concrete steps, shoved the door open and showed his badge to the man on the night desk. Within minutes, he had the name, phone number and address of the witness who'd reported an assault on L Street near the Capitol. The good Samaritan was a woman, a clerk for the State Forestry Department.

Tom went to a phone on a corner desk and called her, even though it was nearly 11:30.

"Tom Cavanaugh, police. I'm sorry to wake you, ma'am, but this is important. Can I come over and talk to you? I'd like to get your statement right now."

Tom heard the desk sergeant say, "What the hell?" to his back as he fled out the door.

The witness lived between East Lawn Cemetery and Cal State Sacramento, just off Folsom Boulevard.

The woman opened the door a few inches after his knock. African-American in her fifties. Tom showed his ID and apologized for the late call. She stammered and stalled, said her place was a mess, then said something in a muffled voice to someone else. She looked closely at the wallet badge and Tom's face, her gaze shifting between the two several times. Finally, she pulled the door open wide and motioned him in.

He was shown into a modest living room, accepted a cup of coffee, and slipped into an easy chair. He saw a black man of about the same age moving about in the kitchen. The woman, in electric blue cotton sweats, sat opposite Tom on a leather sofa, with her own cup of coffee. It trembled slightly in her hand.

Tom knew he had to quell his impatience. He smiled. "This is much better than I get at work," he said after taking a sip.

"Better'n I get at work too, you better believe. Now, listen, officer, I don't wanta get involved in any trouble. I waited half an hour before calling in, 'cause I was a little scared. But after thinking it over, I knew I had to. What else could I do? Nobody's got a right to abuse a woman like that."

"You did the right thing, ma'am. We're grateful. Now, please tell me everything you saw."

"Well, I already told the desk sergeant—"

"I know, but please take it from the top again."

"Well, there was this dark blue van, no windows in the back—"

"Cargo van. Did you get the make?"

"Sorry, no. I'm not real familiar with vans."

"License number?"

"No. I'm sorry."

"That's all right."

"This happened awful fast and I wasn't all that close. They were white California plates, though."

"Then what did you see?"

"This tall woman—"

"Tall?" *Shit.*

"Yes, five-eight or nine, gray pants. Late twenties or early thirties. She goes over to the van and, um, starts talking to someone in the passenger side. Then this guy comes up behind her and grabs her. Yanks her back real hard. Puts one hand over her face, the other around her body. She fights him—"

Good girl, Tom thought.

"—but he takes and like shoves her inside the back, slams the door, and runs back to the front. Then the van takes off, you know. That's pretty much it. Feel sorry for the poor woman. I don't like people gettin' knocked around like that."

Her description of the victim and her charcoal gray slacks fit Cass perfectly. Tom hoped he didn't look as sick as he felt.

"You all right, sir?"

"Um, yes. What did the man look like?"

"He was tall, like you, white fella. Huskier than you, though. Didn't get a good look at him."

"What was he wearing?"

The woman shifted in her chair, crossed her feet. "Can't really say. A long-sleeved shirt, I think, and light-colored pants."

"Jeans?"

"Not jeans. Light-colored pants. Maybe gray, maybe khaki. Can't say for sure."

"Anything else? Was he wearing glasses? A hat?"

"Dark sunglasses. And a baseball cap, now I think about it, yes sir, a baseball cap, dark blue or black."

This went on a few minutes more but Tom got little else.

"Would you mind repeating these things to our Crimes Against Persons Unit?"

"I guess not, but why? You're the police."

"Right, but this isn't my specialty. And the FBI may want your statement too."

"The FBI?" Her eyes widening.

"Maybe. Kidnapping often becomes a federal crime after twenty-four hours."

Questions swirled as Tom drove away. *Why do this in broad daylight?* Answer: Because the days are longer now and Cass is—was—almost always home before dark. *But why use a vehicle with visible license plates?* Because they were stolen, had to be.

He headed to the scene at Fourteenth and L, just up from the Capitol. It was after one when he surveyed both sides of L, the sidewalk, the bench at a bus stop, the walkway leading to the garage entrance. He found nothing, not a shoe, not a button from Cass's jacket. He knelt and checked the ground around a tiny patch of shrubbery, found only a sticky soda cup and a wadded-up gum wrapper.

He stood and paced up and down the street. *Here. It happened right here. Damn.* He stomped a foot on the pavement. Traffic was almost nonexistent. The mercury vapor streetlight hummed faintly. A bus rumbled by. One passenger, bored-looking driver.

Tom reached home a few minutes before two. He walked into the bedroom, leaving the light off. He looked around, knowing he wouldn't go to bed, wouldn't sleep. Glancing at the bed, he thought wistfully about the times Cass had accused him of hogging the covers. The green numerals on the face of the clock radio, Cass's clock radio, glared at him. Their glow looked like an eye, a sorrowful, accusing eye.

He got out of there and prowled the house, looking at magazines without really seeing, tossing them aside. He remembered Cass saying, "Where there's a rare old jewel, there's always a curse." Maybe she'd actually been right.

He went out to the back yard, where stood a liquidambar tree and some rose bushes he and Cass had planted. The lawn he enjoyed watering and fertilizing was soft beneath his feet as he sauntered around aimlessly, listening to the night. Sometimes he could think better out here. Somewhere a night bird called, a whippoorwill maybe.

Shortly after six he fed Orbison, downed a cup of instant coffee, had a hurried shower, and took a cab to the capital garage to get Cass's Porsche, using the extra set of keys.

Since he didn't have the electronic key card, he told the parking attendant that Cass had been called out of town and he was picking up the car at her request. The attendant, a young Asian woman who knew Cass's car, said that wasn't good enough, she couldn't let him take it.

Tom shoved his police ID in her face and snapped, "Open the goddamned gate." The attendant complied, but glared at him and picked up a phone as he drove through.

While he drove back toward Land Park, eyes burning from lack of sleep, he hoped he could clear this up fast and not have to make explanations to certain people. Nevertheless, a mental list began forming of those he might have to call before long. Cass's parents and her sister Jan. Those would be the toughest calls to make. His father. What he wanted from him was help, ideas, a suggestion he could build on. He'd have to be careful with that call—didn't want to put a burden of guilt on the frail old cop for getting them into this in the first place with his darn emerald.

The Crimes Against Persons Unit, which dealt with kidnapping, had been in existence only a year. Tom had little faith in it. Obviously they hadn't even done a follow-up interview yet. What did they know? Sacramento didn't have kidnappings.

CHAPTER TWENTY-THREE

Consciousness inched across Cass's mind. She reached for Tom. Then her memory gears engaged. There was no Tom. Wherever he was, he wasn't here.

She was lying on a worn leather sofa in a small, alien room. She looked around. It hadn't been a dream. She'd really been kidnapped.

Hey, she really *could* look around. Her face wasn't covered. Hands and feet weren't tied. She was in a small windowless room. The air was musty, stale. An old-fashioned, frosted-glass fixture hung from the ceiling, dimly lighting the room. Gray cement-block walls. A stairway with wooden hand rails and thick plank steps leading up to a door. On a small picnic table, a bottle of water, a plate of doughnuts—and her purse.

Her head was woozy, her gray slacks and tunic vest rumpled, underwear sweaty, and she needed a bath.

She slipped her stockinged but shoeless feet to the floor. It was cold and damp. A concrete slab floor, with a few occasional rugs thrown here and there. Her low-heeled shoes were parked side by side on the floor beside the sofa. The cobwebbed ceiling consisted of wide planks supported by thick wood beams. She was in a cellar, she concluded. *Cellar, ha! Delete the "ar."*

Full mental clarity kicked in and she rushed to the table, snapped open the purse. Everything seemed to be there—wallet, compact, makeup, car keys, box of tissues, two pill bottles, a scattering of coins and business cards, even her organizer. Everything but her pistol and mobile phone of course. And her pen. They didn't want her writing notes. She also noticed that the mirror had been removed from her compact. *Great, they won't even let me look at my face.*

She checked the contents of her wallet. Money, credit cards, driver's license, snapshots of Tom and her parents—it all seemed to be there. She couldn't remember how much money she'd had, but the amount seemed about right. She couldn't bear to look at the picture of Tom. What she needed was the *real thing.*

Slowly, softly, she mounted the stairs. One of the plank treads creaked beneath her feet, but they seemed solid enough. She tried the knob on the thick, sturdy door, knowing it would be locked. It was.

She returned to the table, uncapped the water bottle, sniffed it, took a tentative drink. The water was fine, delicious in fact. She took a bigger drink, fished an aspirin bottle from her purse, shook out two tablets, and swallowed them with another gulp.

Now she surveyed the room more thoroughly. In addition to the couch, there was an old overstuffed chair in a corner, a battered gunmetal gray file cabinet in another, lots of dust and dirt everywhere. She noticed that fine flecks of sawdust were mixed in with the dust. Odd. A colony of spiders had set up house in the high corners and the space beneath the stairs. Dark stains smudged the ceiling boards, above fleecy nets of spider webs, as if oil had seeped through from above.

She walked to the file cabinet and tried the doors. Locked. There were a couple of old *Time* magazines on top of the cabinet. The mailing labels! No, they'd been ripped off. Madonna peered at her from one of the covers, Pope John Paul II from the other.

She found nothing anywhere that she could use as a weapon, no silverware, no tools, not even a broom. There was no sign, either, of the hood or the bindings they'd used on her. No clock, nothing to indicate, wait—her watch. It was right there on her left wrist, just where it was supposed to be. Ten-twenty, it said.

Where the devil was she?

She slumped down on the sofa and tears formed in her eyes. "Another fine mess you've gotten us into, Nesbit," she said, sounding like Oliver Hardy. Like Stan Laurel, she wasn't amused.

In the morning, Tom rushed downtown to the Crimes Against Persons Unit. He hadn't met Lieutenant Jefferson Hayes, but he'd heard about him. Everyone had. Hayes had been an all-Pac Ten running back at UCLA. He'd earned his spurs in the jungles below Adams Boulevard, a cool hand who'd finally had enough patrol the day he was shot in the hip by a twelve-year-old. He'd gone on to become a homicide detective.

Now he was in Sacramento, heading its kidnap unit. Never mind that he was unqualified. The scuttlebutt around the department, which was probably unfair, was that Hayes had been appointed by Chief Pulaski, under pressure from the mayor, for PC reasons. So Jefferson Hayes, the celebrity cop, had taken a kidnapping course, then started.

During the introductions, Hayes said, "Call me Jefferson. Do *not* call me Jeff. I don't go for candy-ass nicknames."

"Would we get along better if you called me Thomas?"

Hayes smiled at that, and poured coffee in two mugs from his own pot. Tom spotted autographed pictures on the wall of Hayes with Ronald Reagan and with Steven Spielberg.

"What can I do?" Tom sank into the chair in front of the desk. "Where do we start?"

"I heard you already started." A red-and-black striped tie was loosened at Hayes' tree-trunk neck. His coffee-with-cream skin was several shades darker than Tom's and his bulked-up arms and chest seemed to be trying to escape from his white shirt. "You gotta cool your jets, man." He placed a mug before Tom and another in front of himself before sitting.

Hayes then spent a few minutes pontificating on textbook

procedure, stalling, Tom believed, because he wasn't sure where or how to start.

"Yes, right, but what do we do now? We've got to get going." Tom drank off some of his coffee. "Maybe I could get a temporary transfer to you, till we get Cass back."

"I could use the manpower, but not on this. You too personally involved, man. No, you gonna have to hold up, and let us handle this. Didn't appreciate you going out in the middle of the night to interrogate my witness."

"You hadn't even done a follow-up interview."

"We're doing that today."

"Today?" Tom leaned forward. "This happened *yesterday*. Follow-ups have got to be done right away, while memory's fresh. Witnesses forget things."

"Don't tell me how to do my job."

"My fiancée's been kidnapped. We've got to move."

"Smart mouth ain't gonna help, Cavanaugh." Hayes got up and placed both hands flat on the desk, leaning forward, his physical strength all too obvious. Tom eased back in his chair. "What you did was way outta line."

"Look, no offense"—Tom leaning forward again—"but this unit hasn't been in business all that long. Don't thumb your nose at good police input."

"I know you're panicky, man. I understand your impatience, but don't be comin' in here with an attitude. We're gonna solve this mother, and we're gonna get your woman back. Yeah, and we're gonna make a reputation for this unit that hasn't—like you say—been in business all that long. Got it? Now, the best thing you can do is go on back to chasin' druggies, an' I'll let you know."

"I want to take part. Isn't there something? Don't you have some questions for me?"

"I said I'll let you know, *Sergeant*."

Jefferson Hayes was the one with an attitude. "Yes, *Lieutenant*."

Tom got to his feet, resisting a temptation to salute. "I hear you." And left.

Cass made another circuit of the room, looking more closely this time. A heater was built into a wall, its metal grille-work facing into the room. A large nail had been hammered into the mortar between two cement blocks at about eye level. She guessed it might once have held up a dart board, because of the small nicks in the cement in a wide circle.

There were cleaner, lighter-colored geometric shapes on the floor. Those probably had been made by furniture removed before her arrival. They'd straightened up, but not *cleaned* up.

She bent down and felt behind the file cabinet for anything—a dart, maybe?—but came up with only a stubby, tooth-marked pencil. Her fingertips were coated with dust. She went to the table and put the pencil in her purse.

She was back on the sofa several minutes later when she heard a knocking on the door. A muffled voice called, "Get on the couch. The lights are going off."

Cass sat there, unmoving, heart pounding, waiting to see what would happen next.

The light flicked on and off a couple of times, like the curtain-call warning at a theater. Seconds later it went off for good, and she heard a key in the door. It creaked open, and a strong flashlight beam probed the room. It found her, stabbed at her face, made her squint. The beam jiggled as the holder of the flashlight came down the stairs. The light swung crazily around the room, then settled on the table.

Cass saw the silhouettes of two people. One placed a couple of bowls or dishes on the table.

"Here's some food for you, dear," said the female voice she knew from the van. "And you can wash up if you like."

"Just great," Cass snapped. "You're so good to me. What about a bathroom? Is there a toilet around here?"

"You can have a potty break after lunch," the woman said. This must be Madame X, the photographer, Cass thought. The other silhouette was larger and moved like a man. That person put something on the table too.

"This isn't fun for us, either, your highness." The woman again. "The sooner lover boy comes through, the sooner this will be over for all of us."

This will be over. Those words chilled Cass. Her hands shook.

The light and its shadow people lurched up the stairs, one shape disappearing through the door, the other remaining perfectly outlined for a moment by dim light from beyond the opening. This was definitely a woman, medium height, short hair. The woman from the van, Cass was sure of it. The same two people who'd overpowered her were now her jailers.

"When you're done eating and ready for the bathroom, knock twice on the door. We'll be making a phone call to lover boy pretty soon too."

Why did she say "lover boy" with such contempt? Cass wondered.

"This light will be turned on every morning at seven, off every night at ten," the voice said. *Every night*? How many damn nights was she going to be locked up here?

The door closed. Cass heard the click of the lock and the clunk of a deadbolt driving shut. The sound hit her like a punch.

Why don't they want me to see them? she thought. So I couldn't identify them later, of course. Does that mean something, like they do plan to free me at some point? Maybe it's more than that. Have I seen them before, is that it? Do I know them?

The table bore a sandwich on a paper plate, a plastic cup of potato salad, and a chilled can of soda. A plastic fork stuck out of the potato salad, and there were paper napkins. The untouched doughnuts were gone.

Cass also saw a basin of water, a bar of soap, and a hand towel. The water was actually lukewarm. She'd expected cold. She scrubbed her hands and forearms, rubbing the soap on liberally, then washed her face with her hands—there was no wash cloth. After toweling off, she felt slightly better, and was willing to try some food.

The sandwich was turkey and lettuce. She tried it cautiously at first, but surprised herself by finishing it off quickly. Her watch told her it was noon—all she'd eaten in the past twenty-four hours had been a few fries in the van. Although angry and afraid, she was hungry. She consumed several bites of potato salad, washing it down with cola.

Feeling less bad if not better, Cass returned to the sofa and plopped down. The darn thing would be warmer if it was covered with fabric instead of this cheap leather.

Tom had dreaded calling his father, but it went better than he'd expected. Desmond Cavanaugh concentrated on the problem at hand and only once did he say, "I'm sorry I got you into this."

"I don't know a lot about kidnap procedure," he said. "That's a little outside my area, but they'll be contacting you, and soon. Whatever you do, just cooperate. They don't want to hurt Cassandra . . ." There was a long pause. "They just want the emerald. So forget about me and my damn promise to the old field marshal. Cooperate and get your woman back. She's worth more . . . well, I don't have to tell you."

The old man with the rickety heart sounded weak and tired.

"Can I drive over and see you, Dad? Maybe fire up the old van and charge the battery for you?" Tom hadn't meant that, just said it to be nice.

"No, you stay there, Thomas, do what you have to do. As for the van, maybe I should've had you sell it for me after all."

"What do you mean, Dad?"

"It's gone. Stolen."

"What?"

"When my nurse came over this morning, the garage door was jimmied open and the van was gone. Novato PD was out here to take a report and check out the garage."

Anxiety swirled in Tom's stomach. His father's van, a cargo van, was dark blue and bore white California plates.

CHAPTER TWENTY-FOUR

Good, the pros are getting involved, Tom told himself after getting a call from a local FBI agent.

They met that afternoon in a coffee shop on Fruitridge Road. Tom had sometimes worked with the FBI, but hadn't met Zack Elwell before. He didn't look like your typical, slick FBI man. Big, but looking out of shape. His brown suit was lumpy and Yasser Arafat chins hung beneath his jaw. Black horn-rimmed glasses completed the image.

Special Agent Elwell moved with confidence, though. He led the way, picking a corner booth. He sat first, facing outward so that, Tom figured, he could survey the front door and the whole room. The place smelled of frying hamburger.

"I'm glad you guys are getting into this."

"Are you now?" The words and tone surprising. Elwell stared at him for a few silent seconds before saying, "How long have you been a cop?"

"Going on fifteen years."

"Three years longer than I've been with the Bureau."

The jukebox was playing *Born to Lose*. Tom liked Ray Charles. Cass did too. He remembered a snippet of conversation, just after Charles had won another Grammy.

"I'll bet he's a happy camper," Cass had said.

"He's probably saying, 'All this fuss, I just can't see it.' "

Cass had given him a Bronx jeer and said, "I'll turn a blind eye to that one."

"Nasty business," Elwell was saying, snapping Tom back to the present. "I'm real sorry about it. How long had you known Ms. Nesbit?"

The use of the past perfect cut deeply. "Over three years. She's my life, Elwell," Tom said, playing idly with a fork. "We're engaged, but I'm sure you know that."

"Yes. This must be tough for you." Elwell moved the napkin dispenser, lining it up perfectly with the salt and pepper shakers.

A waitress appeared. "What'll it be, fellas?" They each ordered coffee.

"Out of curiosity, where were you when she disappeared?" Elwell asked after the waitress sauntered off.

Tom had been waiting for that. The husband or boyfriend were always Suspect No. 1 in a case like this. "At a cop party. Tons of witnesses."

"Good for you. No offense, Cavanaugh, but you're the logical place to start."

"No offense?" Tom leaned forward aggressively.

"Good alibi, but you or whoever did this had to have helpers," Elwell said. "You've been living together. Her folks have some money—you don't. Your father is a middle-class cop on a pension. You're an investigator, what would you do in my shoes?"

"Oh, for crying out loud, I thought you guys were experts." Tom started to get up, but Elwell clamped a hand on his arm. Steel grip. Tom was reminded that some NFL linemen were very strong despite being fat. He sat again. "If that's all you have—"

"How about this? Your father's van matches the description of the kidnap van, right down the line. You took that statement yourself, even though it wasn't your place to do so."

Apprehension chilled Tom as the waitress returned with their coffee. He realized he was fidgeting and willed himself to sit still.

The girl left. After a strained silence Elwell said, "Your father reported his van stolen just before the disappearance, and it was dumped shortly afterward. Know whose fingerprints are on it?" His thick black eyebrows arched. "Yours. The cops found three strands of reddish hair in the back, which might match your fiancée's. I'll have them send a tech over to your home, check her hairbrushes and so on. I hope you'll cooperate, but you know we'll do it, either way."

"Oh, I'll cooperate. We're on the *same side!*" Tom scrunched his face in exasperation. "As for those damn prints, of course my prints were there. I've driven that van a lot. I know you got plenty of other prints too. Several people have driven that van since Dad got sick."

Elwell smiled. It reminded Tom of the disingenuous smile he'd gotten from Doctor Gerhard in Vienna.

Elwell took a sip of coffee. "Between us, I don't think you did it. You got a good record and your chief thinks the world of you, but I gotta look at all the possibilities. I've seen a lot of solid-appearing citizens get involved in some pretty sordid stuff. You have too, haven't you? Things aren't always what they seem."

"Hey, I called the desk at the station house that night." Tom glanced around, realized he'd said that too loud.

"I know."

"You think I'd kidnap my own fiancée, using my own father's van?"

"No, not really."

"What've I done with Cass then? Where did I park her? Who's watching her for me? This is all too stupid for belief."

"Not so stupid." Elwell toyed with a package of sweetener.

"What am I going to do, demand ransom money from Cass's folks?"

"I doubt it," Elwell said, but Tom saw a "who knows?" look on his face. "We put a tap on their phone today."

"Why tell me that? Now I'll be sure not to call their house when I demand money." Tom looked away, blew some air from his mouth, and looked back. "I'm your suspect, then?"

"Not really, as I been saying, but there are too many facts to ignore, and I got nothing else to go on yet."

Tom let out another sigh. "Are you gonna Miranda me? Never mind, I know my rights. Well, come on over to the house then. Let's get it out of the way. You can look at anything, take all the samples of fabric and hair and anything else you want."

"I don't do that. The cops will send a lab guy."

"So, do we have anything else to talk about?"

"I have to tell you not to leave town."

Hands on hips, Cass surveyed her prison. The cold gray walls made her shudder.

She returned to the sofa and shut her eyes. She thought about her church upbringing. "Hear my cry, for I am very low," she quoted from Psalms. "Rescue me from my persecutors, for they are too strong for me. Bring me out of prison . . ."

Thought about the day she met Tom. And the first time they'd made love—it had been after they'd patched up a misunderstanding. She'd taken him to dinner to apologize. Afterward, well . . .

God, I'll go crazy if I think about things like that. Concentrate on getting out of here, she told herself.

She jumped to her feet. God might help, but Cass wasn't going to wait for Him.

She made a circuit of the whole room; looked at the nail on the wall. It had held up—what?—a mirror, a dart board, a picture? She reached up and took hold of the nail. It didn't budge. She tried to work it back and forth, using all the strength in her wrists and hands. Did it move slightly? She kept trying. In a minute or two, she was convinced it had loosened some.

If I can get that nail out, maybe I could use it to break open the lock on the door. Was it a twelve-penny? No, bigger. A sixteen. Cass knew something about hammers and nails from the restoration work she'd done on two different houses. Tom had worked with her on the second, the house they now owned.

She thought about the silly squabble over the nylons. *So stupid of me. Why'd I have to go and snap at him like that?*

Tom slumped on the sofa, Orbison at his feet.

"It's my fault, buckaroo," Tom said. "I should've picked her up every day after work . . . So, what do I do now?" He stroked the top of the cat's head. "You seem to be the only friend I have left in the world." Orbison purred and rubbed against his ankle, then hopped into Tom's lap.

"Somebody took Dad's van, kidnapped Cass in broad daylight so they'd be seen, hauled her someplace, then dumped the van. Who the *hell?*"

Orbison looked up at him, cocking his head in the funny way he had. His pupils, which outdoors were vertical black slits, were dilated into deep ovals and appeared full of understanding.

Tom leaned back, closed his eyes and focused on Cass. She was a strong and brave woman, but she must feel scared and alone. They'd found that they often thought of each other at exactly the same times during the day, even though miles apart, doing their own jobs. Just as Tom would reach for the phone to call her, it would ring, and it would be Cass calling him.

"Cass, I'm with you," he whispered. "Always. I'll come and get you somehow. I'll be there. Please know that. Please hear me."

It was a warm night, but not hot enough for air-conditioning, and the windows were open. The smell of young oak and hackberry leaves and fresh-cut grass drifted in. From the park, a few blocks away, he heard the calliope, as sometimes happened when the wind was right. "*. . . He'd marry the girl with the strawberry curl and the band played on.*"

Where *was* the girl with the strawberry curl?

Cass had glanced at the two *Time* magazines. German scientists might be getting healthy fees to help Iran develop a nuclear bomb.

Controversy swirling around Salman Rushdie's book, *Satanic Verses*. A little story about *Buffalo Springfield*.

Stop this! she told herself. Don't sit on your fanny looking at old magazines. Figure out how to get out of here.

She closed her eyes and concentrated. *Tom, I need you. Please get this message. I need you, need you.*

The blinking of the overhead lights startled her. They winked on and off three times, then off to stay, a repeat of the earlier routine. Again came the unlocking of the door and the flashlight beam probing the room and finding her on the sofa.

"How's your photography?" Cass said, going on the offensive, though almost blinded by the flashlight beam. "Taken any pictures lately?"

"What are you, a mind reader?" Madame X answered. "Stay like that on the couch for a second. Give us a little smile." Asking the impossible.

A brighter burst of light exploded, followed by a huge after-image hanging in Cass's eyes—a full moon on steroids. She heard the whir of a Polaroid camera winding.

"Just in case we need to show lover boy you're alive and well," Madame X said. "Let's hope we don't need to, that he comes to the party when he hears your voice."

Her voice? The thought of talking to Tom lifted Cass, even though she knew it would be a highly restrained ransom call. Maybe with a gun at her temple.

"We'll do that tomorrow. We'll let him sweat it out another night first."

"No," Cass pleaded. "Today. I want to talk to him now!"

"Sorry, sugar, tomorrow. Now it's time for your potty break. First, your little headdress. Hold still, be a good girl, and we won't tie your hands."

Cass let the hood be placed over her head. Even blind, climbing those steps, getting out of this cellar for a few minutes, using an honest-to-goodness bathroom, would be a welcome change.

She'd sensed the presence of a second person in the room. The hand that gripped her arm and guided her up the steps was a man's—surely the same man who'd drugged and captured her. The creep who'd fondled her face. Who was he? She only knew he had strong hands.

Looking downward as far as possible, till her eyes hurt, she managed to see her feet and the wooden treads of the stairs through the small gap at the bottom of the hood. It was the same way she'd been able to see Madame X's unique watch-ring the night before. Or whenever that was. Cass was losing track of time.

One of the treads creaked again. The third one. She salted that knowledge away. She saw the bottom of the door frame, then stepped onto linoleum—warm to her stockinged feet after the concrete of the basement. She caught the unmistakable smell of sawdust again and heard the faint rumble of distant machinery.

Map this out in your mind, she told herself. As she was pushed forward, she counted her paces—twelve—before she was steered to the right. Six more steps, then the man stopped her. She heard a door open.

"When you hear this door close," she heard the woman say from several feet away, "you can take off your bonnet. Knock on the door when you're finished. If you don't knock in five minutes, we're coming in."

Cass was nudged forward a couple of steps. She heard the door close. And lock.

She lifted the hood. Sudden light shocked her eyes. They took several seconds to adjust. She saw that the hood was a thick black flannel bag with a drawstring at the opening. Like a kid's marble bag, only bigger.

She found herself in a small, spartan bathroom, like a gas station's. It had a toilet with a brown stain at the bottom, a paper-towel dispenser on the wall, a frosted glass window—closed, of course—and a sink with a liquid soap dispenser. She tried to raise the window but it was nailed shut. Of course. She went to the sink. A small, water-spotted mirror hung above it and she saw the weary face of a woman she hardly recognized. Bloodshot eyes with purplish half-moons beneath them, worry creases in the forehead. No makeup, but what the hell.

For the next couple of minutes, while making good use of the toilet and sink, Cass thought about what Madame X had said about Tom coming to the party.

Tom was making lists at his desk. His green-shaded Tiffany lamp threw a splash of light over his notepad. One column was headed SUSPECTS and another, NEXT STEPS. Random notes were scrawled at the bottom of the page, things like VAN - WHO? and LAW FIRM –HUTCHINSON'S CLIENTS.

He concentrated on the lists, trying to shut out distractions, such as Special Agent Elwell's ridiculous assertions, and Jefferson Hayes' attitude, which was probably based on inexperience and insecurity. Hayes' M.O. was to bluff it out and not ask for help. Bad approach for a cop.

Okay then, Tom would be his own one-man band. He scrawled several new items on his list. Some he underlined, some got question marks, others were crossed out almost as fast as they were written.

In bed hours later, he was walking into a cornfield when it suddenly caught fire on its perimeters. The flames advanced rapidly on one side, then a bullet came from another, tracking him like a missile. Both closed in, the bullet much faster than the flames.

He snapped awake with a jolt, astonished to find he'd actually fallen asleep. The faint light in the bedroom was a murky haze of gray. Again the glow from the numerals on Cass's clock radio looked like a sad green eye. Something besides the dream had wakened him, something triggered in his subconscious.

He glanced around the dark bedroom and suddenly—*good God*—saw Cass's face. The face was transparent, suspended in space like a hologram, indistinct as if veiled in gauze. There was no mistaking it. The vision stared at him pleadingly. Through it, in the faint light, he could see a chair and dresser. No neck, no shoulders. Just that lovely, ghostly face. The hair, the eyes, the nose . . . without question it was Cass.

Orbison was meowing and pacing, his tail swishing like a berserk metronome.

Tom squinted to focus better, but as he did, the vision began to fade. "Cass, no . . ."

Her mouth opened. The facial expression—eyes widening, eyebrows frowning into a W—became one of entreaty. "Help me," it said wordlessly, fading. The vision faded more, then flew apart in a thousand silver sparks like a fireworks burst.

Orbison hopped on the bed and rubbed against Tom's forearm, the agitated tail swishing across his face.

"You saw her too, Orby?"

CHAPTER TWENTY-FIVE

Cass was prodded back into her cell, and Madame X said they would bring a chamber pot she could use from now on as her toilet. "We can't be bothered bringing you upstairs every few hours."

Cass groaned, and Madame X snarled, "Oh, poor princess. You can shit on the floor for all I care."

"Bitch," Cass muttered. After the hood was jerked off and her captors left, she went to the old leather couch. The couch was now her most familiar—almost comforting—retreat. Although cold and lumpy, it seemed like hers, and she had so very little left. She slumped onto it and shook her head.

An old memory flooded in. It was Thanksgiving and the family had gathered at her grandparents' home in South Pasadena. She had gone up to use the second-floor bathroom.

Cass hadn't started kindergarten yet, must have been about four. She wore a green and white jumper, bought new for the occasion.

She excused herself like the perfect little lady she'd been taught to be, and skipped up the stairs to the bathroom. She clicked the lock as she knew Mom and Grandma always did. The only trouble was, she couldn't *un*-click it when the time came. Her little hands just couldn't get that strong silver handle to rotate to the straight-up position and free her.

The bathroom was large and sunny, with lacy yellow window curtains, but in her panic to leave it and rejoin the family, it seemed to shrink. She sobbed. The walls closed in. She started to scream. She'd never been claustrophobic before.

After a ghastly eternity, she heard her father's voice outside the door, first telling her not to worry, then how to turn the knob.

She *knew* how to turn the knob, but the dumb thing wouldn't go. His tone gradually changed. "Anyone can turn that knob! Come on, Cassie, what are you doing wrong? Stop that crying." Which only made her cry more. And the room continued to shrink. Total, black terror now.

A tapping came at the window. Cass turned, eyes and mouth open wide with fright, expecting to see the bogey man. Instead, it was her grandfather. He'd placed a tall ladder against the side of the house and climbed up. One hand was supporting himself on the sill and the other was raising the window. Rescue!

In another minute he'd squeezed through and, wise old man that he was—he must have been *fifty!*—gave Cass a long warm embrace before turning the lock and opening the door. Her sobs of joy got tears all over the front of his clean white holiday shirt. She'd always loved her grandfather, but never more than at that moment.

Her grandfather had died two years ago.

Tom called Cass's parents' home in Los Angeles. He'd agonized over this for two days, but it couldn't be put off any longer. While the phone rang, he thought about the emerald. He was starting to call it the Green Monster. *I should've just thrown the damn thing in the river. Too late now. Too late.*

He was startled by Ty Nesbit's "Hello."

"It's Tom, Mr. Nesbit."

"Call me Ty. How's the career going, son?"

"At the moment, sir . . . Ty . . . not so good. I can't think of any easy way to say this, so I'll just . . . well, Cass is missing. Possibly kidnapped."

"What! Kidnapped?"

"We're not sure. It's looking that way."

"When? How?"

"A couple of days ago. On a public street apparently, not

far from the Capitol." Tom proceeded to tell Ty Nesbit what he knew.

At one point the man said, "Just a minute, Tom," followed by a muffled aside: "It's Tom, dear . . . Tom Cavanaugh . . . No, no, nothing's the matter . . . No, I can't put Cass on the line. She's . . . she's not there just now."

"This will be hard on your wife," Tom said, regaining Nesbit's attention. "But Cass will be okay. I swear that to you. I'll get her back."

"You could be mistaken. The witness saw"—Nesbit lowered his voice—"someone else, some other woman about her size. Cass could be visiting someone and forgot to tell you. Maybe she's down here, seeing her sister Jan. I'm sure it's something like that."

"Go away for two days without telling me? You know Cass wouldn't do that."

"Okay, let's say she *was* kidnapped. Why? *Why?* What's the"—Nesbit lowered his voice again, to a near whisper—"uh, motive? What are they after? Are they enemies of the governor? Do they want ransom money from me? Will they be contacting me?"

Tom reluctantly told him about the Maria Theresa Emerald. The explanation was interrupted twice by Edith Nesbit, demanding to know what they were talking about. "I'll tell you in a minute, dear. Now for Pete's sake, go watch TV or something."

Then, back to Tom: "What do you mean *you* will get her back? There are kidnap specialists, the FBI and so forth."

"Well—"

"Listen, I'm coming up there."

"No point in that, sir . . . Ty. What could you do?"

"I have some connections."

"With all respect, they wouldn't help. Not on this."

"But I'd be there when you"—his voice broke a little—"when you get my baby back." Tom felt his pain, shared his pain.

"Damn it, do whatever they ask. Cooperate, Nick, er, Tom." That slip hit Tom hard. "Give them the goddamned emerald right now. Nothing, *nothing* is worth any stupid risk."

"I know, Ty, I *know*. I'm very sorry I had to tell you this. I'll keep you posted and, believe me, I'll get her back. I'll get these bastards."

Tom rang off and pictured Edith Nesbit falling to pieces and crying that Cass should have stayed with that nice respectable Nick Race. He also wondered how long it would take Ty Nesbit to go to the FBI. Or to arrive on Tom's doorstep.

Cass's dinner came. Even though her watch worked fine, she didn't look at it. Time was meaning less and less.

The meal was two pieces of fried chicken from a takeout, plus a roll and a small tub of cole slaw. She searched the box for a receipt that might include the name of a town. There wasn't one.

Nibbling listlessly on a drumstick, she noticed something new in the corner of the room, a sturdy clay pot, more than a foot in diameter. On the floor beside it was a roll of toilet paper.

"Oh, crap, my new potty," she murmured. "Well, how about that, I made a joke. Good sign, I guess."

She ate about half the meal, drank some water, returned to the couch, and examined her feet. Her knee-high hose were worn through on the soles, so she pulled them off and hurled them toward the chamber pot. The bottoms of her feet were black with dirt.

She shrugged and moved to one of the throw rugs, reclined on her back, and did some crunches. Instead of counting, she thought about what she could say to Tom on the phone the next day. She wouldn't be given much time.

A small spider marched across the floor. Cass flinched for a second—hated spiders—then sat up and crushed it beneath a heel. And instantly regretted it. A small creature dead by her hand. Well, foot. A death here in this basement, this dungeon. She looked at that simple, dreadful thought, and shivered. *I'm sorry, little insect lady, I'm sorry.*

Tom got a call from a friend at Tower Records—he'd forgotten he'd called this guy after the trip to Washington.

"Tom," he said, "on that Roy Orbison song, it's 'Pretty woman, *that* I'd like to meet.' "

"*That?* Damn, well then, I lost a bet, but thanks." After hanging up, he said, "You were right, Cass. I owe you a dinner in Paris. What was the name of that pricey restaurant you mentioned? I *will* pay off, you know. You'll be back with me and we'll go to Paris." He sank into a chair and tried to believe his own words.

Without giving it thought, he picked up the remote and clicked on the big-screen TV that was a gift from Roy Oakley. A ball game was on. The Giants were playing the Dodgers. Or was it the Cubs? Somebody with team names across their chests in blue script. A week ago he would have sat and watched—not now. He shut it off with an angry jab of his finger and returned to his list of suspects.

Mary Savage is a hell of a photographer, he told himself, but an honest cop. Why is she so darn interested in me? I assume that because as a woman executive in a traditionally male organization she doesn't have many men friends, especially in Homicide. A social need. Also, that she wants to learn more about how male cops think and operate. Am I off base on that? A forty-year-old executive out to break the glass ceiling, a Type A woman who's discovered that, hey, men aren't total monsters after all and maybe my life needs one. That's what Mary Savage is. A kidnapper and a precious-gem obsessive is what she *isn't*. I think.

Manny Díaz, formerly one of the governor's bodyguards. Now there's a crooked cop. Ex-cop now, a fugitive on the lam. Díaz must hate my guts, would probably do anything he could to get to me.

Tom glanced back at the TV and thought about its donor. Roy Oakley—was he a possibility? He knows about the emerald and he had access to Dad's van. Drove it recently to keep the battery up. Was aware that I'd done the same. He definitely had the opportunity to set me up with that van. He also was a good photographer. The highly competitive Roy Oakley, old Twenty-Five-for-Twenty-Five, who loved beating Dad at trap shooting. Maybe he also loved beating him out of that precious emerald? But Oakley was an ex-cop. He wouldn't be dumb enough to abandon the van where it could be quickly found. Or was that deliberate?

Could I ask Dad about this? Tell him of my suspicions about Oakley? Not from here, anyway. The damn FBI might be monitoring my calls, and I'm not supposed to leave town.

Jesus, is that Elwell jerk for real? Does he really think I'm in on this? Kidnapping my own fiancée to grab some ransom money from her folks? I'd have to live out my days in Brazil or someplace. He's crazy. Maybe crazy is where I'm headed. Driving myself to nutso land.

The lights flicked on and off, followed by the now-familiar flashlight-and-hood routine. As she was led up the stairs, Cass again noted the creaky step. Once inside, she counted her paces. Instead of twelve steps forward and six right, which led to the bathroom, it was twenty-eight forward, ten left, twelve forward, eight right.

Through the slim opening at the bottom of the hood, she saw her dirty bare feet step through another doorway onto a wooden floor. The strong hands steered her again. She'd begun calling their owner The Shadow. He maneuvered her into a chair, a swivel chair with armrests.

"We're calling lover boy," Madame X said. "Now listen, when we get him on the line, tell him you're okay and you're being treated fine. Tell him to cooperate with us, nothing else.

No conversation, no funny business. Short and sweet. If you try anything, I'll beat the hell out of you. And I'll really enjoy it."

To emphasize her point, The Shadow's strong hands grabbed Cass and twisted her right arm behind her back and up. Electric pain ran up her arm and shoulder. The sick bastard! One of those same hands had stroked her cheek in the van a few nights before, she was sure of it.

"That's just a little sample," the man said. "Believe me you'll hurt much worse if you get smart on the phone, so do as you're told." Grimacing with pain, Cass realized it was the first time she'd heard The Shadow speak. He let go of her arm. *God, the relief!*

She leaned forward, resting her arms on what must have been a desktop. She heard numbers being tapped on a phone. Through the tiny gap, she saw one of her elbows, and a matchbook. She slowly inched her arm closer and covered it with her hand. She heard The Shadow's voice again and hoped these people were too busy placing the call to notice that she'd palmed the matchbook.

"Sergeant Cavanaugh, please." Cass thought The Shadow wasn't using his normal voice. It sounded forced, altered from what she'd heard earlier. A few seconds passed.

"Mr. Cavanaugh. Have we finally found your pressure point? . . . Oh, you know who it is. There's someone here with something to say to you." With mixed anxiety and yearning, Cass's heart raced. The phone was pushed to her ear and mouth. "Talk," the man hissed.

"Tom, it's me, Cass."

"Cass—"

"Don't say anything. I'm okay. They're treating me okay. Do what they say. Please. Trust in the Lord and everything will be all right. Second Chronicles 2:8."

Cass was wrenched from the phone—as she knew she would be. A hard slap stung her face, then another. The hood didn't buffer the blows much. A dozen hornets were loose in her ears.

"You bitch!" The woman speaking. "We warned you." Cass was slapped again. Felt like her cheek had been ironed. She started to black out, fought against it.

Tom replayed the episode in his mind.

"For you, Tom," April the Cop had said. "Line Three."

"Who is it?" He seldom asked that, but he was doing many things differently these days.

"I dunno. Some guy."

Tom picked up his phone. "Cavanaugh."

"Mr. Cavanaugh," a man's voice said, cutting each word carefully from his mouth. "Have we finally found your pressure point?"

"Who is this?"

"Oh, you know who it is."

Tom cupped a hand over the voice piece.

"April! Trace!" He wished they had that new caller ID, though this probably was from a stolen mobile phone.

"There's someone here with something to say to you."

An apprehensive pause. Tom's breathing slowed. He sensed Cass's presence on the line even before she spoke. Then he heard, "Tom, it's me, Cass." His heart jumped. The voice sounded strained, guarded, but wonderful.

"Cass—"

"Don't say anything. I'm okay. They're treating me okay. Do what they say. Please. Trust in the Lord and everything will be all right. Second Chronicles 2:8."

Tom heard a scuffling sound, followed by a muffled silence as if a hand had been clamped over the speaker. Then: "You see, Mr. Cavanaugh, she's all right. For *now*, anyway. But don't be stupid again. We'll get back to you." A hard click, then a dial tone.

He'd scribbled "OK. II CHRON 2:8" on the pad in front of him.

"Did you get that, April? April!"

"Sorry, Tom, not enough time. Another few seconds would've done it."

"I want the tape as soon as possible."

"Sure thing."

"What was that you said to him?" the man snarled at Cass.

"Just a Bible verse." She wasn't going to let herself cry, but she was close to it. "Something to encourage him."

"What was it? Second Chronicles something. What was it?"

The strong hands hauled Cass from the chair and slammed her back against a wall. She slid slowly to the floor. Someone kicked her in the thigh.

"Second Chronicles 9:7, you bastard." She grabbed at the foot that kicked her. Blinded by the hood, she missed.

"What the hell does that say?" the man shouted.

"Look it up." Cass as angry as the hornets in her ears.

"No, you tell me. Exactly."

"She didn't say 9:7 before," the woman said. "It was something else, 5:8 or something. It ended with an eight."

"Baloney. I said Second Chronicles 9:7." Cass shouting. " 'Happy are thy men, and happy are these thy servants.' It was just a way of saying everything's cool."

"Get a Bible!"All pretense at disguise gone from the man's voice. Cass trying to determine if it sounded familiar.

"Where am I going to get a Bible?"

"I don't know, just get one. She's probably lying, but we need to check. Throw her downstairs. No food for her tonight."

Do I know that voice? Is it familiar? No, not familiar, just odd in some way.

"Anybody have a Bible around here?" Tom called out.

"Sure," Luke Monelli answered. "Right next to my cassock

and beads."

"Want to talk about it?" It was April, touching Tom's shoulder. He hadn't realized that she'd come into his cubicle. "It was them, wasn't it?"

"No and yes," he said. "Thanks, April, but I need a few minutes."

He closed his eyes and rested his face in his hands for several seconds. He took a deep breath and looked around. He reached for his phone book and looked up the Sacramento Public Library. He punched in the number. A woman answered and Tom asked if someone could look up a passage from the Bible.

"Oh, sure, that's not at all a strange request," she said. "You should hear some of the calls we get. Now, do you want the Protestant Bible or the Catholic?"

"King James, I think." Wasn't that the version Cass had studied?

A couple of minutes later the woman was reading to Tom from Chapter Two of Second Chronicles: " 'Send me also cedar trees, fir trees, and algum trees, out of Lebanon: for I know that thy servants can skill to cut timber in Lebanon; and, behold, my servants shall be with thy servants.' "

"Is that what you wanted, sir?"

"Is that the whole eighth verse?"

"Yes sir."

"That's it, then. Could you repeat it, please, a little slower? I'm taking this down."

After he hung up, Tom's emotions were a whirlpool as he re-read his notes.

That night with Orbison on his lap, his ex-wife Sharon crossed Tom's mind. That didn't happen much anymore, but when it did he couldn't help comparing her to Cass—not that there was any comparison. There were times in that misbegotten marriage when he'd have been glad to have had Sharon kidnapped. Awful thought, but he'd known for quite awhile now that Cass was the only woman he'd really loved. His hands became fists. He thought about Sharon's cheating, and about how expensive the divorce had been. Tom hadn't heard from her in years—which was fine with him.

He brushed thoughts of Sharon aside and checked his notes against the text in the Bible he'd found on one of their bookshelves. It matched. *Send me also cedar trees . . . thy servants can skill to cut timber in Lebanon.*

"What is she telling us, buckaroo? Is she in the woods? She's scared out of her mind, and still cool enough to give us this. She probably caught hell for saying that. I'll kill the bastards who've done this!" Orbison stared at him.

"Fir trees, cedar trees. Cut timber. Cedars of Lebanon. What is she telling us? A lumber yard? A sawmill?"

Cass had no appetite so going without dinner was hardly punishment. Her neck ached from being slammed into that wall; her thigh too, where she'd been kicked. She knew she'd have a hell of a bruise.

She reached in her pants pocket for the matchbook she'd snatched during the phone call. Maybe it would bear the name of a bar or restaurant, give some clue as to where she was. She held it up. REST AT THE BEST. ARAPAHOE LODGE, BRECKENRIDGE, COLO. *Damn.* She couldn't possibly be in Colorado. She slipped it back in her pocket. She had matches and two magazines. Could she make something of that?

She looked around the gray cellar. Longed to see the moon, a star, a tree, anything outside, even a McDonald's golden arch. Instead, her tired eyes saw only the hostile concrete walls, the cobwebby ceiling, and the rude furnishings of her dungeon.

Her gaze stopped at the sixteen-penny nail in the wall. She went to it and worked it back and forth, back and forth. It surprised her how much this aggravated the soreness in her neck. The nail was definitely looser now, but the stubborn thing just wouldn't come out. At last, she gave up and shambled back to the lumpy couch, her fingers stiff and red with indentations from the nail head. This had become a mission. She'd get that damn nail out yet.

As if on cue, the light went out. Ten o'clock. Must be curfew. The darkness was total. In the shroud of blackness, she imagined the walls moving inward, as she had in her grandparents' bathroom years ago. She curled up in a fetal position, her hands cupped around her jaw. I'm going to die here, she thought.

CHAPTER TWENTY-SIX

Three a.m. In fitful, blanket-slinging semi-sleep, Tom processed a jumble of words. "Gum trees, fir trees, cedar trees. Skill to cut timber. Woods. Lumber yard. Sawmill."

Five a.m. He gave up on sleep, got up, swallowed an aspirin, and plopped down at the kitchen table, chin in hands. Orbison ambled over and began rubbing himself against Tom's ankle and the chair leg.

"Wait!" Tom blurted. Orbison looked up. "Roy Oakley, Dad's old shooting buddy. He owns a lumber mill, buckaroo. Not only owns a lumber mill but knows about the emerald."

Seven-thirty a.m. Tom dropped coins in the slot to call his father. Figuring the FBI could listen in on calls from his house, he was in a phone booth nearby in Land Park. It seemed to take an hour to get a real operator. Like everyone else these days, the phone company was automating and downsizing.

"Deposit ninety cents for the first three minutes."

"Dad," Tom said when his father's frail voice answered. "This may sound weird, but where is Roy's lumber mill?"

"Why do you ask, Thomas?" Desmond Cavanaugh sounding not only weak, but oddly cold and guarded.

"I just need to know. What town is it in, or close to?"

"I had some company yesterday."

Huh? Why did he say that? Tom wondered. Is his mind starting to go? "That's nice, Dad. Please, though, this is important. Roy's lumber mill?"

"No, Roy didn't visit me yesterday. It was someone else. A very good listener."

A good listener? Ah, Agent Elwell had been there, Tom thought, and Dad believes his line is tapped.

"Oh, I'll bet it was my uncle. Yes, he's a good listener, my uncle."

"Yes. Say, Thomas, I called the bank the other day to check my balance. It always bugs me the way they ask for your mother's maiden name."

"Huh?"

"Your mother's maiden name, son, your mother's maiden name."

Tom was confused again. "Yeah, Dad, that's frustrating, but I guess they have to be careful."

"Speaking of being careful, remember that time you got caught off base against Petaluma High? I always warned you not to take too long a lead."

"Yeah, geez, that was a long time ago."

A chime sounded. "Deposit fifty cents for the next three minutes," said a cold, synthesized voice. Tom dropped in his last two quarters. Two more chimes rang out.

"Yes, a long time, but you still play some softball, don't you?"

"Sure, you know that."

"There you go. Don't take too long a lead. Especially at Field Twenty-Five. That'd be a mistake."

You can't lead off in softball, Tom thought. Dad knows that. "Field Twenty-Five?"

"Yes, that one can fool you. Keep it in mind."

"Okay, Dad, I will. But about Roy. He hasn't been around lately?"

"You're taking a long lead again."

"Oh." A few seconds lapsed. "Well, Dad, I'm out of change, so I'd better get going. Maybe I should check my own bank balance. I'll probably have to give 'em my mother's maiden name too."

"Probably will."

"So long, Dad."

"Good luck, son."

Just before hanging up, Tom said, "What's *your* mother's maiden name, Elwell?"

Several cars passed as he hiked the four blocks back to his house. The work day was beginning, people who lived around Land Park heading to their jobs. While he walked, Tom examined the coded conversation he'd just had.

The FBI had been to see his father, whose phone was probably tapped. Field Twenty-Five. His father thought Tom was off base in suspecting Oakley, dubbed "Old Twenty-Five-for-Twenty-Five" for his trap-shooting prowess. But what about his mother's maiden name? What was that about? Tom's mother's surname had been Weaver. Weaver?

It struck him later, after reaching home. *Weaverville.* Oakley's lumber mill was near Weaverville.

Weaverville was a small town on Highway 299 between Mount Shasta and the coast, two hundred miles from Sacramento. And Tom was forbidden to leave town.

Cass was lying awake, trying to think, to plan, anything to ward off the terrible hovering blackness telling her this could be the last day of her life.

I'm going to beat these people, she thought. I have to. I don't know who they are, but they despise me, especially Madame X. She hates me, feels inferior, has something against me. Who the devil is she? Whatever her problem is, I'm going to out-psych her. Doing what they're doing, these people have to be nervous. I'll play on that, show them how in control I am, how confident I am—even though that's a big lie.

She reflected on the man's voice. When he dropped the disguised tone, he'd sounded slightly nasal, lower Midwest. She wasn't certain; he'd been angry, but there'd been a bit of twang, the kind you heard in southern Illinois or Missouri.

She had slipped the matchbook beneath the sofa. The way this room was cleaned—ha!—no place could be safer. Sometime this morning she'd have that big nail under there too.

The light came on at seven o'clock, chasing away the goblins of the dark. Shortly after, the on-and-off ritual took place, followed by the flashlight.

"Breakfast," the woman grumped in the darkness.

"I sure could go for a workout," Cass said. "Lift a few weights, spend ten or twelve minutes on the treadmill, swim some laps. How about you? I'll bet you could too. Say, do you usually tip Charlotte for all the clean towels? I never know if that's appropriate. I usually leave her some money about half the time. Charlotte's neat, isn't she?"

"Shut up."

I'm getting to her. Good.

"Why won't you talk about our gym? I really miss it. It's a great place—but you know that. Wish I had a picture of it, don't you? But then you *do* have pictures of it, don't you?"

"I said shut the hell up!"

In the shadows cast by the flashlight, Cass could see someone in the corner, lifting the chamber pot. Good, they were going to empty it. This place must stink but she couldn't tell anymore.

Tom pulled a California road map from the desk. He was going to look up Weaverville. He'd peeled back only one fold of the map when the phone rang.

"Detective Sergeant Cavanaugh? This is Dot, Chief Pulaski's assistant. The chief wants to see you right away."

"Me? At headquarters?"

"Yes, right away, no matter what you're working on."

Tony Pulaski had come from someplace in Pennsylvania three years ago when the old chief retired. A search firm had screened candidates, and Pulaski, who was about fifty, had a good record back East. He'd worked his way up through the ranks and was known as a tough cop. Tom liked him—he'd been a strong supporter of the Narcotics Unit.

In the downtown station, Dot greeted Tom in the chief's outer office and told him to go right in.

Tom liked Dot. She was in her late thirties and was pretty in a plump sort of way. It was all over the department that she was into dating matchups from the newspaper personals. He recalled the moment he'd started liking her. He'd said, "Dot, is your last name Matrix by any chance?" Without skipping a beat, she'd answered, "No. It's Com."

Pulaski shook hands briskly and motioned Tom to the chair opposite his polished mahogany desk. He had gray-blue eyes and thinning, razor-cut brown hair. His dark suit jacket hung from a hat rack behind him. His monogrammed white shirt didn't hide his strong shoulders and muscular arms. By comparison, Tom looked like a bum in his usual narc grunge.

"Cavanaugh, no point beating around the bush." No small talk here, no offer of coffee. "We're putting you on administrative leave."

CHAPTER TWENTY-SEVEN

ass's breakfast was a dry, packaged danish and a styrofoam cup of something pretending to be coffee. At least it contained caffeine, the first she'd had in days, so she drank it greedily. She also devoured the entire danish. Having been denied food the night before, she'd been hungry.

She reclined on a throw rug, did some pelvic tilts and obliques, the pull on her abdominal muscles feeling good. She rolled over on her stomach and did thirty press-ups. Next, she stood and ran in place, breathing deep and pumping up her heart rate. She finished by doing ten squats.

The water in the basin was a day old, cold and filmy with yesterday's soap. She washed her hands and face anyway, removing at least the facial perspiration from her workout. She figured she must smell like a basketball team after double overtime. If only she could take a bath and change into clean clothing. What luxury. Fresh underwear would be a godsend.

She couldn't do a damn thing about that, so she turned to the nail in the wall. After a few hours of sleep and an intake of calories, she felt stronger.

She twisted the stubborn nail back and forth. The concrete really had a grip on it, but it was slightly looser with each determined twist. She put all the strength left in her wrists, forearms and shoulders into the effort.

It came out! The nail popped from the wall so suddenly Cass almost fell on her back. When she regained her balance, she tossed the nail up and down a few times, getting a feel for it. It was almost five inches long. It felt good in her hand. Like a dagger.

This was an achievement, maybe not much of one, but even

a small victory was good. She went to the couch and slipped the nail underneath, beside her matchbook and pencil stub. Her small arsenal was growing.

She gave the metal wall heater a close inspection. What was behind that grilled facing? There had to be a hole in the wall for wiring or a gas line. How big would that hole be? Large enough for an adult human to crawl through? Not likely. Besides, she didn't see any way to pry that thing from the wall. Four large Phillips screws, covered by several coats of paint, secured it. Her nail would be useless. She needed something sharp and flat like a chisel to scrape that paint off, then a Phillips screwdriver. Or else a crowbar. No, the heater held no promise as an escape route.

She decided it was time for a walk. She stretched a little, did some leg lifts, then, staying close to the walls, strode around and around the room at a brisk pace, counting her steps. Fifteen, sixteen, seventeen. It was such a boring route, she reversed direction a couple of times. She was breathing old and stale air, but it couldn't be helped. Forty, forty-one, forty-two. She had to keep in shape. That would help her mind as well as her body. As she walked, the soreness in her thigh and neck began to dissipate. Another small success.

Tom stared at the chief, dumbstruck.

"This is temporary, of course," Pulaski said.

"Why? I don't get this."

"This isn't fun for me either, Cavanaugh. We all think the world of you. You're a good cop with a fine record, but—"

"And I've been on the force a lot longer than Jefferson Hayes."

Pulaski's eyes narrowed. "What's Lieutenant Hayes got to do with this?"

"You've been talking to the FBI too, haven't you?"

"Don't interrogate me, Cavanaugh."

"Who's pressuring you?"

"I said don't interrogate me!"

"You guys aren't gonna back me up? You're buying into this cockamamie theory of Elwell's?"

"Who?"

Right. Play dumb, Chief. "The FBI. Special Agent Elwell."

"Elwell? Oh yeah, I met the little guy once."

Little guy? Tom wondered.

"But dammit, no. The FBI? You've got it all wrong, Cavanaugh." Pulaski raised his hands, palms outward. "It's just that till this thing is cleared up and the governor's aide is back safe and sound, it's best if you had some time off."

"The person you call the governor's aide is my fiancée!"

"Of course, your fiancée. Fine woman, and naturally you're distracted right now. Can't give the department your best. This is nothing personal."

"Administrative leave? I haven't shot anybody, nothing like that. This is screwy. The union will be all over you."

"I'm not concerned about the POA. My concern is getting your fiancée back."

"Is the governor leaning on you too, as well as the FBI?" Tom knew how paranoid that sounded.

"Oh, please, Cavanaugh, give me some credit."

"Okay. How long will I be off?"

"Until I say." Pulaski smiled a non-smile. "Hopefully this situation will end fast and well."

"And meanwhile, I'm a suspect." Tom's fists clenched so tight his forearms ached. "Unbelievable! Well, then, I guess I'll go out to the location and pick up some of my stuff."

"No, don't do that. If you have some personal items out there, one of your colleagues can bring them to you."

"And you'll want the department car, of course?"

"I'm afraid so. You drove it here?"

Tom nodded.

"I'll have someone take you home. I'll have to take your firearm and badge too."

"Of course you will." Tom stood so fast he almost knocked his chair over. He flipped his badge on the desk in front of the chief, then his 9-millimeter Ruger. He wasn't going to volunteer that he had an extra badge at home. Also, he still had two guns of his own, a .357 Magnum and a .25-caliber Astra.

He pulled a key ring from his pocket and removed the keys to the department Chevy—ignition and trunk. He tossed them on the desk with an insolent snap of the wrist. "I guess I'm out of here, Chief."

Pulaski was known as a tough man, one who couldn't be bought, who would keep the department as free of corruption as it could be. Why, then, had he wimped out, furloughed him under pressure? And who had turned those screws? The FBI? The governor? Someone else?

"We'll have you back in no time," Pulaski said.

"An ousted cop with a kidnapped girlfriend, suspected of doing the kidnapping himself. I'm having a hell of a week," Tom snapped as he turned and left.

Storming through the outer office, he caught the chief's assistant, seated at a computer, gazing at him. "Don't feel sorry for me, Dot, I don't need it."

Cass knew how to shim a lock with a credit card, something she'd learned from Tom. Standing at the top of the stairs and studying the door, she believed she could handle this one. The problem was the deadbolt. If she could dig out around the bolt's lock slot in the door frame maybe, using the large nail, she could force the bolt out into the open position.

It was her only idea. She went to the door, careful to step over that noisy third tread, and began to whittle away at the door frame with her nail. Could they hear her? She felt sweat droplets form on her brow. Would they burst through that door and beat the crap out of her again?

It was slow work. She knew it would take a long time. Still, the overhead light was always off when her captors were in the room, and maybe they wouldn't spot the damage with their flashlight. This was a longshot, but the only shot she had.

The wood was fairly hard. She had no idea what kind it was, but it sure wasn't soft pine. Within fifteen minutes, when her hands and fingers needed a break, she had gouged two small holes in the frame, a fraction of an inch apart. Later she'd try to connect them and make the resulting single hole bigger and deeper. She scooped up the small wood flakes she'd created and stuck them under the couch.

Tom hadn't even asked if the administrative leave was with or without pay. He wasn't sure of his legal rights on that, but he would sure as hell find out. He'd sometimes felt himself miscast as a cop. He should have been a history teacher. Maybe it's not too late, he thought, during the short ride home in a black and white. He said very little to the young patrolman at the wheel.

The department will want me back, he thought, when I get this thing over with and Cass is safe and the FBI and Pulaski are humiliated. If this is what fourteen years' service as a cop gets me, I should say "screw 'em" and just turn to teaching. He wondered if he could get a job at Sac State or maybe one of the community colleges.

He was thirty-eight. He could probably get a teaching credential in two years. Maybe life really could start at forty. He was pissed off at law enforcement. At Chief Pulaski, Special Agent Elwell, Lieutenant Hayes. Even at the young cop beside him at the wheel. When they reached his house, Tom hopped out quickly. Didn't even say thanks.

Hell, Pulaski had done him a favor, he told himself as he loped toward the front door. He wouldn't have to worry about druggers any more. He could concentrate one hundred percent on getting Cass back.

He went through the day's mail. One of the items was a large manila envelope from the Cal State Sacramento History Department. He opened it and pulled out a sheaf of photocopied papers clipped beneath a cover note. The note was from a graduate teaching assistant, who said she was responding to Tom's request and that this was material about Sutter from her master's thesis. He flipped through the pages, noticing that several passages were marked with yellow Hi-Liter.

The doorbell sounded. He tossed the papers down on his desk with the rest of the mail, walked to the door and searched through the peephole. *What is Debbie Hamilton doing here?*

He opened the door and repeated aloud, "Debbie, what are you doing here?" *Dumb thing to say.*

"Calling on a friend. Is that okay?"

"Sure, sure, come on in. I was just surprised to see you. Thanks for coming by."

Tom closed the door. The rookie cop flashed a high-voltage smile and hugged him. Orbison, watching this from his perch on a chair where he'd been catnapping, looked surprised, Tom thought. *Good thing Orby can't talk.*

Debbie carried a canvas tote bag and was out of uniform, way out, wearing a washed silk pants outfit, midnight blue, and high heels that made her much taller than her five-foot-three.

"You're pretty brave, Debbie, coming to see a discredited old cop. Want a glass of wine or something?"

"Sure, whatever you have."

Tom led the way into the kitchen, where he pulled a bottle of chardonnay from the refrigerator. "Whatcha got there?" he asked, indicating the tote bag.

"Your stuff from the boonies."

"I thought April—"

"I told April I'd bring it to you."

Tom remembered the remark Debbie had made at the party, how she wished she'd met him first.

"Plus something else," she said softly.

"Uh, what?"*A teddy? Condoms?*

"The tape of your phone call from the bad guy. April wanted you to have it. She'd have her fanny in a sling if they knew she'd pulled that for you."

"Good old April."

While Tom poured the wine, Debbie produced several of Tom's personal effects from The Hole, including snapshots taken down from his cork board, and an audio cassette.

"You're great," Tom said as they clinked glasses.

Orbison circled Debbie's feet, sniffing at the unfamiliar scent. The cat looked up and winked, Tom could have sworn it.

"You sure this place isn't bugged?" Debbie said quietly.

"Pretty sure. Been over everything with the proverbial fine tooth comb."

Tom took the items and placed them on the counter. He didn't look at the snapshots of Cass. They would only feed the hurt in his heart. He wasn't sure what to do next. "Are you hungry?" he asked.

"I took a chance and ordered pizza. I figured you wouldn't be cooking tonight." Debbie folded her hands nervously in front of her. "Was that, um, okay?"

"You ordered pizza?"

"Sausage and mushrooms. It'll be here pretty soon. Was that, like, stupid? Maybe I should've called you first."

"No, no, that's fine. Fine, hell, it's great, thanks. In fact, I was going to ask a favor of either you or April—I guess it'll be you, since you're here and all. We can talk about it over pizza."

"Tom," Debbie said, looking him straight in the eye, "on top of everything else you've been through, you're getting screwed big time by the gutless department. You need a friend and, like I keep saying, I'm a friend. I know you're not available, that you're head over heels—end of story. Don't be uptight about me, okay? Now what's the favor you need?"

The doorbell rang, and Tom fumbled for his wallet.

"No, no, we're covered. I put it on my Visa. Take care of the tip if you want."

"Debbie, this is so darn nice, I don't know what to say."

"Just say I'm great again."

They talked for several minutes over pizza and wine. Debbie paused, her glass held high, and gazed at Tom as if he were under a microscope. It made him uneasy.

"Penny for your thoughts," he said.

"I was just, you know, this business has cost you a lot, hasn't it?" She put her glass down. "Your face was always so warm and full of fun."

He thought he saw a tear form in one of her eyes. "I admire you, Tom, always have," she said hesitantly. "Cass Nesbit is one lucky woman. My heart aches for you both. I really hope you'll be safely back together real soon."

Tom nodded, pursed his lips. He was touched.

"You'll do it, somehow, I know you will, you're a great cop." She took a sip of wine. "So what's your next move? How can I help?"

"Well, my car is at a mechanic's out on Auburn Boulevard, close to Fulton, and—"

"What's the problem?"

"Nothing. Just making it look like it's being serviced. The mechanic is an old friend. I took the trolley back home after dropping it off."

"Were you tailed?"

"I was real careful. Now here's the favor, Debbie. If you could pick me up tomorrow night at the golf course in Land Park, the parking lot out in front, and take me back there, to the garage, that'd be great."

"And then you'll head out to, where exactly?"

"A place called Weaverville."

"Weaverville?"

"Yeah, up near Shasta."

Later, when he walked her to the door, he didn't resist when Debbie hugged him again—but was surprised when she kissed his cheek.

"I wouldn't do that out in front," she said, placing a hand on his chest. She stepped back and opened the door. "Well, I'm out of here, coach, see you tomorrow night." On the porch, she looked back over her shoulder. "I wish . . ." She smiled mysteriously and walked away.

Cass lost her train of thought. Something puzzled her for a moment but she couldn't put her finger on it. She refocused on the problem at hand.

Okay, first, this smells and sounds like a lumber mill.

Second, this couple—whoever they are, Madame X and The Shadow—couldn't tell all the workers here what they're doing. "Listen up, folks, we've kidnapped a state official and are holding her hostage so we can steal a rare emerald." No way.

So, third, if I can get out of here, I won't be facing thirty or forty people trying to recapture me, only two or so. *I hope.*

My objective, then: get out of this place. My tactics: disable the deadbolt, shim the lock, sneak out of whatever building this is, "borrow" a vehicle or walk into the woods, assuming that I'm in the woods.

What's the likelihood that one or both of them is watching this door from the other side? Pretty likely, but the two of them can't watch it twenty-four hours a day. So, if I can get that door open, I'll go out when it's least likely to be guarded. Real late, two or three a.m.

Okay, Nesbit, it's a plan—let's get to work.

With that, she climbed the stairs and began picking at the door frame again, enlarging the holes she'd started in hopes of tunneling into the deadbolt's lock slot.

Tom sat at his desk and glanced at the papers from Sac State. Some Hi-Lited matter near the bottom of the first page caught his eye.

"Sutter's empire was collapsing as squatters, lawmen of dubious character, and other flotsam of the Gold Rush were making it impossible to hold onto his more than 50,000 acres. In the spring of 1861, though, the visit of Prince Rudolf, brother-in-law of the Austrian Archduke Maximilian, buoyed the colonel's spirits. The young prince spent two months as Sutter's guest, and his interest in American farming and cattle-breeding diverted and revived the old man. Sutter enjoyed the opportunity to once again speak German, his half-forgotten native tongue. Rudolf studied the fort, the farms, trading posts, even river navigation as practiced by American pioneers. An expert horseman, he rode all over the Sacramento River Valley. He took a great liking to a tree-shaded spot on the banks of the river about twenty miles north of Sutter's Fort, and made camp there for several days. Sutter supposedly said, 'If you fancy that place so much, I'll give it to you.' The visit ended with news of the firing on Fort Sumter. If there was to be Civil War, the prince said, it was his duty to observe it first-hand for the Emperor."

If he went straight from here to the Confederacy in 1861, that means the emerald was here! With him. In Sacramento!

This was great stuff, but Tom wasn't going to dwell on it, not tonight. One thing and one thing only was important now. He tossed the papers down, picked up the tape Debbie had brought, and went to the den. It was good of April to make this dupe for him, he thought as he slipped it into a cassette player.

" . . . There's someone here with something to say to you."

"They're treating me okay. Do what they say. Please. Trust in the Lord and everything will be all right. Second Chronicles 2:8."

He rewound the tape and listened again. He searched back in his mind to the phone conversation with his father. *Your mother's maiden name.* Cass must be in Roy Oakley's lumber mill at Weaverville, even though his father had cautioned him not to get off base on Field 25, meaning, "It's not Oakley." *But Dad must be wrong. Everything points to Oakley.* Yes, he would go to Weaverville tomorrow night.

He'd been told not to leave town, but he hadn't agreed. He'd given no answer at all when Elwell had told him that.

While getting ready for bed, Tom found a Roy Orbison song running through his head. *Only the Lonely.*

CHAPTER TWENTY-EIGHT

Tom tossed fitfully on the bed. His temples began to throb. He felt himself beginning a slow fall, sinking right through the bed as if mattress, box springs and frame were warm quicksand.

He saw himself trudging along in a blue coat, smudged with Virginia dirt and mud. Tarnished brass buttons fastened the coat all the way to the neck. One of the buttons was coming loose—he'd have to remember to re-sew it. A blue forage cap perched on his head, its flat top slanting forward.

The Twelfth Massachusetts was marching through Washington City, having just crossed the Potomac on the Long Bridge. Tom saw numerous construction sites and lots of makeshift scaffolding. The place smelled like mud and spoiling food. A bad odor, but still better than the reek of an army encampment or the deep, eye-stinging smell of a body-littered battlefield. God, how he hated the stench of decaying flesh.

Someone hurled a potato. Directly in front of Tom, it whacked Hiram Hannah in the ear. "Go on home, you Billy Yanks," the antagonist called out. "Desist your hopeless war."

"I'll show that secesh son of a bitch," Hannah declared, and began to leave the ranks.

Tom grabbed him. "No, Hiram, he's not worth it. The captain will have your ass." Hannah grumbled, but got back in step. Several men—Union sympathizers, no doubt—ran up and shoved the troublemaker.

"This looks like a dirty, wide-open boomtown, "one of the soldiers said. "Near as many secessionists as Union folks."

"Whole place looks to be under construction."

"Everything 'cept the Washington Monument over there. That stubby ol' thing looks like a cut-off pecker, don't it?"

"They ain't goan finish it till the war's over."

"Have any of you boneheads spied Father Abraham?"

"Nope. He's prob'ly havin' hisself a tea party with old Seward."

Once out of Washington, tramping northwest through the Maryland countryside, their reception grew warmer. Cheering farm wives in sun bonnets and pretty girls in calico dresses waved the flag at them as they approached South Mountain. The ladies gave them hunks of fresh bread and tin cups of cold spring water. "Thank you, ma'am. Thank you kindly."

"Whoever told us that Maryland's nothing but Rebel traitors was dead wrong, as far as I can see," Tom said.

A rumor spread through the ranks about a woman in Frederick. When Rebel cavalry was there a few days before, she supposedly waved the flag at them and yelled, "Shoot, if you must, this old gray head, but spare your country's flag." Tom figured it was just a story, like so many others in this damned war, but it made him feel good anyway.

Whenever they reached the crest of a hill, he saw the march as the movement of a long blue snake, slithering forward as far as he could see, in clouds of dust. Those moments were rare, though. Most of the time the army's hike across Maryland offered nothing more to his tired eyes than the dusty back of the man in front of him, his rifle and haversack swinging in step over his sloping shoulders.

The whole thing played back in his mind. The glorious ceremony on the Common two years ago when the ladies of Boston presented them their majestic silk battle flag bearing the Massachusetts coat of arms. What ignorant boys they had been, infatuated, believing that war meant glory and the adoration of girls and ladies.

At First Bull Run, they learned that glory was out of date. That first brutal, chaotic clash of arms left many of them dead. Amongst them, their first commander, Colonel Fletcher Webster, son of the great Daniel Webster himself.

This last month had been aspecial hard for the Army of the Potomac. First, the defeat at Manassas—now being called Second Bull Run—when old Bobby Lee had outfoxed and outflanked the Union generals. Again! The retreat to Washington and now the hot, dusty trek westward across the fields and hills of Maryland. They'd done a powerful lot of marching the last few weeks.

Somewhere along the way they'd heard the grand news that Little Mac was back. President Lincoln had turned again to George McClellan to lead the army in this next scrap against Lee. Everybody was happy about that. Little Mac was the one man this army loved, the one man it would fight for.

Finally they reached this pitiful little stream that nobody'd ever heard of: Antietam Creek.

They made supper and it was pretty awful, as usual: sowbelly, hardtack and a potato. Later, when the regimental band played Taps, Tom silently sang along with the words he'd supplied himself. Go to bed. Go to bed. That means you, that means you, that means you. Sleep tonight . . . for tomorrow . . . you may be dead.

He placed his bedroll on a soft grassy spot, sheltered by a huge chestnut tree, half a mile east of the creek. He carefully removed rocks and twigs and sticker balls before spreading out. Still, a hard spot found his lower back during the night, and he tossed and squirmed, thinking, always thinking, never able to shut out images of battle.

Early morning now. A hot September morning filled with dense air holding little promise of autumn.

Thunder muttered in the sky, the man-made thunder of artillery. His right hand gripped his almost-new Sharps rifle, which fired .58-caliber, percussion-cap bullets. Fifty-eight caliber. No wonder so many men were mangled, so many amputations made. He'd seen precious few "minor wounds." This war between the states was a dreadful war, an almighty dreadful war.

The battle had started an hour ago, maybe half a mile ahead. He heard the bass booms of many cannon, the tenor cracks of the rifles and muskets, the inexpressibly haunting wail of the Rebel Yell, the urgent shouts of frantic officers. It was considerable of a fight all right.

The first battered stragglers came tottering back through the encampment, hollow-eyed, dusty, bloody, desperate for sanctuary. "It's a butcher shop up there, a bloody butcher shop," one of them screamed. Poor fella like to be losing his mind.

And then the order came. "Company C, Twelfth Massachusetts, form Line of Battle. Company C, prepare to advance." Tom and scores of others were on their feet, falling in with their comrades.

"Dress up," a sergeant shouted, "dress ranks." Soon they were tramping forward in parade step. The colors were out in front. The boys on the snare drums had begun their rattling sound. Ketrack-ketrack, ketrack-a-tack-a-tack. Attack, Tom. Attack, Tom. Attack attack attack, Tom.

It took ten minutes for the Twelfth to ford Antietam Creek at a low spot a scout had picked. Tom was soaking wet halfway up his thighs. His socks squished inside his shoes as he climbed a small rise. He hated to go into battle wet, but it seemed he always did.

To the left, farmland sloped downhill toward the creek. He saw a whitewashed barn and a row of bee hives in the distance. To the right, maybe half a mile, slightly higher ground, a large clump of woods spat flame and smoke. Stonewall Jackson's artillery. Dead ahead, a pitiful cornfield.

A blanket of acrid smoke covered the ground to about eye level. Black powder. "Wheel right! Twelfth Mass, wheel right!" On they tramped, into the cornfield.

For a moment, he spied Private Seth Gladding, as big as

life, moving forward with everyone else. Tom shook his head—couldn't believe his eyes. Old Seth Gladding went to his reward at Manassas. I saw him carried off to the meat wagon. How in the name of mercy could he be here? Has this war gotten so far beyond human bounds that the dead are rising up to fight again? Or am I just losing my mind?

The corn—what was left of it—was high, tasseled, ready for harvest. Tom had to step around the bodies of wounded and dying men, some with arms outstretched, begging for water, or to be finished off with a merciful bullet. The cries of torn men and shattered horses alike broke your heart.

Came now the Rebel fire, the whipcracks of their bullets and Minié balls tearing through the corn like a hailstorm. Men were falling, friends from Worcester and Grafton, bluenoses from Beacon Hill and manservants from Southie. But on they went, the men of the Twelfth Massachusetts—most of them, some of them.

In the distance, through a momentary gap in the haze, he glimpsed a small whitewashed chapel. Clouds of gray-black smoke blossomed out from Rebel artillery posted in front of it.

"Twelfth Mass, form on me, take that church, that's the objective, boys, that church. Let's show those God-damned Rebs what Massachusetts men can do." He saw an officer flashing a sword toward the enemy. Bright sunlight reflected off it. Few wounds were ever inflicted by swords. They were just props for officers to flourish in theatrical displays of authority.

The noise—of rifle and cannon fire, screaming men and horses—must have been deafening, but Tom no longer heard it. His consciousness had somehow turned off the frenzied sounds of the battlefield. He trudged forward in the unearthly silence. A bullet sliced through his left sleeve and nicked the skin, but on he went. His arm stung a little, but there wasn't much pain. He pressed forward, into a bizarre hell of silent screams, soundless puffs of smoke.

A Johnny Reb appeared forty paces ahead, grimy cap on a young head, uniform more butternut than gray. The Rebel was taking aim with his musket, one eye closed. Tom fired instinctively. A red splash appeared where the Reb's mouth had been, and he saw agony in the boy's eyes as the rest of the face fell backward, slowly it seemed, evaporating from his line of sight. Tom crouched and reloaded. "Better him than me."

Time meant nothing. "Fall back," someone shouted. "Fall back." He was hearing things again. Odd, that.

Like automatons, Tom and the others around him obeyed, those who still could, stepping backward as the firestorm raged over them. A bullet splintered his rifle stock. Slivers of wood stung his face.

Then, above everything else, a shrill voice. "Rally to me, men, rally to me. We can take 'em now, right now. This is our moment." From the corner of his eye, Tom saw a red-faced, white-bearded officer, an old man by the look of him, sword upraised defiantly, gesticulating toward the church. It was General Mansfield.

Tom was about to step forward when the old man's chest exploded like a burst watermelon. He tumbled backward. For an instant, their eyes met, before the old man vanished among the ravaged cornstalks.

Tom shouted, "Mansfield, Mansfield," and others began to pick it up. The chant grew in strength, rising above the ruined field like a cloud. The battered ranks found new energy and resolve. Tom started forward. So did the men around him. "Mansfield, Mansfield." The church grew as they surged ahead.

That was when he saw a bullet coming at him. Strange. He'd never seen a bullet in flight before, didn't know it could be done. It was being drawn directly toward him, slowly, inexorably, as if his body were a magnet. Straight at his chest. He tried to duck, tried to throw himself down, tried to twist away—but he couldn't. He was caught in an enormous kind of web.

He could tell now that it was some sort of fabric that held him. He fought against it. Twisted and wrenched himself, trying to pull free from the entanglement. The bullet kept coming. Sweat drizzled down his face and chest.

A voice said, "Now let's check the morning commute on our freeways." At last, he pulled loose from the tangle, which turned out to be sheets and a blanket. He glanced over at Cass's side of the bed. It was empty—cold and empty.

Tom lay there for several minutes, trying to bring his mind back to some kind of order. At last, he pulled himself to his feet and stumbled toward the bathroom.

He stepped on something. He looked down and saw a tarnished brass button. He looked at it for several seconds in total confusion.

He stooped to pick it up. It must be the button that had come off his blazer a few weeks before. He couldn't remember if he'd sewn it back on. He took a closer look. His eyes jumped. The button in his hand was scratched and tarnished. It was imprinted with the letters U.S. His spine ran cold. It was an old Army button.

CHAPTER TWENTY-NINE

Cass had worked deeply into the door frame and believed she was close to reaching the deadbolt. A sudden thought: *Oh God, what if the deadbolt has a metal sleeve?* If the bolt was slotted in a brass jacket instead of a simple tunnel bored in the wood, she'd be screwed. *Please, no,* she prayed as she worked on.

With a precision developed over painstaking hours, she pushed the nail into the wood again, turning it in a screwing motion as she pressed. Then she pried it upward, levering, and another small flake of wood popped loose—just as the light blinked off.

She scampered down the steps in her bare feet, silently, she hoped, and made for the couch. The light blinked again. By the third blink, Cass was placing the nail and a small handful of wood flakes under the couch. She had just settled onto the couch when the door opened and a flashlight beam found her.

Madame X and The Shadow came down the steps and began slamming containers on the table. "You were right," Madame X said. "Second Chronicles 9:7 says what you said, 'Happy are your servants' and all that crap. But that's not what you told lover boy. What was it?"

"I told you, drop it," The Shadow said in a faked bass voice. "It's done with."

They're getting on each other's nerves.

"I just want to get this damned thing over with." Madame X.

"Shh." The Shadow.

"Children, children, mustn't bicker." Cass.

"Shut up!" Madame X. "Put the light on the bitch."

Before she could brace herself, Cass was slapped hard across the cheek. She flung a counterpunch at Madame X with all the strength she could muster. In the dark, it was off the mark, glancing off the shoulder blade. But it had to have stung.

"Get out of here," The Shadow snarled, forgetting to disguise his voice and obviously not talking to Cass. Her cheek aflame, Cass saw the silhouette of the woman she hated stalking up the stairs. Even in the dark, Madame X's anger at The Shadow showed in the way she stomped.

The man followed, but stopped in the doorway. The beam fastened on Cass's face for a few infuriating seconds. Then it jabbed at every part of the room, inspecting walls, floor, the table, even the treads of the stairway. Don't look at the door frame, Cass prayed.

The light blinked out and the door slammed shut. The room was black and silent.

Except for the pounding of Cass's heart.

Tom had only begun to ponder the tarnished brass button and his bizarre dream when the phone rang.

It was Lan Nguyen, the computer whiz. He said he had interesting news. Tom cut him off, took Lan's number and said he would call right back—which he soon did from a phone booth. Whether puzzled by that or not, Lan announced that he'd broken into the computer network at Curry, Bickford & Marshall in San Francisco.

"They considered it a secure database. Ha. It took me about six minutes," he said, self-satisfied. "I was able to print out Fred Hutchinson's billings for January, February and March." Hutchinson was the attorney who'd called Tom.

"Perfect." Since Tom didn't have a fax at home, and he couldn't use the police machines, he asked Lan to send the purloined documents to a Kinko's, giving him a fax number he'd already looked up. Lan agreed, sounding caught up in a spirit of clandestine adventure.

"I'll be waiting at the store," Tom said, thanking him. "Incidentally, I'll mail you a check today."

"That's not necessary, Mr. Cavanaugh."

"Of course it is. I was a starving college student once myself. And remember, this is just between you and me."

"Right, Mr. Cavanaugh," Lan said conspiratorially.

Driving to the Kinko's, something suddenly occurred to Tom. Cass had given him the Civil War button he'd found on the bedroom floor. Knowing he was a history buff, she'd bought it for him a month ago at an antique shop in Folsom. He'd placed the button on top of the dresser—and forgotten about it, like a dummy. He slapped his forehead with the heel of his hand. The button hadn't slipped through some seam in time torn open by that weird dream.

An hour later he was sitting at the rolltop desk. The Tiffany lamp illuminated the fax pages and an envelope addressed to Lan in Princeton, New Jersey. Tom had just written him a check for two hundred dollars.

Fred Hutchinson's recent billings had his full attention. The lawyer had billed twenty-one clients in February and March, and twenty-four in January. Seventeen were businesses; seven were individuals.

Tom studied the names of the businesses and the person billed at each location, hoping to find Roy Oakley or a lumber mill. He didn't. Nor were any of the businesses located far north of San Francisco, as was Oakley's mill. Disappointing.

That left the seven individuals. Three of them were in the San Francisco area, and the others were in Modesto, Los Angeles, La Jolla and Santa Barbara.

He thought about the Los Angeles postmarks on the envelopes that had carried the photos of Cass. Hutchinson's client in L.A.

was a woman who'd been billed for eight hours of consultation and other services related to a lawsuit. A date was listed with each charge, but not a specific time of day.

The Modesto client was a Robert Angus. Modesto was a farm town in the Central Valley, three hundred miles or so from L.A. and its mailboxes. Angus had been billed for a telephone call on March 29, the day before Hutchinson had called Tom with the offer to buy the Maria Theresa Emerald. Tom put a checkmark beside Angus's name.

A Kurt Neumann was the La Jolla client. Tom, who'd gone to San Diego State on a basketball scholarship, knew La Jolla, an upscale section of San Diego. Neumann's billings puzzled him. The services had been light each month, just a few telephone consultations. But there was a two-thousand dollar monthly retainer. Neumann was paying good money just to have Hutchinson handy.

Tom scanned the dates of the calls. One jumped out at him, March 30, the very day that attorney Hutchinson had called Tom with the brazen offer. He splashed a checkmark by Neumann's name.

The fourth client was a Wilson Judge, who owned an art gallery in Santa Barbara. Anyone who dealt in paintings might also have an interest in gems. Tom put a checkmark by that name too. The man apparently was being defended by Hutchinson in a suit brought by a painter who'd displayed at the gallery on consignment and claimed he'd been shorted on his payments. Just the kind of thing someone who'd steal Austria's crown jewels might do.

Wilson Judge. Kurt Neumann. Tom's lips pursed, his forehead scrunched. One of those two could be behind the offer to buy the emerald. Which one? Probably Judge, he thought. An art dealer. Sure.

He picked up the envelope addressed to Lan Nguyen and smiled for the first time in days.

* * *

At the downtown police station, Dot told Chief Pulaski he had a call. Pulaski picked up his phone and listened for a second. "Weaverville?" he said. "Where's that?"

The light was on again. Cass saw her meal: a peanut butter sandwich and an apple.

How she longed for an exquisite, full-course dinner at a good restaurant, with a bottle of cabernet—1982 would be nice. She began daydreaming about menu selections. Veal cordon bleu would be wonderful. So would chicken cacciatore, or salmon Florentine, or lobster. Even a nice little slab of filet mignon, with sautéed mushrooms. And a huge dish of chocolate ice cream for dessert. She picked up the apple, wiped it on her slacks, and bit into it.

She retrieved her nail again and went back to work. Dig in, lever out, dig in, lever out. This went on for God knows how long. Every now and then she stopped, carried the wood shavings to the couch, rubbed some life into her fingers, then went back and dug some more.

An hour later, she was finished. She had connected the two holes she'd dug, forming a bigger one that intersected with the deadbolt's lock slot. And which—*thank you, God*—was merely a tunnel drilled in the hard wood, not a metal jacket.

There was just enough room to slip her sixteen-penny nail in against the end of the bolt. She wouldn't try it now. Once she forced the deadbolt into the open position, it would be beyond her grasp and she'd have no way to slide it back again. The game would be lost if they found the deadbolt open.

She would have to make her escape attempt late tonight, without a trial run. It would either work, then and there, or it wouldn't. She couldn't bear to think of failing in her one shot at it. Once out of the cellar, she'd let her eyes adjust, then try to find an outer door.

She remembered that the bathroom was a few steps forward, then right, and that the office was farther forward, then left, forward again, then right. Except for that, she knew nothing of the layout, nor even what kind of building she was in.

She went to the couch and placed her last handful of shavings beneath it, along with her precious nail. She massaged the stiff red fingers of her right hand. There was nothing to do now but wait, and get some sleep, if possible. She tried to slow her breathing.

Tom had stepped out for a taco and a Pepsi. Back home, he parked at the curb and got out. He scanned the neighborhood as usual. A white compact car he didn't recognize was parked three doors down. That bothered him a little.

He hiked up the walk and stepped inside. As he closed the door, even before he heard Orbison's deep-throated guttural growl of displeasure, Tom knew something was very wrong.

"Move to the center of the room and hold your hands out where I can see them," a voice demanded. Tom slowly obeyed. He saw Orbison on the second step of the stairs, hair frozen upright, tail twitching, eyes dilated into angry black disks.

Reaching the middle of the room, holding his hands partway up and away from his body as if debating, Tom turned to face the intruder, who held a gun on him. The guy was standing in the north corner, the darkest part of the room in daytime.

The man was Latino, medium build—and Tom knew him.

Manuel Díaz had been the head of the governor's security unit until a year ago, when he'd fled to Mexico.

"Manny, be careful now. I've got a pistol in my waistband. The safety's on. I won't touch it."

"Smart man. My shot would be in your heart before you could reach it."

Díaz was mostly bald and the fringe of hair along the sides was grayer than Tom remembered. His pistol was aimed directly at Tom's chest, his kill zone. It looked like a Walther P99. "What do you want?"

"Just to deliver a message, Cavanaugh. You don't seem to take notes seriously, so my employer wanted this one sent personally."

"And who's your employer, Manny?"

"Fuck that! Here's the message. You've got two days, man. In two days you'll get instructions. Follow them and everything'll be okay. Screw around, and you get Cass's head in a gunny sack."

Tom's hands clenched by themselves—he had to force his fingers to straighten out.

Díaz backed toward the door, still aiming the pistol. "Two days," he said, finding the doorknob behind him without turning. "Come outside to follow me and I'll kill you."

He fired. Tom ducked. Orbison leapt three feet straight up. The room echoed from the blast. The bullet had smashed dead center through a framed Monet reproduction on the wall.

"You crazy bastard!"

"Follow me and you're dead. Stay right where you are for two minutes."

Orbison, who'd made re-entry, bared his teeth and hissed like a tiger, his back arched into a dome.

Díaz opened the door and was gone.

Tom pulled out his Astra, flipped the safety off and dashed to the back door. As he sprinted along the side of the house, he heard a car driving off. He reached the front yard and saw a small white car disappearing down the block, too far off to make out the model or number.

Back inside, he calmed Orbison with some friendly stroking and a saucer of milk. Next, he called the Sacramento field office of the FBI and asked for Special Agent Elwell.

"He's not in," came the answer. "Away from the office for awhile. Care to leave a message?" Tom didn't.

What did that mean? Was Elwell taking a few days off, or was he in the field, maybe personally directing surveillance of their prime kidnap suspect?

Tom had hoped to meet with Elwell, tell him a *real* suspect had broken into his home and left a message by shooting up a painting. Also, to give him the new information about Oakley and ask why no lab techs had ever come by to check for samples of Cass's hair. He had to get these dumb feds pointed in the right direction.

Now that would have to wait. He was going to Weaverville. Tonight.

Tom stood in a dark corner of the golf course parking lot waiting for Debbie Hamilton. Leaning against a gnarled oak tree, he tried to control his simmering anger at Manny Díaz. He wanted to kill Díaz, kill his employer, Roy Oakley or whomever, and take Cass off to a mountaintop somewhere. Wyoming, Nepal, Neptune.

How far I've come from my former, simple life, he thought bitterly. The history-reading basketball player and rookie cop was someone else altogether from the beleaguered Tom Cavanaugh who now was about to drive two hundred miles by night to try to find the woman who meant more to him than anything.

The incredible battlefield experience of the night before resurfaced. Had that been a dream or what? There was so much exact detail, names and faces and places. He was like Billy Pilgrim in Vonnegut's *Slaughterhouse Five*, slipping a cog in time.

He was glad when Debbie drove up in her red Explorer a minute later.

"You okay?" she said as Tom hopped in. "You look kind of spaced."

"Yeah, I'm fine, Debbie. I know this sounds weird, but take some back streets to the 160. Make a lot of turns." *When everyone's out to get you, paranoia's just good thinking.*

They didn't say much during the fifteen minutes it took to

reach his car. He was grateful Debbie wasn't being talkative, and he silently thanked her for understanding.

"I owe you," he said when they reached the garage. He leaned over and squeezed her hand before jumping out.

"Don't worry about it, soldier. Be careful."

Tom closed the door. As his young friend drove off into the night, he felt very alone.

Before heading north on Interstate 5, he stopped at an ATM. He would pay cash for food, gas and anything else he might need. The FBI could trace ATM withdrawals, and that's why he made this one here, before leaving town.

It would take around four hours to reach Weaverville. As his Honda devoured mile after mile on the flat, northward stretch of I-5, he thought about Roy Oakley. Why hadn't his name been on Fred Hutchinson's client list? When could Oakley have met that bastard Manny Díaz? Hector Esparza in the El Paso FBI office had said that Díaz was hiding in Mexico City but often sneaked back into the U.S. *No kidding!*

Am I going on a wild goose chase, only to be thrown in a federal lockup when I get back? Should I be going to Santa Barbara instead, to check out Wilson Judge's art gallery? Could Dad be right, that Oakley's innocent of this business? But just about everything points to Oakley. He had access to Dad's van, knows about the emerald, owns a damn sawmill.

I'll find the mill, he told himself, reconnoiter in the dark, make a plan once I see the layout, and spring Cass out of there just before dawn when they'll be least alert.

Fingers of lightning were flashing far off to the northeast, where the Sierra range met the Cascades. On his radio, Charlie Pride was singing, *Anybody Goin' to San Antone?* "Wrong direction, pardner," Tom said.

After he turned west on State 299 and passed Whiskeytown Lake, he found himself corkscrewing through one mountain pass after another. Flat fields of valley corn and alfalfa that he hadn't seen in the dark but knew were there, had given way to ponderosa and Jeffrey pines that he *could* see—they grew right up to the road's edge, the trunks ghostly in his headlights. The white lines streaked past.

Two bright dots burst into view, reflected in the headlights, surrounded by a khaki-colored blur. A deer, just feet ahead. Tom punched the brakes. The car fishtailed. The deer skidded past. A flash image of its frightened face burned into Tom's mind. Full size, no antlers. A doe. The two passenger-side wheels kicked up gravel from the shoulder, but he kept control and got the car straightened out.

Thank God, he thought. I would've killed her for sure, and totaled the car in the bargain.

The adrenaline surge from the close call erased any drowsiness. Although he'd been awake for eighteen hours, he was alertness itself for the remaining twenty minutes it took to reach Weaverville.

The town was heralded by a signpost announcing motels and service clubs, but nothing about a lumber mill. Only a few lights shone along the main drag at this hour. A time-and-temperature sign in front of a bank read 1:02 a.m. and forty-five degrees, a chilly April night in the mountains.

A place called the New York Saloon was still open, but Tom wanted caffeine, not alcohol. He pulled in at an all-night coffee shop and stepped into the bracing night air, which smelled of pine trees and, faintly, charred wood. Above him, a dazzling bowl of stars seemed almost close enough to touch.

A quick cup of coffee, some directions, and he'd be off to the lumber mill.

A bell on the door jangled as he entered. The tables were empty. A solitary customer sat on a stool at the counter. Strong arms, thirties, red baseball cap, sleeveless jacket. He obviously drove the logging truck parked outside. The man turned his head and sized Tom up.

A motherly, gray-haired waitress appeared from the kitchen and said, "What'll you have, friend, coffee?" The catsup stain on the front of her mint green apron looked like a Rorschach test. "Mind reader," Tom said, taking a seat two stools down from the truck driver. "Black, please."

A cup was filled and plunked down in front of him, coffee sloshing over into the saucer, which was chipped.

"Thanks." Tom placed a paper napkin in the saucer to soak up the overflow. "I almost hit a deer a few miles back."

"Gotta watch close for 'em," the waitress said. "They come out this time of night, looking for water."

"Don't I know it." Tom took a sip of coffee, surprisingly good. "Say, can you tell me where the lumber mill is?" The truck driver gave him a sidelong look.

"You another reporter?" the waitress asked, taking Tom by surprise.

"Reporter? No, friend of the owner."

"Not too close a friend, I guess, else you'd know that Trinity Pine burned down last week."

"What?" The mill had been destroyed? And *before* Cass had disappeared? Tom's shoulders sagged.

"Yep, 'bout a total loss."

"Trinity Pine? Is that Roy Oakley's place? Oakley's the guy I know."

"Only sawmill we got—or did have. Wha'd you say your name was?"

"Tom," he said. "Tom Carpenter. From San Rafael."

"Pleased to meet you, Tom. I'm Lucy." The waitress stuck out a dishwater-red hand. She had a nice smile. Tom figured she'd been pretty a few years ago.

"Well, Lucy, you've just given me quite a shock. You say it burned a week ago?"

"Yep, week ago Saturday."

Cass had disappeared later, on Monday. "I was supposed to meet Roy around dawn to do some hunting."

"Hunting? What kinda hunting? Ain't nothin' in season right now that I know of."

"Bird hunting. We shoot 'em with cameras."

"You could shoot those little shitters with shotguns for all I care," the truck driver said, speaking for the first time. "'Specially if you were after spotted owls. And I'd give you some extra shells."

"That spotted owl's not exactly a friend of the industry, is he?" Tom said, smiling at the stranger. Turning back to the waitress: "But listen, Lucy, are you sure we're talking about Roy Oakley's mill?" He took another sip of the good coffee.

"It was run by Buck O'Toole. He's been the manager for years."

"Good old Buck," Tom said. He'd never heard of the man.

"But it seems to me the owner *was* named Oakley. Flat-lander. Big fella? Older fella? Shotgun shooter?"

"That's right. He lives in San Francisco."

"We're talkin' about Trinity Pine, then. The only sawmill we had. We figured Greenpeace mighta torched it, but now they say bad wiring. State Fire people been over the place real close."

Tom's hands balled into tight fists. Already this hadn't been a good day, and it wasn't two hours old.

He figured he'd better get some sleep, since the sawmill was a goner. Even though Cass had vanished before the fire, he was going to check the place out—he'd come all this way. He asked Lucy to recommend a motel.

He had two days till Manny Díaz' deadline.

CHAPTER THIRTY

S haken by a bad dream she couldn't remember—just knew it had been bad—Cass was more determined than ever to break out.

She climbed the stairs by feel, avoiding the creaky third step. She used four matches practicing the maneuver of holding the nail while striking a flame in the dark for her attempt to unbolt the door. She was right-handed and hadn't succeeded in striking a match with her left hand. Okay then, Plan B. Hold the matchbook in her left hand, strike the match with her right, and clamp the nail in her teeth. Get a good flame going, switch the nail to her right hand, and grip the matchbook with her teeth. It was awkward, but it worked.

She struck a match with her right hand as rehearsed, and concentrated to form a mental picture of the door before the flame burned out. She'd be in trouble if she dropped the nail or the matchbook now. At best, they'd be hard to find at her feet in the dark. If they fell between the steps into the cobwebby void under the stairs, she'd never be able to retrieve them till the light went on in the morning.

Irksome shadows flickered as she peered into the hole she'd dug in the door frame. Heat suddenly singed the tips of her right thumb and forefinger. She shook the match out violently. To blow it out would mean dropping the nail from her mouth.

Now, in the dark, with a picture of the door in her mind's eye, Cass rearranged things, grasping the nail with her right hand and slipping it against the end of the deadbolt. This was the moment of truth. There had been no way to practice the actual levering of the cylinder with the nail until now.

She pushed gently at first, then more firmly, but nothing

happened. She took a deep breath and tried again. Still nothing.

On her third attempt, the deadbolt moved, but stopped with a dangerously loud metallic clunk. It hadn't opened. The bolt in fact had moved very little. She tried again, but it was no use—the deadbolt remained lodged in place.

Cass didn't move, trying to control her frustration and her breathing. She listened carefully for footsteps or any other sound outside the door. What was wrong? Why wouldn't this damn thing slide open?

With sickening realization, she remembered a deadbolt that she'd installed in her old house. The cylinder didn't simply slide open and shut—it had to be rotated ninety degrees. There was a catch on the bolt, nestled in a lock slot, and to release it, the bolt had to turn. This must be that kind of deadbolt. If so, how could she possibly turn the dumb thing?

She felt she'd been kicked in the stomach. She'd come this close, only to . . . Damn!

Back to the drawing board.

Navigating by feel, she padded down the steps. The treads made little noise under her barefoot weight, which once had been a hundred and thirty pounds. She guessed she was six or seven pounds below that now. Across the concrete, back to the sofa, to think through this new problem.

She struck another precious match to check the time. One-thirty. *Okay, Nesbit, what can we do about turning that damned bolt ninety degrees?*

She made a mental list of the stuff in her purse. Eyelash curlers? No. Tweezers? Maybe. Yes, tweezers. Maybe they would open wide enough to grasp the deadbolt. The bolt was smooth, but she could wrap the tweezers in tissue for a better grip.

It took a couple of minutes and two matches to find them. Now there were only ten matches left. Back at the top of the stairs, she used two more before she got the tweezers positioned around the cylinder. This had been hard to do, and the scratching sounds they made seemed deafening.

With a firm grip on the tweezers, she twisted again.

The tissue slipped and tore beneath the tweezers. It was too soft.

She slumped to the top step and sat there in the blackness. What else could she do? She'd been so close. How could she possibly clench that damn thing and make it turn?

She remembered the chair. Its fabric was coarser than tissue. Without wasting a precious match, she felt her way to the chair, reached behind it where a rip wasn't likely to be noticed. Using the nail, she sliced into the fabric. It took a minute or two and more nail jabs to tear loose a small strip. Then, using teeth and fingers, she trimmed it down to less than half an inch in width.

Back up the stairs again. Too much time has passed. She used another match getting the tweezers and her scrap of cloth positioned around the cylinder. Hard to do. What she needed was a third hand.

At last the tweezers had a firm grip and she twisted them. Her nerve endings danced electrically. Beads of sweat chilled her forehead.

The cylinder turned. She twisted more and felt it slip out of its lock slot.

This time when she pried at the end of the deadbolt with the nail, she felt it give. A little more pressure and it slid over. Still a little more and it was out!

The battle was half won. Cass had conquered the deadbolt— now for the conventional lock. She went back down to her purse. Put away the nail, tweezers and piece of cloth, and pulled out a credit card. Back at the door again, she fumbled with matches and the plastic card.

She was down to her last three matches, when—success!— the tumbler moved. Too loud for comfort, of course, but she'd shimmed open the lock. *Bless you, Tom Cavanaugh, for showing me that trick.*

She returned to the table for what she hoped would be the last time ever, collected her shoes and purse, replaced the credit card in her wallet, and slipped the nail in a pants pocket. Less than half her peanut butter sandwich remained, but she stuck that in her other pocket. Shoes in hand, she mounted the stairs again, her breathing erratic.

Well, here goes, she told herself, and started to turn the door knob.

Tom found the motel. It was vintage Forties: a row of small wooden cottages strung out behind a stucco office with a neon sign announcing **VAC NCY**. The driveway was gravel. After a persistent stabbing of the night buzzer, the door was opened by a sleepy person of indeterminate age and gender, an immense bowling ball wrapped in a scruffy robe. The tiny office smelled of old linoleum and cigarette smoke.

The bowling ball grumped, "Room Six. Twenty-seven bucks," before Tom could say he needed a room. He peeled off three tens and said, "Keep it."

The bedspread had cigarette burns on it. He climbed in anyway. The pillows were clean, at least. He lay there, thinking about the evil behind all this. Who the hell lusted after the emerald so much he'd harm Cass to get it? He pictured the terrible punishment he would exact upon this person. At last, drowsiness set in.

Where is he? What has happened? Pain cuts deep into his arm.

Someone steadies his head, gives him water. From a wooden canteen. Hard to see, the light so bright. Sunlight. Water delicious.

Can see a little better now. Face before him that of a man. About his own age. Sunburned face, cobalt blue eyes, neatly trimmed Vandyke on his chin. Peaked military hat, forest green with a band of red. Unfamiliar. Nothing like it in the Union Army, the Rebel either, for that matter. Tunic the same green color. Fine wool, by the looks of it. Gold shoulder boards.

He remembers now. The cornfield. Bullet coming at him.

"A wound most serious you have, but I think not mortal," the man is saying. "Your arm, surely she is broken." Strange accent. Is it Dutch? French? "My obligation as a Belgian officer, to give you water, give aid to the wounded and the dying."

"Belgian? . . . in . . ." It hurts to talk. ". . . Maryland?"

"Not to speak, please, you are weak. But Belgian I am, yes, a guest of your adversaries, the Confederates, oui?*"*

Wounded and dying.

"Am I . . . dying?"

"I think not. You must not to speak now. Permit Rudolf to comfort you."

Tom notices a cloth pouch strapped to the Belgian's waist. The pouch seems to quiver. It gives off something, a glow, an aura. Shimmering green light. It seems to reach out to him. The pain is forgotten.

"You . . . you must . . . return it." Why is Tom saying this? "It's your . . . duty." The words come unbidden. Seem to be dictated by the glow coming from that pouch. Speaking is slow and painful, but there's no stopping these words. "Be rid of . . . your . . . covetous . . . thoughts."

"Quiet now! You must rest."

"Return it. You must. It's . . . your . . . duty."

"You are a reader of ze mind, mon ami? *What are you, my poor wounded friend? A mystic? What of this gem do you know?"*

Tom's pain returns in full measure. Feels like he's swallowed broken glass. Lungs feel full of sand. The light fades.

"You must . . . your duty."

* * *

Cass was ready now. Barefoot and carrying her shoes and purse in her left hand, she pushed the door open. It creaked. *Of course.* She'd persuaded herself that if she ran into The Shadow, damn it, she'd stab him with her nail, kick him in the nuts, anything.

She stepped forward slowly while her eyes adjusted, fearing the worst. Light coming from somewhere around a corner dimly lit the hallway. She saw a metal folding chair leaning against the wall, unoccupied. She took a deep breath and listened closely. Heard nothing but an unfriendly silence. The place smelled of old wood and varnish.

Looking down the long, dim hallway that faced her—she'd seen too many movies—she imagined an electric chair at the end of it. She started forward on tiptoes, heart thudding like a kettle drum. To the right, through an open door, she saw the bathroom she'd used, how long ago?

As she passed a closed door on the left she caught sight of something at her feet. A cord stretched across the hallway, about a foot off the floor, tied to tin cans at each end. A primitive trip-wire alarm. Thank God she'd seen it in time. What a racket that would have made.

Holding her breath, she stepped gingerly over the cord and continued on. She ignored another corridor that led off to the right. It took about a century to reach the end of the hallway, where she peeked both ways, her eyes open as wide as they could go.

To the right stood doors that probably led to offices, likely including the one where she'd talked to Tom on the phone. To the left, an open area.

Suddenly she heard a clanking sound from behind one of the doors. Her nerve endings jangled. A couple of footsteps and water running from a tap. *Jesus!* Somebody was in there, maybe making coffee.

Her forehead felt clammy and her hands quivered involuntarily— she willed them to be still and not to drop her shoes. She tiptoed toward the open area and soon found herself in a reception room with a high counter, two chairs, a small table strewn with magazines and newspapers—and a door to the outside. A sign on the counter said Applicants to the Left, Visitors to the Right.

Cass crept to the door, glanced all about, and tried the knob. The palm of her right hand was damp but the door opened easily, though with a squeak that was much too loud.

She stepped out into a gravel parking lot. A mercury vapor light on the building and another on a pole formed two pools of purple-white brightness. The nights were shorter now but the first light of dawn was still far off. She slipped into her low-heeled shoes, her lungs filling with cool air smelling of burned charcoal. Still, it was the best air she'd breathed in a long time.

She could see that she'd been imprisoned in a long, low, cement-block office building. Two pickup trucks and an old Volkswagen were parked in front. Across the lot, fifty yards away, stood an empty logging truck, and beyond that, a large cone-shaped building with thin smoke wisping from a hole in the top. Somewhere a dog barked.

A sign in front of the building read: **EMPIRE LUMBER**. So that was the name of her jail. She didn't stop to ponder it—she had to make tracks.

Her first step made a loud crunch. She darted across the parking lot toward an opening in the wood-rail fence surrounding the lot. A single railroad track crossed the yard and, beyond that was a narrow asphalt roadway and a clump of pine trees.

She ran faster—until a Doberman pinscher exploded from the darkness like a cannon shot. It cut her off at the entrance, jumping, snarling, and baring foamy Dracula teeth.

Kurt Neumann handed his empty coffee cup to a flight attendant and turned back to the shopping guide. The crystal goblets were nice, but not good enough for a man of his taste. He closed the in-flight magazine and slipped it in the flap in front of him. He gazed out the plane's window. Snow quilted the higher peaks of the Sierra. It would be cold tonight at Cameron Flats.

Neumann would land in Sacramento in a few minutes, then he'd drive to the mill.

He thought about the woman he'd recruited for this endeavor. It was a gift from the gods when he'd met her by chance at the Del Mar Racetrack. Smart, greedy, ruthless, absolutely ideal for this project, this satisfying revenge he was about to enact upon the cop who'd destroyed his wife—and his life.

Neumann would have the greatest treasure he'd yet collected. And he'd *manage* the hell out of Tom Cavanaugh's woman.

CHAPTER THIRTY-ONE

Cass took a step backward, but stopped. Against all her instincts—which were screaming "run like mad"—she knew she had to hold her ground. She had worked with a dog trainer one summer while in college.

"Halt, sit," she commanded. "Sit, stay." But the dog continued to squirm and snarl, its tapered ears pinned back in attack mode. It was black with rust-brown markings. Its fearsome, snapping jaws the focal point of a long, lean head.

Don't show fear, Cass told herself. "Sit, stay, damn you." She felt like a Christian in the Roman Colloseum.

The dog only continued its sound and fury. Each snarling jump brought those knife-like teeth closer. She knew the dog would take a chunk out of her at any second. *Some escape. I haven't even made it out of the parking lot.*

"Sit, stay, damn you," she demanded, leaning forward in her own attack mode, surprising herself with her language. This time the dog's rage seemed less genuine. The animal acted confused. *Standing up to him must have been the thing to do.*

"Sit, sit." Suddenly her tormentor obeyed. The dog actually sat. Okay now, uh, reward him, right?

"Good boy," Cass said, "good boy." Her hand shaking, she reached out fearfully and let the dog sniff her fingers. After a few seconds of that, she pulled the remains of her peanut butter sandwich from a pocket and offered it. The Doberman wolfed it down in one big gulp. Cass forced herself to stroke his head. Transformed, the dog wiggled his powerful body in delight and licked her hand with a slavering tongue.

"You big fake." Cass wiped dog slobber on her filthy pinstriped slacks. "Call your bluff and you're just an old softy." The dog began nuzzling her ankles. *Great, now he loves me.*

Across the parking lot, the door opened and a man rushed out, hurriedly tucking a denim shirt into his jeans. "You, lady, come here," he shouted. She recognized the voice. The Shadow. Mister Strong Hands. The asshole who'd fondled her cheek a few nights ago.

"Sic 'em, boy, attack," Cass yelled at the dog. She bolted for the woods, running faster than she ever had on a softball diamond. She didn't look back to see if the dog obeyed.

Low branches lashed at her as she dashed deep among the trees, in a direction she hoped was away from the road. She ran without letup for several minutes, thrashing through underbrush, stumbling over roots, her clothes snagging. Her heart hammered and her breath came in great ragged gulps. She had no idea where she was or how far she'd gone into the woods.

Some time after slowing her pace from a jog to a fast walk, faint light began to appear in the treetops. Not enough to keep her from stepping on briars and other nasty things, but also, she hoped, not enough light to help someone trail her.

Her watch told her that she'd been moving for two hours. She stopped every few minutes to listen for sounds of pursuit. Heard only the usual woods sounds—birdsong, bees droning, squirrels scurrying about. She prayed she wouldn't come across a snake. Hated snakes.

Cass remembered a Girl Scout day trip in the San Bernardino Mountains twenty years ago. She'd gotten separated from the troop and wandered in the woods, hopelessly lost, for an hour that seemed like a month. When she finally stumbled upon the others, she said, with false bravado, "Where have you guys been?" She remembered fighting off the tears that threatened to erupt when the troop leader hugged her.

Slant sunlight cut through the trees stronger now. It was just after six. She looked for familiar landmarks in the terrain but saw none. There were several kinds of pines in these woods.

And black oaks too, leafed out in the bright green of spring. Other trees—she didn't know what kind. Golden poppies and mustard plants were blooming yellow. The air was cool, pleasant and full of fragrance.

Tom woke with a start, thinking about Cass. Something—he didn't know what—had shocked him out of sleep.

At first, he didn't know where he was, but then he remembered: the motel room in Weaverville. Awake now—after what, two hours' sleep?—he lay there, pondering in tangled thoughts all that had happened.

He finally got back to sleep. When he awoke a second time, it was close to six. He got into his clothes and made for the door.

He found Trinity Pine a few minutes later and ignored the yellow tape strung across the entrance. The gate lay trampled on the ground, crushed, he guessed, by a fire truck. The sawmill had occupied several acres. Two once-large buildings were reduced to stark, blackened rubble, but three smaller sheds remained intact.

As he approached the first of these corrugated-tin outbuildings, a man appeared in the pink early light, wearing a green uniform with official-looking yellow patches on his chest and shoulder. Rent-a-cop.

"What can I do for you, mister?" he said, squinting, a hand resting on a belt-hung radio like it was a weapon.

Although he'd given a badge to Chief Pulaski, Tom had another, and he showed it, saying, "I'm a cop."

"What kinda cop?"

"Detective, Sacramento," Tom said as the badge was examined.

"Pretty far off the reservation, ain't you?"

"Pretty far, but the owner here is a friend of mine. Roy Oakley asked me to have a look around."

"At this time o' day?"

"I'm a morning person. Any problem with that?"

"Well—"

"I'll put in a word with Oakley, tell him you're doing a good job out here."

"Well, okay, Mister Detective. Don't know what you're gonna find, though. Sheriff's been all over this place top to bottom. State Fire too."

"I'll look, just the same."

"Suit yourself. If you want some coffee, holler. I got a thermos over at the pickup."

Tom spent ninety minutes poking around. He checked the ruins of the main structures, but gave special attention to the still-standing outbuildings. He even scrutinized the log pond, which still floated scores of unsawed tree trunks. There was no sign of Cass, or that she'd ever been there. Not a scrap of fabric, a button from a jacket, not anything.

Tom asked the rent-a-cop if there were any other sawmills around here.

"Nope, this the only one in this whole area."

Where the hell is she? Tom thought. Persuaded that Cass hadn't been there and there was nothing more to see, he made fists as he shambled toward the car.

What now? he thought, The FBI will know soon enough that I've been in Weaverville. Fatigue ground over him like an avalanche.

Who would have thought, Tom Cavanaugh, a man on the run? *I'm fucked*, he told himself as he started toward Santa Barbara and Wilson Judge's art gallery.

Cass sat against a tree to rest and take stock of her situation. Well, she'd done it! She'd escaped. She was *free*, a fantastic feeling.

But where the devil was she? People lost in the woods lost their lives—it happened all the time.

Through a gap in the trees, she saw rolling hills of green and bronze, and a substantial ridge a few miles away. A jet high above painted a thin ribbon of white on the dawn sky.

She felt a mess and knew she looked it too. She'd have to find a town soon or at least someplace with a phone, but leaning against this tree was comfortable. So very comfortable. The forest sounds began to meld into one pleasant hum.

And she fell asleep.

She dreamed of an alien forest—trees with lobster claws for branches. Strange, hideous animals. And snakes.

A beetle crawling on her neck startled her awake. She leaped up and brushed it off. Thank God it wasn't a snake. Her neck was stiff, her hands and feet cold, but otherwise she was okay. She looked at her watch. Eight o'clock. My God, she thought, I slept two hours. *Stupid! Lucky I didn't wake up in chains back in that cellar.* She got up and resumed her trek.

Coming up on a slight rise, she noticed some wild berry bushes in a low spot a few feet away. Those are blackberries, she thought. They must be good to eat. Hell, at this point, even her shoes were starting to look edible.

She picked a berry and bit into it carefully, testing it on her tongue. Not quite ripe, but close enough. Deciding they wouldn't kill her, she proceeded to devour several of them. Not very filling but better than nothing.

With stains on her fingers and probably her lips—*Why did those SOB's have to take my mirror?*—Cass started walking again.

Sometime later, she found herself on a downhill slope in less wooded terrain. The cloud cover was heavier now, but there was still enough sun to guess at the direction of her course: northwest.

Fearful of being exposed in the open for long, she began darting from one sheltered spot to the next. The countryside seemed to have eyes, all trained on this torn and bedraggled intruder.

Once or twice she thought she heard a truck or car in the distance. She weighed the pros and cons of finding a road and decided it was the thing to do. The whole world wasn't against her, just a dishonest man and woman and maybe a few of their hirelings. If she couldn't find a house with a phone, then a road and a kindly traveler offered the next best hope of deliverance.

As the woods grew thinner, she moved slower and surveyed the surroundings with greater care. Why couldn't she see Mount Shasta or Mount Lassen, or one of the fingers of Oroville Lake, something familiar? Where was she?

Then she saw the road, half a mile away, beyond a sloping, fenced pasture. The road twisted through two visible curves, flanked on the far side by a ribbon of trees. It seemed to follow a river or creek. Cars and trucks occasionally whined past in each direction, but the road wasn't particularly busy—didn't seem to be a main highway. The cloud cover was solid now, the sky gone from topaz to pewter, but Cass knew it wouldn't rain. Not in late April.

She didn't like the idea of crossing that wide-open pasture, but it couldn't be helped. Two horses, one the color of her auburn hair, the other as black as her fears, glanced at her as if she were a minor curiosity and returned to their grazing. Out in the open now, she found herself surrounded by hills. The long, uneven ridge she'd glimpsed earlier rose up behind the road and rolled on in each direction for miles. In the distance, far beyond the ridge, a mountain peak thrust against the ashen sky. She didn't recognize it.

She began to cross the pasture. A gash of lightning suddenly stabbed at a far hill, followed by a crack of thunder. The air filled with the scorched smell of ozone.

A blue pickup truck crawled slowly along the road as if the driver was looking for something. *Oh oh.* Cass crouched down and stayed perfectly still.

When the truck was out of sight, she waited two full minutes before moving on. At the far side of the pasture, a barbed wire fence separated her from a shallow ditch bordering the road. The four strands were more than a foot apart and she pushed two of them wider to slip through. She snagged her jacket in the process, leaving an inch or two of fabric behind. *These clothes are totaled.*

Then the rain began to fall.

"Thanks," she told the heavens, deciding it would be useless to hold her purse over her head, as she stepped into the ditch beside the road. Her right foot sank in a muddy spot, soaking the foot up to the ankle. "Even better." She frowned at the dark sky again. "You've got some sense of humor."

Two minutes later, she saw a white sedan approaching from the—was it west?—its windshield wipers slapping like metronomes. It looked innocent enough. Cass waved her arms.

The car rolled to a stop and the window hummed down. A gray-haired man wearing glasses and a green V-neck sweater leaned over and raised his eyebrows in a silent "Yes?"

"I've had an accident. Can you help me, please?"

"Of course, you poor soul. Hop in."

"I'm soaked."

"Don't worry about the car seat. This is a rental. Shall I take you to a doctor?"

"No, no. I just need to use a phone."

Cass slipped in and sat down. The man wore sharply creased gray slacks and a nice cologne. Paco Rabanne, she thought. A foot clad in an Italian loafer rested on the brake pedal. He wore no socks.

CHAPTER THIRTY-TWO

Tom wove his way back through the Trinity Alps. He was weary from lack of sleep even before he reached I-5 to head south. His eyes and hands drove by themselves. Twice he caught himself starting to doze, the car drifting onto the shoulder. Each time it shocked him awake for awhile, but it didn't last.

He tried to stay alert by concentrating on his mission. *Skill to cut timber*. There aren't any sawmills around Santa Barbara that I know of, he thought. But maybe the guy's a woodworking hobbyist, and he's got Cass locked up in his shop.

Cass noticed a rental car sticker on the windshield as she pulled the seatbelt around her and buckled it.

"What happened to you?" the man said.

"I don't mean to be rude, but I don't want to talk about it. Just want to find a phone." She clutched her purse to her chest like a shield.

"You say there's been an accident?" The man pushed a button, locking all the doors with a loud clunk.

"More like a beating."

"A beating? How terrible. But you still have your purse. If it was a robbery attempt, you must have fought them off."

Cass didn't answer. *Why the hell won't this guy just shut up?* They rounded a curve, going uphill. The rain slackened off.

"The rainy season is usually over by this time of year," the man said, flicking off the windshield wipers.

"Sir, I just need a telephone."

"There's one up ahead. I'm taking you there now, but you'll need some dry things."

"Just a phone," Cass snapped. Several seconds passed before she added, "I'm sorry. I'm usually more polite." She exhaled deeply. "I've had a bad experience."

"Of course. We'll say no more about it." While the words were polite, the way the man's eyes examined her made Cass recoil. There was something lascivious in those glances.

They rounded another bend and turned through a wide opening in a rail fence. Into the gravel parking lot of Empire Lumber.

Cass bolted upright, straining against the seatbelt. The tires crunching on gravel made the same sound she'd heard the night she first arrived here in that van. "No, no, not here!"

"But of course here. I know this place. There's a phone."

"No, I said not here." Cass tried frantically to open the locked door.

"They'll take good care of you here, my dear."

A blue pickup truck wheeled into the lot and screeched to a stop. The big man Cass had seen earlier at the office jumped out, nodded grimly at the gray-haired driver and went to the passenger door, an embarrassed grimace on his face.

The driver released the locks and the other man opened the passenger-side door and leaned in close to Cass. "Sloppy work, Wickersham," the driver snarled at him. "I'm very disappointed in you. I knew she'd have to reach that road eventually, but you—"

"Sorry, Neumann, geez."

Damn, Cass thought, so this creep had just been lying in wait for me. Her hands became claws. Still buckled in, she tried to gouge the big guy's face. He deflected her hand and threw a strong left arm across her neck, throwing her back against the seat.

She bit his wrist, adrenaline driving the teeth through the skin. His blood was thick and bitter on her tongue. She hoped this was the same wrist and arm that took liberties with her a few nights ago.

The man's other hand plunged against her thigh. She felt a

sharp jab like a bee sting.

When the guy stepped back, Cass saw a hypodermic syringe in his right hand. He put his left wrist to his mouth and sucked on the spot where she'd bit him. His eyes spewed hatred.

In Cass's eyes, the man began to reel. The parking lot and the whole building swayed, the trees, everything. She grew nauseous, couldn't hold her head up. Tiny points of light exploded and swirled in her eyes. A kaleidoscope of delirium.

She was barely aware of the gray-haired man unfastening her seat belt. Funny, she couldn't feel her legs. Everything happening now with comic slowness. Being pulled across the parking lot. Someone—two people?—propping her up by the arms and shoulders. Worthless feet not working. Hee hee. Going back to her funny gray building. The dog, that huge black Dober, Dober, whatever, levitating up so sluggishly, licking at her hands and arms, then floating back to the ground.

A pool of darkness wrapped around her.

A cold wind seemed to gust through Tom's mind. He flashed on Cass. A telepathic cry for help? *Hang on babe, I'll be there. Hang on.* He was barely aware of the eighteen-wheeler he was passing.

He stopped for gas in Stockton and bought a shrink-wrapped sandwich from a machine. He left I-5 at the Gilroy cutoff to head south on U.S. 101. Hours later, when he stopped for coffee after dark in Santa Maria, he realized with a shock that he couldn't recall going through Salinas or Paso Robles at all.

His hands quivered from hours of gripping the wheel. His eyes were sandy. He used both hands to steady the coffee cup as he ingested the caffeine he needed to keep going. His only thoughts all day had been about Cass. He tossed the empty cup at a trash can and climbed back behind the wheel.

Cass awoke slowly, in a woozy, druggy hangover that was now all too familiar. Her right thigh ached where she'd been jabbed again. If she lived through this nightmare, she'd never take anesthesia, ever, not even for open heart surgery. When she realized she was waking up, she deliberately kept her eyes closed. She recognized the musty smell of damp concrete and old dirt. She didn't want to see that terrible gray cellar. Not now, not ever. How could she survive a second imprisonment here? She would keep her eyes closed forever.

Forever lasted less than five minutes. Curiosity overcame anguish and she opened her eyes, blinked a few times, and squinted until they adjusted. She saw she was lying on the floor and her hands were bound behind her. Her feet were free. The floor was hard and cold. Couldn't the bastards at least have put her on the sofa? She wasn't bound by a soft fabric this time. It was tape, she believed. Wrapped tight. Her hands were numb; she could barely feel them.

A banshee wail filled the room. It throbbed off the walls. At first she didn't know where the sound was coming from, but at last realized it was from her own throat. She'd been unconsciously keening her acid despair.

CHAPTER THIRTY-THREE

Tom finally reached Santa Barbara about eleven and pulled off on Mission Street. He'd driven seven hundred hard miles since leaving Sacramento the night before. He took a motel room and paid in advance. He could barely keep his eyes open. Deciding he needed rest more than food, he fell across the bed fully clothed.

He hears the rapping of snare drums and sees that terrible cornfield at Antietam, puffs of smoke rising beyond the battered stalks from Rebel cannon fire.

He woke with a start when a tiny Latina maid opened the door. "Not now," he said. "Give me an hour, please."

He looked at his watch—My God, he'd slept for eight hours—got up, took a phone book from the night stand, and looked up the address of the Judge Gallery. He jotted it down on a motel scratch pad.

Walking half a block to a convenience store, he bought a throwaway razor, toothbrush, tube of toothpaste and a map of Santa Barbara. He returned to the room, took a shower and shaved before searching out a quick breakfast.

He found the Judge Gallery in Montecito, an upscale suburb. The small, elegant shop had a red brick facade and a forest green awning above arched windows.

And Wilson Judge was at least eighty years old.

The man's movements and speech were slow. He made Tom think of a wounded stork. Paintings and prints were arranged along the walls and elsewhere on easels and stands. Small sculptures were placed here and there. The paintings ran from Neoclassicism and Impressionism to realistic California land and seascapes. Nothing that was non-representational. Not a Rivera or Chagall in sight. Some vases turned out to be reproductions of fifteenth-century Yuan Dynasty porcelains. Tom noticed a curtained doorway in the back.

"I suppose I am what you would call a romantic," Judge rasped in answer to a question, gripping a hardwood cane. His speech struck Tom as meticulously precise, not California-like. When they exchanged names, Tom said he was Roger Lawrence from San Diego. As they chatted, Tom learned that Judge was widowed. This had been his shop since the 1940s, he said, and he'd once owned another in San Francisco, but had sold it. "My traveling days are quite over, Mr. Lawrence."

"You're lucky to be able to combine business with your personal interest," Tom said. "Hobbies are great. Mine is history—oh, and carpentry. There's nothing like building something with wood you've selected and cut yourself."

"I wouldn't know. I would surely bang my finger with the hammer."

Tom couldn't imagine those slender, shaky fingers handling a level or a saw, let alone a hammer. Or lighting a cigarette, for that matter, but that's just what they did next. It surprised him to see the old man pull a cigarette from a gold case. When he flicked his lighter, Tom was tempted to reach over and help to steady the shaky hands.

"Have you always been interested in paintings?"

"Oh yes, I studied art history at Stanford, just before the war. World War II, that is," he added with a chuckle. "I served in the Coast Guard and spent the whole war right out here, looking for Japanese submarines off Santa Barbara. Now they come in here peaceably, the Japanese, and I don't shoot anything at them except Visa slips." He laughed again. "Anyway, I fell in love with this area and have been here ever since. As I said, I'm a romantic."

"You chased Japanese subs? How fascinating. The I-17 was

really something, wasn't it?"

"The I-17? I don't know what . . . oh, excuse me a minute," Judge said, distracted by a UPS delivery man unloading a package out at the curb. He placed his cigarette in a crystal tray, and hobbled outside, his cane tapping with each step, and drew the driver into conversation.

Tom seized the opportunity to slip past the curtain and sneak a peek at the back room. There was a small desk stacked with papers, several crates, and an open door revealing a small bathroom.

He saw a few unassembled picture frames but no carpentry tools, no cut lumber. And no place to hide a prisoner, even if the old man had been physically capable of abducting anybody. He saw Judge's home address on an invoice, memorized it, and hurried back into the main room.

"I'm expecting a package from those people," Judge said a minute later, "but that young man doesn't know anything about it. I must call their office. Now then, what can I show you?"

"I like watercolors, and this is a pretty interesting landscape here," Tom said, indicating a mountain scene with a storm breaking over a solitary cabin. It seemed to symbolize the direction his life had taken. "How much is it?"

"My glasses. Now what've I done with my glasses?"

"In your shirt pocket there, sir."

"Oh yes, thank you. Now, those are by a local artist, a very talented young woman. I am trying to help her get established. She's done some nice things along the waterfront."

Tom admired a painting of a fishing boat unloading its catch at what was probably a local pier. The muted colors and the treatment of the boats and clouds in the background caught his fancy.

"Have you ever been interested in gems or jewelry?" he asked, noting that Judge wore no rings or bracelets.

"No, paintings are my passion."

"Have you ever heard of the Maria Theresa Emerald?"

"The Maria . . . no. The Hope Diamond, of course, and the Star of Africa, but that's about the extent of it. What is this emerald you mentioned?"

"It's supposed to be one of the Austrian crown jewels. I heard about it from my father." Did he catch a slight change in the man's eyes? Knowing Judge had current business with that law firm whose billings he'd seen, Tom asked, "Do you ever have problems with your suppliers? People trying to cheat you?"

"From time to time. Oddly enough, I am pursuing a lawsuit right now. I find that unpleasant, but occasionally I must. The nephew of an old classmate of mine, a lawyer, handles those, as a favor to me."

Tom repeated Judge's home address in his mind so he wouldn't forget. "It's good to have a lawyer you can trust," he said.

"I don't know the man well. He is rather a hustler type. I suppose lawyers have to be that way today. I think he only helps me out because his uncle asks him to."

Tom picked out a small watercolor that was marked seventy dollars.

"I'll only charge you sixty," Judge said, "because I have enjoyed having you here. I like to see young people interested in painting."

Tom handed him three twenties. After Judge wrapped the watercolor, Tom thanked him and left.

The day was dry and hot. A Santa Ana wind was blowing, pushed to the coast from the east. Tom remembered the waiter at the ski resort in Garmisch and his garbled Chandler. "People go a little crazy. It's on nights like this that stifled little husbands feel the edge of a kitchen knife and contemplate their wives' necks."

The memory spooked him as he searched for Judge's street in a graceful, shady section of Montecito. When he found it, the two-story house was stately and rambling, with a red tile roof, pillared veranda, and well-tended lawn and flower gardens.

Tom parked a hundred yards away, approached and knocked on Judge's front door as if he had business there. After waiting a minute, he walked around to the rear grounds, an expanse much too great to be called a back yard. The 49ers could scrimmage in here. The grounds contained a blue and white gazebo and an old, unfilled swimming pool.

He found the alarm system, disabled it, popped open a window and slipped in, envisioning the headlines: **Fired Cop Caught Breaking and Entering**. He hoped to hell there wasn't an interior motion sensor alarm. He didn't know much about those.

Apparently there wasn't.

He spent thirty minutes inspecting the house. It was expensively furnished, and several original oils graced the walls. In the master bedroom he found two photos of a handsome, gray-haired woman, presumably Judge's late wife. There was something sad about Judge living alone in this immense old house.

He examined the four bedrooms, three baths, a den, an exquisite dining room, a utility room, and a three-car garage that sported only a red Oldsmobile dating from the Sixties. The garage didn't contain as much as a saw or wood chisel. Tom had even checked a cobwebby overhead crawl space he'd found above the den.

Nothing on the premises matched Cass's Bible verse. There was no sign of her and nothing to indicate she'd ever been there.

Just as he was about to leave, he heard the wail of a siren, followed by the screech of rubber on the driveway.

Apparently there *was* a motion sensor.

CHAPTER THIRTY-FOUR

The dim overhead light in Cass's cellar was on. Her mind wasn't focusing well, but she knew something was different, very different. Then it struck her. No wonder she wasn't on her old leather sofa. The room was empty—entirely empty. No easy chair, no file cabinet, no picnic table, no chamber pot, and certainly no sofa.

The room was as barren as her hopes. Why the hell had they hauled all this stuff away? They must be really pissed at me.

Tom thought there probably were two cops out there and one would cover the back door. That was the procedure. He was in the hall next to the bedroom where he'd gained entry. He crept into that room, sweat beads popping out on his brow. No sooner had he flattened himself against the wall next to the window than he saw a woman in a blue uniform rush past, unsnapping the leather holster on her hip.

He silently counted to five, then slid the window up and hopped out. Forty feet away stood a copse of trees and a whitewashed wood fence about five feet high. Tom dashed across that space, grasped the top of the fence with both hands, swung a leg up and pulled himself over.

He landed in a neighbor's flower bed and found himself face to face with a wide-eyed woman in overalls. She gasped, dropped a garden trowel, and backed off.

"Who-who are you? What's going on at Mr. Judge's?"

Tom flashed his badge. "Possible house prowl. Seen anybody suspicious around here?"

"Uh, gosh, um . . . no."

"We thought he might have cut through here." Tom put the badge away quickly. "Keep your eyes open, ma'am. Give us a call if you see anything out of the ordinary. Don't bother those two cops over there. They're cadets. Best you call the station house."

He made for the street.

"Will this be on the news tonight, officer?" she called after him.

Tom raised his hands in a "Who knows?" gesture without turning around.

Reaching the sidewalk, he strolled casually back to his car. "Santa Barbara!" he muttered, feeling lower than Death Valley. He didn't speed up till he was two blocks away.

Back on the freeway heading north, he flipped on the radio.

"*Mama said there'd be days like this*," the Shirelles sang. "*There'd be days like this, my mama said . . .*"

It was dark when Tom finally reached Sacramento and the Land Park neighborhood. He drove past his house twice, looking for stakeout cars or anything else suspicious. He fully expected to be arrested.

The first time, he thought he saw a flicker of light moving inside the house. On the second pass, he was sure. Someone was in there with a flashlight.

He parked the car a few doors down. His .357 Magnum was drawn as he entered the circle of blackness created by the old oak tree in the front yard. He circled the house stealthily, walking on his toes. Whoever was in there was in the rear now, in the kitchen.

The back door was just off the kitchen, separated from it by a small alcove used as a pantry, which contained floor-to-ceiling shelves and a bottled water dispenser.

Tom tried the door. It was unlocked. The prowler must have gained entry here. Tom gently pulled the door open and sprang into the black alcove, the .357 out in front of him, gripped by both hands, the safety off.

"Don't move," he shouted.

He saw the flashlight drop in an arc of light and heard it crash to the floor.

"Don't shoot." A woman's voice, a familiar voice.

"Mrs. Potter?"

"Tom? It's you?" his neighbor gasped. "You scared me to death."

"I'm real sorry, Mrs. P." Tom stepped into the room, shoved the pistol under his belt and hugged the widow's trembling body. "Didn't mean to frighten you. When a cop comes home and sees a flashlight in his dark house, his training kicks in."

"The power was out for an hour today," she said, still breathing hard. "Your circuit breakers must have clicked off. I couldn't find them to save my life, so I had to use my flashlight to feed our cat here. Didn't know if you'd be home tonight or not."

Tom felt terrible. The gray-haired widow was a wonderful neighbor and practically family.

"The circuit box is in the garage. I'll go reset 'em. Are you sure you're okay?"

"Yes, I'm all right now." She stepped back and rested a hand on her chest. "This is a pretty sturdy old heart. When did you say Cass will be back?"

"Soon, Mrs. P. Very soon." *I hope.*

Later, after microwaving some frozen lasagna, Tom stroked Orbison, who purred out his appreciation. "I guess I've still got two friends around here," he said, "you and Mrs. Potter."

That night, thinking back to his trip to Washington, he concocted a plan.

By now Tom would rather have a root canal than another long drive, but in the morning he was back behind the wheel. This time, after a stop at his safe deposit box at the bank, he was making the ninety-mile trip down I-80 to San Francisco. He found himself humming Willie Nelson's *On the Road Again*.

After crossing the Bay Bridge, he took the first exit, passed Market Street, turned left on California, and stopped in front of No. 685, the Federated Bank of Switzerland. The curb was red but he pulled down his visor, showing Sacramento Police ID. He was inside the bank for almost an hour.

Driving back to Sacramento, he felt a little better. At least one important item was checked off his list.

After stopping for a taco and a Pepsi in Davis, he got home about two o'clock. When he opened the front door, something immediately caught his eye: a small slip of paper, lying on the floor beneath the mail slot. He scooped it up and saw the now familiar laser-printed capitals. GO TO THE CORNER OF 16TH AND J AT 3:00 P.M.

"This is it, Orby," he said to his cat. "We're getting down to the short hairs."

Tom arrived at 16th and J two minutes before three. He found himself in front of Memorial Auditorium, a yellow brick affair that had reopened after renovations to satisfy the earthquake codes.

"They don't make 'em like they used to," he'd told Cass one night when they'd gone to a basketball game.

"This place has a lot more character than Arco Arena," she had answered.

A stream of cars passed but few pedestrians. At two minutes past three, a dirty white minicompact stopped at the curb and a spiky-haired teenager hopped out. Baggy denims, black high-top sneakers, tattoos, nose ring. He swaggered up to Tom and handed him an envelope. "Here, man."

Tom grabbed his arm.

"No man, back off. Don't ask me nothin'."

Realizing this errand boy wouldn't know anything about Cass, Tom let him go. Besides, he probably had a switch blade as long as the Tower Bridge.

The boy jumped behind the wheel and squealed away, leaving a cloud of scorched rubber. The car had no plates. Tom had memorized the kid's appearance but knew it would lead to nothing. That punk had been hired to deliver the envelope and nothing else. He probably hadn't even seen the person who gave him his orders.

As he walked to his car, Tom looked around closely, as usual. He didn't think he was being followed or observed.

He slid behind the wheel and stared at the envelope. It was the same square invitation-style envelope he'd seen twice before from these people. He ripped it open.

The laser-printed message said: BE AT PAY PHONE AT GAS STATION MARCONI & FULTON 3:20. ALONE. ANSER ON 3RD RING. Tom pondered the misspelling.

Three-twenty. They're clever. That gives me no time to round up some help. These people learned something that Saturday morning at the zoo, didn't they? He had enough time to get there by 3:20 but none to spare.

He found the phone booth with no trouble, but a post-it note said OUT-OF-ORDER. Another clever touch, making sure no one else would be using the phone at the appointed time.

He looked at his watch. 3:18. The next two minutes dragged. He jumped when at last the phone rang. During the first two rings, he looked around carefully, and leaned into the privacy shell. He answered on the third ring.

"Yes?"

"Cavanaugh?"

"No, it's the Easter Bunny."

"Listen, funny man, do you want that woman back or not?" The voice sounded vaguely familiar.

"You know I do. Well . . . It's your dime."

"The exchange will be made at an abandoned farm up near Nicolaus."

Who was this? Tom thought maybe he'd heard that voice before. It wasn't Roy Oakley, he was sure of that.

"It's on the old Garden Highway, just off 99, the road to Yuba City. When you get off 99, take a left at the T, and go one-point-eight miles. Pass under the high-power lines. You'll see a green farmhouse, a red barn and a couple of small outbuildings on the left-hand side of the road. You got that?"

"Yeah."

"That's the place. Friday night at eight. Come alone and unarmed. Pull any stunts and we'll hand you your girlfriend's head. Soon as we have the item and verify it's the real thing, you'll get your lady back, simple as that. You got it?"

"I heard you."

"Don't be dumb again. If you—"

"I'll be there. I don't want you people armed, either." Tom hung up, still trying to place the voice. He pulled a card from his wallet and jotted down the directions he'd just been given. Highway 99, left at the T, all that.

Thoughts tumbled over one another as he drove home. When he reached the house, he couldn't remember any of the turns or stops he must have made to get there.

He pulled a beer from the refrigerator, popped it open, and sank into a kitchen chair. For the next ten minutes he focused on all that had happened and what he'd do next.

The handoff would be a tricky thing. Was there any way he could have backup at that farm without screwing it up and further endangering Cass? He'd like to discuss this with his father.

He walked to his rolltop desk, pulled out the phone book and looked up the art department at American River College. He called a friend, an instructor there, and they spoke for a few minutes, during which Tom said, "Yes, I have some photos."

After he hung up, he made up his mind. He'd go to Novato to talk things over with his father. He no longer worried about leaving town. If he could drive as far as Weaverville and Santa Barbara without getting locked up by the feds, he could sure as hell do the sixty miles to Novato.

He wolfed down a peanut butter sandwich, put some food in Orbison's bowl, and left.

Driving to Novato, he detoured out of the way to check out the abandoned farm near Nicolaus. Nicolaus was twenty-five miles and a century out of town, a country hamlet withering in the age of freeways and corporate farming.

The directions he'd been given on the phone proved precise, down to the last tenth of a mile. The farm and its buildings were exactly where he was told they'd be, on the left side of the road on land rising gently eastward from a levee along the Sacramento River.

He rolled past without slowing down. Late afternoon sun burnished the house and barn, the outbuildings, and two round metal silos with conical tops like coolie hats. He was tempted to stop for a closer look, but the place was probably being watched.

As he drove away, he made a mental note to call a real estate agent he knew and see if he could find out who owned this place. Then, a haunting thought. That graduate student's report said that Prince Rudolf had grown fond of a tree-shaded spot just east of the river about twenty miles north of Sutter's Fort. *Which would be right about here!*

Reaching Novato by seven, he parked a block from his father's house and approached on foot in the twilight, relieved that Roy Oakley's Jeep wasn't there.

Once inside, Tom spent an hour discussing the situation with his dad after turning the volume up high on the TV. Even with that precaution, some of their communication was by writing. Reading one of Tom's notes, his father's eyes widened in shock and he whispered hoarsely, "The farm is *where?*"

After Tom left, Desmond Cavanaugh reached over to the night stand and pulled the phone into his lap. Resting a moment from the effort, he tapped some numbers and said, "You get your ass over here right now. No screwing around. Right now!"

His temples throbbed as he shakily replaced the receiver. His heartbeat was erratic, the room reeling. He gulped huge bites of air through his mouth to supplement the oxygen force-fed to his nose by plastic tubes.

Finally, the dizziness abated and he began to breathe more normally. *Just hold out one more day, you used-up old ticker*. As he lay in his lonely bed waiting for his telephone command to be carried out, memories flooded his old cop's mind. Memories of baby Tom nursing at his mother's breast. Memories of the toddler he became, falling often but his little jaw set in determination. Determination that he would walk for himself, walk like his older brother Michael could walk.

As the boys grew, Tom thought he'd kept his resentment of Michael to himself, but his father had seen it. He remembered Tom's frustration over all the time he'd spent instructing Michael. How Tom had taken up basketball because he, the father, knew more about football and baseball and had concentrated on teaching those games to Michael.

Maybe Tom had been right; perhaps he'd unconsciously favored his first born, giving Michael the best of his time and attention. But, God knows, he hadn't meant to. He hoped that now, all these years later, Tom had come to know it hadn't been intentional.

Then it was Tom's first date. The shy, furtive phone calls to the girl, taking pains that other family members didn't listen in. Then the senior prom and the excitement of his first rented tuxedo. His mother helping him tie the tie because he was embarrassed to let his father do it.

Tears formed in Desmond Cavanaugh's eyes. Now Tom was going off to San Diego State, whereas Michael had stayed close to home, going to Cal, just across the bay. Tom surprising the hell out of him by becoming a cop, following in his footsteps. He was never able to tell Tom how much he'd hurt for him when his ill-fated marriage to Sharon had fallen apart.

More tears now as he recalled some of Tom's eloquent graveside words at his mother's funeral. "Rest well, dear lady, you're the kindest person I ever knew." God, how Desmond Cavanaugh missed that good woman.

Then came Cass. He'd liked Cass more every time he'd seen her. Unfailing good humor, magnetic personality, great inner strength. How he wished he could live to see Tom marry her. And now this terrible mess he'd gotten them into over the emerald. He wished he'd never been an MP in Germany and that he'd never heard of that place called Nuremberg.

Desmond Cavanaugh prayed to God that this business would end well. He twisted his mouth angrily and shook his head. His oxygen tubes jiggled. If it was the last thing he did, he'd do everything he could to help it end well. And it probably *would* be the last thing he'd do.

CHAPTER THIRTY-FIVE

C ass searched the room again with her eyes. Even her purse was gone. She'd managed to keep it with her so long, and now she didn't even have that. She noticed with a shock that she was wearing baggy denim pants that she'd never seen before. *Somebody changed my pants? Jesus God, that pisses me off.* Her top, now sweaty and torn, was the same silk blouse she'd worn for days.

What had happened after that man pulled up to the lumber mill? She tried to piece it together, tried hard, but it wasn't coming. Her memory bank held only shadowy snippets of being dragged across the parking lot, and the dog, that huge black Doberman, her new friend—ha!—romping at her side. That's where her thin tape of memory ran out.

It was nearly ten when Tom dragged himself up the steps of his home. Fighting off fatigue, he called the real estate agent who'd sold Cass and him their house. He apologized for the hour, described the farm near Nicolaus, and asked the agent if he could find out who owned it.

Next, he called the FBI office and left a voice message for Agent Elwell. He said there were several new developments and it was urgent that they meet the next day, Thursday. He repeated his phone number twice, although he knew very well that Elwell already had it.

In the morning when Elwell hadn't called by eleven, Tom said, "The hell with it." He'd been talking to himself a lot lately. "Try to do it yourself and they nail your ass—try to cooperate and they ignore you." He made two calls. The first was to Dick McAuliffe, his ex-cop friend who owned a helicopter school. The second was to an acquaintance who owned a photo lab. "Yeah, late this afternoon. Great."

Tom went to the dining room table and began cleaning his Smith & Wesson .357 Magnum and his .25-caliber Astra ankle gun, although neither needed it.

He collected his camera, a telephoto lens, and a pair of binoculars, and drove toward Sacramento Executive Airport. He had company. A beige sedan had picked him up a block from home and remained in his rearview mirror all the way along Freeport Boulevard, always hanging back with two or three cars in between, but always there.

Inside the small parking lot, Tom made a couple of quick turns, and stopped a hundred yards from the administration building. He looked all about, then spotted the sedan. It was two rows over, moving slowly.

He inched his Honda through a small pedestrian gate. One of his side mirrors scraped, but he got through into a smaller lot marked AUTHORIZED PERSONNEL ONLY. In his rearview mirror, he soon saw the sedan blocked, unable to get through the tiny opening. Tom gunned past a row of private hangars and sheds, out another exit and back onto Freeport.

Ten minutes later he returned a second time and drove directly into the hangar at Dick McAuliffe's helicopter school. He was pretty sure he'd gotten in clean.

Before long, he and McAuliffe were airborne. They clamored north toward the little town of Nicolaus, the Robinson 44 helicopter passing a mile east of Sacramento's main airport. They followed Highway 99 over patchy flat farmland, sectioned out in corn, alfalfa and rice. The sun was bright and it was hot under the plexiglass bubble, even with an open hatch.

When they reached the farm, Tom shouted over the rotor wash for McAuliffe to hover several hundred yards to the south. This was far enough away, he hoped, that the helicopter's numbers couldn't be read from the farm, but close enough to conduct his surveillance. The slapping of the blades could be heard for miles but that couldn't be helped.

He knew he could have made this recon unnoticed in a fixed-wing plane at a higher altitude, but he wouldn't have been able to make the drops he'd planned at just the right spots. So he'd decided, what the hell, let 'em see the copter.

Although the farm buildings looked to be vacant, crops were being grown there—you didn't waste good valley farmland. Tom saw a field of spring corn, another of alfalfa, and a rectangle of nut trees, probably almonds. The bottomland nearest the river was growing rice. The acreage there was diked off geometrically and flooded.

He lifted his binoculars to his eyes, thinking, *this could be the most important piece of real estate in my life*. The farmhouse, a faded green, two-story clapboard job with a pillared front porch, was boarded up and had a sad air about it. A barn and a stable, both wanting for paint. An old-fashioned windmill. Two round tin grain silos. A weathered chicken coop with a sagging roof that was about to call it a day.

But there was something that didn't belong. A small white chapel. Sending a shiver through him. It looked like the old Dunkard Church at Antietam. Some God-fearing farmer must have built that chapel for his workers.

Tom pulled out his camera, attached the telephoto, and began clicking off pictures. He didn't see any people, not even a farmhand, but assumed someone was there, staring at the helicopter.

Two-story farmhouse. Click. Windmill. Barn. Click. Stable. Click. Fenced-in livestock pen. Chicken coop. Click. A kid's rope swing dangling from a big walnut tree in the yard. Click.

Untended, weed-choked garden plot. Click. Chapel. Click. Click again. And so on for twenty-four frames.

He put the camera down and propped a notepad on his knee. McAuliffe watched curiously while maneuvering the cyclic control and anti-torque pedals to keep the R44 in a static hover.

Tom began sketching. He made the map as complete as possible, including fences, gates and trees, estimating the distances between each. At last, he looked over and gave McAuliffe a hand signal. The chopper wheeled north, behind the farmhouse, and hovered over a spot between the house and one of the silos.

Beside the house, behind an untrimmed hedge deep in shade, a pair of binoculars was lowered, and a man moved slowly toward the copter's new position. He was careful to stay in the shade.

Tom dropped a military smoke marker from the open door, and the copter immediately swung to the south. When a large billow of diversionary green smoke roiled up from the open ground between the house and silo, Tom dropped a small cloth satchel into the cornfield. It fell into the corn at a spot opposite the front of the barn. The copter wheeled out over the Garden Highway and clattered toward Sacramento.

"John Singleton Mosby," Tom said.

"Huh?"

"Oh, nothing, Dick." Colonel John Singleton Mosby was a Confederate cavalryman who'd led a band of guerrillas behind Union lines in the Civil War. It was said that Mosby once hid military supplies in a place where he expected to need them in a future battle.

Driving east on Fair Oaks Boulevard later that afternoon, Tom got an uneasy feeling about Orbison. Maybe he'd find his cat dead when he got home. Killed by *them*. His stomach churned. They didn't have to do that to show they meant business. He *knew* that. He hoped to hell this premonition was all wrong.

He pulled into a strip mall in front of a photo lab owned by a man with whom he sometimes played pickup basketball at the Y. Tom's roll of 35-millimeter Tri-X, black and white film was in the pocket of his denim shirt.

Thirty minutes later, using a loupe for magnification, he checked a sheet of contact prints, squinting against the glass like a jeweler. With a grease pencil, he marked several shots for enlargement. On five of the frames, he asked for extreme blowups, cropping as tight as possible on certain features.

His friend entered the darkroom to make the prints. A red bulb above the door winked on when he closed it.

Tom took a seat at a metal table and pulled from his shirt pocket the map he'd drawn of the farm. He pushed aside a pile of transparencies and a light box to give him room. He studied the map for several minutes. Added a few lines and made some notes in the margin, drawing arrows from two of them to specific features on the map.

He borrowed the phone and called the art department at American River College.

When the darkroom door opened and Tom saw the prints, he was not unsatisfied with his amateur debut in aerial reconnaissance.

"I owe you," he said.

"Damn right, sixty bucks and a beer."

"You've got a raincheck on the beer, but here's the sixty," Tom said, writing out a check. Were they monitoring his checking account? At this point he didn't give a damn anymore. He left with a sackful of eight-by-ten and eleven-by-fourteen prints.

Minutes later, as he walked toward his front door, he feared he might find Orbison's bloody body hanging by the tail from the portico. But it wasn't. Inside, healthy as ever, Orbison lay curled up on a sofa.

"Meet King Paranoia," Tom said, tossing his sack of photos on the dining room table. He quickly spread them out, alongside his sketched map of the farm. Orbison, who'd hopped on a cane-backed chair, pawed curiously at one of the prints, and gave Tom a what-are-you-up-to look.

"That's what I've got to figure out, buckaroo." Various parts of the farm looked up at Tom from the table in stark black and white, defiantly it seemed, daring him to draw up his plan. It was Thursday evening. Whatever he came up with would either succeed or fail tomorrow night.

If it came down to a fight, he'd be alone against several men. He pulled a Civil War encyclopedia from a bookshelf and turned to Stonewall Jackson's Shenandoah Valley campaign of 1862. Against enormous odds, Jackson and his one little Confederate army faced the three separate Union armies of Banks, McDowell and Fremont. By adept maneuvering, he outflanked and defeated them all, one by one.

Tom made a few notes, put the book away, and began to study his photos and map. He started to make a notation on the map when something in an eleven-by-fourteen caught his eye. Twin points of light, like cat's eyes in the dark. They appeared in some shrubbery beside the farmhouse. Tom rummaged in his desk until he found a large magnifying glass. He looked closely at the two bright specks. *Very dark and grainy. Hard to tell, but they could be eyeglasses.* His mouth formed a grim smile. *Or binoculars.*

"Who are you?" he said.

CHAPTER THIRTY-SIX

om again called his art instructor friend at American River College. "That's great," he said, and made arrangements to come by the instructor's office in the morning.

He put his map and photos aside, went to the bookshelf and scanned the rows until he found Kerenyi's *The Gods of the Greeks*. He pulled it open and checked the index for Cassandra, the Trojan woman who could foretell the future. Cassandra's powers enabled her to see what the Greeks were up to, and she warned her people not to accept that wooden horse, to keep the gates closed. When they didn't listen and Troy fell, Cassandra was kidnapped and taken to Greece as a slave. And then was murdered by Aegisthus.

Tom tossed the book aside. He went to the bedroom and got out his pistols.

Cass awoke to someone shaking her shoulders. When she opened her eyes, she found herself staring into a black ski mask. She shuddered and gasped. Madame X had a hand on her shoulder and was prodding her out of an edgy sleep. Cass saw that she'd been sleeping sitting up, her back propped against a wall, hands still taped behind her. She felt stiff all over.

"I brought you some soup," Madame X said. "It's all they'll let you have. You bit the hell out of Dave, er, the guy. They're pretty ticked off."

"Oh, poor babies." Cass was woozy. Her leg ached where she'd been jabbed. She'd persuaded herself that if she lived through this nightmare, she'd never, ever, let a needle pierce her flesh again. *Dave*? The woman had said Dave.

"Come on now, eat your soup. It's going to have to hold you for awhile, but this will all be over tomorrow."

"Tomorrow?" Cass said weakly, catching a whiff of something smelling like chicken broth.

"Yeah, tomorrow. It's all set. Lover boy's got the word. Open up, princess."

Madame X lifted a spoon to Cass's lips. She accepted it slowly and held it, her tongue and mouth tasting with great caution. Weak chicken noodle soup, probably from a can. Well, better than nothing. In fact, pretty good. She swallowed, then parted her lips for another spoonful.

As the hand came up with the spoon, Cass saw the elegant gold ring on the index finger, the ring with a miniature watch inlaid upon it.

"I don't know how the hell you dug out around that deadbolt," Madame X said. "That was pretty amazing. They're really pissed, I can tell you."

Why did she say *they*, not *we*? Cass wondered. Who else is in this besides Madame X and The Shadow? Oh right, the gray-haired man who drove her here.

"You're not such a bad kid after all. Tougher'n shit, that's for sure."

Why was this woman dropping some of her bluster? Even sounding a little sympathetic.

Cass took another swallow of the lukewarm soup, and another. She still felt weak and sick, but the warmth and nourishment helped some.

Like crashing cymbals, her mind hit on something. *Hell!* She'd seen The Shadow's face. And she'd had an even better look at the guy who gave her a ride. She could identify them. They'd never release her now. They'd have to get rid of her. And Madame X knew it. That's why the change had come over her.

Damn, it would've been better if she hadn't been able to sneak out. She lost her appetite, shook her head at the next offered spoonful.

"I don't suppose you could cut this tape off my wrists?"

"No way. They'd never let me."

"For awhile at least? Let me get some feeling back in my hands, then tape me up again."

"Huh uh, no can do."

Cass had a terrible thirst, despite the soup. Which reminded her, she didn't have to pee right now, but knew she would before long, and there was no chamber pot. She didn't even want to think about *that*.

The brown eyes behind the ski mask were troubled. Cass stared into them, searching deeply. Somehow she knew this woman.

The two faces, inches apart, one pale and worn, the other masked in black wool, inspected each other for several seconds. They looked deeper than the unblinking eyes, far behind the corneas and pupils and retinas. They understood. Each had a terrible knowledge, a dread of things to come.

For Tom, the time for sober reflection was over. Now he was focused. He'd thought a lot in the last two weeks about his life and what it meant, what purpose he was serving here. A couple of times, he'd pulled a quotation from his memory bank. James Stewart, in the old Civil War film, *Shenandoah*. "If we don't try, we don't do, and if we don't do, why are we here?"

Tom was going to try. And do. He was in his old gray Honda, driving north on State 70-99. To get Cass. To get his life back. *Their lives*.

In his head, he went over the layout again, and his plan. He'd memorized every detail of the farm, had studied the photo blowups until they were etched in his mind. He wished he could have backup, but that would blow everything. He'd tried to think of every plan *they* could use. Every possible way they could position themselves. Where vehicles could be placed. And people. How possible escape routes could be blocked. He'd thought of everything. Hadn't he?

The days were long now with Daylight Time in effect. It was after seven, but the sun was still up, just over the ridges east of Lake Berryessa, casting evening shadows on the towns of Woodland and Knights Landing—and Nicolaus. And the old farm across the Garden Highway from the river.

He wore jeans and a loose cotton shirt. On the seat beside him was a small cheap flash camera and a brown paper sack looking as innocent as a school kid's lunch. It weighed more than a sack lunch, though. Inside was a hard, cold, dangerous polyhedron.

He was on full alert. He eyed every car and truck suspiciously. Some flying bugs splattered themselves to death on his windshield.

The brightness faded as he approached the fork where 99 parted from 70. The sun had dipped behind the Vaca Hills but some daylight remained. A thin scattering of clouds reflected deep golds and reds above the horizon, but Tom barely noticed. He could admire sunsets the rest of his life, but not tonight.

He turned left at the fork. Roadside stands and small farm buildings blurred past. At last his turnoff came into view. The sky had descended into a moody purple by the time he took the Nicolaus ramp. He flicked on the headlights. Had he been followed? He didn't think so. He'd watched very closely. He turned left at the T and drove toward his destiny.

He ran down his mental checklist again. He was as ready as he'd ever be.

The car passed beneath the high-tension wires that brought electricity to the Bay Area from distant dynamos in the mountains, and the high, grass-covered levee on his right that held back the Sacramento River during flood seasons. He thought about the farm just ahead. Was Cass there? She'd better be. Was she all right?

She'd better be.

It was nearly dark now, the headlights forming a pool of light in front of the car. Tom flipped on the high beams and saw a jackrabbit scurry across the road. That's right, he thought, hustle home to your family. They'll be glad to see you. That's what I'm doing too, buddy, hustling to my family. My future family. My future . . . period.

Reflectors on the roadside fence danced in the high beams as he approached the farm. His hands clenched and unclenched on the steering wheel.

One-point-eight miles. He slowed as the farm came into view. A white rail fence circled the farm yard, with a broad gate in front. The gate was open. Tom turned onto the gravel driveway. He rolled down the window and soft spring air swept in a pungent mix of smells: wet earth, growing plants, manure, diesel fuel. Over the crunch of tires turning slowly on gravel, he heard the croak of a frog.

The boarded-up house, with a flower bed grown wild and a huge walnut tree in front, loomed ghostly and cold on the left. The rope swing he'd seen from the air hung limp from the tree. On the right, beyond the windmill, a cornfield stretched off to the east. The car moved at a crawl as he scrutinized the ground. In the rear stood the barn, the other outbuildings, the beginnings of an alfalfa field. He felt the hair on the back of his neck bristle as he spotted the white stucco chapel straight ahead on a small rise. The one he'd seen in his dreams.

A pole light near the windmill threw out a puddle of mercury-vapor brightness. So did another light on the barn. It was murky in between and would get more so as total night descended.

He saw two cars, a small white compact a hundred yards ahead, parked in the driveway, and a dark limousine much farther back, near the chapel, the limo partially hidden by rows of corn. The gravel stopped back there and the driveway became a dirt lane that bent off to the right, into the fields. He tried not to let the uncanny resemblance to the Battlefield at Antietam unnerve him. All this place needed was some old brass cannon and granite monuments.

There was just enough light for Tom, in the rearview mirror, to see another vehicle, a dark van, pull into the driveway behind him. Its lights were out. It made a sharp ninety-degree turn, and backed up a few feet to block the drive. He had expected something like that.

Almost to the farmhouse now. He braked the car to a stop, clicked off the lights, and let the engine run another few seconds, an old battery-saving habit, before shutting it off. Then he slipped the keys in his pocket. He controlled his breathing and told himself to stay calm.

He scanned the terrain slowly, thoroughly, left to right, and, in the mirror, took another look at the van blocking his escape route. The white compact car was seventy yards ahead, facing in his direction.

He thought Cass was probably in the limo in the rear.

He gathered up the camera from the seat beside him, strapped it around his neck and right shoulder, picked up the paper sack and waited. He placed his left hand on the door handle. It was their move now. After a long moment a man stepped out of the driver's side of the small car up ahead.

The guy stood in shadow between the two snowy patches of light. His silhouette was tall and bulky, with major shoulders. Looked like a steelworker or a tight end. Facing Tom's car, his hatless head an oval of blackness, the man took three steps forward. Then the passenger door opened and a second man got out. This guy was much smaller, and Tom caught a glint of eyeglasses reflected in the light from the barn as he stood and faced forward.

"Cavanaugh," called the one who looked like a tight end.

The crickets and frogs, who'd been making quite a din, stopped their evening concert as if the voice had been a conductor's baton.

Here we go.

As Tom opened the door and stepped out, he adjusted the shoulder strap so the camera hung behind him. He knew hidden guns were trained on him. A warm breeze from the east kissed his face. It was the *Föhn*, or at least California's version of it. The wind with its overabundance of positive ions that made people go crazy.

He stepped slowly forward, as did the two men facing him. They approached each other like gunfighters in an old Western. Feet crunched on gravel. There was no other sound anywhere. Three or four seconds passed.

"You have it?" The Tight End called.

Tom answered by holding up the sack in his right hand. "She's here, right?"

"Yeah. You'd better be unarmed."

"I said I'd be. You better be too."

In his left hand, the smaller of the two men carried what looked like a flashlight. He was taking mincing little steps, frightened steps.

When they were forty feet apart, the Tight End stopped, his face still in shadow, backlit by the light on the barn. The smaller man hesitated, then continued on. He wore a suit and tie. At last he reached Tom, who'd never seen this little guy before.

"Pat him down like I showed you," the Tight End commanded. "Be sure he hasn't got a gun."

"I have to do this, sir," the little man said as he felt Tom's ribs, hips and pockets. The hands were small and delicate. Tom figured he wasn't comfortable touching people.

"Is he clean?" the Tight End barked. "Be sure."

"Y-yes."

"Okay, Cavanaugh, show him what you've got. He's a jeweler.

He'll check it out."

"Not till I see Cass, he won't."

"She's here, I told you. We made a deal."

"I want her right up here. With us. Now."

The Tight End turned, put two fingers in his mouth and whistled. The profile was vaguely familiar. Tom knew that man.

Far to the rear, near the little chapel, the limousine sat black and ominous-looking. Someone stepped from the limo, hesitated, and finally started slowly forward. It was too far for Tom to tell if it was Cass, but he could see it was a woman's size and shape when the form was momentarily silhouetted against the much lighter chapel. He knew individual walking patterns were distinctive, hard to disguise. But this person seemed to be in pain or great fear, or both. Seemed to be stumbling, feeling her way blindly. The arms weren't swinging with the footsteps. They were behind the body. Probably tied behind her.

It must be Cass, he persuaded himself.

"Okay, that's your woman back there."

"She's not close enough."

The Tight End whistled again and the woman moved ahead, still slowly, favoring her right leg. An ankle injury? She was almost even with the barn now and her face would soon be bathed in light. Then he'd know. It took forever for the slow-moving form to come out of the inky shadow of the barn, but at last it did.

A dark hood covered her face. She wore the same pinstriped suit slacks Cass had worn the day she disappeared. Now they were ragged and torn.

"Close enough," the Tight End called, and the woman stopped. "There she is. Now let's see the emerald."

"Cass," Tom shouted. "Cass, are you all right?"

No answer.

"Take off the hood," Tom called.

"No can do. We can't let her know where she is. You can see

it's her, damn it."

She took another step forward. The auburn hair jutting from the bottom of the hood was unmistakably Cass's. *She's been through hell,* Tom thought, *but thank God she's alive.*

"Cass, are you all right?"he repeated.

"Yes," she answered in a hoarse croak.

"You're sure? Say something else."

"Yes." Again, a mere rasp.

They've hurt her. Beat her up pretty bad. Damn it, they'll pay for this.

Swallowing needles of anger, Tom handed the sack to the small man, who took it and gingerly opened it. He pulled out a small block of something wrapped in tissue paper. He tore away the paper and balanced the stone in his hand. Green rays danced from it, glittering in the distant light from the barn. The man pushed his glasses up on his forehead. He pulled a jeweler's loupe from a suit pocket and turned on a flashlight.

He turned the stone over and over, examining it closely.

Jesus, he was taking forever. Tom's heart beating now like a Civil War drum, a furious tattoo against his chest. *Ketrack-ketrack-ketrack. Attack, Tom. Attack, Tom. Attack Attack Attack, Tom.*

"This is rather good," the man said at last. Softly. "Not a bad fake." Then, loud enough so the Tight End could hear, "This is a nice bauble, but it's not an emerald."

CHAPTER THIRTY-SEVEN

T he hell it isn't," Tom shouted. "What are you guys trying to pull?"

"What are *you* trying to pull?" the Tight End bellowed, reaching a shadowy hand across his chest. For a gun no doubt.

Tom dived to his right, rolling in the dirt at the side of the lane, just as he'd practiced in his mind. When he came up, he was beside the cornfield. "Cass, get down," he yelled.

He hoped the camera hadn't broken. He crouched against the first row of corn, low enough so the stalks shaded him from the yard light behind him.

"That's the Austrian emerald, pal," he shouted. "No pipsqueak jeweler can tell you different. Now let's have Cass."

The Tight End took a few steps backward.

"Get out of there, Cass. Run."

Too late. The Tight End grabbed her by the arm and moved behind her. She was still a hostage—and now a shield. He tugged her off the roadway, stepping back into the shadow of the barn, but not before Tom saw the pistol in his right hand.

"What about it, Crabtree?" the Tight End called to the jeweler.

"It, it's . . . not the Maria Theresa, or any other emerald. It's a fake. It . . . it's glass."

A gunshot. A bullet kicked up dust inches from Tom's leg. The shot had come from *behind* him. He dived into the rows of corn. One of the punks in the van blocking the lane had tried to take him out! The bastards. The goddamn Rebels.

"Knock it off," the Tight End shouted. "Hold your fire, damn it. Crabtree, you sure?" Tom still hadn't got a good look at the big man's face, but the voice was familiar, maybe the guy who'd called him.

"Y-yes, yes," came the jeweler's quavering answer. The gunshot had scared the bejesus out of him. "N-no question at all." Tom, a few feet inside the field, could see the little man in the center of the lane, exposed and shaking.

Tom began crawling on hands and knees, searching. At last his right hand found what he was after.

"Cavanaugh, you lying bastard," the Tight End screamed. "We told you, no more bullshit. You've got exactly thirty seconds to come out of there with that rock."

Tom opened the cloth satchel he'd dropped from Dick McAuliffe's helicopter and pulled out his .357 Magnum. He scurried deeper into the field. After about forty feet, he turned and moved parallel to the driveway, to get behind Cass and the big bastard with the gun in her back. This was harder, because now he was cutting across the rows. It took time to step between stalks quietly.

When he figured he'd gone far enough, he turned and crept up a row. He'd almost reached the driveway when he heard the Tight End. "That's it. Thirty seconds. You've had it, Cavanaugh. Waste the field, boys!"

More gunshots. Tom knew they couldn't see him. They were firing blindly, trying for a lucky hit. He poked his head out for a look. Cass and her captor were still in the shadow of the barn. Bullets sang through the air. *Whap, whap, whap!* Hitting cornstalks and dirt.

"Over here, buddy," Tom shouted.

The Tight End turned and saw him. As he did, Tom clicked the camera's shutter with his right hand, shielding his eyes with his left—the Magnum was tucked in his belt. The flash popped. The Tight End was blinded.

"Cass, go! Run toward my voice." Tom had just accomplished two things. Pinpointing his enemy, and disabling him—for a few seconds anyway. Trouble was, he'd given away his own position. He jumped two feet to the side and clicked off another picture. This time the flash caught the Tight End crouching, confused, with Cass several feet away, moving awkwardly, hands lashed behind her.

It took Tom two seconds to pull out the Magnum and fire twice, and another to dive to the ground. He heard, "Shit! Ah, damn it," as he rolled back among the cornstalks. He'd hit the big man somewhere, but how bad?

More shots tracked Tom. The people shooting at him were some distance away, firing on the run, coming from each side and getting closer. They'd expect him to move east, he guessed, away from the farmhouse and barn, so he ran the other way, back west toward the highway. This time he shoved through the corn, his sounds covered by gunfire and shouts.

Cornfield. Bullets. Tom grew dizzy as he ran. His mind swirled. He thought he heard a sergeant's voice. A sergeant in the Twelfth Massachusetts.

More bullets peppered the field. He was starting to lose focus. *Hold on*, he told himself. He had to keep hold of reality till he finished this business, got Cass back. Have to make them pay. Have to get Cass back . . . get Cass back . . . get . . . who was Cass?

A hot breeze rife with a bittersweet stench trembles across his senses and quickly dies. The night rushes at him, opening like the mouth of a tunnel. A blur of energy envelops him. Make them pay. Make them pay for Second Bull Run.

He takes stock of his situation. He's hit and wounded that big damned Rebel. But, Judas Priest, now he's hemmed in. The Rebs have this whole shebang surrounded. Is this the end of the line for Company C? They've been through so blasted much together.

He swivels his head, scanning the whole field.

All right, there! He has one of the Rebs now. He's in the field, coming up from the east, the rear of the farm. Tom sees him clearly. And this fella sees him. He's rushing him, dashing with his shoulders hunched low, pistol drawn.

Pistol? All-fired peculiar. Why isn't the Reb carrying a rifle or musket? He was closer now.

How many shots left in the revolver? Tom stares at the Magnum. What the devil is this?

He's used a revolver before—Samuel Colt's new cap and ball revolver—but he's never seen one like this. Not in the Twelfth Mass.

The Rebel raises his pistol and fires. Tom sees the bullet coming at him. Strange. He's never seen a bullet in flight before, didn't know it could be done. It's being drawn directly toward him, slowly, inexorably, as if his body were a magnet. He tries to duck, tries to throw himself down, tries twisting away—but he can't.

It tears through his left biceps. He drops lower, feeling the hot blood, but not the pain. Not yet. He knows that will come soon enough.

In the darkness, forlorn, numb and queasy, Cass felt a sudden jolt in her arm. *What just happened?* Her senses had long been dulled, but now they snapped keenly alert. She could see nothing, but there'd been a clear jab of pain in her arm. *How long have I been out of it? And where am I? What just happened?*

Tom is hit. Knows he has to do something right now, to defeat this foe. An oblique rondelle! I'll try an oblique rondelle, like Stonewall Jackson at Front Royal.

He jumps up, reveals himself, takes a step to his left, ducks and pivots to the right in one quick motion. He raises his head for a peek—good, the Rebel has reacted to the feint. Tom fires while his enemy is off balance. The Reb appears to bounce off a glass wall, pistol flying, arms askew, and plummets into the corn. It worked,

Tom has hit him.

"T'other way, corporal. Look t'other way. Another one's a-comin' yonder."

Who said that? Tom turns.

A second Rebel is running toward him.

In the dim light Tom can make out long curly hair bouncing on the Reb's neck as he runs. Thank God for the warning, but where in Hades did it come from? Tom can't see anybody else from Company C anywhere.

This pretty boy is advancing from the opposite direction, and drawing close. Tom, his left sleeve slick with blood, raises his revolver, ready to fire when the Johnny gets close enough.

An old man suddenly appears. Rises right up out of the rows of corn. Has a white beard and carries a rifle, no, a shotgun. He levels it at that swamp-ass, long-haired Reb, just as the Reb likewise takes aim.

General Mansfield!

Mansfield fires both barrels, a two-foot sheet of flame gushes, and Pretty Boy's torso detonates in an inky spray. His body flies backward, limp as a rag doll, and vanishes among the cornstalks.

"Mansfield, Mansfield," Tom whoops. "We'll take that church yet, boys." Everything will be all right now. They'll win this damned battle. Twelfth Mass will carry the day and take that church.

"Mansfield, Mansfield."

CHAPTER THIRTY-EIGHT

The Tight End was hurting. Dragging his right leg, he stumped after his hostage, following her toward the front of the barn. Good thing she hadn't run toward Cavanaugh's voice. He'd been hit somewhere above the knee. The wound wouldn't kill him, but Kurt Neumann *would*—if he didn't get that woman back. Pain stabbed at his thigh with every step, but he couldn't let everything fall apart now. Neumann would have his ass on a skewer.

He'd almost caught up with the woman when he heard a shotgun blast. He turned and saw an old man with white whiskers, side-lit by the barn light. The geezer was standing in the cornfield, eighty feet away. He'd just blown away one of the Tight End's best men. Who the hell was this old guy and where had he come from? He was reloading now, and turning this way. He'd seen him. Could shotgun fire carry this far with effect? The Tight End didn't know.

He had no qualms about killing an old man, especially one who'd just wasted one of his men. He leveled his pistol and fired twice. Both shots struck home.

Tom is about to move forward, to rout General Hood and his Texans, to take that church, when he hears shots from the side. He looks left just as General Mansfield's chest explodes. Their eyes meet for an instant before the old man vanishes among the cornstalks as if swallowed by a sinkhole.

"Mansfield. Mansfield."

Tom dashes through the corn, punishing stalks, crushing them aside, running toward the Rebel with the big shoulders who'd shot the general. Mansfield had been directly between them, so Tom comes on him first.

The general is on his knees. Glassy eyes complain at Tom, as if requiring him to explain. The old man's chest bears two ragged black holes. He makes a sound like water gurgling over rocks, and then falls forward—his death plunge. Tom reaches out, but catches only a shoulder patch, which tears away under the falling man's weight. The general is certainly gone, or will be within seconds. Tom can do no good here. He has to pursue the killer, whose form is hobbling around the corner of the barn.

Unconsciously shoving the shoulder patch in his pocket, Tom bolts to the end of the field and tears across a gravel roadway toward the front of the barn, trying to ignore the pain growing fast in his arm.

He has but one thing in mind now: avenge Mansfield. Let the others rush the church and fight the Rebs. But there is something else. What is it? A visceral scrap of data in the temporal lobe, trying to get through to him, trying to tell him something else. Something about the woman? Yes, the woman, she's important. He has to help her but isn't sure why, as he reaches the front of the barn.

The big man had just limped around the corner, out of sight on the north side of the building. Instead of following—the big guy would expect that—Tom will go counterclockwise around the barn and cut him off.

He's moving on instinct, a solitary patrol soldier on a kill-or-be-killed mission. The battlefield is strangely quiet now. Battlefield? He dashes along the side of the barn that faced the driveway. It's a deep barn, more than a hundred feet long.

He reaches the end, turns the corner, and steps into the darkest dark he's ever known. Into something else, something both ancient and new, washing over him like cold water. He feels as if he's being squeezed through a narrow tunnel. Again the rank but sweet smell, in his nostrils for a moment, then gone.

Tom shook his head. He felt as if he'd just slipped out of a deep hypnotic sleep. Senses awakened. He became aware of the barn and realized that he was behind it. It was ice black out here.

He knew that he was Tom Cavanaugh, a Sacramento cop, knew he'd just seen an old man killed, an old man who'd somehow appeared and saved his life.

Cass. He had to rescue Cass. Rescue her so he could spend the next forty or fifty years with her.

Tom's left arm was really hurting now, a throbbing drumbeat of pain, and he remembered that he'd been trying to outflank the big guy who'd kidnapped Cass.

He reached the barn's far corner, clutching the revolver in his right hand. The Tight End would be around that corner, and Cass too.

He waited several seconds, calming his rushed breathing and willing his eyes to dilate more. He smelled dry grass and cow manure. But he heard nothing, absolutely nothing. The world had come to a standstill, except for the hammering pain in his arm, pulsating in time with the beating of his heart. At last, dropping in an exaggerated crouch, he peeked around the edge. No one. A sliver of light from the front of the barn spilled around the far corner. And there was no one.

He crept silently up the north side of the barn. He stopped every few strides and listened. Then he stepped on a twig. *Damn.* It cracked loudly.

Halfway along, he discovered a door, one that swung outward. It was open a few inches. He stared at the door. Cass and the Tight End were in there. Nowhere else they could be. The guy's eyes would be accustomed to the dark by now. Tom wished he knew how bad the guy was hurt. Going in would be tricky—damned dangerous. But he had to do it.

He knelt and searched around on the ground with his left

hand—it hurt to do that. After several seconds he found what he needed, a rock.

He took a deep breath. This was it.

With his right hand, he slipped the Magnum's muzzle beneath the handle and levered the rickety door open. With his left hand he lobbed the rock inside. It hit something with a crash and there was an immediate gunshot.

He dived through the door, tucked his shoulder, struck hard dirt, and rolled to his left. He almost cried out, this hurt him so much. Another gunshot. The sound of old wood splintering.

Tom lay there, trying not to breathe. He was in deep blackness compared to the open doorway. He knew the Tight End, who was in here somewhere, wouldn't be able to see him for a few seconds. Pale, slatted light seeped in through broken boards.

The camera remained strapped around Tom's neck. He hated to make even a slight movement, but he gripped the camera and slowly swung it around in front of himself. His right hand still holding the revolver, he snapped the shutter left-handed. He didn't shield his eyes this time—needed to see what he illuminated.

In the flash a huge room appeared beneath a half upper floor, a hay mow. The Tight End frozen near the center of the room, Cass was crouched several feet away against a low stall, still bound and hooded. Tom lunged to the right to avoid the gunshot that came instantly, as he knew it would. In the same fluid movement, he fired twice, aiming directly at the point of the muzzle flash he'd just seen. Black room, bursts of sound, stabs of light.

One shot spat back in answer—but it didn't hit close. In fact, the muzzle flash showed the big man had fired in the wrong direction entirely. Tom heard a crashing sound as if something or someone fell through the rotted boards of the stall he'd seen. He realized the guy hadn't fired at him at all. Cass! The bastard had shot at Cass. *No!*

He must have smoked the big guy with his two body shots at

close range. He'd fired straight at the muzzle flash. This close, he told himself, he couldn't have missed. He'd have to trust he was right because he couldn't wait a second more to see about Cass.

He stepped to the side door and shoved it all the way open, throwing in more light. Groping along the wall, he found a light switch just inside the door and flipped it on.

Overhead, three dusty bulbs blinked on with weak yellowish light.

Cass had crashed through a flimsy old stall, where her body lay unmoving among moldy straw and broken gray slats. Stabbed with panic, Tom rushed to her side. Her chest was streaked with blood.

CHAPTER THIRTY-NINE

It wasn't Cass.

This woman was slightly shorter. Her voice—the scratchy "yes" he'd heard minutes before, come to think of it, hadn't sounded right either. The wound was chilling, a gaping, bloody mess in her torso.

He hoped to hell he hadn't shot this woman. It had to have been the Tight End . . . Still, Tom wished, like he'd never wished anything before, that he hadn't fired that second shot.

Who was this poor soul? This woman lying here with duct tape lashed around her wrists? He pulled back the hood. And blinked.

It was Sharon! My God, *his former wife*. Tom felt his mouth drop open.

He saw that some of Cass's hair had been taped to the bottom of the hood, so it would be seen. How had Sharon found these guys? Or had they found her, learned that she was his ex?

The chocolate brown eyes, glassy, stared at him. There was recognition there. Her lips parted, and a sound like cracking ice came from deep within.

"Sharon," Tom whispered. He felt her neck for a pulse. Couldn't find one. He placed his hand gently behind her head and supported it. He hadn't been so close to this face in years.

"Sharon, how come?"

She tried to speak. "Straight."

"What?"

Sharon smiled slightly. "You . . . you . . . always . . . so straight." Her head made a slight downward motion, maybe an attempt to nod.

"Cam . . ." It was no more than a whisper. Panic filled her eyes. She was trying to get breath, but couldn't.

"Cam . . ."

What was she trying to say? "Cam? What's that?"

A sigh of air gurgled from her mouth. He felt the life force slip away, the head go limp. He sat there for several seconds, frozen by the impact of the moment, staring at the once familiar face.

He hadn't loved Sharon in a long time, but she'd been a big part of his life for awhile and he was sad, deeply sad. She hadn't been a bad woman. She'd just had wrong ideas about him, had tried to mold him into something he wasn't, something he could never be.

He'd lost track of Sharon a long time ago. Last he'd heard she was living in San Diego. Greed must have led her to this pitiful end. They'd used her, got what they could from her—like sneaking those photos of Cass; she'd been a good photographer—then disposed of her. Forced her to play the role of Cass in one final degrading act, played out here in a crumbling old barn.

He pulled up the sleeve of her blouse. Her arm bore a needle mark. They'd drugged her. No wonder she'd moved so sluggishly in the roadway.

Feeling sick from his crown to his toes, he turned to the man he'd shot in the dark. His first shot had struck home, in the center of the chest. He stared at the face.

Another shock.

A dead hand still gripping a 9-millimeter Beretta, it was Elwell, Zack Elwell, the FBI agent. Except that he could be no FBI agent.

There was no satisfaction. *Well, Cavanaugh, you've killed a man.*

He searched the pockets for identification. No wallet, no driver's license, nothing on him except a big gold ring and a small scrap of paper.

Tom recognized the ring. It was inlaid with a miniature watch. He'd bought that ring for Sharon fourteen years ago. The scum not only drugged and then murdered her—he had, hadn't he?—but he'd robbed her too. Tom looked at the scrap of paper. EMPIRE LUMBER, CAMERON FLATS was scribbled on it, along with a phone number.

He stuffed the note and the ring in a pants pocket. Using his teeth and his left hand—*Ow! God, it hurt*—he tore off half the sleeve from his good arm. He fastened a crude pressure wrap over the wound in his left arm, again with the help of his teeth, thinking all the while about Sharon.

His second shot couldn't have been fifteen feet off the mark, could it? And Elwell's last shot had been fired in her direction. Deliberately, right?

Tom feared he might never know. The bullet that killed Sharon would be deformed. It would be hard to tell whether it came from his .357 or this guy's 9-millimeter. The difference was something like three-thousandths of an inch, a tough call for even a top forensics man, which this county maybe didn't have.

No time for that now. He picked up his revolver and ran through the open door into the night. And headlong into someone. They collided fiercely and the other person fell.

"D-don't shoot," the jeweler stammered. "Don't shoot me. There are enough d-dead men out here." Vomit soiled the front of his jacket.

"Who's alive out here? Who else?"

"As, as far as I know, only the m-man in the limo."

Tom brushed past the jeweler and moved across the front of the barn, scanning the terrain as far as he could see in each direction. No sign of movement anywhere. He jogged across the gravel drive into the cornfield.

The name Mansfield popped into his mind—he didn't know why. Something about the cornfield made him shiver, even though it was a warm night.

He found the man, his chest shot open as Sharon's had been.

His killer must have fired hollow points. Even in the bad light, Tom recognized the face and its white goatee. It was Roy Oakley! His father's shooting buddy. What the hell was *he* doing here?

Old Twenty-Five-for-Twenty-Five's last shot had been a good one. It had saved his life. Tom had more questions than answers, but couldn't think about them now.

It took a few more minutes to find Pretty Boy, whoever he was. Mansfield's, or rather Oakley's, double shotgun blast had left the long-haired punk anything but pretty.

When he was certain that Oakley and this other guy were beyond help, Tom left the field and started toward the limousine, but it wasn't there.

"Where's the limo?" he called to the jeweler.

"I, I don't know. It was th-there a minute ago."

Tom scanned the long driveway in both directions. He went up on tiptoes and stretched his neck. The limousine was gone.

"Who was in it?"

"A driver. I didn't know him."

"Anyone else?"

"The woman with the hood and the, uh, young man with the long hair were there, but they got out before, before he was, you know, shot."

"Come here, then." His Magnum still in hand, Tom led the jeweler up the lane to his Honda.

"Faster." Tom was antsy. Had to get moving. When they reached the car, he said, "Here, tighten this dressing on my arm. Make a knot."

After the jeweler complied, Tom pulled a pair of handcuffs from the glove box. He motioned for the guy to sit on the ground, next to the cornfield.

"Oh, please, please don't leave me here alone with all these d-dead people."

Tom ignored the pleading and cuffed the little man to a post, tossing the key on the driveway just beyond his reach.

"Don't go anywhere," he said, jumping into the car. "I'll send someone for you." The engine coughed to life and he turned around in a squeal of rubber and gravel and headed toward the gate. He swerved around the van blocking the drive, smashing through the old, untended flower garden. He hit the Garden Highway and speeded up.

As he neared Highway 99, he came to a teenage boy riding a horse. Tom slowed and pulled alongside, rolling down the window.

"Police emergency," he shouted. "Call the Sutter County Sheriff's Department and tell them to get to that farmhouse back there, the deserted one on the left, with paramedics. "There's been a shooting."

"Cool," the boy said. As Tom roared away, he saw the kid heading toward the town of Nicolaus, urging speed out of his horse.

Empire Lumber, Cameron Flats. That's what Sharon had been trying to say: Cameron Flats. That was a small town in the hills, somewhere near Grass Valley, wasn't it? Calm yourself and figure out where you're going, he told himself.

When he reached the state highway, he pulled off on the shoulder and yanked a map from the glove box. Now where the devil was Cameron Flats? In a few seconds he found it. There, quite a long way up State 49, in a remote part of the northern Sierra foothills. He'd go to Marysville, take Highway 20 to Nevada City, then north on 49. He'd better get gas in Marysville. He faced an hour or more of driving and most of it would be on winding, two-lane roads.

He put the map away and pulled out. A deputy's car, with so many flashing lights it looked like it was invading from Mars, whined past in the opposite direction, speeding toward the farm.

Tom stopped at a convenience store in Marysville to gas up the hard-worked Honda. He'd put the car through hell the past few weeks.

The attendant, a tiny Middle Eastern woman, must have seen what a mess he was: the shirt sleeve torn from one arm, the other arm a stiff, bleeding mess, his face smudged with dirt, corn silk in his hair, probably. "What happened?" she said. "I'm calling 911."

"No," Tom snapped. "I'm the police." He showed his wallet ID. "Just help me get filled up."

Whereupon the woman hopped out from behind the cash register and pumped the gas herself. Tom snatched some paper towels and blotted his arm.

Cass hadn't seen anyone, not Madame X or any other living soul, for more than a day. She didn't know when she'd last eaten. She hadn't slept much, knew she was reaching the end of her endurance. Somehow, though her senses had all but deserted her, she discovered there were brass rivets on the back pockets of her pants, these pants she'd never seen before. She figured the stuff binding her hands behind her was duct tape, judging by its stickiness and texture.

So she began rubbing her wrists up and down, scuffing the tape against one of the brads. *Ow! This is cutting my skin as much as the tape, but I already feel so damn bad, the heck with it.* She scraped away for two or three minutes at a time, rested, and scraped some more.

About the time she felt a rip in the tape and thought one strong twist of her wrists could break it, the door opened. A man appeared in the doorway. Medium height, dark complexion, bald except for a fringe of hair and a ponytail. Eyes remote and black. About her age. He carried a small pistol. Cass realized it looked very much like her own LadySmith, the one they'd stolen from her. *Great, they're going to kill me with my own gun. Make it look like suicide.*

She recognized him. It was Manny Díaz, the ex-bodyguard for the governor. She'd known Díaz and had liked him—until his fall from grace a year ago.

"Manny? Manny Díaz, is that you?"

"Afraid so, Cass, live and in person. A lot has changed. Now come with me."

"Why, Manny? How come you're a part of this?"

"Like I said, a lot has changed," he uttered with a scowl. "You were always so cute, weren't you? Little Goody Two Shoes, Maggie's favorite. Big college girl."

He was so different, so cold and angry. He used to bring her doughnuts.

"Then you and that guy of yours screwed me up good. I used to like you, Cass . . . I don't like anybody now. Come on!" he commanded, motioning with the pistol.

Cass obeyed. As she climbed the stairs in her bare feet, she noticed the damage she'd done to the door frame in her futile escape. Seeing it only made her feel worse.

When she entered the hallway, she saw the older man with the close-cut gray hair, the one who'd picked her up along the road and brought her back here. He was standing at the far end of the hall like a model for a seniors' catalog. Crisp golf shirt, tailored slacks.

"Take her up the hill," he said. "To the old air shaft."

"I know," Díaz said.

"You won't get away with this." Cass glared at the old man. "Tom will cut your guts out."

The man laughed mirthlessly and stepped out of sight.

Díaz shoved Cass down a corridor to the right. "Don't have to be so rough, Manny," she said. "By the way, I like the ponytail. Looks good on you."

"Shut up."

Cass wished she still had that big nail, but—like her purse and slacks—it was long gone.

When they arrived at a back door Díaz reached around her, opened it, and pushed her out into the night. She found herself facing a huge fenced yard. Lights were on here and there. She caught a combination of smells: petroleum, damp earth, fresh-cut lumber. The mill was deathly quiet. Maybe it's the weekend, she thought. Yeah, the weekend, all the workers gone. *The perfect time to commit murder unnoticed.*

Forklifts and trucks were parked every which way in the rectangular yard and open sheds on each side held stacks of boards. Beyond the yard, logs floated in a pond next to a tall, tin-roofed building. That would be the millhouse, Cass figured, where the big saws were. The upper of its two levels faced the parking lot she'd run through in her brief escape. A long concrete ramp extended steeply down to the water.

The gravelly dirt bit at the bottoms of her feet. Each time she turned her head something felt wrong. What was it? Aha, her hair didn't flounce against her ears as it always did. Had they cut her already-short hair while she was unconscious? If so, whatever for?

It was getting cold. She had no idea of the time, but it felt late. Then she laughed inwardly. *Late? Yeah, it's late.*

She saw a gate in the wire fence that enclosed the yard. She occasionally had to step over small scraps of wood as she walked, Díaz shoving her in the back to prod her whenever she slowed.

They reached the fence. A hill rose off to the left. Díaz went ahead of her to open the gate. In that instant, Cass twisted her wrists as hard as she could. The frayed tape snapped. Her wrists were free.

Díaz was having trouble with the gate. "Damn it. Don't they ever use this rusty son of a bitch?" He'd unlocked a padlock, but the gate still hadn't opened. While he fussed with it, Cass reached down and picked up a tattered wooden slat. She clasped it behind her with both hands as Díaz kicked the gate. It creaked open.

"Go on out there," he said, and Cass complied, keeping her hands behind her as if they were still bound. She stepped through the opening. In the half-light from the mill yard, the hill facing her was long and round-topped, with some brush and a few scrubby trees.

"We're going up there," Díaz said.

Cass advanced, keeping a few feet away from Díaz. She didn't want him getting a close look at her hands or what she had in them. It wasn't much of a weapon, but it was something.

CHAPTER FORTY

As white lines streaked past in the road, Tom tried to think about what had happened in the cornfield, anything to take his mind off the searing pain in his left arm. Parts of the experience were blacked out, like someone else had filled in for him. He thought about the voice that had warned him, like some guardian spirit.

And General Mansfield, who'd appeared out of nowhere and then was shot down. Tom had a powerful sense that he'd experienced all that before. But then General Mansfield had turned out to be Roy Oakley, who was very much of this place and time. Tom shook his head. Oakley. Oakley had saved his life. His suspicions about him had been all wrong. But what the hell was he doing out there at that farm?

He thought about something easier to handle: Elwell, or whatever his name was. That guy hadn't been any FBI agent. That's why he'd never been in when he'd called. These people were good—they'd probably learned that the real Elwell was away on assignment and wouldn't be in if Tom tried to reach him.

Overriding all of that was the crushing sense of guilt he felt about Sharon. The shock of finding her mixed up in this and dying in his arms was transcended by the possibility, slight though it was, that he might have shot her.

At Grass Valley, he turned onto the mountain road that would take him to Cameron Flats. Above Nevada City the road twisted endlessly, the double yellow lines looping on and on like never-ending crime-scene tape.

He thought about the arrogance of Fred Hutchinson, the lawyer from Curry, Bickford & Marshall. Suddenly it hit him, why that firm's name had somehow seemed familiar. Marshall, that was the key! Ben Marshall was the lawyer who'd got Kurt Richter off on that Colombian drug sting a few years back, Tom's first big drug bust.

Richter. Kurt Richter. He was behind this. How did he ever find out about the emerald? And where the hell was he? He'd cleared out of Sacramento after his release, and probably created a new identity for himself somewhere.

Tom remembered the cold hatred Richter's eyes had glowered at him as he'd left the courtroom.

Ben Marshall must have become a partner in the San Francisco firm and got his name on the letterhead. Sloppy of Fred Hutchinson to call from his own office. Marshall would be furious. Not to mention Richter. Richter, whose eyes had said, "Someday, you bastard, some day. . . ." Richter, who now had Cass.

It struck Tom that one of Fred Hutchinson's clients was a Kurt Neumann. *Kurt?* Hmm.

The hill smelled of wild juniper and sagebrush. As they neared the crest, Cass stumbled on a rock and Díaz took her by the elbow to steady her. She still kept her hands behind her, out of his sight. "There's an old mine deep under this hill," he said. "It's been sealed off for years with tons of rock at both openings. There's an air shaft on top, hidden by underbrush."

"Thanks for sharing that, Manny."

"Oh, there's more. It's seventy feet straight down. We're almost there—to the opening of the shaft." His laugh was vicious.

Cass's wrists pulsed with pain, hundreds of needles stabbing them. Anyway, they were no longer numb. Having feeling is good, she told herself, even if the feeling is pain. She wished she'd been able to rub the wrists to get the blood circulating faster, but at least they were no longer bound. Her only advantage lay in Díaz not knowing that.

The hill was faintly illuminated by a sliver of moon in the west. It was quiet up here. Besides their own footsteps, all she could hear was a night bird calling in the distance. *God, I envy that bird, free, able to fly wherever it wants.*

"Manny, this is ridiculous. What's happened to you? You used to be such a sweetheart. I used to say you were the second-best cop I ever knew."

"Give it up, bitch. Save your breath."

"You'll never get away with this. Forget this, let's drive to town. I'll testify for you, get Governor Maggie to intercede too. You can get a life again."

"Ha. Governor Maggie. Some Mexican."

"Come on, Manny, get real."

"Stop," Díaz snarled. "Far enough." Cass watched him kneel to one knee, feeling with his left hand, his right still holding her LadySmith. He pushed small bushes aside. "Ah, here," he said and stood up. "No one's ever going to find you." Again, the sadistic laugh.

He's really going to do this.

Her instinct to live erupted. *No, goddammit, no.* As Díaz turned to face her and grabbed her shoulders, Cass drove a knee into his groin as she'd learned in self-defense class. He groaned and reached down.

She shot her right hand upward and thrust the small slat into his belly. She felt it penetrate. But she was weak from hunger and sleep loss; the improvised dagger hadn't gone in very far.

"Jesus, you bitch. You stabbed me. Jesus God, I'm bleeding."

She tried to twist the slat and drive it deeper, but he struck her on the scalp with the pistol.

Cass fell, her skull burning with pain.

"You're gonna be one dead bitch when I throw you in there." He raised the pistol to fire.

* * *

Cameron Flats was a tiny burg, a sundry collection of roadside businesses and clapboard houses with steep tin roofs. Pulling up in front of a small café, Tom jumped from the car, leaving the motor running. As he reached the door, a biker came out, all hair and leather and metal.

"Where's the lumber mill?" Tom demanded.

"Jesus, ain't you a sight. What happened, man?"

"Empire Lumber. Where is it?"

A tattooed hand pointed. "Up this road about two miles. It's closed, man."

"Thanks."

Tom hopped back behind the wheel and peeled onto the highway, leaving behind a billow of dust.

The biker watched the taillights disappear out of town and shook his head. The last few seconds had provided the most excitement he'd seen in Cameron Flats in a long time. *Wonder what's goin' on up at the mill?* He strode toward his Harley.

Cass stabbed out blindly for Diaz's leg but missed. Then she heard something rushing through the brush. The gray-haired man? No, it was moving too fast. Inhumanly fast.

The snarling Doberman shot through the air. It landed on Díaz's chest in a flash of fur and teeth. They both tumbled backward in a writhing tangle. They thrashed wildly on the ground, just above the hole, the dog's throat making a grinding, hacksaw sound.

Díaz suddenly shouted, "Help me, help me. I'm slipping." He'd slid partway into the shaft. "Grab my hand." His arm was outstretched, his eyes pleading. Cass heard the dog yelp in pain, far below.

She instinctively scooted backward, but stopped. She no longer heard the dog.

"Please. Can't hold—"

Cass hesitated. Had a moment of internal struggle. Finally, she leaned forward and extended her hand. Their fingers touched for a second, but his slid away. She could no longer see him. She heard a gruesome scream and a muffled crash that seemed to come from the center of the earth. Both beasts were gone.

CHAPTER FORTY-ONE

Cass sat there a moment, heart racing, her mind not wanting to accept what her eyes had just seen.

She crawled several feet back from the hole. She had none of Tom's acrophobia, but that terrible opening in the earth gave her the willies. A painful lump was growing on her head.

She heard footsteps. Was it Tom at last? She turned. It was that damn gray-haired man. He was coming up the hill and carrying a gun. Hers was probably down there with Manny Díaz, her would-be assassin, and her savior, the dog.

"Any problem up there?" the man called. "Let's get on with it, Díaz. We've got to get down to the farm."

Cass started crawling backward, hoping to find concealment somewhere on the hill. The slice of moon was almost down but still threw too much light.

If she could make it off the hill unseen, maybe she could circle behind this guy and get back into the lumber mill. Plenty of places to hide there—and phones. She might even drive off in one of the trucks she'd seen in the yard.

"Díaz, answer me, damn you. I'm not at all pleased with you people."

Cass continued to slither backwards, trying to be quiet. She wanted no part of the gray-haired man. Why wouldn't that damn moon go down? Her eyes were fully adjusted to the dim light—and she knew his were too.

"What's wrong?" Alarm in the man's voice. "Where are you?"

He was near the crest of the hill, and Cass wasn't very far down the other side. She was moving again, keeping low on all fours, when her foot dislodged a rock. It began rolling down the hill.

The man stopped and looked in her direction.

Cass lay stock still, hoping he couldn't see her. He was staring straight at her. Just possibly, though, he was only looking in the direction of the sound. Don't move, she thought. Don't even breathe.

"There you are, my dear."

Cass bit on her lower lip.

"You keep turning up like a bad penny, isn't that the saying? What's happened to my friend Díaz?"

Cass caught sight of the man's gun again. It glinted in the faint light as he took a step in her direction.

"You and your fiancé have been such a nuisance. I never wanted to hurt anyone. I made him a handsome offer for the jewel, you know. It could have been so clean and simple. It's too late for that now."

Cass's hand brushed against a rock. She probed it with her fingers. It was about the size of a softball; she threw softballs very well. She picked it up and hurled it at him, jumping up and to the side as she did. She sprinted down the hill toward the log pond, bounding like a leopard. If she could reach the water, she might have a chance.

She zigged and zagged, changing direction every couple of steps, painfully stripping the torn tape from her wrists as she ran. She heard a gunshot and the whang of a ricochet. The slope of the hill added to her speed. More shots zinged past. Hitting close.

Her hands became fists as she ran. She was furious with herself for ever walking over to that van. Dying out here alone and cold in the middle of the night, far away from Tom.

She reached the pond and dived in on the run. It was a flying leap. Her left arm struck a log and she sank deep, pain throbbing in her forearm.

She'd planned to dive deep anyway, but not like that. Fortunately, the buoyant log had spun and turned when she hit and the impact was nothing like running into a tree. She swam away from the bank, submerged, kicking strongly. She'd been swimming laps at the health club, but hadn't had much underwater practice. How far could she go before she'd have to surface?

Down here, a few feet below the surface, the water was cold, icy cold. This stuff came right down out of the Sierra snows. It was ink black down here. Couldn't see a thing. Something brushed against her face. *Just a fish, I hope.*

Her lungs were about to burst. How much longer could she hold off this primal craving to inhale? When she couldn't last another second, she kicked to the surface and popped her head up for a look and a quick gulp of air. She found herself near the center of the pond, surrounded by hundreds of floating logs. Lucky she hadn't hit another coming up.

She'd hoped that water was flowing from the pond and she could float out with it, but she didn't see a dam or sluice gate.

A bullet slapped a log, kicking up a shower of splinters close to her face. She dived.

Now that she had her bearings, she made for the opposite bank, which was close to the mill yard. And the lights that were on there. She weighed pros and cons. How many times had the man fired? At least four or five, possibly six. She had no idea how many rounds that pistol held.

Her hand struck something—mud, she realized. She'd reached the far bank. She clambered up the slope, slimy with water weeds, gasping for air.

Where was the gray-haired man? Ah, now she saw him, a couple of hundred feet away. Water dribbled down her face and arms, her pants and frayed silk blouse were glued to her cold body, mud oozed between her toes, goosebumps forming everywhere. *Keep moving.*

Although her soaked clothes were heavy, she ran zigzag toward the millhouse, as fast as she could. She heard the man fire again from across the pond. Cass knew most pistols weren't accurate at this range. Still, she changed direction every couple of steps till she reached the millhouse. She knew the gray-haired man would waste no time coming around the pond after her. She stepped on a small rock, pain bit deep into her right foot, and she staggered the last few feet to the building.

Shivering, hugging a side wall of the millhouse, she tried to catch her breath. She shook her foot and hoped it wasn't cut, just bruised.

She knew she had to keep going, and waited just a few seconds before taking off. Dashed through the open gate into the mill yard, made a quick turn and ducked into the first storage shed she came to. Inside, she felt her way along a high stack of boards, toward the rear.

The shed wasn't illuminated and very little light seeped in from the yard. This was good. She couldn't be seen back here.

When she reached the back of the shed, she stopped and listened for sounds. She heard no footsteps, but that only worried her more. Where was that old bastard? As her eyes adjusted, she noticed a back door.

She waited at least a minute, letting her breathing slow. She rubbed her foot, her wrists, her arms. She didn't know which was worse, her injuries or the cold. She had to fight with her teeth to keep them from chattering.

Hearing nothing, she tiptoed to the door and tried the handle. With a push, the door swung open to the outside.

She crept behind the row of sheds toward the office building, her eyes gradually seeing more and more. She halted every few steps, searching with eyes and ears. *Now I know how hunted animals feel.* The bottoms of her feet throbbed. Must be scraped raw.

She rested a minute pondering her next move. Return to the big yard and try starting one of the trucks? No. Too exposed out there; the old bastard would gun her down before she could get away. She'd just have to make it back to the office, work around it on one side or the other, and go back into the same woods she'd fled into before.

Off she went, moving cautiously. At last she reached the back of the cement-block building that twice had been her prison.

She started around the corner, toward an open area maybe a hundred feet wide, between the office and the millhouse. The two buildings were linked by a narrow catwalk spanning a steep dropoff to the log pond.

Loose gravel and strips of pine bark littered the ground. They might as well have been a bed of nails—Cass's bleeding feet were beyond hurting.

She came face to face with the gray-haired man.

"Not again!" she screamed. After all she'd been through, this was more than she could take. The guy must have seen her reach the office and—*damn*—circled around the other side to cut her off.

"You've been such a nuisance," the man said, and jabbed his pistol into her ribs. "Now get up on that catwalk. We're going over to the millhouse."

Why doesn't he just shoot me now? Cass wondered. Does he think he's going to rape me in there before killing me? She turned and shambled up the steel steps, angry as all hell. When she stepped onto the catwalk, the man prodded her in the back with his gun. "Keep moving!"

She walked forward, shivering, dripping water onto the metal latticework flooring. The narrow footbridge had sides of widely spaced steel rods, the hand rail on top wide and flat to her touch. At the far end, a hundred feet ahead, stood a side door to the mill.

She crossed slowly, her battered feet testing the cold, spiny metal. The dropoff to the log pond was quite a precipice, deeper than she'd first realized. She hesitated. For an instant she thought about jumping, but no, she'd probably break her neck.

The gun jabbed her ribs again. "Keep moving, girlie. We're almost there."

Girlie? That pissed her off. Less than fifteen feet from the door, she halted defiantly.

Rounding the last bend, Tom saw the office with its EMPIRE LUMBER sign and the opening in the rail fence. He cut the engine and let the car roll to a quiet halt just outside the gravel parking lot.

He picked up his Magnum, now reloaded, got out, and started across the lot.

"I'm not taking another step," Cass said.

"Oh, but you are." Another jab of the gun.

"Stop that, you son of a bitch. Who the hell do you think you are? You're never going to get what you're after if you kill me." But she knew he *had* to kill her. She could identify him.

As the man shoved her toward the door her toes stubbed on the steel mesh and she fell, landing roughly. One leg dangled between the railings, out into space.

The man stepped over her, turned the knob and opened the door. He grabbed Cass's forearm and hauled her to her feet.

Tom reaches the front of the office building. He hears voices. Following the sounds, he dashes around the side, spots the catwalk and two shadowy figures at the far end. A man is shoving a woman through the door into the upper level of the millhouse. Cass! It's just a brief glimpse in bad light—she was ragged and wet—but there's no doubt. He's found her.

He runs to the base of the catwalk and bounds up the little steps. At the landing, he swings out onto the webbed steel and strides forward. He can see right through this thing.

There below him, far below, lies an arm of the pond and part of a concrete ramp. His stomach quivers. His steps slow. *Not my damned acrophobia. Not now.* The catwalk seems to reel. He clamps an unsteady hand to the railing for support. *Don't look down.* He shoves the Magnum beneath his belt, tightens his grip on the rail, and tells himself his fear of heights is stupid. If he were in a plane, he'd be fine. He tries to persuade himself this is like clasping the yoke of a Cessna 172.

Fighting stubborn feet and legs, he forces himself forward with hand-over-hand grips on the rail. He figures weakness from blood loss is only adding to his vertigo. At least the queasiness makes him forget the pain in his left arm.

He focuses on the door. There's a window in its upper half. He hopes Cass's captor, Richter or whoever the bastard is, is too busy concentrating on her to look out and see him.

He gets to the door at last, sucks in a deep breath, reaches out for the knob. I might get shot in the next couple of seconds, he thinks. *So what's new? Wouldn't be the first time tonight.*

The door opens quietly, a happy surprise. He enters in a crouch. A massive saw dominates a cavernous room smelling of sawdust and machine oil. Banks of overhead fluorescent lights are off, but smaller wall fixtures throw a soft gold glow.

He sights Cass and the man. They're moving beyond the saw, near a rear opening and a chain-belt chute leading down to the pond.

Still crouching, Tom approaches on tiptoes, his Magnum extended in front of him.

In front of the mill, another car pulled up next to Tom's and stopped. The door swung open and an old man stepped out and began to walk carefully as if this were unfamiliar ground. He picked his way around the corner to the main entrance at the front of the millhouse.

CHAPTER FORTY-TWO

If he could edge closer without being seen, Tom was thinking, and if Cass wasn't directly in front of the guy, he could get position on him and end this thing fast. Or, worst case, shoot him in the leg if he had to.

With all this in mind, he moved forward slowly, stepping lightly, hunkered low, gaining concealment from the big saw. He saw a door at the far side of the room. The gray-haired man was prodding Cass toward it. Tom didn't like that. What did the bastard have in mind? What was he planning to do in there?

Okay, neither of them was looking his way. This was working. *Now*. Tom jumped out of his crouch, stepped around the end of the saw and called out, "Stop right there. Put the gun down."

Cass gasped in stunned surprise. "Tom!" she blurted, and took a step. She stumbled on something—*damn*—lost balance and fell back against Neumann or whatever his name was.

The guy threw an arm around her, making her a shield. "Cavanaugh," he blurted. "You can't be here, it's not possible." Obviously this guy expected that Tom had been dealt with back at the farm, as Sharon had.

"Tom!" Cass cried. "You're hurt."

"Wickersham wouldn't have told you about this mill," the guy said, his pistol hand twitching dangerously close to Cass's head. "Has he got the emerald? Is he all right?"

Assuming he meant the Tight End, Tom said, "He was lying down last time I saw him."

"The emerald. Does Wickersham have it?"

Tom didn't answer, just gave him a cold stare.

"You should have taken my offer."

"It wasn't mine to sell, mister. Now put the gun down."

"Where is it?" Neumann shifting his weight from foot to foot.

"In Austria, or on its way. A Swiss bank is taking care of it."

"A what!"

"Sorry, Mister Kurt Richter, client of Ben Marshall."

Tom saw confusion on Cass's face. All these names. Obviously she made no sense of it.

"You *are* Kurt Richter, aren't you?" Tom said.

"Not anymore. You destroyed that man, and his wife too. Now I want that emerald. Where is it? No more lies about Swiss banks." Madly waving the pistol. "I must have it. I *have* to have it. You do have it, you do. You must."

"Believe me, Richter, Neumann or whatever you call yourself, I don't."

"You *know* this creep?" Cass said.

"The gun. Put it down," Tom repeated. "Now! This is over."

"Like hell it is." Neumann's arm relaxed a bit when he said that. Cass pushed herself back against him hard and jabbed an elbow into his stomach. He staggered but in her weakened state she wasn't able to knock him down. He shook her off.

Tom leveled his Magnum at Neumann, but he'd grabbed Cass again and whipped the muzzle of his pistol against her neck.

"No!" Tom shouted.

"Kurt, do not do this," someone said. The voice came from the shadows, a voice as old as time. Tom saw an old man slip into the light and say, "This has gone too far, Kurt."

"They destroyed the chance of my life," Neumann snarled.

"It has gone too far. This must stop here."

"This is not your business, Judge."

Judge? Tom now recognized the old man. It was Wilson Judge, the art dealer from Santa Barbara. *What the hell?*

"Kurt!" It was a go-to-your-room tone.

"Keep out of this, you stupid old picture-framer."

"No one calls a German *Oberst* an old picture-framer," the old voice insisted, "not even you, child."

Tom didn't dare fire—Cass was too close to Neumann. He started to shout "Get back" when the flash of a pistol shot lit the room. Tom grabbed Cass and pulled her down. He wasn't sure which of the two had fired. He only knew he hadn't been hit.

Neumann reeled backward.

Wilson Judge stepped forward. "Kurt, Kurt," he murmured, as Neumann, clutching his chest, tottered. He stumbled and fell on his back onto the log chute.

Tom moved to the opening and watched Neumann slide head first, twenty or thirty feet, till his face disappeared in the cold water of the pond.

One of his loafers bounced down the chute behind him, as if looking for the foot it had just deserted. It stopped against a knee.

Bubbles gurgled up from the water. Neumann's legs, splayed at cockeyed angles just out of the water, formed twisted shadows in the weak light. A shroud of silence settled over the mill.

Hell, Tom thought, he's drowning. Damn, I've got to go down there and get him. He stepped close to the chute and was about to start down when Judge fired twice more. Water jumped where Neumann's head was submerged. And turned red.

The old man's body sagged as if firing that pistol had spent the last of his energy.

"My son." He began to weep.

Tom went over and took the pistol from the unresisting bony fingers.

"My son."

Cass rushed to Tom and fell against him, some of his blood getting on her tattered blouse. Who cared?

CHAPTER FORTY-THREE

Floating in a fog of sedation, Tom vaguely sensed men in lab coats bending over him, doing things to his arm. He recalled the words "her slight concussion" from someone and, oh yes, "strange bullet we dug out of this fella's left femur. Big and roundish—looked very old." There was a filmy memory of someone taking his temperature, putting a pill in his mouth and giving him water. These images swirled in and out of his cognitive grasp like confetti on a breeze.

He felt a prick of pain in the crook of his elbow and realized a nurse was pulling a needle from it. He looked at her groggily and croaked, "What—"

"Removing your IV drip," she said. "You've been getting blood for awhile."

"You were a couple of quarts low," a more familiar voice said from across the room.

The sunlight streaming through the window made Tom squint, but its golden glow looked good. "What time is it?"

"Almost ten," the nurse said. "We didn't get you in here till after two, so we let you be a sleepyhead this morning."

He seemed to have a cannonball for a left arm. Then he saw that it was encased in an elbow-to-shoulder cast and immobilized by a sling.

He looked over at the next bed and saw Cass, staring at him, propped up by an elbow. How long had she been awake, gazing at him? She was pale, dark half-moons underscored her eyes, and her right temple wore a large bandage. But to Tom she'd never looked better.

"It's about time you looked over here at the Creature from the Black Lagoon," she said.

"Cass, it's really you, thank God. Sorry I didn't see you right away. I'm still pretty foggy. Had all kinds of creepy dreams."

"You were tossing and turning like mad and mumbling some weird stuff."

Tom hears a voice. "Give the woman a hug, soldier. Tell her of the powerful love you have for her." It sounds like General Mansfield.

"I will, I will."

"You will what?" Cass asked.

"Give you a big hug and tell you how much I love you." He glanced down at the cast encasing the arm strapped to his side. "Except I guess you'll have to do the hugging."

Cass came over and did just that. Her cheek next to his, she said, "And just how much *do* you love me?"

"A whole heck of a lot, lady."

The nurse, standing near the door, smiled. Tom asked her to push their beds closer. Over the next hour he and Cass held hands, snuggled as best they could, and described their ordeals.

"My God," Tom said, "I'm so darned relieved to see you. You're in pretty good shape, considering."

"Don't be so sure. I couldn't stand to have the lights off in here last night. I've never been afraid of the dark, but after . . . Well, now I've got another phobia: needles. I don't ever want another needle stuck into me. They wanted to give me a shot of something last night, but I said no way. I swallowed a sleeping pill instead." Cass made a face. "I guess you figured out Second Chronicles 2:8? 'Thy servants can skill to cut timber.' "

"Yeah, but you could have said, 'I pine for you.' "

"Ho! That would have got me worse than just kicked around." She went on to tell about her futile escape and about Manny Díaz and the old mine shaft.

"I'll have to go and see his wife Maria then," Tom said. "That won't be easy." Cass softly stroked his neck.

The catching-up was often interrupted by visits from doctors, nurses, and the real FBI.

Chief Pulaski also showed up. Tom tensed and frowned when he saw him.

"Ms. Nesbit, it's a great relief to see you. I'm so glad your injuries are not major." Turning to Tom, he said, "You came through, fella, just as I knew you would."

"What's that supposed to mean?"

"I have a confession to make. I had more confidence in you than our new Crimes Against Persons Unit, so I put you on leave to turn you loose on this. I knew you'd go after it whole hog and do a good job."

"You faked my firing?" Tom's free hand made a fist. "That's stupid."

"You were never fired. Look, I couldn't officially put you on leave, could I? I realize it was a dirty trick, but the ends justified the means, don't you think?" He held up his hands, palms out. "I had you tailed. She found out you'd cased—"

"She?"

"Yes. She learned you'd cased that farm by car and helicopter. PO-2 Hamilton, it was. Debbie Hamilton."

"What?" Tom's mouth dropped open.

"Great young cop. I'm giving her a nice promotion."

"Okay this time," Cass threw in, "but I don't want that little cutie following him anymore, Chief."

"Word of honor," Pulaski said with a grin. "I understand they're keeping you both another night. Detective Norfleet will come around tomorrow to drive you home—his personal request. Your old job will be waiting for you, fella, after some rest and therapy to get that arm back in shape." Pulaski tapped the cast lightly.

"Huh," Tom grunted. "Lotsa luck on that."

"We need you, Tom. Things will look better when you're more rested up."

"You think so?"

After Pulaski left, Tom recalled that someone had warned him in the cornfield, called out that another guy was coming after him. Could that have been Debbie Hamilton?

Out of the blue, Cass said, "Ginger Vitus."

"Dental hygienist," Tom answered.

Cass grinned and nodded. Tom laughed out loud.

Mike Norfleet came to pick them up the next day. A nurse rolled Cass to the front door in a wheelchair, where she got up hesitantly, still wearing hospital booties. Her tender feet had scarcely begun to heal. She and Tom hobbled beside Norfleet to his car, parked in a red zone. Her left arm was linked with Tom's good right arm, but it was hard to tell who was supporting whom.

"You guys look like American Garlic, that farm couple."

"What?"

"The painting, that pitchfork thing." Same old Norfleet, dumb as an ox and smart as hell. "Hey, I like your new haircut, Cassie. Where'd ya get that, on the base?"

Cass laughed. "It does look pretty boot camp, doesn't it?"

Mrs. Potter and Orbison greeted them at home. The neighbor had a pot of tea waiting for them.

"Or maybe you'd rather just go right upstairs," she said. "I'll serve it to you in bed if you like."

"Mrs. P, you're a gem," Cass said, then glanced slyly at Tom. "But I think I'll go to the bathroom first and wash out some nylons."

Bewilderment filled the neighbor's face and Tom started to throw both arms up in surrender, forgetting about his sling. "Ouch."

Later, Cass was sorting through a mound of mail. Tom, who

was listening to messages on the answering machine, glanced over and noticed Orbison rubbing against her ankle. Bonded more closely to Tom, the cat had never done that before. Must have sensed that this was much more than the usual homecoming.

One of the messages was from the real estate agent.

"You owe me, Tom. I had to call in a favor from a title company. Got them to run a search on that farm you asked about. I'll drop off the printout whenever you like. It goes all the way back to a Mexican land grant to Sutter in 1840. The Sutter estate sold it in 1871 to a Belgian, a Prince Rudolf Kessler, and it's been passed down in his family ever since. His great-great-granddaughter May Kessler Oakley had title till she died four years ago, then it went over to her husband, Roy Howard Oakley . . ."

"Oakley!" Tom made it sound like an expletive.

"Back in the 1870s, the prince built a chapel on it, supposedly a replica of one he'd seen in the Civil War."

Tom trembled the way he had at the Antietam Battlefield. He had to sit down.

CHAPTER FORTY-FOUR

W hen he and Cass entered his father's bedroom, Tom felt something had changed. The oxygen machine still hummed away in a corner, and its tubes still led to the prone figure in the bed. But the old man seemed stronger, a little more alive, but also uncharacteristically tense.

After handshakes, hugs and kisses, Tom began his story. He explained that Neumann, nee Richter, had started as a minor player in the international art black market. And, being the shark that he was, soon got into the big time. His contacts in Mexico had led him to Manny Díaz, the fugitive state cop.

"I'm so sorry I got you both into this mess. I had no idea—"

"Forget it, Dad, who could have known? Now this—"

"No, stop right there, Thomas, there's something I have to say. You weren't off base on Oakley after all. You see, he owned that farm—"

"I know—"

Desmond Cavanaugh put up a trembling hand. "Hear me out, son. His wife loved that farm but Oakley didn't. When she died, he rented it to Dave Wickersham, but he got tired of the farm and moved back to town about a year ago. It's been vacant ever since and Oakley was trying to decide what to do with it. Roy knew about the emerald—me and my big mouth—and he also knew this Kurt Neumann character. They'd made some investments together. Oakley didn't know how to fence a big emerald, but Neumann did, so he decided the two of them could team up and split it. In all my life I've never misjudged a man so badly."

His eyes angry, Desmond Cavanaugh stopped and struggled

for breath. "I'm so sorry, son," he managed. A tear made its way onto his cheek. At last he went on. "When you were here the other day and said where the handoff would be, it all fell into place. As soon as you left, I called Oakley and told him to haul his evil butt right over here. I told him he was the lowest kind of bastard and he'd better make this right or I'd kill him."

Cass gasped. "Kill him?"

"Oh yes." Desmond Cavanaugh pulled a .38 from beneath the covers to emphasize the point. Cass gasped again.

"I had this thing leveled right between his eyes. Oakley said he didn't know it had gone so far as kidnap—his face kind of fell apart before my eyes. Said he thought the world of you, Cassandra, that he'd get his best shotgun and go right on out there. Asked if I could find it in my heart to forgive him. Not in a million damn years, I said."

"Wow," Tom uttered. "So that's why he was there."

"Can you ever forgive *me*?" his father said in little more than a whisper.

"There's nothing to forgive, Mister C," Cass said, and bent down to kiss his cheek.

Tom fetched him a glass of water from the kitchen before continuing.

"Wilson Judge's real name is Willi Richter. The German word for *judge* is Richter. Simple, huh? He entered the U.S. from Uruguay thirty years ago on forged papers and set himself up in Santa Barbara. He'd hightailed it out of Europe when Nazi Germany was falling apart and built a new identity for himself. He made a fortune in art in South America, dealing both above and below board. I knew there was something funny when he claimed he was in our Coast Guard on antisubmarine duty."

"Why?" Cass asked.

"Because he didn't know about the I-17 when I brought it up."

"What's that, a freeway?"

"No, the I-17 was the Japanese submarine that fired on Santa Barbara during the war. Any real Coast Guard antisub guy would know about the I-17."

"My man, the historian," Cass said.

"That's me." Tom grinned. "Now, Doctor Gerhard, the slimy little curator at the art museum in Vienna, was one of Judge's confederates. Gerhard was deep into a neo-Nazi ring of art thieves. When he suspected we had the Maria Theresa Emerald, he told Judge—"

"No," Desmond Cavanaugh put in, "it had to be the other way around. I never told Oakley about the emerald till just before your trip, so *he* must have told Richter, who told Judge, and Judge told your curator in Vienna."

"Oh, sure." Tom slapped his forehead with the flat of his good hand. "And so Doctor Gerhard was just waiting for me, like a spider."

"More than that, son. He probably had you tailed from the moment you got off the plane."

Tom remembered the eavesdroppers at dinner in Garmisch and how his hotel room drawer had been rearranged. "That snake. Well, the Austrian police are taking care of him now."

"You pieced this together very well, Thomas. Good police work."

"Mister C, you wouldn't believe your son," Cass said. "Interviewing that old man Judge in the middle of the night."

"Interviewing? That was interrogation."

"Interview, interrogate, whatever, while Tom's practically bleeding to death. And here I am, freezing cold, the headache from hell, nothing to eat in three days, trying to persuade some hairy biker to call an ambulance."

"Hey, that dude gave me directions to the mill. I'm glad he followed me out there."

"We almost had a new dog, you know. A Doberman."

"Orbison would have loved that."

"Cassandra, you went through hell," Tom's father said. "You're a strong woman. I'm proud of you. Great addition to the family."

"Oh, Mister C," she said, and kissed his cheek again.

"Call me Des. You're wearing your hair shorter, I see."

"Yeah," Cass said with a curious smile. "My boy-cut."

"Well, it looks good on you. Now, Thomas, suppose you explain this." He held up a newspaper opened to a story on the second page.

Tom took the paper and began reading.

SWISS BANK RETURNS RARE JEWEL TO AUSTRIA
Maria Theresa Emerald was Stolen by Nazis

ZURICH (Reuters)—A Swiss bank which had been under fire in recent years for allegedly keeping funds deposited by Jews before and during the Holocaust, today announced it had uncovered one of Austria's Crown Jewels and was returning it to that nation's Hofburg royal palace.

Officers of the Federated Bank of Switzerland said the Maria Theresa Emerald was found in a lock box linked to a numbered account that had belonged to an official of the Nazi Third Reich. Europe-watchers said the move marked a public relations comeback for the embattled bank.

In a news conference, the bank announced that, "The emerald was uncovered in our search of German accounts from the World War II period, part of our unflagging efforts to return funds to those with rightful claims. Swiss and Austrian experts have authenticated the gem as one of the Austrian Crown Jewels. We are pleased to make this restitution . . ."

Tom put the paper down, his lopsided smile broader than it had been in weeks.

"What a beautiful pack of lies. I went to college with a guy who's now a PR man in Washington. He gave me the idea, said a Swiss bank that needed to score some points in the court of public opinion—that's how he phrased it—would love to return it for us."

"You saw this PR guy when we were in Washington?" Cass asked, eyebrows raised.

"Sneaky, aren't I? And I went to the bank's San Francisco office last week."

Tom's father smiled. "Excellent work, son. Well, Field Marshal Keitel can rest in peace now, his duty done."

"Back when we broke up Neumann's drug deal and he was still known as Richter," Tom said, "he owned some property in the foothills, but I didn't know that included Empire Lumber. Now here's the amazing thing: old Judge told me Neumann never knew that he was his father. Judge said he never let on because he felt so guilty over abandoning him and his mother at the end of the war."

"And he ended up killing him? His own son?"

"Judge said he was tired of the whole thing, years of living a lie, and deeply disappointed that his son turned out to be even worse than he was. He said it was time to end it, couldn't stand the thought of any more murders on his hands."

"Thank God," Cass and Tom's father said together.

"He also said nobody could call a German *Oberst*—that's colonel—a stupid old picture-framer. He stood very straight when he said that, and I could just picture him in uniform."

"I don't know if I should bring up Sharon," Desmond Cavanaugh said.

Wild gunfire again in a dark barn. Tom put his good hand over his eyes, wondering if this reel would play over and over again the rest of his life. Fortunately, the Sutter County sheriff's report had concluded that Sharon's death resulted from "gunshot trauma inflicted by the kidnap suspect Wickersham." The rifling marks on the bullet had proved that.

"Madame X," Cass said. "You know, at the end she was sorry for getting into it."

"Sharon was wearing your slacks," Tom said, "and even some of your hair, trying to fool me. She must've run into Neumann in San Diego. She was always trying to get close to money." Tom stopped and looked at his feelings a moment. He bit his lower lip. "I don't want to talk about her."

He sank into the old leather chair, his arm starting to ache. "I know you were betrayed, Dad, but I'm sorry old Twenty-Five-for-Twenty-Five died. He saved my bacon."

"Well, at least the old bastard went out with his boots on. In a way, he always missed being a cop in his later years. Maybe he died happy at that."

"When I saw him," Tom said, "I thought he was . . . well, somebody a lot older."

Desmond Cavanaugh's brow wrinkled in puzzlement.

"Tom, I asked you once before," Cass said, "if you believed in reincarnation. I repeat the question."

"Maybe, Cass. Yeah, maybe."

Tom's father still looked perplexed. "You'll go back on the force, of course, when you're healed up?"

"I don't know, Dad, I really don't know. Pulaski's stunt leaves a sour taste."

"Don't make a hasty decision, Thomas. You've got some time to think about it. Now, what did you learn about Wickersham, the so-called FBI man?"

"Yeah, Tom, the Shadow."

"The Shadow, Cass?"

"That's what I called the lovely gentleman."

"I called him the Tight End. He used to be a cop in Wichita, but he came out here and started doing dirty jobs for Neumann. Being an ex-cop, he faked the routine of grilling me as a suspect real well. I'm mad at myself for buying into that." Tom made a fist and whacked his thigh. "I didn't even ask him for ID. Wickersham did his homework. The real Zack Elwell is on loan in Canada."

"He was pond scum," Cass said. "He beat me up pretty good when I couldn't fight back. I wish I'd killed him myself."

"Cass!" Tom uttered.

"I do," she said, her jaw set defiantly.

"I'm surrounded by killers," Tom said, looking at each of them. "Well," he went on, "the FBI wasn't even in on it at first. If the state line's not crossed, kidnaps aren't automatically federal cases. They're involved now, of course, cleaning things up. They have old Judge in a federal lockup."

"What was it you gave Wickersham if not the emerald?"

"A counterfeit made by an art instructor at American River. He used some green epoxy and did some fancy sculpting."

"What about the flash camera?"

"I got that idea from Alfred Hitchcock in *Rear Window*. James Stewart used flashbulbs to blind the killer, remember? By the way, my film is due back tomorrow."

"Think General Mansfield will be on it?" Cass asked with a sly grin.

Desmond Cavanaugh's face showed even more confusion.

"You never know. We should have some interesting shots."

"Oh," Cass said, pulling something from her purse. "I found this in your jeans when I ran some laundry this morning." She handed Tom a small rectangle of coarse blue woolen material, stitched on each side with faded yellow piping. In the center were two embroidered stars, also yellow. "What is it, anyway?"

"Let me see that," Desmond Cavanaugh said. "Why, it looks like a shoulder patch from an old uniform, a major general's, I'd say. Where the devil did you get this?"